MY HONORABLE BROTHER

MY HONORABLE BROTHER

A Thriller

BOB WEINTRAUB

YUCCA

Copyright © 2015 by Bob Weintraub

All rights reserved. No part of this book may be reproduced in any manner without the express written consent of the publisher, except in the case of brief excerpts in critical reviews or articles. All inquiries should be addressed to Yucca Publishing, 307 West 36th Street, 11th Floor, New York, NY 10018.

Yucca Publishing books may be purchased in bulk at special discounts for sales promotion, corporate gifts, fund-raising, or educational purposes. Special editions can also be created to specifications. For details, contact the Special Sales Department, Yucca Publishing, 307 West 36th Street, 11th Floor, New York, NY 10018 or yucca@skyhorsepublishing.com.

Yucca Publishing® is an imprint of Skyhorse Publishing, Inc.®, a Delaware corporation.

Visit our website at www.yuccapub.com.

10 9 8 7 6 5 4 3 2 1

Library of Congress Cataloging-in-Publication Data is available on file.

Cover design by Yucca Publishing

Print ISBN: 978-1-63158-018-5
Ebook ISBN: 978-1-63158-031-4

Printed in the United States of America

FOR SANDRA, MY EVERYTHING

1

AT THE LAST MINUTE he decided to put on his sweat suit and go for a jog before breakfast. Doug Fiore knew he had to shower anyway before meeting with the judge at two o'clock, so it made sense to get his exercise out of the way now. In the bathroom, he wet the two spots on his face, one on his cheek and the other on his chin, where he nicked them while shaving too quickly, carefully pushing away the toilet paper he used to stop the bleeding.

"Oh, fuck," he said out loud when the second cut occurred, and Grace knocked on the door, reminding him that Susan, their fourteen-year-old daughter was still in her room. His foul language was a response to knowing that the Columbia Law School alumni magazine was doing an article on him and sending a photographer to his office at Walters, Cassidy & Breen the next day to take pictures. He didn't want them spoiled by what might look like adolescent zits.

When he went downstairs, Grace was at the refrigerator getting the eggs and vegetables she needed to make Doug his regular Sunday morning omelet. The frying pan on the stove was filled with onion slices sizzling in melted butter.

"Honey," he said, "would you hold up making breakfast for about an hour. I'm going to do my running and then I'll clean up and get dressed. I've got to see Tom Raymond this afternoon about his case."

"This afternoon? What time are you talking about, Doug?"

"He said he could do it at two, and that would give us a couple of hours to work before the Patriots come on at four. He never misses one of their games."

Grace stopped what she was doing and looked at him, her hands moving to her hips. "Have you forgotten that we're going to my brother's party this afternoon and we have to leave here by one o'clock?"

"Oh hell, I thought that was next week."

"No, it's today. I reminded you a few days ago, right here in the kitchen."

"Well, I got it mixed up. Damn." Doug disliked going to one of Grace's brother's parties as much as he disliked Walter, her brother. "Don't call me Wally," as he often referred to him, drank too much too quickly and inevitably started to rant about the "good old days" when Reagan was in the White House and how he saved America from everything that was evil, both foreign and domestic.

"Tom's case is going before the Ethics Commission on Thursday and I really have to spend more time with him to be sure we're ready. Your brother's not going to miss me if I'm not there."

"That's not the point," Grace answered. "Walter invites these same people all the time—you know that—and you weren't there for the July cookout. They'll think we're separated or something if I'm alone again. It wouldn't matter what excuse I gave for you, Doug. It'll be embarrassing for me."

Fiore went over and embraced his wife who willingly moved into his arms. He thought about the wonderful time they had the night before, dining at the new restaurant in the Biltmore Hotel, enjoying the hit musical at the Trinity Theatre and later, back home, having an exciting hour of sex. Even though he was having an affair with one of his law partners at that time, he loved Grace very much and tried his best to keep her happy.

"Okay, honey," he said. "I'm not going to spoil your day. The judge will have to find some time for me after work one night this week. Or maybe he can see me tonight, after seven, when the game's over. We'll definitely be home by then. I'll call him now."

At breakfast, Grace asked Doug to tell her what Tom Raymond's case was about. As soon as he began to speak, his voice became louder without his realizing it. "It's about how easy it is for a piece of trash to malign a good man and smear his name in the community."

"Please, Doug," she interrupted, "spell it out for me, but don't get upset."

"I'll try to make a long story short," he answered, then paused several seconds before continuing. "Tom was the judge in a criminal case involving this guy named Blackburn. Tom found against him and sentenced him to three years in jail. He's still serving time now. A few months ago Blackburn got to see the warden and accused Tom of offering to throw out his case if he came up with five thousand dollars. Blackburn said he couldn't put his hands on the money at the time. The warden didn't believe a word of it but felt he had to cover himself and reported it to the Attorney General's office."

"How would Tom ever come to be alone with this Blackburn person to even offer a deal like that?" Grace asked.

"Good question, just what the A.G.'s office wanted to know. The answer is that Blackburn said he did it through Tom's clerk, a guy named Timilty, who called him on the phone during the trial."

"Did the clerk confirm it?"

Doug shook his head. "He neither confirmed it nor denied it. Unfortunately for Tom, the clerk had died several months earlier, so what Blackburn said couldn't be refuted. I suspect that miserable son of a bitch heard about Timilty, waited a while and then went to the warden with his story. Anyway, the A.G. decided to refer the case to the State Ethics Commission with the understanding that his office could get back into it, depending on the finding."

"Well, with Tom being a judge, I'm sure he'd have more credibility than Blackburn. I mean it's just a 'he said/he said' case, right?"

"No, it's not. There's Tom on one side, but Blackburn has a number of witnesses lined up to lie to the Commission and say what he wants them to say. I'm sure we'll hear testimony that he was trying to borrow money from them at the time with a story that the judge was ready to take a bribe. The Commission has made their names available to me—they're all bottom of the barrel types—and I've been able to find out a lot about them from a good source, so it should be interesting."

"Poor Tom," she said. "And with two kids in college I suppose it will cost him more than he can afford to defend himself."

"No, I'm doing it pro bono. I spoke to the Executive Committee about it and got their approval. Our firm doesn't do any criminal work so there's no chance of any conflict in the future with one of our lawyers representing someone in Tom's courtroom."

"That's wonderful. I'll be rooting for both of you."

They each turned to a different section of the *Sunday Providence Herald*, he to the sports page and she to the local news.

Minutes later Grace asked, "Why would this be in the paper, Doug?"

He stopped reading and looked at her. "What is it?"

Grace leaned over the paper which lay on the table. "It says that the police entered the Pawtucket Avenue dining establishment run by the Tarantino family on suspicion that there was illegal gambling taking place, but found nothing of the sort, only a room full of people having dinner." She paused and looked up at Doug. "I assume they mean it was a police raid, even though that word isn't used in the story. But if the police were wrong, and the Tarantinos weren't charged with anything, why is there even a mention of it in the paper? That's like telling us that a man in the street walked past a Rottweiler and the dog didn't bite him."

"Very good, honey, I like that analogy. It sounds like the cops were embarrassed but still wanted to give the Tarantinos some bad publicity. If there's gambling going on, they want the public to worry about being caught in a raid, so they'll stay away. Gerry Quinn, the Chief of Police, was probably able to talk the right editor at the *Herald* into throwing that little piece of news into the paper. Don't forget that the *Herald* has always been against gambling in its editorials."

Doug took satisfaction in knowing that he played a significant role in the failure encountered by the police the night before. As was the case numerous times over a period of twenty years, he had taken a coded message received from Joe Gaudette, a captain in the Providence Police, and passed it on immediately to someone in the Tarantino office on Atwells Avenue. Gaudette, a trusted friend of Sal Tarantino, the Mafia head in Rhode Island, couldn't make any suspicious phone call from police headquarters on the same day that Gerry Quinn ordered his officers to raid a Tarantino club where casino gambling was known to take place. But then circumstances gave the Family an opening that allowed Gaudette to use Fiore as a middleman for messages, whose meaning he never knew, to be relayed to the Tarantinos. He realized now that the message he received and passed on Saturday was a warning to the Tarantinos that there would be a raid at the Pawtucket Avenue location Saturday night. It was a dangerous role he agreed to play years earlier when he was just a young associate looking to get ahead, but there was no denying it paid off for him . . . big time. He knew that being Managing Partner of his firm was only part of the reward.

On the way to her brother's home in Little Compton, Grace asked, "What arrangement did you make with Tom Raymond?"

"He's coming to the office at six o'clock on Tuesday. That photographer from Columbia is supposed to show up between five and six tomorrow and then I've got the Executive Committee staying late for a meeting. I expect to be home by ten at the latest." Fiore knew that he would steer the meeting to an end by seven-thirty and then hurry over to the Howard Johnson Motel in Seekonk where Carol, his mistress, would already be in bed, waiting for him.

"Is that about Tom?"

It took Doug a few seconds to get back on track. "No, it's a whole different issue," he said. "Some of the partners have been lobbying for us to lay off a bunch of associates at the end of the year. Everyone can see from the monthly spreadsheets that billable hours have been way down consistently. They know that could mean no Christmas bonuses and maybe even cuts in salary for next year, and that's making them unhappy."

"But the whole country's in a recession. They wouldn't be the only unhappy ones."

"That's right, but they figure that if we let about ten or twelve associates go, the money we save can be spread around for the partners."

"That doesn't sound very collegial to me."

"You're right. It stinks. It's the sort of thing that gives lawyers a bad name and makes us the butt of so many jokes. I'll do whatever I can to convince the Committee to vote it down if it gets proposed at the partners meeting."

"Do you have a sense right now of how the Committee would vote? Does it have to be unanimous?"

"No, I need three of the five, including myself. Right now my best guess is that Ed Jackson's vote is the crucial one."

"But even if the Committee supports you, that's no guarantee the partners would go along with it. Money is the root of you know what."

"I know, and I'd have to convince them it's wrong to hurt the associates just to make the partners a little richer. Some of those young guys have families and mortgages. Besides, we've trained them to be good lawyers and we'll need them when business picks up."

"Oh, that reminds me," Grace said, "you had a call this morning while you were out running. I totally forgot about it."

"Who was it?"

He didn't leave his name and seemed to be in a hurry to get off the phone right away when I told him you weren't home. He said to tell you that your friend wants to speak to you. I asked him if you'd know which friend he meant, and he just said 'Yes' and hung up."

Fiore knew that the caller was Joe Gaudette and he was telling Doug that Sandy Tarantino, Sal's son and Doug's college roommate for four years, wanted a meeting with him. Nine months had passed since the last time the two of them were together, and he understood that Sandy had something important to discuss if a meeting was necessary. He wondered at first whether it had anything to do with the police presence at the Pawtucket Avenue establishment the night before, but dismissed that thought since he had relayed Gaudette's coded message and it was acted upon. Still, he knew that Sandy would not want to be kept waiting once he told Gaudette to set things up. Fiore had to find out how soon the meeting would take place.

"That was from my biggest client," he said. "Sunday's just another work day for him. He probably told someone in his office to get me on the phone. He may even be in a hurry to see me tomorrow. I'll stop at the mall and call back." As he drove, Fiore thought about the matters he was handling for the Tarantinos and questioned whether he had done anything to upset them. That was always his first thought whenever Sandy summoned him to a meeting. He had a lot of homework to do before seeing his old friend.

2

The stocky man looking out the window wore a black pinstripe Armani suit over a fine white Egyptian cotton shirt and red paisley necktie selected from a catalog mailed monthly by an exclusive designer men's shop in Milan. He took in the view around him a few seconds longer before answering the question put to him by the junior United States Senator from Rhode Island.

"You can do whatever you like, Senator," he said, turning away from the window. "Go back to your jewelry factory if you want. And if that's not good enough anymore, set yourself up as a consultant or a lobbyist." Sandy Tarantino's voice was gruff, as if fighting its way through some bronchial congestion. "Do something with the influence you've got. Use the fucking connections you've made here in the last five years. Or maybe you want to take some time off. My family will carry you for a while. Like I said before, we're trying to make this easy for you."

The Senator was peeved, and it showed when he spoke. "Your father never said I'd have to quit after one term. If Sal told me that, I might not even have bothered to run."

Tarantino walked over to one of the chairs in front of Spence Hardiman's desk and sat down. He stared hard at the white-haired man, twenty years his senior, before speaking. "That's bullshit, Senator. You'd have jumped at the chance to come here if the goddam term had been for just a year. And my father never gave you any guarantees when he financed your campaign."

Hardiman was having a difficult time keeping himself under control. The phone call he received from the elder Tarantino a few days earlier was friendly. Sal just said that his son would be in Washington to see him. Hardiman assumed the Family needed his help on some matter and that he'd solve the problem by speaking to the right person. But instead, the cocky young man with the menacing half smile had wasted no time in telling him that the Tarantinos didn't want him to run for a second term.

"We want John Sacco out of the Statehouse after next year," Sandy said. "There's one hell of an issue on casino gambling coming up and our thinking is he'd probably be against us on it. The Family never put anything more than chump change in Sacco's campaign so there's nothing he owes us. We've got to have our own man in the governor's chair, someone we can count on to veto any bill that would hurt us. So Sacco's got to find a place he'd rather be than Providence. That's right here, Senator, where you're sitting. My father's sorry you have to move out, but that's the way it is."

Hardiman tried to find out more about the gambling matter. He wanted Sandy to feel he still had plenty of influence in what went on in Rhode Island. "Believe me," he said, pointing his thumb at his chest, "there's guys in both the House and Senate back there I can still control. They'll do what I tell 'em."

"Forget it, Senator. The decision's already been made. Sal's not taking any chances. He's got to know the governor's in our pocket when we need him."

Hardiman began to feel nauseous. He wanted Tarantino out of his office. He was being pushed hard to agree to something he wanted no part of. It would be better to get his old friend Sal on the telephone and talk about it. Maybe he *could* get the Tarantinos the help they needed, even if they didn't think so. But goddammit, being a United States Senator meant everything to him and he couldn't let this kid just walk in and change his life on the spot.

The Senator got up from behind his massive oak desk and walked over to where Tarantino was sitting. He anticipated that his movement would prompt Sandy into getting up also and that he'd be able to walk him to the door. When Tarantino ignored his approach, Hardiman wasn't sure what to do. He took a couple of steps backwards, pushed aside some papers on the corner of the desk and sat down, somewhat tentatively. Unaware of his body language, he folded his arms together in front of him while he considered his next move.

"I'm glad I finally got to meet you today, Sandy," Hardiman began, shaking his head up and down slightly for emphasis. "Sal has spoken to me about you any number of times. He's proud of you and knows the Family will be in good hands when it's time for you to take his place."

Tarantino didn't say anything. He thought he knew where Hardiman was going with this. But one of the lessons his father had taught him was never to speak too soon. "Sometimes," Sal had cautioned him, "they'll know just from looking at your face that you're not happy with what they're saying and they'll change it halfway through. So be patient. Don't interrupt. You'll always get your chance to talk."

Hardiman was becoming uncomfortable with Tarantino's silence and the fact that his effort to be friendly didn't have any effect. The ominous smile was still visible on his visitor's face. "I'm sure this isn't something that has to be decided today," he continued. "I'll think over everything you've said and give Sal a call. Tell him he can expect to hear from me in a few days."

Tarantino started to get up. Hardiman thought the meeting was finally over. But just as the Senator began moving away from his desk, Sandy was on top of him, grabbing his shirt and tie just a few inches below the older man's neck. Hardiman couldn't believe what was happening. He felt stabs of pain as Tarantino's strong hold on him seemed to be pulling hairs from his chest.

"We're not asking you to do us a favor, Senator," Sandy hissed into his face. Hardiman could feel a few drops of spittle land on his cheek. "You're goddam through here when your term's up. That's been decided. My old man got you elected and now he's telling you it's over. Don't give us any of that 'I'll call him later shit.' There's nothing to talk about."

Tarantino kept a tight grasp on Hardiman while he spoke. But as he held on, his hand shook back and forth so that his knuckles kept pounding into the Senator's chest. Hardiman thought about shouting for help but was afraid to do it. He knew things would get a lot worse for him if Sal's son were arrested in his office for an assault. There'd be no way to stop the publicity and Sal Tarantino would become his enemy. That's one thing he didn't want. He'd just have to hope this nightmare was almost over.

Suddenly, as if he'd read the Senator's thoughts, Tarantino's free hand whipped across Hardiman's face, slapping his left cheek with a force that made the Senator's head jerk back. The blow would have sent him sprawling on the floor if Sandy hadn't been holding onto his shirt and tie.
    "Do you understand me now?" Sandy asked. He kept his voice low. "We'll give you the time frame to announce to the folks back home that you've decided not to run for a second term. My father will let you know. So get used to the fact that you won't be campaigning again next year. Do you hear me loud and clear, Senator?"
    Hardiman had to swallow before he could answer. "Yes, yes," he said. "Okay."
    At that, Tarantino released his hold. Tears had filled Hardiman's eyes just seconds after he'd been struck and were slowly rolling down his cheeks. He seemed oblivious to it and made no effort to wipe them away. Tarantino walked over to the closet where he hung his suit jacket earlier, slipped it off the hanger and put it on. He looked in the mirror on the back side of the closet door and straightened the knot in his tie before returning to where Hardiman stood. The Senator hadn't moved.
    "Don't do anything stupid, Senator. Just listen to what my father tells you. Because if you don't, you know what can happen. We wouldn't want it to come to that—you and Sal have known each other a long time—but business is business. Sometimes things get out of hand."
    Tarantino hesitated a few moments before extending his right hand to the Senator. "Thanks for the meeting," he said.
    Like a beaten fighter who has gotten up off the canvas dazed and unsteady on his feet, Hardiman shook the hand that had just disrupted his world. "Okay," was all he could say again.

3

At seven o'clock on a raw evening in early December, Doug Fiore hurried down the steps of the Spalding National Bank building. He was wearing a black Burberry raincoat and carrying the extra-large size briefcase favored by litigation lawyers. A Yellow Cab was waiting for him at the curb. Fiore looked younger than his forty-four years, and his handsome face still showed evidence of the flattering tan he acquired in St. Maarten over a five-day Thanksgiving holiday. He said nothing on entering the back seat of the late model Chevrolet, but noticed that the driver was Asian. *Probably one of those Vietnamese who've been moving into the west end of Providence,* he thought. He had driven through that neighborhood on several occasions and felt sorry for the people, mostly new immigrants, who were crowded into the many dilapidated buildings there.

The cab drove east along Kennedy Plaza and took a left turn in front of the United States District Courthouse. One block later it turned left again along the far side of the plaza and onto Sabin Street. It passed the rear entrance of the *Providence Herald* building and slowed down for several groups of pedestrians crossing the street, headed for the hockey game at the Civic Center between the hometown Bruins and the visiting team from New Haven. Accelerating slightly, the Chevy made a right turn onto Atwells Avenue, but stopped almost immediately for a traffic light just beyond the Holiday Inn at the entrance to Interstate 95. The driver crossed the bridge over the highway and passed under the pineapple-topped concrete arch dominating the entrance to Federal Hill. This was the area known informally in the city as the Italian section, but to Rhode Island law enforcement agencies and the FBI, it was the backyard of the Mob.

Fiore leaned forward slightly as he looked out at the passing storefronts. He was tense most of the day, thinking about the meeting he was summoned to attend. When he returned Joe Gaudette's call, he was given a choice of two dates, a week apart, for the meeting. The later time was more convenient for him, but Fiore didn't want to chance displeasing Tarantino by keeping him waiting. He quickly decided to cancel the dinner date he had with a client and be available earlier.

The taxi moved down Atwells Avenue. Its left headlight illuminated the center strip, painted green, white and red, the colors of the Italian flag. Soon the low commercial buildings in the heart of the shopping district gave way to a disorganized mixture of single family and two family homes that alternated with four and six unit apartment houses. Fiore hardly noticed as the driver turned left and traveled several blocks before making another turn onto Broadway. But his attention returned as the cab suddenly slowed and began entering a wide driveway. The building was an old Victorian. It had two flights of stairs leading to an entrance in front, and a side door on the lower driveway level that received most of the traffic. Fiore had been there several times in the past. The dark green awnings that provided shelter from the rain at both entrances informed the public in large white letters, visible at night in the glare of several spotlights, that the establishment was the Vincent A. Milano Funeral Home.

The driver eased past the entrance and continued on into the parking lot. Fiore reached for his briefcase on the seat beside him, his anxiety increasing. As the cab made a slow U-turn in the large yard and headed back toward the street, he counted a dozen other vehicles parked there. The Chevrolet came to a stop, and an attendant wearing a heavy black woolen coat and a Russian style fur hat that partially covered his ears opened the passenger door for him.

"Good evening, sir," he said, and continued without waiting for a response. "The wake is being held in the first room on the right. Toilet facilities are at the end of the hallway." The words were spoken in a monotone, as if prerecorded. Fiore thanked him and entered the building, uncertain what to do next. The sign on a metal stand at the entrance to the room on his right indicated that a wake was in progress for a Dominic Sabatini. The name meant nothing to him. Still, as Gaudette didn't tell him where Sandy Tarantino would be, and as he saw no activity farther down the corridor, he joined the mourners in the room.

Gray, metal folding chairs were set out along the walls on three sides. Fiore saw several faces turn in his direction as he entered, then look away when they didn't recognize him. Sandy Tarantino was not in the room. He took off his raincoat and draped it over one of the chairs. He placed his briefcase on the floor, under the same chair, and hesitated for a few moments, as if waiting for someone to approach him. When no one did, he silently cursed to himself about having to be where he was, but took a deep breath and walked toward the front of the room.

The casket rested on a low platform built against the far wall. It was almost totally surrounded by bouquets of flowers, several in the form of a wreath. A woman, dressed entirely in black, her face covered by a veil, sat on a dark vinyl chair immediately to the left of the bier. Her hands were folded in her lap, her head bent forward slightly. Fiore guessed that she was Sabatini's widow.

He knelt before the casket and crossed himself, but did not look at the body. He closed his eyes and remained in that position for less than half a minute. When he got up and started to turn away, the woman spoke. "Thank you for coming," she said softly. Fiore caught himself quickly, moved to where she sat and said he was sorry for her loss. He could see through the veil that she was somewhere in her forties, close to his own age.

"Did my husband go to you for legal work, Mr. Fiore?" she asked. Her voice was just above a whisper.

Fiore was momentarily confused. He was certain he had never seen her before, but she obviously knew who he was. He searched his brain for a connection to the name "Sabatini," but came up empty. Suddenly, the flash of a smile on her face made him realize that she was playing a game for his benefit. It must have to do with Sandy, he thought, and knew he had to go along with it.

"Yes, he did," he answered, smiling momentarily himself. "On several occasions."

"I'm glad he went to the best." She took his hand, as if she were being consoled and was thanking him for something kind he said. "Down the hall there's a door marked 'Employees Only.' It's just after the ladies room. Go in there and wait. But please, first express your condolences to Dominic's family. That's them sitting by the window." She let go of his hand and raised her voice slightly. "It was very nice of you to come. God bless you."

"Thanks," he replied. Fiore considered acknowledging her role with a wink, but reminded himself that she was still mourning a dead husband. He made a mental note to find Sabatini's obituary in the newspaper and perhaps send a donation in his memory to a local charity. "Take care," he said, and walked over to the window.

A man sat between two women, all of them elderly. The women were both overweight and looked uncomfortable on the small chairs they occupied. One held a man's white handkerchief in her hand and used it alternately to dab at her tears and blow her nose. The other held a large pocketbook on her lap with both hands. The man's wide, striped tie was long out of fashion. It was knotted poorly at his neck, revealing the unbuttoned top button of his shirt. Fiore shook hands with each of them and offered his sympathy. He assumed that two of them were Sabatini's parents and that the other woman was either a close aunt or the dead man's godmother. They said nothing to him in response, but just moved their heads up and down as he played out the mourner's role for their benefit by assuring them that he would always treasure his friendship with "Dom."

Fiore retrieved his coat and briefcase and found the room to which he was directed. A ceiling light was on when he entered and closed the door behind him. A long glass-topped wooden table occupied the center of the room, surrounded by eight red plastic chairs, the kind that could be stacked one on top of the other. Although functional, they were totally out of place next to the imposing table made from a fine-grained dark wood.

The room had no windows. There was an old Whirlpool refrigerator to his left. The droning sound it gave off seemed hardly worth its obviously small capacity. A food-market shopping cart to one side of the refrigerator contained opened packages of small paper cups, paper plates, plastic utensils and napkins. He guessed that the funeral home employees used the room for lunch or a quick snack at break time. There was nothing there to encourage them to linger when they finished eating. Mahogany paneling extended from the crown molding below the ceiling all the way to the baseboard on all four walls, interrupted only by a narrow piece of chair rail about three feet above the floor. Fiore assumed that the elegant space, not visible from the outside, was planned originally to host clandestine meetings.

"Hello, good buddy."

Fiore was startled. He turned around quickly, in time to catch Sandy Tarantino pushing a panel back against the wall. Nothing on that section of mahogany identified it as a door. He was certain that someone would have to open it again from the other side when their meeting was over.

Doug moved quickly to greet his friend. "Sandy. Good to see you."

Tarantino took Fiore's outstretched hand and held it firmly in his own as he shook it. The vise-like grip into which Doug's fingers had entered reminded him again of the strength of his former roommate, the only member of the Princeton wrestling team who didn't lose a single fall in four years of varsity competition.

"I'm great, Doug, just great. Thanks for coming tonight. Sorry about all the intrigue, but I had no idea where we'd meet when Joe set up the date with you."

He walked over to the door, pushed the button in the handle to lock it and steered Fiore over to the table where they took seats across from each other. "The guy they're waking is Dominic Sabatini," Sandy said. "He was the construction worker you may have read about who had the ditch collapse on him in Pawtucket a few days ago. The poor bastard suffocated before they could dig him out. We grew up on the same street. I even dated his wife a couple of times in high school. She was one knockout broad in those days. I called and told her to use this place when I heard about Dom. He had some life insurance through his union—something like ten grand—but we'll help her out with what she needs until she's back on her feet. That fucking construction company he worked for is going to pay through the nose for this. Fiore understood that the company's immediate problem would come from the Tarantinos.

"Anyhow," Sandy continued, "I had one of the guys show Barbara Sabatini your picture and tell her what to say to you. You never know

My Honorable Brother • 15

who's watching, Doug. I assume I'm being followed everywhere I go. And it's a wake, so any of them could just walk in here like they know the Sabatini family and look around. That's why I wanted to be sure you paid your respects. If you're ever asked what you did after you spoke to the widow, your answer is that you went upstairs to say 'Hello' to your good friend Vincent and then took a cab back downtown. He'd swear to the same thing."

Tarantino got up and started moving back and forth along his side of the table. "I've got to exercise this left leg a little. There's a problem with some discs in my back and it shoots pain through my knee like it was a torn cartilage or something. They're scheduling me for an MRI. Ever had one, Doug?"

"No," he said. He rapped the side of the table with his knuckles. "No reason for one yet. Knock on wood."

"It's murder if you're claustrophobic like me. You're like a torpedo they shove into a hole in a machine. It's pitch-black in there and you can't move. If I didn't take some Xanax, I'd be screaming for them to pull me right out. I've been through it six times already. My wife calls me 'The King of the MRIs.'" Sandy laughed and Doug smiled back.

Fiore looked at the man he first met twenty-five years earlier, in the second semester of their freshman year in college. Sandy was probably thirty pounds heavier now than in those days, up to about 220, Doug guessed. He still wore the beard and mustache he initially showed off to Fiore about seven or eight years ago. His face was slightly flabbier than back then, especially in the jowls, and the black hair he combed straight back started from higher on his forehead. But the eyes that always grabbed your attention and said, "Look right here, you fucker, when you're talking to me" hadn't changed at all. They were the color of the darkest roast coffee beans, ready as always to pull you into a sinkhole.

The two of them took the same political science elective that second semester. They were part of a study group with several other classmates but didn't socialize otherwise. When the Brown University basketball team played at Princeton, they were both in the sparse crowd that showed up to watch. At halftime they bumped into each other and discovered that each had roots in Rhode Island.

After that, they began meeting at the athletic center a couple of nights a week for some one-on-one basketball, and their friendship grew. Tarantino had his own car, a three-year-old Plymouth coupe, and Fiore drove to Providence with him for several weekends at home. Doug intended to live in a dormitory again for his sophomore year, but Sandy called him during the summer and suggested they share an off-campus apartment.

"You can use my car when you need it," he said, sensing Fiore's hesitation.

That clinched it. "You've got yourself a roommate," Doug said.

They kept the same apartment for three years. But back in Rhode Island during summer breaks, neither ever visited the other at home. Fiore recalled that when they briefly discussed their families, Sandy said only that his father was in life insurance.

Together, they made frequent trips into New York and loved everything the City had to offer. Partying and chasing girls came naturally and easily, and they made many friends at Columbia and NYU. They never bothered reserving hotel rooms on those trips. There was always someone who would let them crash. When they went their separate ways with girls after a party, the standing arrangement was to meet the next day at noon at the main entrance to Madison Square Garden. That location was chosen with the hope that the Celtics would be in town to play the Knicks, and if they were doubly lucky, to get their hands on two tickets to the game.

As graduation from Princeton approached, Sandy and Doug both knew they wanted to go on to law school at Columbia, if it accepted them. With excellent college records and high LSAT scores, each applied to just Columbia and one "safe" school.

"Fuck it," Sandy said sarcastically, "if I can't get into Columbia or BU with these grades, I'll follow my father into the life insurance business." They laughed at that, but Vietnam was still going strong in 1969, and Fiore often questioned whether they could get deferments. Doug reminded his roommate that if both law schools rejected them, they'd be buying life insurance instead of selling it and marching off to Vietnam. Tarantino never seemed worried about it, and asked Doug at one point for the address of his local draft board. By the time they had their degrees from Princeton, deferments came through for both of them. Fiore was never aware of the pressure Sandy's father put on the officials of the two boards to make sure that his son and his son's best friend weren't drafted.

Columbia admitted them both. They rented an apartment within walking distance, at the corner of Broadway and 84th Street. Although the first year was difficult, they finished near the top of the class and still found time for fun. When exams were over, they returned to Providence to spend the summer clerking in law firms. Each was selected to serve on the *Columbia Law Review* in the fall, and that helped open doors to the better law firms. Fiore chose Walters, Cassidy & Breen from the three offers of employment he received. It was the second largest in Rhode Island, and gave him the chance to pick up experience in several different areas of the law.

Sandy told Doug he took a job with Tecci & Tecci, two brothers who had a small office just above the Roma Pasticceria on Federal Hill. Doug knew the location because the Roma was the best Italian bakery on Atwells Avenue. But when he checked the lawyers' directory to find out more about the firm, he discovered that it wasn't listed. No one he spoke to at WC&B ever had a case with the Teccis. Most assumed it was a Mom and Pop type office that drafted wills, did some immigration work and handled personal injury claims for people in the neighborhood. Doug couldn't understand what Sandy hoped to get out of that experience.

A month into his clerkship, Fiore read about the sudden death of Anthony Buscatelli, head of the Rhode Island crime family. Buscatelli's fatal heart attack was the subject of a large bold headline in the *Providence Herald* the morning after his demise. The story reminded readers that his only son died several years earlier in an automobile accident. "It remains to be seen," the report concluded, "who will assume leadership of the Rhode Island Mafia."

About a week later, following the wake and funeral which were attended by well-known Mob figures from New York, New Jersey and Massachusetts, word filtered across Interstate 95 to the *Herald* newsroom that Salvatore Tarantino was chosen to replace Buscatelli. Doug noted the similarity of the surname to his roommate's when he saw the article in the paper. As he read what was written about the State's new "crime boss," he was stunned to learn that Tarantino had two children, "a daughter, Ottavia, and a son, Salvatore Michael, known as Sandy."

Fiore waited two days before calling Tecci & Tecci, still uncertain of what to say to his roommate about what he now knew. The man who took the call told him that Sandy was unavailable, and Doug left word for him to call back. When the call wasn't returned after a week he tried again, but a different male voice informed him that Tarantino was out of the office and hadn't said when he'd be back.

Fiore was alone in the firm's library at eight o'clock on a Friday night when the switchboard operator paged him for a telephone call. He guessed that it was one of his basketball playing friends wanting to know if he'd be at the "Y" in time for his pick-up team's nine o'clock game. He gave his hunch a shot. "Hello, Butchie," he said into the receiver, and recognized Tarantino's answering laugh immediately.

"No, it's not Butchie. Goddammit, Doug, if I thought you were going to become a fucking big firm nerd workaholic, I'd never have studied for exams with you and given you the benefit of my probing and incisive intellect. If that's what you're going to do in this life, it'll be better if you flunk out of law school and become a more meaningful member of society."

"Funny guy," Doug answered. "Shit, Sandy, I called you almost three weeks ago. Where've you been?"

The levity in Tarantino's voice disappeared immediately. "Busy, Doug, really busy." There was a pause. "I guess you read the article, huh?"

"Yeah, I read it. And all these years you wanted me to believe that your old man was in the life insurance business."

Since the story about the senior Tarantino first appeared, Fiore hadn't thought about Sandy's past references to his father's occupation. But at that moment he suddenly recognized the subtle humor in a Mafia captain, and possibly a hit man for all he knew, being characterized as a life insurance salesman. Something in his gut told him that Sandy was aware of the connection he just made between the phony story he was given in the past and the reality of the situation. He was right.

"I'm sorry, good buddy," Sandy said, "but the truth just wouldn't have made for great conversation. And I was sensitive enough about it to want to be accepted for who I was, not feared or rejected because of my family. You probably wouldn't have told me to go fuck myself as many times as you did, often to my benefit, if you wondered how thin-skinned I was or whether my father taught me how to use a little muscle to win an argument. That's the way it had to be." Then the flippancy

My Honorable Brother • 19

returned again: "Anyhow, the next time you tell me to go fuck myself, I may have to have you iced."

Fiore laughed. "I'll try and remember that." He countered with his own jab at humor. "I guess every great friendship has to be tested, and it looks like ours failed miserably."

Tarantino hesitated but didn't take the bait. His voice became serious. "Listen, it's going to be a while before the two of us can sit down and talk about things. What's happened to my father is changing my life in a lot of ways. Right now I'm at the lowest rung of the apprenticeship-training program. There's an awful lot I've got to learn, especially in the time that's left before it's back to school."

"Yeah, we've got to decide when to leave for New York."

"That's the main thing I called you about. I'm through with Columbia. My father wants me close to home so we can talk face to face every day. Don't ask me to explain that. It gets complicated and he won't take 'No' for an answer. Anyhow, I'm transferring to BU in September. If there was a law school in Providence, I'd be staying right here. You've got to understand that not everyone who worked for Tony Buscatelli is overjoyed with Sal Tarantino taking over the operation. He's worried about a few of the unhappy ones going off half-cocked and doing something stupid before he gets established. That's why I have to have protection whenever I'm away from home. I fought like hell against it, but my dad shot down every argument I made. It wasn't exactly like moot court, if you know what I mean."

Fiore smiled and took advantage of the pause that followed Sandy's last words. "Look, all I know about your father is the stuff that was in the paper. There was nothing there about him ever spending time in prison or being indicted for anything. I assume he must have some brains if they made him head of the Family. But any way you look at it, it's still the Mafia, crime incorporated as far as the public's concerned. Are you telling me you're going to be part of that just because you're Sal Tarantino's son?"

Sandy anticipated the question. "Not exactly, Doug. I've drawn some lines that I won't cross, and my father feels the same way I do. We'll talk about it when I see you, and I'll fill in all the details, but not now. Listen, when you get back to New York, let me know your address if you don't stay in the same place. Don't worry, I'll keep in touch. A guy in my position never knows when he may need a good lawyer."

"Do you want me to say anything if anyone in class asks about you?"

"No sweat. Just tell them I decided I'd be happier selling insurance than chasing ambulances. Don't say anything about BU And do me a favor, okay?"

"Sure. What?"

"Make it whole life, not term insurance."

"You're a real comedian. Listen, Sandy, take care of yourself, okay?"

"I will, old buddy. Thanks." He took a deep breath and raised his voice sharply. "Now get back to work, you fucking nerd."

"Go fu . . ." But before Doug could get the words out, he heard the click at the other end.

4

Fiore watched as Tarantino took a bottle of white wine out of the refrigerator and pulled two paper cups from a package in the shopping cart. He brought the cups over to the table and filled them.

"It's a Soave Bolla," he said. "Good stuff. But I didn't ask you to come so you could hear me complain about my health."

Sandy sat down, pushing his back into the wide slats of the plastic chair as firmly as he could, his feet flat on the thinly carpeted floor for additional support. He knew it was time to get down to business. He raised his cup. "Salut."

"Salut," Fiore responded, and made a motion with his own cup toward Sandy before taking a sip.

"Question for you Doug. Have you been to any of the slot machine parlors that have opened around the State?"

Fiore wasn't sure whether this was more small talk or whether the evening's agenda had begun. "No, I haven't," he said. "I just heard about them in the last month or so. But you know me. I like sure things, not stupid bets. I probably haven't spent ten dollars on lottery tickets since they started selling them twenty years ago, or whenever it was."

"Smart man. That probably means you haven't lost any money on the Jets either. What a fucked-up football team that is. But let me tell you something you may not know. Do you have any idea how the slots got started in Rhode Island?"

Fiore shook his head. "No idea at all."

"Then I think you'll find this interesting." Tarantino took another sip of wine before continuing. "I'll try and make a long story short, so bear with me. The first parlor—it was really what we'd both call a joint—opened up in Newport. The guy behind it was some relative of the mayor there. He offered to give back forty percent of the net to the town. The town didn't have to do a thing for its money except look the other way and let him stay open. The place was right on Thames Street. That meant every tourist who went window-shopping along the main drag could see it, step inside and leave a few bucks there. You know how hard up Newport's been for money. The teachers there went on strike for six weeks last fall before they caught on that they weren't going to get more than a token raise if they picketed forever. Narragansett Sailboat and P. P. Cummings both shut down within the last fifteen months, and they were two of the biggest boat makers in the State. Unemployment in Newport was running at something like ten percent. That's a hell of a lot of people out of work, looking for benefits. And benefits cost money. So the mayor said 'Okay,' to his cousin, or whatever he is, and told the cops to stay away from the place. The money probably gets entered on the town's books as some sort of fee or taxes."

"I didn't know they had them in Newport," Fiore said.

"Yeah, they do." Sandy took a deep breath. "Then, about three months later, another slots parlor opened up in Westerly. Same story. A poor town that the recession was making poorer every day. The biggest employer there is the Bromfield Company. It makes those camouflage uniforms for the Defense Department. It got into financial trouble, went bankrupt and laid off a couple hundred people while the lawyers are getting it reorganized. Again, the town is getting a big piece of the money pie from the parlor operator who picked up on what was happening in Newport. So everybody's happy, especially the local politicians who don't have to talk about raising taxes. The cops make believe there's still a convenience store at that location. Only in Westerly, instead of catering to tourists with money to blow, it's different. There, it's a case of someone local with just five bucks in his pocket, or her pocket, to give the ladies their due, throwing eight or ten quarters into a slot machine hoping to make a great big ten dollar hit. Five minutes later they're wondering what they can put on the table for dinner with what they've got left. But the way they see it, the odds of having three oranges come up on a one-armed bandit are still better than hitting four out of six numbers in the lottery."

"It's sad," Fiore said. "Half the stores on the main drag in Westerly are boarded up. It'll be a disaster area if Bromfield can't make it back."

Tarantino picked up his wine again and held it in his hand as he continued talking. "The story gets even better," he said. "Just after the slots got started in Westerly, a State rep filed a bill in the House to allow casino gambling in Rhode Island. He's talking about craps, roulette, blackjack, the whole thing, at the option of each town. The difference, of course, is that the city or town would run the operation and take all the profits instead of sharing it with some entrepreneur who came out of the woodwork to make a fast buck." Sandy took a sip from his cup and put it down again.

"The Senate got pretty much the same bill a week later, courtesy of Millard Brickman, that great statesman from Warren."

"Not the brightest bulb in the room," Fiore interjected.

"That's no secret," Tarantino answered. "He probably thinks the town could open up a Las Vegas style casino just a mile off the Swansea/Warren exit on I 195 and catch everyone from Rhode Island and Massachusetts driving toward the beaches and the Cape. Anyway, it looks right now like the House would go for the legislation while the Senate's against it. But neither one is anxious to have a vote too soon. The smart money says there won't be a vote on any of the bills until after the election next November.

"Meanwhile, two other slots have opened since the legislation was introduced, one right up the road in Pawtucket. And believe it or not, while gambling is still illegal in this great little state of ours unless you're betting the lottery, every one of those joints is being allowed to operate."

Sandy got up and began pacing along his side of the table again. "No one is doing a damn thing about it. Every town needs the money so bad they just shut their eyes and stick out their hands, palms up. And someone with clout has told the State Police to look the other way. So tell me, Doug, how do you think my old man feels when the cops drive right past an illegal-as-hell slot parlor on the way to harassing a room full of people at one of our Family's private clubs?" He didn't wait for an answer. "What really pisses me off is that they show no fucking appreciation for what my father's done in the years he's been running things. You can't compare the sources of our income today to what they were under Tony Buscatelli twenty years ago."

"I know that," Fiore said.

"Anyhow, the slot machines aren't the big issue. They hurt our take because it's another option the gamblers have if they feel like a little action and don't want to come to one of our clubs. But it would cripple us if the State decides to get into blackjack, craps and roulette, the heavy stuff. I've told you before, that's a big part of what the Family relies on for our basic operating income. That, and the sports betting. Competition from the State would give my Family one hell of a problem. All our investments in legitimate businesses are gravy when things are going well. It's where the bonuses come from. But we've had some big losers in the last few years too. We can't afford to kiss that kind of gambling money goodbye. What some of these Statehouse morons are talking about doing could even start a little war within the Tarantino family if there was any kind of push from one group to get back into drugs or prostitution."

Fiore listened to everything carefully and thought he saw where Sandy was heading. "We've got two lawyers in my firm who hold seats in the House," he said. "I can talk to them when the time's right, if this ever comes up for a vote. I'll even twist their arms if I've got something to use, but I can't guarantee they'd vote against it. And I've never lobbied for anything up at the Statehouse, so I don't think I'd do a very good job at it."

Sandy smiled. "Good try, Doug, but you're not even warm. Here comes the bottom line." He continued pacing as he spoke. Fiore leaned forward in anticipation, resting his arms on the table. "My father knows there's got to be a strong voice in Rhode Island against the State going into gaming operations. And it has to be the voice of morality. It has to convince the people that the State would just be encouraging the poorest members of society, the ones who gamble the most and can't afford it, to go even deeper into the hole by making casino games available to them all over the place. Gambling is a sickness, a disease, and they shouldn't be exposed to it every time they walk out their front doors.

"That speaker would have to make our so-called leaders understand that eventually those folks will become wards of the State. They'll have to be fed, clothed, housed and given health care out of public funds. It will end up costing the taxpayers more than what the State takes in from gambling."

"That's for sure," Fiore said.

"And besides, there's the bureaucracy that would have to be set up to run it. You know what that means. It'll be full of former politicos and other hacks who'll get all the good jobs through their friends in power, whether or not they're qualified. If some commission says it can oversee casino gaming with 200 employees, you can bet your ass there'll be twice as many feeding at the trough within two or three years."

Sandy was standing behind his chair, his hands pressed against the top of it. He looked down at his friend and waited until he caught his eye. "That's the message that has to get delivered, Doug. It's pro Tarantino family all the way, but no one will be thinking of us when they hear it. They'll be too concerned and upset about the idea of their own tax dollars going to support the people who live on the edge. What they'll be saying is, 'Don't take my hard-earned money and spend it on welfare.' And the argument that will persuade them from supporting any casino bill has to come from one person."

Fiore had no idea whom Sandy had in mind. "Who?" he asked.

"The Governor of Rhode Island."

It wasn't registering. Doug felt like a deer caught in the headlights. He looked blankly at Sandy for several seconds before speaking.

"I don't get it. What have I got to do with John Sacco, or vice versa? I always thought he was against gambling. Wouldn't he veto any casino bill that passed?"

Tarantino answered immediately, as if he and Doug were reading from the same script. "A year ago I would have said you were right. Sacco used to say he didn't want to depend on any gambling revenue to pay the State's bills. But he hasn't done a thing to keep slots shops from opening up and he hasn't said a fucking word to discourage the casino bills from going forward in the House and Senate." Sandy slammed his hand down on the table when he swore. "He's either getting something out of it himself or he changed his mind about gambling. That's been the bad news for us. But the good news is on the way. As soon as Spence Hardiman announces that he's tired of Washington politics and doesn't want to go back for another term in the Senate, Sacco will be a candidate for that job. Maybe the only one on the Republican side, maybe not. So we're going to get him out of the Statehouse, whether he wins Hardiman's seat or not. Rhode Island will elect a new governor."

"That's one giant 'if' of a scenario," Fiore replied, "but even if you were right about it . . . ."

Tarantino cut him off. "We think you're the best man for that job."

Fiore was stunned. He looked at his friend, certain of the big grin he'd see momentarily, followed by the boisterous laugh and the words, "Just kidding, just kidding, don't have a goddam heart attack for Christ sakes." But none of it happened, and as the seconds passed he realized that Sandy was serious.

"Come on," he said, still unbelieving, "you want me to run for governor?"

"You sure are a quick study." Sandy smiled. "I make the motion and the Tarantino family seconds it."

Fiore shook his head back and forth several times, almost involuntarily. "But I've never held a political office," he reasoned. "I haven't run for anything in my life, including dog catcher. No one knows who the hell I am. I'd get a hundred votes from Federal Hill and fifty more from my family."

"You're wrong, good buddy." Sandy sat down again. He forgot about his back problems and leaned forward toward Doug. "In today's world, the fact that you've never been in politics is a great big plus. The public hates those guys, especially the ones who want to hang on forever. One of your biggest selling points will be that you're coming forward out of a sense of duty, just like the good old 'Founding Fathers' wanted. On top of that you pledge to serve no more than two terms in the governor's chair under any circumstances.

"The people will love it, just wait and see. You don't have any name recognition today, but by the time you become a candidate next year, we'll have a campaign ready to roll and the money to drive it. I've already discussed it with this super guy I want to bring in to put the entire thing together. I mean he's someone who's been through it all before, the whole pressure cooker, from beginning to end. He goes all the way back to Reagan's campaign for governor of California. He helped put him in the White House twice and was co-director for Bush's election in '88. He's the one they credit for getting Bill Weld elected governor in Massachusetts. And let me tell you, Weld never ran for anything before that and was the longest shot on the board going into the primaries. It can be done, Doug. It just takes a good candidate, a manager who knows what the fuck he's doing, lots of money and a ton of work."

Fiore was still overwhelmed. "Who else do you expect to run for governor if Sacco doesn't?" he asked.

"There's no 'if' with Sacco, Doug, or with Hardiman either. Trust me on that. Your competition in the primary will probably come from Richie Cardella. Two good Italian boys fighting it out. Then we don't have to worry about the voters being prejudiced, right?"

Tarantino laughed, and kept talking. "Cardella won't be any pushover. He had four years as Attorney General after he gave up his seat in the House. Richie won a couple of big cases as AG that got plenty of coverage all over the State. Remember the serial killer who swore that Jesus kept telling him in his dreams to strangle those women? Richie put him away for life. Neighborhood crime will be a big issue in the election. To tell you the truth, if we thought he'd be against legalizing casino gambling, we'd have no problem with him." Sandy paused. "But he's not . . . and we do . . . in spades."

"How do you know his position?" Fiore asked.

"Because we've checked carefully, carefully and quietly. He voted for the lottery when he served in the House. He also made a few speeches about gambling being a necessary source of income for the State, that it was better than trying to raise taxes every year. We also found out that his law firm was retained as a consultant by several Senators to draft a revised casino gambling bill they plan to introduce at some time. No doubt about it, he's in deep on the other side."

Fiore no longer looked as if he was listening to a story he couldn't understand. The shock of hearing himself referred to as the next governor had finally passed. He realized that he was already beginning to like the idea. He'd been up against Cardella in some cases over the years. They were corporate matters, not criminal, but he didn't think the former Attorney General was any great shakes as a lawyer.

"What Democrats do you see in the race?" he asked.

"Only one," Sandy said. "Bruce Singer's got it all to himself. The Party has to go with him, even if he blew his race in the primary two years ago. Singer was lieutenant governor for two terms when Frank Lindgren was in the governor's chair, and he made a lot of friends. Ed

McGurty never expected to beat Singer in that primary. He was in it just to get a lot of publicity for his Mercedes dealership at the expense of his contributors. It probably shocked the shit out of him to win it.

"And Singer learned that you can't lay down on the campaign just because everyone tells you your opponent is an asshole. You don't put in the time on the stump, you suffer the consequences. But Sacco murdered McGurty in the general election. That's why the Democrats feel they don't owe him anything next time around, and they know Singer's a much better candidate. I doubt he'll have anyone running against him in the primary. That means he won't have any mud getting thrown at him until he's up against you, if you knock off Cardella. That's too bad, but there's nothing we can do about it."

Tarantino was up again, moving around. He stopped to pour more wine into both cups and returned the bottle to the refrigerator. He retrieved his cup from the table and continued walking. "What do you think, old buddy?" he asked, standing near the panel that opened earlier to let him into the room. His tone of voice indicated that he wanted a quick "Yes" from his former roommate.

"Christ, Sandy, I don't know what to say. I'm not going to tell you it turns me off. In fact, it sounds real good. It's flattering as hell and I'd probably love the job if I could get elected." Fiore pictured himself sitting at the desk in the large corner office of the Statehouse. "One thing I know is that four years in the governor's office wouldn't hurt when I got back to the firm. I'm sure a lot of good business would follow me there. But first I've got to talk to my wife and a few of my partners. It's a big decision and I need their input on it. How soon do you need an answer?"

Sandy hesitated a few moments. "Before I respond to that, I want to tell you something else. There's nothing that says you'd have to get out of politics if you did serve two terms in the Statehouse. That pledge I mentioned was limited to running for governor. And it sounds like you forgot that Rhode Island's joining the rest of the country and making governor a four-year term instead of two. So it could work out to be eight years for you if you wanted it. The point I'm making is that four years from now Jim Hanover's third term in the Senate will be up and he'll be sixty-seven years old. He's already had a couple of heart attacks. Chances of his wanting another six years or the people sending him back to Washington are getting more remote all the time. It's just a thought, Doug, but maybe you wouldn't be happy in that national spotlight anyway." Sandy winked at his good friend as he finished the sentence.

"As far as letting us know if you want to go for it, do you still remember that conversation we had nineteen years ago in Doctor Feeney's office at Mount Hope Hospital?" Fiore remembered it well. It was the first phone call he ever received from Joe Gaudette who told him that Sandy wanted to see him. Doug was in his third full year as an associate at Walters, Cassidy & Breen. He and Grace were married for six months at the time. Gaudette explained that he scheduled Doug for a routine physical by an internist named John Feeney at Mount Hope Hospital, and that Tarantino would see him there. On the day of the appointment, while Fiore waited for the doctor in the examining room, half undressed and wondering whether he'd actually be seen by Feeney, Sandy came in. He took only a minute to ask Doug about his personal life before starting to explain how the Family, under Sal Tarantino, was moving out of most of the illegal activities Anthony Buscatelli had favored, including drugs and prostitution.

"This is my contribution, with my father's consent. We're turning our attention to investments in legitimate local businesses that need a financial boost." But the problem, he said, was that those companies were afraid of seeing their names dragged into the newspaper every time the *Herald* did a story on the Tarantino family and how it made its money.

"It's a public relations problem, Doug," he recalled Sandy telling him. "The point we try to make with these outfits is that my father is taking the Family in an entirely different direction, away from the things it's always been associated with. In time we'll be pretty much like any other venture capital company looking for businesses that have a good product or service and need money. I do a good selling job with them one-on-one and there's a list of companies that are definitely interested. But one of the things we've got to avoid like the plague during the transition is being embarrassed by the police in the media."

That's when Fiore learned that Joe Gaudette was a captain in the State Police and was an old trusted friend of Sal Tarantino's. "Gaudette's desk job lets him find out when the police plan to bust into one of the Family's private gambling clubs," Sandy explained. "But he usually doesn't get that information until just before they're planning the raid. At that point he can't risk making phone calls to the pols we're friendly with on the Hill." Then Sandy informed him that the Teamsters Union had just organized everyone in the State Police under the rank of lieutenant.

"That gives us a new way to handle the situation," Sandy said. "You'll be receiving a call from Superintendent Halliday asking your firm to represent management in negotiating the labor agreement with the Union. Your firm will report to Gaudette. Once the negotiations get started, Joe will be able to speak to you any time he wants, probably after he's checked in with the labor lawyer you'll have handling the case. There'll be some code words for any message he wants you to get through to us right away. You'll be completely in the dark about what's going on because you won't know the code. But when the cops show up at our club that night, hopefully all they'll find will be a crowd of people having a good time over dinner. No gambling, no laws broken, no story for the papers or TV. That's what I need from you, Doug. Aside from Joe, you're the only other person outside the Family that we can trust a hundred percent."

The quid pro quo, Sandy told him, would demonstrate the Family's appreciation. "We'll see you get all the legal work for the companies we invest in." To show what that involved, he proceeded to preview two of the construction firms with which the Tarantinos were ready to close investment deals. He made sure Doug understood that the amount of legal work and billable hours that would come from representing them was huge.

Fiore recalled that even at that early stage of his career he didn't want to be just another lawyer at Walters, Cassidy & Breen. He looked forward to being able to move into a power position when his time came; to lead, not follow. He remembered the words his father drummed into him when he was in high school and Anthony Fiore was already concerned about his son being admitted to an Ivy League college: "Good grades will get you where you want to go," he said, "and then, after college, wherever you are, you want to fight to become king of the hill, to get as much power as you can and to fight like hell to stay there."

Years later the talk was very much the same whenever he was home on break from Columbia. "Work your ass off," his father told him. "These three years can make you or break you. Do whatever it takes to get to the top of your class so the big firms—the ones that pay big money—will want to hire you. Get close to the lawyers who have the power. Do favors for the right people and never—I mean *never*—talk out against the ones who run the firm. They can help you if some bastard there tries to walk all over you. At some point they'll be looking for friendly faces to replace them when they step down. You want to be one of those people because power in the firm will come with it. Power is the magic word, Doug. And when you have it, don't be afraid to use it. The lawyers in your firm can do what you say either because they love you or because they're scared shitless of you. Either way, you're on top and you do what you have to do to stay there."

Although Fiore had little respect for his father because of his temper, surly disposition and heavy-handed discipline, he understood that the words were coming from his heart and were intended to make Doug's life easier and more rewarding. He knew that his father, a lathe operator at the same tool-making plant for over twenty-five years, made all the mistakes he was warning his son against: bad-mouthing a series of job stewards in his desire to be appointed to the position himself, and then, while serving on the negotiating committee for a new contract, trying to persuade other members of the committee to reject the deal that the union representative strongly recommended. From that point on, it was made clear to him that he would never serve on the negotiating committee again and would not be considered to fill a job steward opening. Anthony Fiore realized then that if he ever had a reason to file a grievance against his employer, especially if he was suspended or discharged for some alleged misconduct, he would not be able to count on strong support from his union. He knew that all that was left for him to do at the plant was run his lathe and shut his mouth.

Doug wanted to be part of the inner circle that made the important decisions for the firm and eventually become "numero uno" among his peers. It was something he thought about often, although he wanted to achieve his goal through respect, not fear. In a quiet way, he tried to find out all he could about the other associates at the firm so as to determine which of them would make valuable allies for him in the years ahead.

Fiore realized, as he listened to Sandy in Dr. Feeney's examining room, that he was being presented with an opportunity on a silver platter to achieve his goal. It didn't take a genius to see that the business he received from the Tarantinos would make him stand out from other associates and give him a power base. It would probably be the best chance he'd ever get. There didn't seem to be much risk, as Sandy said, but he couldn't kid himself about whether it was legal or ethical. If it was ever discovered that he helped the Tarantinos avoid a raid on an illegal activity or outsmart the police in some other way, his license to practice law would be suspended, at the very least. He might even be disbarred. This was a career decision—he had to face that fact—one that could make him or possibly destroy him.

"It's a good deal for you, Doug. Don't pass it up."

He wouldn't. He decided it was worth the risk. "I'm your man," he told Sandy.

* * *

The knock at the door came just as Fiore recollected the commitment he made to Sandy Tarantino in Dr. Feeney's office that day.

"Who is it?" Sandy asked.

"It's Johnny."

"Let him in, Doug. The door's locked."

Fiore opened the door and a man who looked to be about retirement age came in. He wore a black suit, the standard uniform for someone in the undertaking business.

"Sir, Mr. Milano wanted you to know that the wake is over and everyone has gone."

"Thank you, Johnny. Tell Mr. Milano that my meeting should end in about ten minutes and that I'll knock on the panel when I'm ready to leave."

"Yes, sir, good seeing you again."

"Thank you, Johnny. You take care of yourself."

Fiore locked the door after him and returned to the table. "Yes," he said, "I remember that meeting in Feeney's office like it was yesterday. Pretty much word for word."

"Good," Tarantino said right away. "Then I'm sure you haven't forgotten how I made you act on your gut instead of going home and thinking about it."

"I remember, but . . ."

My Honorable Brother • 33

"And you've never regretted that decision, have you?"

"No, I never have. You and your father have been awfully good to me. The companies you invested in and sent to my firm have been great clients. I've had higher billings than anyone else for the last seven or eight years."

"And where do you think you'd be today if you said 'No' to me that morning?"

"Who knows? I think I would have made partner after eight years but there was always the chance they could have told me to find another home."

"Listen, Doug, if you weren't the managing partner of a hundred-lawyer law firm that's pretty close to being number one in the State, you wouldn't be such an attractive candidate. But you are, and we need you, even more than we needed you back then. This decision could do at least as much for your career as that one. If you're elected governor, that could pave the way for you to go to Washington later on as Rhode Island's junior senator. And once you're there, who knows what might happen after that?"

The words hung in the air. Fiore allowed himself to imagine the possibilities as he looked at his former roommate. He got up and began moving slowly in Sandy's direction. "I know you're right," he said, "but this is a hell of a lot more involved. I've got to discuss it with Grace and my daughter and . . ."

Tarantino held up his hand to cut him off. "Not this one, Doug. There's nothing for you to talk over with your wife or anyone else. It's already a done deal."

"What are you talking about? You just raised it for the first time."

"I know, but you're the guy we've got to have. There's no one else waiting in the wings that we've got a chance to elect. You're the only one we can count on for sure to veto a gambling bill if one makes it through the legislature."

Fiore didn't like the way Sandy was trying to steamroller him into a decision. *What did he mean by calling it a done deal?* he thought. No one would be asked to take a step this big without being given some time to think about it.

"But come on," he said, "I've got commitments to my firm and to some special clients. I don't know what would happen to all the bond work we do for the State if I'm a candidate. I've got to check those things out."

"You're not hearing me, good buddy." The tone of voice registered on Doug immediately. He'd heard his old roommate speak that way a number of times in the past when the next order of business would be a fist to someone's face. He knew it was time to shut up and listen.

Sandy waited until he could catch and hold Fiore's eye. "My father and I are telling you what you have to do. We've been investing in you for twenty years. No one knew for sure there'd be a time when we'd have to cash in that investment, but that's where we're at right now. You'll run for governor, Doug, or every fucking piece of business you've picked up through us will disappear overnight. You wouldn't have much left, would you? No more number one rainmaker managing partner. You'd be back researching cases and writing briefs for everyone else. There are probably some lawyers in that firm who'd just love to see you in that position, or better yet, getting your walking papers. Maybe they're jealous at how fast you made it to the top, with all the power you've got, and they'd enjoy watching you get knocked down."

Tarantino stopped. He could see that what he said took all the fight out of his old friend. There were stronger threats he could make, but now he knew they weren't necessary. Fiore belonged to them already. He continued on, speaking in a less menacing way.

"But we can't force you to run. If you're willing to give up everything, that's your call. I'll have Gaudette get back to you in a few days and ask whether you can keep the appointment with me. You let him know. 'Yes' will mean you've decided to throw your hat in the ring. You with me, Doug?"

Fiore was still absorbing the meaning of what he was just told. He knew there was no sense prolonging the discussion. The shit had hit the fan and there was nothing he could do about it. Regardless of how he felt, he'd given Grace and Susan the good life through his deal with the Tarantinos and he couldn't just take it away from them now. He remembered the old saw that if rape was inevitable, lie back and enjoy it. He nodded his head.

"I understand," he said.

Tarantino moved closer. "You'll see, it'll work out best for everyone. When you get elected, you'll be thanking me every day." He smiled and offered his hand, as if the two of them had just concluded a mutually agreeable transaction. Doug took it and returned the handshake. Sandy wasn't surprised at how limp the other hand felt.

"Wait here for a couple of minutes after I leave the room," Sandy said. "Then go back out the way you came in. The same cab, same driver, will be at the door. I assumed you'd want to go to your car in the Arcade Garage, right?"

Doug shook his head affirmatively. "Yeah."

"Well, his orders are to let you out right where it's parked, whatever floor you're on, not outside the garage. Don't try and tell him anything different because he won't listen to you. We take good care of all our investments, Doug." Sandy winked at him. "As usual, thanks for coming."

He started walking toward the hidden panel at the side of the room. Doug watched him, noticing for the first time how he leaned to his left as he moved forward.

* * *

It was almost midnight when Vincent Milano pulled into Sandy Tarantino's driveway in Barrington and let him off. Sandy knew his father would be awake in bed, watching *The Tonight Show,* and called him before removing his overcoat.

"So how'd it go?" Sal asked.

"No problem," Sandy said. "He had to swallow hard when I showed him the fork in the road, but he knows there's only one way to go if he wants to stay with the good life. He'll be our man."

"Good. Do you still think he'll be up against Cardella in the primary?"

"That's my bet. We know who's calling the shots in the Party. They've got to go with him."

There was silence on the other end of the line, but Sandy could hear the TV in the background. He waited a few moments before speaking. "Did you hear me, Pop?"

"Yeah, I heard. Leno was just telling a joke and I wanted to catch the punch line. Okay, then what you've got to do is put one or two of the boys on Cardella. Have them follow him around. Find out where he goes after work at night. Maybe he's got a favorite bar or restaurant he hangs out at. See who his friends are. Take a table next to him and listen to what he's talking about. We want to know everything we can find out about him in case Fiore needs our help later on. You understand?"

"I'll take care of it tomorrow. What time you coming in?"

"The usual."

"Okay, Pop. Good night." Sandy hung up the phone, took off his coat and went to sit in the darkness of the living room. Doug Fiore was their candidate. Now he had to figure out how they could be sure he would win the primary.

5

GEORGE RYDER WASN'T SURPRISED to find that the hallway leading to his office was still dark. It was only 7:15 a.m.

Minutes earlier, he got off the elevator at the main reception area of Walters, Cassidy & Breen on the thirty-first floor of the Spalding National Bank building, checked his mail slot for messages and slowly climbed the internal spiral staircase that connected the three floors occupied by the firm.

Made of light oak, with the stairs covered in beige industrial carpeting, the staircase was de rigueur for any law firm moving into new quarters in the 1980s. WC&B had committed itself to renting the space about a year before construction came to an end in 1984. The older partners were split on whether it made sense to move from where they were situated for many years to expensive new offices in a building several blocks away. But the younger ones, led by Doug Fiore, helped carry the motion to relocate by voting almost unanimously to sign a lease for ten years with an option for ten more.

Business improved dramatically, year to year, in the second half of the eighties. The partners' soaring earnings allowed them to overlook the fact that overhead increased almost twenty percent after the move was completed. But things changed dramatically when the real estate boom suddenly became a bust at the beginning of the new decade. Although the bankruptcy lawyers were often working seven days a week to keep up with the demands on their time, the recession affected the billable hours and fees for almost every other department of the firm.

A number of associates, part of the groups hired out of law school in 1988 and '89, were let go. When the WC&B Executive Committee reacted to the prolonged slowdown by announcing that the partnership track was being extended from seven years to nine, several other associates resigned and looked for work elsewhere. In 1988, the firm brought eleven new lawyers on board, with much fanfare about challenging Harding & Reynolds as the State's largest law firm. But by 1993, the number of law school graduates it recruited for openings was down to four.

Ryder had stopped at the takeout shop in the lobby for a cup of coffee and a bran muffin. He knew that Anna, the Nicaraguan woman who prepared the pots of coffee in the kitchens on each of the firm's three floors, wouldn't be at work yet. He justified ordering the muffin, which his overweight body didn't need, by telling himself that the fiber it contained was good for him. As he rode up on the elevator, Ryder saw that some of the coffee was leaking out into the bag.

Entering the dark hallway on the thirty-second floor, he was forced to use his right elbow to push the two light switches into their "on" position before walking down the corridor to his office. Ryder was several inches over six feet and weighed in the neighborhood of 260 pounds. Every so often, at his wife's urging, he went on a crash diet and took off anywhere from twenty to thirty pounds. But inevitably his will power deserted him and he started each day at work with the purchase of a muffin or Danish pastry.

Ryder lurched slightly several times as he moved along the corridor. His baggy blue suit had gone too long without being cleaned and pressed. When he reached his office, he dropped his heavy briefcase onto the sofa that sat along a side wall and switched on the light. Several yellow pads were on his desk. He turned one of them over so he could put the wet paper bag down onto its cardboard backing.

The office had a view that overlooked the federal courthouse at one end of Kennedy Plaza. When WC&B first occupied the new building, Ryder chose that location for himself with the seventh highest seniority in the firm. He stood at the window for several seconds while removing his jacket, then hung it up on the plastic hanger he kept behind the door. As he collapsed into the large executive chair at his desk, a sigh of exhaustion escaped from his lips before he was aware of it. He opened the bag and was upset to discover that some coffee had seeped into most of his muffin, turning it soggy. "Damn it!" he grumbled.

George Ryder knew he was in trouble. In the last year and a half his labor practice lost five good clients. Only one of them, a sausage manufacturer, went out of business. It was another victim of society's changing attitude toward eating meat.

A larger client, Bell Coated Plastics, was a victim of Doug Fiore's matter-of-fact approach to the recession. Ryder had done a significant amount of work in guiding the company through a long strike. As a result of the losses it took during the work stoppage, Bell's payments to the firm were not in significant amounts. Confronted with the matter, Ryder assured Fiore that they would be paid in full and urged him to be patient. But Fiore was concerned about the number of clients whose payments for services rendered were already overdue. As a consequence, he lobbied for and got a green light from a majority of his Executive Committee to shut off legal services for clients who were 120 days behind in their accounts unless they paid a quarter of the outstanding balance the next time they needed professional advice. Fiore expected the new policy to help the firm's cash position. Soon afterwards, Ryder was forced to give that message to Harry Bell when he called to discuss a new employee grievance. Bell thanked him for all the help he was given in the past and told Ryder to tell the firm's managing partner to shove his new policy up his ass. So Bell Plastics was gone, but WC&B received a check each month reducing the balance owed. It was the same amount Harry Bell was paying regularly before he rebelled at Fiore's directive and kissed them goodbye.

The other three clients Ryder lost were sold to larger companies based outside of Providence, and their legal work went with them. The law firms benefiting from such corporate takeovers were most always located in the home city of the acquiring company. One of these former clients was a large printing and mailing firm that had several different unions representing various groups of employees. The contract negotiations for each group every two or three years, along with the inevitable grievances that had to be settled or arbitrated, had provided steady work for Ryder.

When George Ryder first joined the firm thirty-two years earlier, it was known as Walters, Holt, Miller & Cassidy. It was his first job after graduating from Harvard Law School. He lacked the confidence and personality for bringing in new clients, but did excellent work within his area of expertise. He quickly earned the trust of those clients whose labor problems were normally handled by lawyers senior to him. As time passed, Ryder inherited a good deal of that work for himself, and when David Miller drowned during a vacation in Florida, he suddenly became the senior labor law specialist. A year later, he was elected to serve on the Executive Committee. It was the same year Doug Fiore became an associate at the firm.

Ryder remained on the Executive Committee for four years, took a year's leave of absence from the firm to have major surgery on his back, and then returned to the firm and his position on the Committee. It was just in time for him to be its only member to vote against shortening the partnership track for Fiore from seven years to six. The Committee's willingness to allow the exception came in response to Fiore's threat to take his burgeoning practice elsewhere.

Ryder recalled how surprised he was when the older lawyers in the firm backed his candidacy for managing partner after Bob Gorman announced that he no longer wished to continue in that role. Gorman, a good friend, saw to it that his Executive Committee recommended Ryder as the candidate to replace him. It was George's twentieth year with WC&B.

His opponent in that election was Steve Breen, a skilled and dynamic litigator who brought his own large practice into the firm five years earlier and was rewarded by having his name included in the renamed partnership. Breen's strength came from the partners who felt that the position should be in the hands of a rainmaker, someone with the ability to attract new business. They preferred a leader who could push the firm in certain directions through an implied threat of taking his important list of clients elsewhere if he wasn't a happy camper.

Ryder expected to lose the election, and was speechless when he learned from Gorman that he was the new managing partner. All of his peers stood and applauded when he entered the meeting room from the lounge where he and Breen were awaiting the results of the vote. But later that same night he learned from an Executive Committee member that almost half the partners voted for his opponent.

Like Gorman before him, Ryder held the position for six years. But unlike his predecessor, he did not resign. Rather, he was voted out of office by his fellow partners—it was 19 to 16, he recalled—who were in favor of certain changes being advocated by his challenger, Doug Fiore.

Ryder got up from his chair and moved uneasily to the window. He didn't want to think back to that election or the infighting that went on between himself and Fiore at the time. He realized, 20/20, that he made a fatal mistake in not recognizing how fast Fiore's star was rising. It would have helped him to inquire, much earlier than he did, whether his announced rival really had all the votes in his pocket that he bragged about. He opened the window to let in some fresh air and sipped the last few drops of coffee. It was already cold. He flipped the cup, basketball style, into the wastebasket next to the wall. Margaret Cardoo walked past his office and waved to him as she said "Good morning." He waved back, silently. Someone else said "Hi, George" a few minutes later, while he was staring out the window, but was gone before Ryder could recognize the voice or return the greeting.

Ryder closed his office door quietly and sat down at his desk. Opening the top drawer, he pulled out the yellow sheet of paper with the numbers he wrote down the day before. It revealed that his billable hours for the entire year, through December 10th, were 982. That was down from 1,351 the year before and 1,668 the year before that. The totals for fees billed out to clients credited to him were just as discouraging. At one time those numbers were counted on to fall somewhere between four and five hundred thousand dollars annually. But the figure reached just $267,000 the prior year and was only $203,000 this year, to date. He was being paid more money than he was bringing in.

Ryder carefully reviewed his list of clients. He saw that a large part of the work he did during the year was for Ocean State Wire & Cable. *God help me*, he told himself, *if I ever lose that account*. The situation he was in forced him to realize that it would be a good idea to call Brad Hanley, Ocean State's president, and invite him to dinner.

The problem was exacerbated by Ryder's knowledge that he had very little work scheduled to do the rest of the month. There was nothing on his calendar for that day or the next. He could hope to hear from one of his clients, or perhaps be asked by Paul Castillo, the firm's junior labor law specialist, to help out on some matter. But Castillo stopped doing that some months earlier, and Ryder suspected that Fiore was behind it. No one had to remind him that as bad as his performance looked on those weekly computer printouts, he was also burdened with the thought that the managing partner of the firm hated his guts. The only question in his mind was how soon Fiore would try to push him out the door.

6

On the same day that Fiore told Joe Gaudette to let their "good friend" know he would "keep the appointment," he was forty minutes late for a date he had with one of his partners. Their meeting was at the Hilton Hotel, two blocks north of T. F. Green International Airport in Warwick. Making his way through the lobby, he noticed on the bulletin board that two companies were hosting Christmas parties for their employees that evening. Several groups of people, drinks in hand, milled around in the open area just beyond the front desk.

Fiore took the elevator to the fourth floor. He found Room 420 at the end of the corridor to his left, and knocked. Playfully, he contorted his face and brought it as close as he could to the peephole on the door. A few moments later he heard the chain lock being released, and the door opened.

"I thought you changed your mind," she said. There was no warmth in the greeting. She held the door while he entered, then closed it and put the safety lock back in place.

Fiore had already thrown both his raincoat and suit jacket on one of the queen-sized beds by the time she was alongside him. "I'm sorry, Carol," he said. "I just couldn't get out of there any sooner." He reached for her shoulders as he spoke, but she pulled away.

She was wearing a white blouse, with a small pocket on each side set off by mother of pearl buttons. Her heavy woolen skirt was multi-pleated in a Scotch plaid, its dominant color a forest green that Fiore found very attractive. Her hair was black, cut medium length. All the features of her face seemed perfectly combined until her profile revealed a slight bump in the middle of her nose. She wore no eye shadow, but had on lipstick the color of a delicate pink rose. At five feet, eight inches tall, she was just two inches shorter than Fiore.

Carol's voice carried a harsh tone when she answered. "Your being sorry isn't enough. I don't intend to be a lady in waiting for you, hanging around a hotel room until you decide to show up. If you can't be on time, have the decency to call and let me know. Then it will be my decision whether or not to stay. Don't think you can take me for granted just because we're lovers." She walked past him, over to the bed near the window, and sat down at the end of it.

Fiore loosened his tie and unbuttoned the top button of his shirt. He was there for sex, not for a fight. He was looking forward to being in bed with her, and didn't want anything to spoil it. But he went through this sort of thing on other occasions with other women and was sure he could talk himself back into her favor. *Besides*, he told himself, *she wants the sex as much as I do.*

Doug sat next to her on the bed and spoke quietly. "Look, I know how you feel. I don't blame you for being upset. But don't think for a second that I'm taking you for granted, because I'm not. If you left before I got here, I would have understood completely. I would have had to rush home and take a cold shower, but that's my problem."

He looked at her and waited until she returned his glance and gave him a slight smile. He knew he was doing well and was confident that everything would soon be on track. "I probably wouldn't have been more than ten minutes late," he went on, "except that Scardino got hold of me and said he had to show me some numbers. Receivables have been God-awful the past couple of months. He wanted to know how I felt about taking out a ninety-day loan from Spalding to tide us over."

Fiore removed the gold cuff links from his shirtsleeves. Each was in the shape of a capital "F." He folded the starched cuffs over twice as he continued speaking. "I had my coat on and was halfway down the hall when he grabbed me. We used the conference room across from the elevator, and I figured it would take ten minutes at the most. But sometimes he has to explain his figures three different ways before I know what he's talking about. When he finished, it was already quarter of eight. I couldn't call you from in there because Frankie stayed and started working on some other stuff. The elevator was waiting for me when I stepped out into the reception area. I grabbed it and got over here as fast as I could." Fiore put his hand on her left shoulder and began massaging it.

Carol waited until his fingers dug deeper into the flesh, anticipating the pleasure it would give her. "You knew I had to be home by ten o'clock tonight," she said. "I've got a husband who may start wondering where I've been. I don't want to feel like we're doing something dirty when we're together. But if there's only enough time to get undressed, make love and rush out of here, how else can I feel?"

"You're right," Doug answered. "I don't want it to be like that either." It didn't matter to him how long they were together as long as he got what he came for. He moved closer and started working the fingers of both hands into the soft part of her neck and around her shoulder blades. Carol bent her head forward and rested her left hand on his thigh.

"Frankie's been putting in a lot of time at night in the office," Doug said. "He tells me he's got a hundred things to finish up before the end of the year. It's no secret he's not the smartest firm administrator in town, but at least he's not afraid of work."

Carol looked at him and shook her head, as if in agreement. "What's no secret is that he's sleeping with Janice what's her name, Dick Birnbaum's secretary. He hangs around at night to be with her."

"Janice Rossman?" Fiore looked at her as if he couldn't believe it.

"That sounds right. She's got long blonde hair. Always wears heavy makeup. She looks like someone just got her ready to go on TV."

He pictured Rossman in his mind's eye. "Yeah, that's her. I thought she was married." He realized his faux pas as soon as the words were out, but if Carol caught it, she let it pass.

"She's either divorced or separated. I believe she has a daughter about twelve years old."

"So how does she get to spend time with Scardino?" he asked.

"Oh, right there, Doug," Carol said, ignoring the question for the moment. "Keep your fingers right there. That feels so good."

He pushed his fingers a little deeper into her skin and pressed down hard. He began moving them around in a small circle.

"Oh, that's wonderful," she sighed, and took her time before answering him. "The gossip about her and Frankie is that she runs out of the office at five o'clock to go home and feed her daughter. Most nights she comes back into town for dinner with him. She lives only ten minutes away, near the Hasbro toy plant in Pawtucket. Once or twice a week he takes her to the Econo Motel in Attleboro. They say it rents out by the hour."

Fiore laughed. "That's transporting a woman into Massachusetts for the purpose of having sex. Christ, I remember how those words about 'crossing state lines' used to scare the shit out of us when we were kids. We used to shack up in some motel in Fall River for a few hours on a Saturday night and we were always afraid the FBI was going to smash the door down just as we had an orgasm."

Carol laughed along with him. Doug moved his hands over her shoulders and down the front of her blouse. He squeezed her breasts for several seconds, cupping and uncupping them, and moved each of his forefingers in a circular motion around the area of her nipples. She leaned back slightly toward him. He kissed her ear and began unbuttoning the blouse. "How do you know all this stuff?" he asked.

"Because the girl is a bimbo." Carol emphasized "bimbo." "She can't keep it to herself. She told at least two other secretaries what was going on, in confidence, of course. And apparently she finds enough reasons to go into Frankie's office half a dozen times a day. She believes in his open door policy but always closes it behind her."

Carol moved her arms back to make it easier for Doug to slip off the blouse. He pushed the ends of her bra together so that the hooks came undone. She reached for the straps and threw it on the chair facing the TV. Doug turned her toward him and they exchanged smiles. He loved her breasts. They were larger and more rounded than his wife's. He put his mouth over one and ran his tongue around the nipple. She started to breathe heavily and he felt her give a mild shudder. He did the same on the other side. He gently pushed her breasts together and let his tongue massage both nipples in a wider circle. She put her hands on the side of his face and kissed the top of his head.

"Why are you still dressed?" she asked. There was a playful urgency in her voice.

Doug got up. He undid his tie and started taking off his shirt. He smiled at Carol, who was pulling the zipper of her plaid skirt down from the waist.

"I've got to hand it to Frankie," he said. "The man is fat, ugly in anyone's book, and has basically no personality. But he finds himself a good-looking blonde to screw around with."

"Look at it the other way, Doug. She may have found herself a little job security in Frankie. Dick Birnbaum's the third lawyer she's worked for in ten months. That probably means she's not the world's greatest secretary." Carol put her hand between his legs. "I think someone down there is ready and waiting."

Her touch excited him. Doug was suddenly anxious to make love. "Fix the bed," he said. Carol pulled the bedspread down and reached for the light switch. He quickly undressed and lay down next to her.

"Who do you think we can bill for this time?" he asked, in mock seriousness. A few seconds later they both laughed at the question. Then she started moving on top of him. "Easy, take it easy," he whispered.

* * *

Doug was in the shower when Carol left the hotel room. She emerged from the elevator and walked toward the lobby, holding the straps of her briefcase in her left hand. At that moment, she heard someone call her name. Panicking for an instant, Carol considered ignoring the greeting, as if too engrossed in other thoughts to have heard it. But she glanced to her left and saw a familiar face rapidly closing in on her. She stopped and smiled at Jeff MacGregor. He was one of several vice presidents in the loan department at Spalding Bank.

Carol represented a number of WC&B clients, including Fiore's two major construction companies, in obtaining loans from Spalding. She and Jeff often spent the better part of a day reviewing the endless number of documents arranged around the perimeter of a long conference table while closing some of those deals. MacGregor was holding hands with a woman wearing a white suit. Carol was certain she recently saw the same outfit hanging in the designer section of Lord & Taylor's.

"Hi, Jeff. Spending the bank's money again?" She started to offer her hand but stopped, realizing he'd have to let go of his companion's to take it.

"Don't I wish it," he answered. "We're celebrating our eleventh anniversary tonight."

"Well, congratulations!" She directed the word and her smile at both of them.

"Carol, I'd like you to meet my wife, Debbie. Debbie, this is Carol Singer, a lawyer at Walters, Cassidy & Breen. She and I often have to do what it takes to make certain that the wheels of progress keep moving forward in this town."

The two women smiled at each other and exchanged pleasantries.

"Working late, huh." Jeff made it more of a statement than a question.

Carol raised the soft leather briefcase in front of her. "Yes, I just got out of a meeting. The law is a jealous lover, as we gals like to say. Trouble is, I've got an even more jealous husband waiting for me at home. If you'll excuse me, I'm going to run. Very nice meeting you, Debbie. I'll see you soon, Jeff. Congratulations again to you both." She waved her hand and hurried off.

"She's some terrific lawyer," Jeff said. They watched Carol moving quickly toward the revolving door at the main entrance. "Her husband's a lawyer too, but he does litigation. Bruce Singer. He was the lieutenant governor for four years under Frank Lindgren."

7

THE HOUSE, A WHITE Victorian with black shutters, stood on Orchard Avenue, five blocks from the edge of the Brown University campus. It was the East Side of Providence, a neighborhood of well-kept older homes. The wealthy professionals who resided there rejected the idea of a tedious daily commute into the city from Barrington, Warwick, and other outlying towns where the homes were newer, leaned heavily to split level ranches and had significantly more lawn to be cared for.

When Brad and Patricia Hanley first moved in, nine years earlier, there was a need for the four large bedrooms, three baths, and spacious family room of which the house boasted. According to the real estate guidelines, the price was more than they could afford. But they envisioned a bright future for themselves because of Brad's new job and borrowed some money from Pat's parents to help swing the deal. They never regretted the decision. Now, however, their oldest child, Christine, accepted a position in Pittsburgh, where the family lived before Brad was hired to be the new president of Ocean State Wire & Cable. And Christine's two younger siblings were away at college.

Pat Hanley looked forward to this time when she and her husband could be alone again. They married when she was nineteen and he was twenty-four. The children came along right away. The youngest, Marie, arrived just sixteen months after Peter and three years after Christine. As a mom, Pat went through her full share of lying awake at night. Brad always fell asleep within minutes after closing his eyes, so the job of waiting up for their kids to get home was hers by default. She listened for the sound of one of the cars pulling into the driveway, followed by the opening and closing of the heavy kitchen door and the footsteps on the stairway. It was only then that she could relax and get some rest.

Later on, as her children went off to college, she discovered that the old cliché was true—"Out of sight, out of mind"—at least when it came time to sleeping at night. But now, Pat was troubled. Brad's day started, as always, with his leaving the house at quarter to seven in the morning. But the twelve-hour workday schedule he was on for so long seemed no longer to exist. Instead, she became used to seeing him return anywhere between 9:00 p.m. and midnight.

Pat urged Brad to come home earlier that night, and he agreed. When he told her not to bother making dinner, she assumed they would be going out to eat. She guessed that he would take her to one of the restaurants on Thayer Street, which ran through the middle of the Brown University campus. Brad always enjoyed being in the company of young people, even if it meant just being able to observe them.

Pat arrived home shortly before five o'clock from her three-day-a-week job at the Werner Medical Lab, where she ran blood tests. Work at the lab had picked up dramatically because of the increasing amount of AIDS testing that was being done. She took a long bath before changing into a pair of black slacks and a white blouse with a multi-colored rhinestone design in front. The children pitched in and gave her the blouse on her last birthday, but this was the first time she wore it. Pat looked at herself in the mirror as she dressed and was pleased with what she saw. The good looks that attracted a long list of boys from the time she was thirteen were still there. They captivated Brad when he first saw her working as a receptionist for a Dayton, Ohio, metallurgy firm. Her brunette hair, still long the way Brad liked it, showed no trace of gray. The several lines around her eyes didn't detract from the luminous blue color that looked out from below long attractive eyelashes. She puckered her lips, blew a kiss at herself and smiled, revealing teeth a movie actress would envy. Turning sideways, she threw her chest out a little and complimented herself on keeping an excellent figure.

Pat hurried downstairs when she heard the back door slam. She was still on her way to the kitchen when Brad called her name and announced that he picked up some food at a Chinese restaurant on the way home. They kissed each other lightly on the lips, as always, and he told her how good she looked. Pat loosened his tie for him and hid her disappointment at not going out for dinner

"How come you're all dressed up?" he asked.

"Oh, I just felt like looking good for my man," she said. "In case there's any competition out there," she added, smiling broadly at him.

"That's something you'll never have to worry about, and I mean never."

They got through the appetizers on small talk: how her day went at the lab; the letter in the mail from their son, letting them know he'd be spending most of the Christmas vacation at his girlfriend's home in Tampa; and the need to do their holiday shopping earlier than usual because they were attending a wedding on Long Island on the twenty-second of the month.

"Okay, my love, what's on your mind?" Brad asked. "Why the early bird special?" He reached for the container of shrimp fried rice and used his fork to shovel it onto his plate.

Pat waited for him to finish before answering. When he passed the container to her, she set it down on the corner of the table. "I'm worried about you, Brad. You can't keep up the hours you've been putting in at the plant the last five months. I hardly get to see you anymore, and I'm afraid you'll work yourself sick."

He smiled. "See what a man has to do to get some attention from his wife?"

"I'm serious, Brad, so no jokes. This is something we have to talk out right now. I know you're under stress, but there's got to be a limit on how much time you spend there."

As she spoke, he took food from each of the other containers, sprinkled a few drops of mustard sauce on top and mixed it in. "Your turn," he said, pushing everything closer to her. Pat knew he wouldn't give her an answer until she scooped some food onto her dish.

"Look," he said, after she helped herself to a little of everything, "I appreciate your concern and I love you for it. But I told you before that I'm trying to do everything I can to keep this year from being a disaster for the company. We've lost money two years out of every three since I took over. At least the red ink has always been a reasonable number. I mean there was always the chance the good year would wipe out most of the losses from the other two. That seemed to satisfy the Platt brothers. Their other businesses in Connecticut made enough money to let them accept the losses at Ocean State and wait for the demand for wire to pick up again.

"But the recession we're in has been hurting everything they own. I can tell they're panicking when I start to get faxes on a regular basis asking me what orders we've got coming in for the next month and how much production we turned out week by week, sometimes day by day. That never used to happen! I can only guess that they're in a cash flow crunch like a lot of other big companies. I'm sure no one in the Connecticut office has forgotten that I bought three percent of this business when we came here. But you'd think from some of their memos that I didn't give a damn about what was happening."

Brad needed time to calm down a little. He went to the refrigerator, took out a bottle of root beer and got a large glass from one of the cabinets. He half filled the teakettle with water, lit the front burner on the stove and brought a cup and tea bag to the table for Pat. He didn't say anything more until he was back in his chair and filled his glass.

"Listen to me, Pat. The numbers for the first six months of the year were the worst we've ever had while I've been here. That's for two reasons. The first is that the Canadian wire plants are bidding everything to our customers at lower prices than what we have to charge just to break even. And the second is that the wire manufacturers in Ohio and Illinois are killing us. Their new facilities are automated. That means low labor costs. And they don't have the heavy freight expenses we're stuck with when we ship from Providence to customers in the Midwest and the West Coast."

Pat started to say something, but he cut her off.

"Let me finish. A lot of what's happening is my fault, and I can't duck it. I got the employees to throw out the goddam Steelworkers Union. I convinced them they'd have better job security because we could run the place more competitively without a thousand union work rules. It was true, and it would have worked.

"But then I screwed up everything. I knew the Tarantinos were nervous about buying thirty-five percent of the company from the Platts, and I was anxious to show them they made a good deal for themselves. If they hadn't come in with that cash when they did, the

Platts might have shut the place down to stop the bleeding. I should have been happy just to get control of everything from the union over a one- or two-year period and have the employees doing things my way. Instead, I began pushing for profits right away. It was an ego thing. I know that now. I was just too stupid to see it then. So I cut wages more than I planned over the first couple of years and made everyone on the factory floor start contributing a piece of what the health plan cost. We showed a good profit the first year because sales took a nice jump at the same time I was cutting costs. The year after that wasn't as good. But I took too much money away from those production people too fast. I might as well have sent out an invitation to the Machinists' Union to come in and represent them."

Caught up in his review of the events that transpired, Brad forgot about the food on his plate. Pat didn't attempt to interrupt him.

"You have no idea how much more it costs to run that place after the contract we signed with the Union three years ago. What a mistake that was. It might not have been so bad if we let them go on strike for a while. I was ready to bring in as many new employees as we could hire if the production people walked out. That would have given us much more leverage in the negotiations with the Union. George Ryder, the lawyer the company uses, was all for my doing just that. But the Tarantinos got the right to call the shots on labor matters when they bought in, and they were against our letting a strike get started. Ryder told me off the record that Doug Fiore, the managing partner of his firm, probably pushed the Tarantinos in that direction. Maybe Fiore wasn't thinking about what was best for Ocean State. Maybe he just didn't want to take a chance on the strike forcing us to close the plant and costing his firm a good client. I hardly know the guy so I can't be sure one way or the other. And maybe Ryder's feeling about Fiore isn't right either. I just don't have the answer."

Hanley finally paused and took a long drink of his root beer. When he finished, he returned the bottle to the refrigerator and sat down again. "I'm just about done," he said. "Since I knew we had to avoid a strike, all we could do to keep the Machinists from robbing us blind was talk tough at the bargaining table and threaten to put a lock on the door if our costs went too high. But the employees weren't afraid of striking, even though they had to worry about losing their jobs if they walked out. They'd had it with me and the company and were ready to risk everything. So they stuck to most of their demands and came away with a hell of a contract. Now, in a couple of months we've got to negotiate with them all over again and who knows how much worse things will get?"

Pat saw the clouds of steam escaping from the kettle and took it off the burner before its whistle began to sound. She brought it to the table and poured a full cup for herself. "I understand everything you said, Brad, but what is it you're doing at work all the time? Why do you have to be there hour after hour?"

The question heightened Brad's frustration, but he took a deep breath and answered as calmly as he could. "I'm there all those hours, Pat, because I'm trying to crack the whip as hard as I can. My presence is important. Hopefully, it makes everyone realize that I'm willing to work at least as hard as what I'm asking them to do. I make sure I'm there when the first shift comes in at seven. Once they get settled, I walk around the plant and observe every one of them at their jobs. I try to have something friendly to say to most of them, but I want them to know I'm watching everything that's being done.

"Before the first shift is through for the day, I go back and check each guy out. They keep their production figures in a notebook next to the machine. I look and see how he's done for the day. If the numbers are on target or even better, I can wave the flag and say a few words. But if they stink, I've got to find out why and make sure the problem gets corrected."

Brad picked at some of the food on his plate. "I hope you're beginning to get the picture," he said. He put down his fork and continued. "Let me tell you the rest. The night shift foremen come in about twenty minutes before their men start work. When they show up, we meet with the first shift foremen to plan production for that night and the next day. We look at the delivery dates that the customers were promised, figure out how long it will take to ship to Chicago or Dallas or Seattle, and decide which orders get pushed to the head of the line.

"When that's done, I go back on the floor and check the night shift guys who are out there. I used to do it only once, but now they know I'll be around a second time before I go home. That keeps them on their toes. It's no secret to them when I'm in the plant. They can see the Buick parked outside in my space."

The words came faster as Brad kept talking. "And when I'm not keeping an eye on production, I'm on the phone to the salesmen in the field who are trying to bring in some new accounts, or I'm listening to our in-house guys call their regular customers. I want to make sure they're pushing as hard as they can for orders. I don't want to see us lose out to the competition for two or three cents a ton. Some of those so-called super salesmen can't seem to learn how to offer a discount on the wire we make fast and cheap in exchange for getting a foot in the door on something the customer has been buying from someone else."

"Please, Brad," Pat interjected at last, "I didn't have to hear all this. Stop and eat your dinner before it gets cold."

"You asked a question," he said. "I'm almost through answering it. I'll heat this stuff up a little if I have to."

He leaned back in the chair and continued. "Other than what I've already covered, I've got to memorize pretty nearly every number on the production printouts. When someone from Platt calls or sends a fax, the answer has to be ready. I sit down with Rusty in accounting almost every day to see what checks came in. We have to decide whether or not it's time to give the customer a call and push for a payment. He and I also figure out what bills to pay, at least in part, so the suppliers don't cut us off. As you can imagine, those sessions are a lot of fun."

Brad stopped, took another deep breath, and looked up at the ceiling. "Oh, yeah," he said, "I still manage to find time for about ten cups of coffee a day and a sandwich at my desk at lunch while I speed read my way through the *Wall Street Journal*."

Pat looked at her husband and didn't know what to say. She wasn't sure whether it was some sort of a welcome release for him to be able to detail his time at the plant as he did, or whether it just added more tension and strain to what had clearly become a very difficult and trying situation for him. She retrieved the kettle from the stove and poured some more hot water over the same tea bag.

"Do you want some?" she asked.

"No thanks." He emptied a little more fried rice on his dish.

She hoped she wasn't about to upset him with the wrong question. "When will it end, Brad?"

"Good question, my love. Maybe a month from now, when Platt gets to see the final figures for the year. Color them deep red. If we get past that, maybe when the union negotiations are over, if we give them anything close to what we did last time. Or if the recession keeps dragging on the way it is, maybe anytime."

"I didn't mean for Ocean State Wire," Pat answered. "I meant for you. When will you stop working so many hours and coming home so late every night?"

Brad felt his wife's compassion. He saw the mist form in her eyes while she waited for him to answer. *How lucky I was to have married her,* he thought. *What would my life have been like without her?*

"Soon, Pat," he said. "As soon as we ship the last product in December. After that I've decided to limit myself to just Tuesday and Thursday nights." He wasn't about to tell her that those were the nights he normally left the plant at six-thirty, drove to Cranston and spent several hours betting on blackjack or craps at a private club run by the Tarantino family.

8

Sal Tarantino used the intercom to call his son into his office. The shades on the windows close to his desk were pulled all the way down, always a sign that he wanted nothing on Atwells Avenue to divert his attention from what he was doing.

"Salvy," he began, as soon as Sandy walked into his office, "I was looking at the numbers for Ocean State Wire & Cable, what we've got through last month. We're taking a bad beating there this year, the worst since we invested in them. Maybe it's time for us to try and get what we can for our thirty-five percent. I don't trust the Platt brothers, especially the older one. We could wake up tomorrow and find out they filed for bankruptcy without warning us. They're going to do what's best for them and not worry about the Tarantino family."

Sandy did not sit down. "I saw the latest profit and loss statement from Ocean State when it came in, Pop. I called Fiore about it, and even told him we were thinking about selling our interest. I let him know it's the worst performing company we've put money into. He told me to sit tight while he tried to get some answers for us. When he called back, he said the company still looks good for the long run, that most of the problem has to do with the recession. He said he asked three different brokers to research the wire industry, and what they told him is that all the producers are hurting, not just Ocean State."

"Have they all got unions?" Sal asked.

"I don't know, Pop."

"Because Ocean State's contract with the goddam Machinists is coming up soon and I don't see where the company's got any room to give the union anything. That could mean a strike if we can't get to the right people, and then the Platts might just say 'Screw it' and shut the place down. Salvy, I want you to stay on top of this situation because it worries me. And see if there are any potential buyers for our shares in the company in case we decide to get out quick."

"Okay, I will."

"And speaking of Fiore, what's with the group you've been trying to put together? Are we getting support from the names on that list?"

"We definitely are. So far, it's looking real good."

"Have you got that campaign manager yet, the one you told me about?"

"Not signed on the dotted line, but we're pretty close. I've still got to work out a few more details. I should know something definite soon."

"Is he expensive?"

"He knows what he's worth."

"How much up front?"

"Forty percent in our case, but that's because Fiore's an absolute nobody right now. This guy likes getting paid, but winning means more to him than the money. Doug will be in good hands if we can wrap him up."

"Good. Okay, I'm taking the rest of the day off."

9

"Come on in, Jenna. Shut the door."

Jenna Richardson returned to the newsroom at four o'clock to file a story before her deadline. Getting the facts kept her on the road overnight at Charlestown Beach in the southernmost part of the State. The four inches of snow that fell that morning on the towns facing Block Island Sound made the driving difficult on her way back to Providence. She was tired and grumpy. She was also disgusted with the fact that the heater in her Toyota Corolla couldn't stand up to a twenty-eight degree day.

The message Richardson found stuck to her telephone was from Dan McMurphy, the *Herald*'s News Editor. "See me ASAP," it said. She intended to drop in on her Toyota dealer and complain like crazy about the eighty-five dollars she paid them a week earlier to make sure she had heat when she needed it. On reflection, Jenna figured it was probably better to go in the morning. The service manager, not yet mentally fatigued by the problems of a new day, might be easier to deal with. McMurphy's summons settled the matter.

"Sit down," Dan told her. "You look pooped. Go stretch out on the couch if you want."

McMurphy's office was enormous. Three chairs faced his desk. Behind it, four large bookcases were filled to overflowing. Books on every shelf lay horizontally on top of those already standing squeezed together. A table on one side of the room comfortably accommodated eight people for a conference. On the opposite wall, two leather sofas sat end to end.

An oriental rug, worn in several spots, sat on top of the room's green wall-to-wall carpeting in the area encompassed by McMurphy's desk and the chairs in front of it.

Colleagues sometimes found it difficult to describe Jenna Richardson. Although not beautiful, she was more than simply attractive. Her face usually appeared pale, a fact accentuated by her dyed blonde hair and reluctance to wear lipstick. It seemed too thin when you looked directly at her, but from an angle her high cheekbones gave it an unusual character. It was often said that she reminded them of a certain European movie actress whose name they couldn't quite recall. She wore her hair long, always unfettered by ribbons or barrettes, with no apology for the dark roots that were visible.

Jenna chose the chair directly opposite McMurphy. She noticed that there were only a handful of cigarette butts in his ashtray. She knew he would never quit smoking, but felt better about the fact that he was cutting down. *He must be pretty close to sixty,* she thought. Did that make it time to listen to the doctor's orders, or was it already too late for help?

Richardson had a deep regard for this man who had been her boss for four years. He knew the news business from top to bottom and needed only seconds to zero in on the most a story had to offer. Best of all, he always found a way for a young reporter to hone her skills when sent to investigate a story and write up what she found. Although the word never passed between them, she considered McMurphy her mentor.

"Pooped doesn't quite do it," she said. "It's some combination of being fatigued, frustrated, exhausted, enervated, weary and worn out. How's that for being a wordsmith?"

McMurphy smiled at her. He had a round, handsome face, with a lot of pink color on his nose and cheeks. His hair was white, rather thin, and brushed straight back without a part on either side. He longed to light up a cigarette at that moment but knew that Jenna would be all over him if he did.

"For me, pooped was always as far as you could go," he answered. "Did you finish the story?"

"Yes, I left it with Milt," she said. "What's cooking?"

McMurphy preferred to have more small talk before getting to the reason for the meeting. He suspected he'd have a fight on his hands and was reluctant to start it so soon. As if anticipating a verbal tug-of-war, he pushed his chair back and set both palms firmly against the front of his desk.

"Jenna, after a good deal of thought, and I don't mean that facetiously, I've decided to change your assignment." He watched her eyes narrow, her face tighten up a little, and waited for any kind of a response.

"Am I going to have to stop and get drunk on the way home today?" she asked, "or is this so bad I'll have to tell the publisher you've been grabbing at my body."

McMurphy chuckled at the question but wasn't surprised by it. He knew and often said that Jenna had the best sense of humor in the newsroom.

"Before you ask," he said, "let me make it clear that I don't have a single complaint about your work. You've been turning out great stuff. Hell, if you weren't, you'd have heard from me about it. But I want you to switch gears and do something else."

Jenna cut him off. "Maybe I never told you, but I've sworn an oath against going into mens' locker rooms. I know I'd never be able to control myself. So no sports beat for me, Dan, no way." She spoke the words with a straight face, not even the hint of a smile. That told him she was concerned and was trying to deflect the blow without yet knowing what it was.

McMurphy wanted the conversation to be akin to a father-daughter discussion. With three grown-up daughters of his own, he had a lot of experience. "It's time for you to sit back and listen, young lady." He talked softly and gave the words a few seconds to do their job. "I'll go right to the bottom line," he said, rocking his chair slightly behind the desk. "This is a political year coming up in Rhode Island and I want you to cover it. Between now and November there could be some big stories happening, a lot of surprises. We need a good investigative reporter out there. Jim Callum's going on a sabbatical as of March first. That means he won't be around for the primaries or the election. I considered everyone in the newsroom for this assignment, I really did. But I decided you're the best person to handle it."

"Why me?" she interrupted loudly, throwing her arms out to the side.

McMurphy remained calm. "I'm getting to that," he said. "Let me finish." He took a deep breath but kept eye contact with Jenna. "I want

Jim to show you the ropes for three or four weeks or however long it takes. Then you'll be on your own, but you can pick his brains as long as he's here." Dan paused. "I chose you because I know you're the persistent type. That's what it takes to find out what's really going on in the Statehouse before our revered leaders are ready to go public with the news. You're the best there is at not taking 'No' for an answer. If there's a story, I know you'll find it."

When Jenna didn't immediately respond, he continued. "But it's like a maze up there, and you've got to learn the territory. Callum's a good teacher. He knows all the players and all the cat and mouse games that go on. Spending some time with him will help you figure out the best way to skin each cat. When you get into it, you may even get to like it." He stopped talking and continued to watch her. After several seconds he added, "In fact, I'll bet you will."

Richardson was stunned. She never once, in four years at the *Herald*, even thought about reporting the political scene. It was distasteful to her, a "Yuk" in her vocabulary. Her dislike for politics had deep roots. She was nine years old when Nixon resigned and would never forget her father watching the drama on television. She readily pictured him raising his voice above the President's as he leaned toward the screen. "That son of a bitch, they ought to shoot the dirty son of a bitch."

Jenna was raised in Brockton, a blue collar town in Massachusetts that consistently gave the Democratic candidate the vast majority of its support. The Bay State was the only state in the country in which Nixon couldn't claim victory when his reelection campaign rolled over George McGovern in 1972. She was the youngest of Bill and Deborah Richardson's three children, the apple of her father's eye. He spent two years in baseball's lower minor leagues before throwing in the towel, but his athletic genes all went to Jenna, who starred in softball, basketball and tennis in high school and college. Her love for the Red Sox matched his, and she accompanied him to Fenway Park on occasional Sundays during the baseball season.

Jenna's bond with her father was strong, and many of his opinions became hers. Listening to him, she grew up distrustful of politicians. Although she followed their comings and goings in the news, she never worked in a political campaign, wore any candidate's button or put an election-inspired bumper sticker on her car. In her view, politicians were just a necessary evil. They were willing to sell their souls with the promises they made. If they never delivered on those promises, so what? Getting elected was all that mattered, and then putting themselves first on whatever agenda they drew up. She certainly didn't want to get to know any of them.

McMurphy's words and his look made Jenna realize that avoiding the assignment was probably impossible. But she felt she still had to fight back, test him, make every effort she could to get out of it. She had folded her arms in front of her after her initial outburst. She kept them that way and leaned forward slightly in her chair when she answered.

"There aren't going to be any big stories in this election, Dan. You know that as well as I do. Spence Hardiman had a good first term. He's going back to the Senate for another six years. The Democrats don't have anyone who could get thirty-five percent of the votes against him. That means John Sacco stays right where he is and goes for another term in the governor's office. Everyone's in love with 'Big John.' Who's going to want to run for his job? Do you think you'll see another car dealer like Ed McGurty step out of the wings? Do the Democrats have someone else willing to throw a pile of money into another futile campaign just to advertise his business? Great! I'm sure no one will want to miss a word he has to say. Especially if he talks about pre-owned cars."

Richardson paused long enough to let the sarcasm sink in. "It's a dead scene, and you know it. The challengers don't have a chance. There won't even be a contest for the two House seats. From everything I've read, Williston has impressed the voters in her first two years in Congress. Besides, this is another year of the woman. She'll win easier than last time. And Droney's got too much influence in Washington now to get beat. He'll promise more jobs and less taxes in every speech he makes, just like he always does. Before the election, he'll bring in Ted Kennedy and a few others to tell us how much he's done for Rhode Island. It's ridiculous. We're sitting here today, in January, and we already know everyone who'll be making a victory speech in November." She paused again, but just for a moment this time. "I know I left out lieutenant governor. If we're not sure who's going to win that race, Dan, no one out there gives a good goddam anyhow."

Jenna was pleased with the argument she made. But she felt it was time to bolster it with another line of attack. The fact that McMurphy hadn't tried to interrupt her was encouraging.

"I've done some pretty good reporting in the last year. The *Herald*'s going to win one or two major awards with my story on the nursing home industry. Now everyone knows what that business is all about and who's been minting money in it. Half a dozen different committees are working on legislation for it at the Statehouse. That's the result of the weeks I spent putting the puzzle together."

She was picking up steam. "Plus there's the story Hank and I turned in on the whole credit union mess. The rest of the media called it a 'bombshell,' Dan, remember? Those are the things that get our investigative team respect from the people who buy the *Herald* every day. That stuff affects their lives. It's real. It's not the phony promises that come out of the mouths of every politician. They're ready to forget or ignore everything they said as soon as the election results are official. I'll tell you what I think, Dan. I think giving me this new assignment is the same as asking me to write off the whole year."

Her last words drove McMurphy out of his chair. He walked over to the conference table, crossed his arms in front of him and looked up at the ceiling as if seeking guidance from above. After half a minute or so he returned to his desk and sat down before saying a word. "Listen to me, Jenna. If I agreed with how you see this election year, I wouldn't be telling you to do this. I wouldn't waste your talent. You've done terrific work and you've sold plenty of papers. But everything in this fat gut of mine tells me you're wrong.

"There's a calm before the storm out there, and I can feel it. Don't ask me how. Twenty years from now you'll be sitting in an editor's chair and you'll know what I mean. It grows on you. Call it experience, call it intuition or anything you want. I'm in my sailboat on a calm sea and there's blue sky all around me. But there's a wind I can feel beginning to pick up from the northeast and it's making me nervous. It's warning me that trouble's on the way. So now I've got to react, know what I mean? I have to make sure I'm on top of things if there's going to be a storm. It's the same thing with this political scene. Things are going to happen in the next ten months—I can feel it in my bones—that you'll regret not covering if you're doing something else. I really believe that."

He went over to where she was sitting and offered his hand. She reached out and let him pull her up. "So I'm glad you've agreed," he said. "You're going to thank me for this before it's over. But if I'm wrong, you'll never have to listen to this speech again, I promise."

Jenna let him see her frustration. "I don't believe this is happening to me. What did I do to disturb the great newspaper gods in the sky?" She turned and headed for the door.

"Jenna," Dan called, still standing by the chair.

She stopped and looked at him.

"If you do a real good job on this, I'll speak to Al Silvano and see if he'll let you cover the Bruins. They've got the healthiest looking locker room in the city." He gave her an exaggerated wink.

10

Terry Reardon gave the bell in the foyer two short rings and then one long one. Moments later the buzzer sounded and he was able to open the front door. Once inside, he quickly climbed the stairs to the third floor condominium Jenna Richardson rented from its owner.

Jenna had called him in the office to break their date. Something was bothering her, she said, and she didn't want to talk about it on the phone. He kept insisting on coming over to her place until she finally gave in.

Reardon had dined with Jenna earlier in the week. It was the night before she left for Charlestown Beach to check out a tip that a resort hotel was operating as a brothel during the slow winter months. They went to the Twin Oaks in Cranston, a favorite among *Herald* employees. The fact that it was always crowded and noisy pleased them. Jenna was in a terrific mood all evening. They laughed at one thing or another for the hour they sat in the cocktail lounge waiting for a table, and all through a leisurely meal. But Terry was expected home at a certain time that night, so they smooched in the parking lot for a while and agreed to see each other at her apartment later in the week.

Ascending the last fourteen steps, Reardon reminded himself that there was no sign of anything troubling her then, and concluded that something happened in the interim. Whatever it was, he had no intention of letting it keep him from getting laid that night.

They met for the first time in September, a little more than four months earlier. The cafeteria at the *Herald* was unusually crowded for lunch that day. Reardon took the last seat at a table for eight, across from a couple of reporters he knew. The conversation, as usual, was hot and heavy about the latest breaking stories. At the end of the table, someone started to bait him about another reporter who was terminated, with Terry's blessing, for excessive absenteeism. The reporter's appeal of his discharge was scheduled for arbitration in three weeks. As Vice President for Labor and Employment, it was Reardon's job to assist the Company's lawyer in putting management's case together and preparing its witnesses.

Ron Lucas was the one raising the issue. "No one who's legitimately ill should ever be let go," he said. To be certain he had everyone's attention, Lucas banged his fist on the table for emphasis. He was the newspaper's senior financial page copy editor. It was clear, almost immediately, that the view he expressed was also the consensus of most of those at the table. Reardon remained silent. He had no intention of being drawn into an argument with the group. But before the issue gave way to another topic of discussion, the *Herald*'s position was defended by a nice-looking blonde at the table. She was someone Terry saw in the building from time to time but never met.

"If he can't come to work and do what he's supposed to do, why blame the paper?" she asked. "If he's got all kinds of problems that keep him out months at a time from one year to the next, is that the *Herald*'s fault? News happens every day, not just when he can be here to report it. I think the Company had a perfect right to let him go."

Reardon was all smiles. He ignored the start of Lucas's immediate rebuttal. "Will someone please introduce me to this spokesman, I mean spokesperson, for enlightened justice" he said.

Someone did, and he took the seat next to Richardson as soon as it became empty. He learned that she went to work in the newsroom just after he was promoted out of his former job as Labor Relations Manager. That explained why he wasn't the one to take her through the Company's orientation program. "I would have turned down the promotion if I knew getting it would make me have to wait all this time to meet you," he told her. Jenna loved it.

Terry Reardon chased skirts. Everyone knew that, and he made no effort to hide it. Sex was a big thing in his life. He enjoyed both the pursuit and the fruits of victory. It was something in his genes, not a game he played because he was unhappy at home. Married fifteen years, with three children, he did most of the things a father of preteen-agers was supposed to do to hold on to his "hero" status with them.

Reardon's wife suspected his infidelity but never had any evidence with which to confront him. At some point in their marriage she decided that it made little sense to keep looking for any. She hoped only to be spared the discovery of some ladies underwear in the glove compartment of his Ford Escort, or some other obvious sign of an amorous adventure. After all, she reasoned, he was a good provider, never abused her or the children, and made love to her as often as she'd let him. Once in a while she tested him by asking for sex on a night when he called with an excuse for staying out late, but when he got home and into bed, he seemed delighted to satisfy her each time.

Richardson also learned of Reardon's reputation early on. She agreed to have dinner with him in downtown Providence several nights after they met. By the time he dropped her at her car in the cheap five-dollar-a-day parking lot several blocks from the *Herald*, she knew he was anxious to become intimate with her. He certainly wasn't handsome, Jenna told herself, but she was amused by him. And there was an attraction in the freckled face with the large pointy ears that gave him the look of a grown-up boy whom Norman Rockwell might have chosen for one of his paintings.

Do I want this, she wondered, *or is it too close to home?*

During the next few days Richardson asked some friends at work about Reardon. What came back in their descriptions of him were the words "womanizer," "Don Juan," and "lecher." She was given the names of several women, still employed at the *Herald*, with whom Terry was openly friendly in the past. But everyone called him "a nice guy" and "fun to be around."

Reardon's marriage wasn't a problem for her. She dated other married men in the past and figured they could play a role in her life until "Mister Right" came along. In the meantime, she liked having a good time and feeling the strong arms of a man around her when she needed to unwind.

Besides, Jenna respected him for the fact that he always wore his wedding band. Unlike others, he never intimated that he was having "trouble" of any sort at home. On their third date she gave him a long preview of the story she just finished writing which McMurphy scheduled to start running in the paper on Sunday. Terry listened attentively and applauded her work. Afterwards, she invited him to her apartment for some coffee. He had two cups, with cream and sugar, when they finished making love.

* * *

Jenna opened the door just as Reardon reached the top landing. He went in, kissed her on the lips and smiled. "Now tell me what's so bad that it could have kept us from getting under the covers," he said.

She wanted to smile herself. Instead, she gave him a feigned look of disgust. "You men are all alike," she said. She took his hand, led him to her small living room and moved inside his arms. "I need a hug, right now," she whispered.

Terry held her close to him for a while, saying nothing, and kissed the side of her neck several times. When he let her go, he leaned forward and kissed her very gently, first around her eyes, then on her cheeks and nose. She found his lips, embraced him again and kissed him hard.

"Okay," Terry said when she started to move away, "no more free love until you let me know what's wrong." He was determined to keep things light.

They sat down on the sofa and she related everything Dan McMurphy said to her that afternoon. Jenna complained again that the whole year would be wasted. "Maybe a lot of other people in the newsroom would kill for that assignment, but I'd like to kill him for choosing me."

Reardon's instincts prevailed. He got up, slipped off his jacket and threw it on the wicker chair across from the couch. He undid the knot in his tie and unbuttoned his shirt collar. Taking the wide end of the tie in his hand, he made a show of pulling it off. As he unbuttoned the rest of his shirt, he exaggerated the movement of his fingers around each button.

"Terry, what are you doing?" Jenna was giggling as she asked the question.

He knew things were going well. This was fun for both of them.

"I've listened to your story, ma'am," he answered. "As I understand it, you want to be an investigative reporter and to hell with writing about politics. But you've got an enemy out there. You're in danger, ma'am, no doubt about it." Terry started to speak from deep in his throat: "I can see that this is a job . . . for Superman." He smiled. "Just hold on a second, ma'am," he continued, "I'm changing into my costume." His shirt was off. He tensed the muscle in his right arm and acted as if it would take a great feat of strength to undo the belt on his trousers. He grabbed one end of it and pretended to pull at it violently before achieving his goal. He followed up by patting his left shoulder, as if congratulating himself on his success. Terry looked over at Jenna. She was laughing and enjoying the performance immensely. He quickly kicked off his loafers, stepped out of his pants and threw them on the chair with his other clothes.

"Now I'm ready for action," he announced.

"What are you going to do to McMurphy dressed like that?" Jenna asked. She had raised her legs up onto the couch.

"McMurphy will have to wait. First I must help a damsel in distress."

Terry went back to the couch and moved Jenna's left leg over to give himself room to sit down. He unbuttoned the flap of her jeans at the waist and yanked the zipper down quickly. He took hold of them at her ankles and began pulling them off. As he did, he let out an exaggerated series of grunts. Jenna laughed louder and put her head down on a pillow in the corner of the sofa so the jeans would slip off easier. Moments later, Terry removed her underpants.

"We're almost out of danger, ma'am. Do you want to fly with that sweater on or off?"

"I'll leave it on until we get to someplace a little warmer, Superman."

"Okay then, time for you to hold on to me tight." He took off his shorts, lay down on the couch and coaxed her on top of him. "Here we go, ma'am, up, up and away."

11

IT WAS ONE HELL of an interesting morning, Doug Fiore told himself. He sat alone at an umbrella-topped table in the lobby of the Spalding Bank building. At 2:15 he came out of the coffee shop where he purchased a cup of chicken soup and half a tuna sandwich for lunch. The umbrellas were there just to provide atmosphere, but the foot traffic going by gave the occupants of the several tables the feeling they were relaxing at a small cafe on the Via Venetto or the Champs Elysee. He took advantage of it to do some serious girl watching.

One of the messages waiting for Fiore when he got to the office that morning was from Dick Birnbaum, a corporate lawyer at WC&B who said he had a matter he wanted to discuss. Birnbaum tried to reach him the day before, in the middle of the afternoon, but Dana Briggs's standing instructions were to tell anyone in the firm who called (with just a few exceptions) that Doug was unable to come to the phone. He invariably let at least half a day go by before he returned any call, and liked to use the time to anticipate what might be on someone else's mind.

Fiore took the *Herald* sports page out of his briefcase after telling Briggs to let Birnbaum know he was free. The Super Bowl was being played that Sunday and he wanted to check on the starting time. He ignored the hype that filled the paper every day for the two weeks before the game, but monitored the predictions the local sports writers made on the outcome. On the final Friday, he always posted his own prediction of the score outside his office door. But he never made a bet on the game, even refusing to back up his forecast of the outcome with a five dollar contribution to the pool set up by the lawyers for the entry coming closest to the actual score.

Birnbaum arrived a few minutes later. He had a scowl on his face and stood by the door to the office, waiting for Fiore to tell him it was all right to close it. He didn't bother to put on his suit jacket before coming. The cuffs of his white shirt were buttoned and the knot of his tie was neatly in place. As soon as he sat down, Birnbaum said that he wanted to have a new secretary.

"I'm up to here with Janice Rossman," he complained, moving his right hand to his eyes.

Fiore reacted with a look of surprise. "What's the trouble?" he asked.

Birnbaum anticipated the question. "First of all, Doug, and probably most important, I can't get her to work any overtime. I don't have to tell you what kind of problems that can give me. Five o'clock comes and she's out the door. Second, she's away from her desk too much, just disappears somewhere, and isn't there when I need her. Third, she makes too many typing mistakes from my dictation, and her spelling is atrocious. Like 'atrocious' would end in 's-h-i-s.' Let me see, fourth, she forgets to give me messages half the time. And finally, a few of my clients have said she comes off sounding rude and impatient to them when they call!"

Birnbaum made a motion with his hand in Fiore's direction. "Is that enough?" he asked. He hoped Doug wouldn't think his question was raised facetiously. "I don't want to bother taking this through the office manager," he continued. "Sometimes it gets very political. I'd just like you to tell Helen Barone to get me a good secretary as soon as possible."

Fiore sat back in his chair and smiled. "I thought the team of Birnbaum and Rossman was going to hit it off," he said. "I'm disappointed."

Birnbaum took Fiore's remark the wrong way and was quick to reply. "My mother always wanted me to marry a Jewish girl, Doug. She said it would kill her if I didn't. Well, she got her wish ten years ago. She doesn't give a damn whether my secretary is Jewish and neither do I." Birnbaum said it without a trace of a smile and got up. "I'm really swamped. I've got to get back to work." He thought the Jewish issue gave him a leg up in the conversation and decided to switch from asking to demanding.

"Tell Helen I want someone who knows what she's doing and can do it after five o'clock."

Fiore didn't say anything to correct the misimpression. He didn't see any reason to embarrass Birnbaum at this point. The change of tone in his voice didn't bother Doug, and he made no promises. He liked Dick Birnbaum and ordinarily would have acceded to the request on the spot, but he was just given an interesting situation to play with and decided to take his time with it. "I'll check it out," he answered.

* * *

Half an hour later Frankie Scardino stuck his head in the door. "Have you got a few minutes?" he asked.

Fiore looked up from a file he was reviewing. "It's too early for me to handle any of this month's numbers," he answered.

Scardino said it was about something else, and took the reply as an invitation to enter. Minutes earlier he had washed his face in the men's room, leaving it somewhat wet, and now mopped his forehead and chin with his handkerchief as if he were wiping off some traces of sweat. He purposely looked agitated, and had checked the look in the mirror before going to Fiore's office. Doug invited him to sit down in the chair closest to the desk and signaled with a nod of his head that he was waiting to hear what was on Frankie's mind.

Scardino said that Kathy Marini, the mail room supervisor, was giving him a hard time. "She's not doing her job the way I want her to. She has her own ideas about directing the different part-timers we employ there."

Fiore knew that Marini's group also included kitchen help who delivered coffee to conference rooms, those who moved furniture around the office and one or two who picked up supplies in the firm's truck. "The problem is," Scardino repeated, "she refuses to do things my way, even after I discussed them with her several times."

"So what do you want?" Fiore asked.

"The bottom line is that I want to let her go before I lose control in those areas."

Fiore was silent while absorbing the request. He thought Marini was pleasant enough and couldn't recall any complaints about her from anyone else. She was a clerk in the firm's library for about three years. Her work there consisted mostly of copying documents, filing the various reporting services that were received each week or assisting one of the attorneys with legal research on the computer. She was promoted to her present job about three months before Scardino came to WC&B as its new comptroller from his position at the Truro Savings Bank. Doug reminded himself that a year had already passed since Scardino joined the firm. He couldn't imagine what Marini was doing differently to get Frankie all worked up. Even though he knew she could be replaced by any number of women in the firm and wouldn't be missed after she was gone, he didn't like the idea of terminating office employees, especially women, who worked well and showed loyalty to the firm. Scardino's request was starting to bother him.

"If you do that, who's going to replace her?" he asked.

Scardino took a deep breath before replying. "I've thought about it a lot. It's my feeling we ought to let Janice Rossman try it. She's been doing a terrific job for Dick Birnbaum, really putting out, and this would be a good reward for her. Besides, it would let me send a message to the other secretaries that there's room to move up in the firm. I'm sure they'd all like to know that."

Fiore listened and chuckled to himself. That told him all he had to know about Marini's performance. He was sure that Rossman was "really putting out" all right, but for Scardino, not Birnbaum. He figured that she probably told Frankie she was going to keep her legs crossed unless he came through for her with a job that paid more money. Doug could sympathize with Scardino's dilemma but decided to play with him a while longer.

"Even if everything you say about Rossman is true, shouldn't we be offering it to one of the gals with more seniority?" he asked.

Scardino said he didn't think that was a good idea. He felt that the women who were at the firm a long time probably had a strong attachment to John Gray, his predecessor, and would have trouble taking orders from him on account of it. Everyone knew that Gray was eased out after twenty-seven years at the firm, replaced within weeks by Scardino.

"Most of the other clericals probably blame me for it, just because I took Gray's place," he said. "Rossman's new blood, and she's got a lot of ambition. I'm sure she'd have no trouble telling everyone who worked under her to do things the way I want them done."

Fiore loved every minute of it. He saw himself as the judge presiding over Rossman's trial. First Birnbaum testified about all her faults. Then Scardino sat in the same chair and told him how great she was. He knew, of course, who was telling the truth. He enjoyed the irony in the fact that letting Frankie guarantee himself a piece of ass for a while longer would make Birnbaum very happy at the same time. Marini was the only loser, and Doug was unhappy about that, but he knew he could ease her pain somewhat.

"Do what you want," he said, "provided Helen Barone comes up with a good secretary to take Rossman's place. I don't want Dick to suffer for one day on account of this." He could barely get the words out with a straight face. Then he suddenly had a new thought. "Ask Marini if she'd like to switch over and work for Birnbaum at the same pay she's getting now. If she doesn't, give her a week's pay for every year she's been here and tell her we'll keep her on our health plan for up to six months." *That should give her two good options,* he thought, *and plenty of time to settle in somewhere else if she chooses to leave.*

Scardino thanked Fiore, assured him he'd take care of both matters and left. As soon as he was out of the office, a big smile crossed his face.

A while later Dana Briggs brought in the mail. She often came around to Fiore's side of the desk when she put it down, informing him of the contents of some of the envelopes she already opened. Dana scolded him, but only mildly, whenever he let his hand get busy on top of her skirt, reminding him that anyone might suddenly open the door.

The two of them slept together off and on for a couple of years before she got married. She was his secretary during the period they were intimate. When she returned from her honeymoon, she asked to be transferred to another lawyer on a different floor. Doug didn't quarrel with her decision, but pushed her to take her old job again when he completed his third year as managing partner. He felt he needed someone who could be his eyes and ears while he was out of the office, and he relied on the confidences they shared in the past as the basis for trusting her completely.

"Frankie's going to give Kathy Marini's job to Janice and let Kathy go if she turns down a position with Dick Birnbaum," he told her. He didn't have to say the last name. Dana had mentioned the apparent liaison between Rossman and Scardino to him just a couple of days after Doug first heard it from Carol Singer.

"I'm not sure you want to know this," Dana said at the time. "I've been keeping this from you, but you may need it later." He expressed surprise when she informed him of the relationship, and was even more confident of her loyalty to him.

"That son of a bitch," was all Dana said now. She was angry at Doug for going along with it, but knew better than to ask him why he did. Instead, she hurried through her discourse on the mail and left.

* * *

The large manila envelope that came by registered mail that same morning caught Fiore's attention first. It was postmarked in Denver, Colorado. The cover letter inside was signed by a Cyril Berman who introduced himself as Doug's campaign manager.

Berman wrote that initial contacts were being made on Fiore's behalf throughout Rhode Island. A select group of people was being told only that if there was going to be a contest for governor, a young lawyer whom they'd be able to wholeheartedly support would be announcing his candidacy in March or April. The name wasn't being released yet to anyone, even unofficially. He was also letting some of them know that the Tarantino family knew the candidate intimately and would do everything it could to get him elected.

The letter from Berman expressed his optimism about the campaign's ability to raise funds once they were able to go public. He urged Fiore to begin reviewing the position papers that were in the envelope. "Let me make it very clear," he wrote, "that you are expected to adopt every one of them as your own, whether you are in agreement with them now or not."

Berman pointed out that Fiore was in an enviable situation. "No opponent can accuse you of waffling on any of these issues because you've never had to speak out on them before. If you are personally unhappy with or opposed to one or more of these positions, you will have ample opportunity while in the governor's office to judiciously amend any stance you have taken. For now, the positions outlined for you are the ones that will win votes."

Berman's cover letter was on a plain piece of white stationery that showed no return address or telephone number. At the end, he informed Fiore that he would continue to communicate with him. The last line read, "I am instructing you to take this letter and have it shredded immediately."

Doug put the letter in a regular envelope and sealed it. He buzzed Dana to come back in and told her to shred it just as it was. He trusted her with everything.

* * *

After returning the other papers to the manila envelope and slipping it inside his briefcase, Fiore looked at the rest of the mail. A small, pink-colored envelope caught his attention, addressed in longhand to "Mr. and Mrs. Douglas Fiore." He turned it over and saw an address on Orchard Avenue in Providence that he didn't recognize.

Fiore inserted the tip of his long silver letter opener into the space left by the unsealed corner of the flap and slit the envelope across the top. The card he removed had a picture of "Uncle Sam" on the front, in full patriotic attire, along with a similarly dressed female. Both were pointing a finger at the reader above the message, "We Want You." It was an invitation for him and Grace to attend a Valentine Day's party being given by Pat and Brad Hanley at their home.

Fiore sat back and thought about it. He knew Brad Hanley for about five years, ever since the Tarantino family bought a strong minority interest in Ocean State Wire & Cable. Hanley's instructions were to call Walters, Cassidy & Breen with any legal problems that arose. There wasn't a great deal of hands-on work for Doug to do for them in that time. But when the wire company's labor contract came up for negotiation a few years back, Fiore assigned the work to George Ryder, and he recalled now that Ryder was also involved in a few arbitration cases for Ocean State. That contract is probably due to be negotiated again, he thought.

Fiore couldn't recall the last time he saw Hanley, although he spoke to him on the telephone occasionally when Sandy Tarantino raised a question about something or other at the plant. Sandy preferred to have Doug get the answers for him. It had all been strictly business between Hanley and himself. There was never a lunch or dinner at which the two of them could relax and get to know each other. Thinking about it, Fiore didn't have an answer as to why he never initiated some personal contact. He decided that there must have been something about Hanley that turned him off.

He did remember meeting Pat Hanley at the plant on one occasion. If his memory was correct, it was the first or second time he went over there after the Tarantinos got involved. She had short brown hair and was quite attractive, but didn't show any interest in talking to him after they were introduced. Now, out of the blue, he and Grace were invited to party with the Hanleys.

"I wonder what's up," he said, the words falling softly from his lips.

* * *

Another unexpected visit that morning came from Bob Gorman. The firm's onetime managing partner and Fiore communicated only on rare occasions. It usually occurred when Gorman took advantage of the safe environment of a partners' meeting to raise a question about some new firm policy that disturbed him. He was afraid of Fiore, disgusted by the way, in his opinion, Doug used the power of his position. He wished the firm had never hired him. Gorman also knew he would always come out the loser if Fiore asked for a partners vote on any policy change he was requesting that Gorman opposed.

For his part, Fiore took to mimicking Gorman in conversations with close friends at the office. "What we used to do around here in a case like that . . ." he would say, in an almost perfect imitation of Gorman's nasal sound. It was always a sure way to produce loud laughter from those who were there for the performance.

I wish that guy would take early retirement and get out of here, Doug often thought, but he knew that Gorman enjoyed his role as one of the senior partners of the firm. Fiore fully expected him to petition the other partners to be allowed to continue working on a part-time basis after he turned sixty-five. "And probably even after he reaches seventy," he muttered in disgust.

Sometimes Fiore wished that he could operate like the general manager of a baseball team. How he'd like to trade away a few of his veteran lawyers for younger prospects at some of the other firms in town. Were that ever to happen, he mused, he certainly knew which lawyers he'd move out "for the good of the team" as quickly as he could. As to Gorman in particular, Doug figured he probably still harbored thoughts of being a kingmaker again someday. His greatest achievement, were he able to pull it off, would be finding and supporting someone in the firm who could get the votes to unseat Fiore as managing partner. There was no love lost between the two of them.

Gorman sat down and crossed one long leg over the other. The move revealed a pair of blue argyle socks. He was uncomfortable being alone with Fiore, which meant avoiding any chitchat and getting straight to the point. Doug was grateful for that because the less time he had to spend with Bob Gorman on any matter, the better he felt.

The thing they were all working for, Gorman began, was to make WC&B the best law firm in Rhode Island. "It's our job to try and maximize income for everyone through hard work," Gorman continued. "It's not good for any partner or associate to be sitting around with a lot of time on his hands if there's work in the office he could be doing."

Fiore understood where the conversation was heading. Gorman was there to make a case for George Ryder. *One dinosaur trying to save another,* he thought. He could sympathize with Gorman's good intentions in trying to help out another partner, but it wasn't going to work with Ryder. Ryder was hanging himself with his low billables, and Doug wasn't going to let anyone loosen the noose.

"There are all kinds of reasons why a lawyer can suddenly find himself with not much to do. I know you're aware of that, Doug. But you're the managing partner. It's up to you to step in if you see that happening and try to spread the work around."

Fiore remained silent. He wanted Gorman to get it over with.

"It happens to all of us from time to time, and right now George is going through it in a bad way."

If there was another George at the firm besides Ryder, Doug would have enjoyed asking, "George who?"

"He looked kind of discouraged when I saw him," Gorman said. "When I asked him what was wrong, he told me he wasn't getting a chance to put in much billable time. George has always been a workhorse, we both know that, but he's lost some good clients in the past couple of years through no fault of his own. It's been tough replacing them, especially in this economy."

Gorman looked directly at Fiore while he spoke. Doug maintained eye contact at first, but then pushed back in his chair and began staring up at the ceiling as Gorman continued speaking.

"What concerns me is that George seems to think Paul Castillo could be giving him some things to handle, but won't do it. So I took a look at the computer reports for the past six months. Castillo is putting in at least 175 billable hours a month, usually closer to 200. Maybe Paul's afraid work will slow down for him, too, one of these days, and wants to hold on to everything he's got, just in case. But that doesn't help George with the problem he's facing right now. Whatever it is, you ought to take a look and see what moves you can make to get George productive again. That's what I always used to do in a case like that, you know."

Fiore was well aware of Gorman's animosity toward him. He wanted to say, "Yes, you asshole, I know."

Gorman was finished with his business and got up. Fiore didn't leave his chair to show him out of the office, nor did he thank him for bringing the matter to his attention.

"I'll see what I can find out, Bob," was all he said as Gorman, after waiting several seconds for a reply, walked toward the door. But Fiore was already very familiar with the facts that were just recited to him. He virtually memorized Ryder's continually declining production numbers on the weekly computer printouts. And as far as Paul Castillo was concerned, he was only doing what Fiore told him to do when Ryder began losing some clients.

*   *   *

Yes, it had been a most interesting morning, Fiore thought, as he finished his lunch on the patio of the building's lobby café and continued to watch the young women moving past in their stylish winter coats and hats. He was satisfied that his decisions that day were good ones, and that to the extent necessary he had exercised the power he possessed as managing partner. Sitting there, he reflected on the events in his life that had brought him to the position he was in.

Fiore was a brilliant student, aided appreciably by an almost photographic memory. His father's words, (the "life and death" importance of Doug getting accepted to an Ivy League college), motivated him into adding a number of extracurricular activities to his high school record outside of basketball. He joined the debating team, proved himself wonderfully adept at outthinking his adversaries on his feet and was elected its president in his senior year. He ingratiated himself with the clique dominated by football players which held most of the student offices and social committee positions. That got him named to a number of those committees himself, and he received a lieutenant colonel's leadership rank in one of the school's military cadet regiments. Fiore joined several clubs whose meetings he scarcely attended, and was brazen enough to pose for yearbook pictures with other clubs in which he never participated. But he claimed membership in those groups on his college applications based on his presence in their photographs. Princeton was the college of his choice, and it accepted him.

In his first year at Princeton, there was something about Sandy Tarantino that Fiore liked right away. Part of it came from the wisecracks Sandy always had ready when he made Doug look foolish on the basketball court by feigning a move in one direction and then having a clear path to the basket for his shot. "How'd you like that one, Mr. Wilt Chamberlain?" he'd say, flashing his smile, or "You looked good on that, Doug, you play a helluva third base."

He recalled the night, during a pickup game, when an opposing player kneed him as he broke toward the basket. Doug hit the floor in pain and lay there for several minutes before he could be helped to his feet. Tarantino supported him as he limped to the sidelines and sat down on a large gymnastics mat someone dragged over from the far end of the field house.

When play resumed, he watched Sandy take quick revenge for the foul by getting in position to find the offending player's Adam's apple with a quick thrust of his arm to the side as they headed down court together. Play stopped again while the gasping victim, on all fours, slowly regained his breath and his composure. Tarantino didn't offer any apologies. Instead, he sat next to Doug as he waited for the game to resume, sending a message to everyone that what happened was no accident.

"I wanted to beat the shit out of the bastard for what he did to you," Sandy said. He held both fists tightly against the front of his waist. "But that ought to wise him up. I don't think he'll keep that knee move in his fucking repertoire."

Fiore witnessed the explosiveness of his roommate's temper on other occasions. He never forgot the party in the Village when a football player from Yale cut in on Tarantino whenever he danced with the pretty blonde from NYU whom he met on an earlier occasion. "I think I'm going to be taking her home tonight, old buddy," Sandy told him, winking as he did. The two of them were in the bathroom of the apartment, taking bottles of beer out of the cold water in the tub.

Later, as Doug and his dance partner were standing in place rubbing against each other, he saw the Yale man approach Sandy and the blonde with a smile on his face. It was as if someone dared him to cut in again and he was already enjoying the joke. When Tarantino felt the hand on his shoulder and saw who it was, he let go of his date gently, as if again acceding to the request. Suddenly, he surprised the Yaley with a combination of punches, the first to his gut, the next to his face, knocking him hard to the floor. Blood began to flow from the victim's nose and two of the women near him screamed. Fiore hurried over to Sandy whose fists were cocked again as he waited to see whether his tormentor would get up and fight back. When it was clear that the Yale man had no intention of submitting himself to more punishment, Doug grabbed one of Sandy's arms and said that it was time to go to another party. No one tried to stop them as they left.

After a while, Fiore was able to understand that what Tarantino always exhibited was a sense of his own physical power. There was a cocksureness about him that was stronger by virtue of his quiet mannerisms than were he any sort of a blowhard. He observed his new friend carefully whenever they spent time together, especially on their long trips back to Providence. When Sandy proposed they room together off-campus in their sophomore year, Doug readily accepted. That arrangement continued into their first year at Columbia Law School when Sandy informed him that they had lucked into a terrific rent-controlled apartment in the West 80s. It was through some friend of his, Sandy said, someone whom Fiore neither met nor heard of before.

Doug matured tremendously during the three years he lived with Sandy at Princeton and the next at Columbia. His roommate's brilliance gave him something to measure himself against on a daily basis. After a while he realized that he didn't have to take a back seat to anyone in any of his classes. He moved to the front of the room in lecture halls and delighted in answering questions in class. It wasn't done to show off his knowledge of the subject matter, but in the hope of stimulating further discussion about something of particular interest to him. Fiore was the leader in study groups at Columbia, while Tarantino shunned the company of others in preparing for class. The other students looked to Doug to resolve issues in dispute between them, and didn't start their discussion and analysis of the assigned cases until he arrived. He was elected Editor-in-Chief of the *Law Review* in his senior year and was the class valedictorian at graduation.

Now, sitting in the Spalding National Bank's lobby, Fiore was proud of himself. He had listened to his father's many speeches over the years on the subject of power and reached the pinnacle. He was the managing partner and primary rainmaker of the second largest law firm in the State. He ran the firm with "an iron hand in a velvet glove," able on most occasions to push the Executive Committee to adopt the new policies he favored or to rescind those that impaired his power.

Fiore was king of the hill and intended to maintain that position. He knew there was an undercurrent within the firm that it could be detrimental to one's job security to get on his bad side. He didn't say anything to encourage or discourage that feeling. But it was his policy not to engage in any infighting with the WC&B senior partners, concerned about the opposition they could muster if put to the test. The only exception he now made to that policy was George Ryder. He knew that Ryder was the sole Executive Committee member who had voted against Doug's becoming a partner a year ahead of schedule. It angered him years later, when he challenged Ryder for the managing partner position, that Ryder refused to resign, forcing the partners to a vote instead, despite Fiore's assurance that a majority was pledged to him. George's stubbornness caused some of Doug's supporters to have to reveal their positions in a debate preceding the vote. Fiore was also displeased that Ryder often opposed various proposals put forth by the Executive Committee with Doug's support, and never seemed to seek his friendship or show him any respect. He worried that Ryder might always be looking for a way to turn the partners against him and elect someone else to run the firm. Fiore comforted himself with the fact that he hadn't gone after Ryder surreptitiously and put him in the position he was in; rather, he waited patiently for the circumstances to arise in which George's value to WC&B would diminish significantly for all to see, and that time had come. Bob Gorman didn't know it yet but his appeal on Ryder's behalf was dead on arrival.

Soon, Fiore realized, he was going to have the chance to run for Governor of Rhode Island. His name and picture would be in the papers and on TV on a regular basis. He anticipated how good it would feel to be recognized everywhere he went. If he lost in the primary or the general election, he had a built-in excuse. "It's because I never attempted to gain public office in the past," he would say. Those who backed him might be disappointed, but they wouldn't be able to blame him for the defeat. Better yet, he'd be able to meet rich bigwigs all over the State and go after their business when he returned to his law practice. *It was just so beautiful,* he thought. The Tarantinos were giving him the opportunity to advertise non-stop for Doug Fiore and it wasn't costing him a dime.

There was no denying that the fickle finger of fate might point his way and get him elected. He'd be governor for at least four years and "Governor" to everyone who addressed him for the rest of his life. It wouldn't matter if he never ran for anything else again.

Fiore also realized that what Sandy told him was true. As governor, he'd have the best shot to go for the US Senate seat if Jim Hanover stepped down at the end of his term. That likely event would let him graduate from the pages of the *Herald* and local TV news to coverage by the national magazines and network news broadcasts. Young, handsome, articulate and a proven vote getter, he might well be just the right candidate to balance out a Presidential ticket. It was no secret that coming from Rhode Island deprived him of any leverage because the State had only a handful of electoral votes to offer, but he was convinced that the qualities he possessed would make him a great campaigner for the Party all around the country. *Whoa,* Doug told himself, *slow down, hold it right there. Let me get to Washington first and then I can start thinking the sky's the limit.*

He was glad the Tarantinos chose him as their candidate. Even though he didn't care whether State-sponsored casino gambling passed or failed, it would not trouble him to speak out against it on their behalf. It was a simple matter for Doug that if people wanted more opportunity to throw their money away at blackjack and craps tables, that was fine. The politicians would be overjoyed at having enough revenue coming in to avoid passing new taxes, but arguing against it would put him on the moral side of the issue. Inasmuch as he had argued many cases before the Court of Appeals, and one at the Supreme Court of the United States, he had no fear of speaking to small or large groups of Rhode Islanders in any environment. No one had to know it was Tarantino money paying for his soapbox, and regardless of where the financing for his campaign came from, Fiore was determined that he would wage a totally clean campaign from beginning to end.

One thought, however, that was troubling him for weeks, wouldn't go away. *It was the reality that he had no voice in whether to go after the governor's chair or not.* Sandy Tarantino began by asking him to do it, as if it were a favor to be granted or refused. But he quickly brushed aside Doug's initial ambivalence by giving him the kind of alternatives that ruled out any decision not to run for office. He would be their candidate or descend from the top rung of the ladder to the bottom very quickly.

Fiore had no doubt about the fact that Sandy could ruin him at any time. Between the two of them, the power was all in Sandy's hands. In this situation, the shoe was on the other foot, and Doug didn't like it. The thought of hearing others snicker, "When Tarantino speaks, Fiore jumps," made his stomach turn. But he knew there was nothing he could do about it. If he wanted to keep his clients and all the power they afforded him, there was no way he could say "No" to the proposal. Once that was understood, Fiore couldn't help worrying about what else he might be "asked" to do down the road.

12

THE GOVERNOR'S APPOINTMENTS SECRETARY told Richardson on the telephone that the interview would be limited to ten minutes. "I'm only letting you in there because you've just taken over the political beat from Callum," he said. He made it sound as if he was acquiescing in a ritual akin to a new ambassador presenting her credentials to the foreign government she would be dealing with on a daily basis.

Richardson asked Callum to make the call for her, but he refused and told her she was on her own. "I've spent over three weeks introducing you to just about every lawmaker up on Smith Hill, their chiefs of staff, administrative assistants and legislative aides. I had you shake hands and exchange business cards with every lobbyist we met in the hallways. I said a good word about you to every clerk or political hack who might ever be able to help you. We've been to the bars that both the Republicans and Democrats hang out at after work. You know the restaurants in town where the Governor likes to have his quiet, informal meetings at night. The same for the Majority Leader of the Senate and the Speaker of the House. For Chrissakes, even the two blind guys who run the take-out shops know who you are. So do the elevator operators, the barbers and the librarians in both chambers. You've got sources up the wazoo for any kind of story you want to write. I've given you the last nine years of my life in twenty-three days. But now you're on your own. If you want to meet with the Governor, call Troy Williams. That's what he's there for. Good luck, Jenna, and try hard not to fuck up."

Callum gave her a big grin when he finished speaking. The gesture sent the message that he knew she'd do fine.

Richardson arrived at the capitol building about ten minutes early. She entered through the north portico and glanced quickly at the famous "Gettysburg Gun" to her left. She remembered learning about it on a tour of the Statehouse when she was a student in the sixth grade. The cannon was last fired at the battle of Gettysburg where it was put out of service permanently by a confederate shell that exploded on it and killed the two Rhode Island cannoneers.

As she climbed the stairs, crafted from white Georgia marble, Jenna told herself that it was good to be early. The Governor might be free before her 3:30 appointment and be ready to talk to her then. She stopped for a few moments in the rotunda to look at the brass replica of the State Seal. It was an anchor mounted on a shield surrounded by a garland of leaves. The word "HOPE" was engraved on the shield, but Jenna was unaware that the single word was the official State motto.

She joined two other women near her in admiring the mural inside the dome of the rotunda. It was about 150 feet above them, she guessed. Part of the painting depicted the Colonists in discussion with some Indians. Jenna recalled that the figure in the middle standing the tallest was Roger Williams, founder of the first permanent white settlement in Providence. She also remembered the point being stressed in school that the land in question was purchased, not taken, from the Narragansett tribe.

As Troy Williams had directed, Richardson proceeded to the State Room, the room that provided entry to the Governor's Executive Chamber. From her seat there, she glanced up often at the crystal chandelier that hung from the ceiling and at the huge portrait of George Washington. It was painted by Gilbert Stuart, another son of Rhode Island who gained fame during Revolutionary times. The portrait was enhanced by an enormous gilded frame and hung over the marble fireplace just outside the entrance to the Governor's office. America's first President stood full length, one hand resting on a table, as he looked almost directly at the artist.

Jenna realized she had wanted this time to relax, breathe deeply and go over in her mind the three or four questions she might be able to ask John Sacco during the brief period allotted her for the interview.

Troy Williams saw her sitting there as he emerged from the inner sanctum carrying an armful of large files. He hurried past her toward the corridor. "Remember, Richardson, ten minutes," he said, without slowing down. *No sex discrimination there,* she told herself, remembering that she also heard him call Jim Callum by his last name alone.

The meeting went very well. Sacco suggested they sit close to each other, on opposite ends of the sofa. Without asking, he poured a cup of coffee for each of them from a white china pot. He expressed his pleasure at knowing she would be covering the political scene around the Statehouse for the rest of the year.

"I suppose Jim Callum probably clued you in on where I go after hours when I want to meet people away from the office." Richardson smiled and admitted that Callum certainly did. "Too formal and stuffy in here for some folks," Sacco said. "Can't get them to open up and tell me what's really on their minds." He also mentioned the names of several executives at the *Herald,* with good things to say about all of them.

The time passed quickly. Before she posed her last key question, Jenna heard a knock on the door and saw Williams look in. She started to get up, but without saying a word, Sacco waved him off. Given a reprieve, she asked the Governor when he expected to announce his intention to seek another term. Sacco didn't answer immediately. Instead, he arose easily from the sofa and walked toward his desk. Jenna realized that it was a question he wanted to think about without having to sit there, looking at her, while she waited for him to respond.

She watched as Sacco changed direction and approached the window at the rear of his office with its view of downtown Providence. The way he carried himself forced her to appreciate the fact that he appeared to be in excellent shape for a man whose next birthday would celebrate six full decades of life. Earlier, as she listened to him speak, Jenna concluded that the Governor had a streak of vanity when it came to his appearance. He was well tanned, had several teeth that were obviously capped, giving him a catching smile, and was impeccably groomed. Jenna made a mental note that he was both a smooth talker and a great dresser.

After contemplating the scene in front of him, Sacco called her over to where he was standing. He pointed at the city skyline a short distance away. "Tell me," he said, "how many people out there do you think took five seconds today to ask themselves when John Sacco would let them know he's running again?"

Richardson knew the question didn't call for an answer.

He looked at her and made a zero with his thumb and forefinger. "That many, Miss Richardson, or Jenna, if I may call you that."

"Please do," she replied.

Sacco moved from the window to his desk and sat down. Jenna took the chair to his left, hoping to continue the interview. He found a thin cigar in the top drawer, tore off the cellophane wrapper and held it between his fingers without making any move to light it.

"This is step five in the eight step plan I'm on to quit," he explained. "But then again this is about the fourth different program I've been on. I keep telling my wife I should be buying better cigars instead of spending the money looking for a cure." His laugh showed off his beautiful teeth.

"The fact is," he said, turning serious again, "I've got much too much work to do to even think about the answer to your question right now. The economy here has improved a little with the changes we've been able to make. It's still what I'd call 'lousy,' although thank goodness it's not nearly as bad as Massachusetts or Connecticut. We're doing everything we can to find jobs for people and get them off the unemployment rolls. I've got law students at ten dollars an hour searching the books for any federal programs we can possibly pull some money out of. I was on the phone half the morning with folks in Washington trying to get some shipbuilding or even ship repair work for Newport. More jobs, Jenna. That's where all my energies are directed, not worrying about whether or not there'll be another campaign out there for John Sacco."

He stood up again. "And there are a few things I've still got to do today," he said, indicating with a sweep of his arm the piles of paper sitting all over the top of his desk. Richardson got up also, and he walked her to the door. They shook hands and she left.

He had avoided her question about his candidacy with an answer that he knew would look very good in print if she chose to use it. But he was completely unaware that as Jenna noted down his words, her eye caught the spines of two books on his desk that were otherwise hidden by the papers resting on them. The one on top was entitled, *The Committees and Subcommittees of the United States Senate*. Under it was a thinner volume called, *A Guide to Househunting in Washington, D.C.*

Jenna wondered why Sacco would have those books on his desk. Was he thinking of running for Hardiman's senate seat? She couldn't believe the Party would let him run against one of their own, an incumbent. Had someone—maybe even Hardiman—told him that the junior senator from Rhode Island intended to step down after one term? *Sonofabitch,* Jenna thought to herself, as she looked down the corridor for a public telephone, *maybe things* are *going to get interesting around here after all.*

13

It was Tommy Arena himself who came up with the idea of wearing a beeper whenever he left the office. It had nothing to do with work.

"What the fuck, I did this job as Secretary Treasurer and business agent of Local 719 for sixteen mother-fucking years before I bought the goddam thing, and anyone who wanted to speak to me bad enough could just leave a fucking message and wait for me to call back."

It was because his wife, Theus, suffered a mild stroke a few months earlier and he wanted to be sure she could reach him any time if she needed help. But he found out that the good ones, models that gave a digital readout of the phone number belonging to the person calling him, were costly. So he put the purchase on his expense account and unknowingly impressed one of the auditors at the Teamster Union headquarters in Washington with his efficiency.

Arena was sixty-three years old and looking forward to retirement in less than two years. He dropped out of school in the middle of the eighth grade, much to the relief of his teachers, and took pleasure in bragging to friends that he never read a book in his life. His parents came to the United States from Sicily and he was the oldest of five children, their only son. He had an olive complexion, with dull, dark brown eyes and thin lips. He rarely smiled, self-conscious of the poor teeth that evidenced his lifelong fear of dentists.

It was just after ten in the morning when his beeper went off. Arena was sitting with a truck driver in a small office at the J.C. Newton

Storage Warehouse. It was a freight forwarding warehouse located a block away from the main post office, just beyond the railroad yards, on the north side of Providence. He got there every Monday morning at seven o'clock and stayed until Newton's employees, members of his local, started their half hour lunch break at eleven-thirty.

The office he occupied was one of four that could be reached from a narrow hallway just inside the customer entrance to the building. Anyone wanting access to that area had first to approach the small window located in the outer office and wait for the near-obese woman who worked there to push back the sliding glass panel. Once she learned the visitor's business, it was her decision whether to press the button that unlocked the door to the corridor.

Jack Newton, who owned and operated the warehouse, had let Arena use that space to conduct his business for the past two years. The room was empty except for an old walnut stained desk and a heavy wooden chair, painted a shiny black. A single window faced the street. It had no shade or blinds. Layers of dirt screened out the light as the sun passed over that side of the building in the morning. The closest building to the warehouse was at least 200 feet away. Arena wasn't concerned about being observed there by anyone else.

The first piece of business he had each Monday morning was with Jack Newton himself. Newton gave Arena a summary of all the freight that was shipped out of the warehouse the prior week. He listed each trucking company that picked up any goods at all, the name of the owner or owner driver, and the total weight of whatever shipments it carried away. Newton then paid Tommy, in cash, two and a half cents for each pound of merchandise that left his premises during those previous five workdays. It was money that bought him protection in the form of Arena's word that Local 719 warehouse employees would never go on strike. The original rate he was assessed was lowered by a half cent a pound when he agreed to let Tommy have free use of the vacant office to make his other collections.

Arena spent the rest of the morning in a succession of brief meetings with a representative from each of the trucking companies that were on the list given him by Newton. They came to his office, one by one. Each presented copies of the bills of lading they were given when they picked up freight at the warehouse during the prior week. The rate for each of them was one and a half cents a pound. That gave them the privilege of being allowed to do business with a warehouse represented by Local 719. All payments were also in cash. Arena made whatever entries he needed for himself on the pages of a large loose-leaf binder. No receipts were ever tendered for the money grudgingly turned over to him.

Some drivers complained when the totals on their own documents didn't match the numbers Arena received from Newton. In those cases, Tommy agreed to have the original bills of lading with him the following Monday, but the protesting driver paid what he was told he owed at that time, subject to a later review.

Every company that handled any shipments out of the Newton warehouse was expected to show up and make its payment that morning. Failure to get there meant a penalty of an additional half-cent per pound when the bill was settled the following week. And at Arena's discretion, the delinquent driver or company might not receive any calls from Newton that week to pick up freight.

On Wednesday and Friday mornings Arena dealt with his other two freight-forwarding clients and the trucking companies that made deliveries for them during the previous week. In those cases, he made brief stops to settle accounts with the warehouses and then set up shop in nearby restaurants. Both were owned by friends of his, and neither opened its doors to the public until 11:00 a.m. By that time Tommy completed his collections for the day from the group of drivers and was enjoying a cappuccino before heading back to his office. He made no reduction from the full rate of three cents a pound for the two freight forwarders with whom he did business in this manner.

Every Friday afternoon, just before five o'clock, a black Jeep Waggoneer pulled into the parking lot next to Local 719's one-story brick building on Rockville Avenue. Several minutes later, when the Union's employees left work for the day through the side door that opened on to the lot, one of the women in the group handed the Jeep's driver a large sealed US Postal Service priority delivery box. Within the hour an accountant at Sal Tarantino's office was recording its contents.

The box contained copies of the delivery records given to Arena by the three freight forwarders for the prior week and exactly half the cash he collected. This arrangement, proposed by Tommy and mutually beneficial to both him and the Tarantinos, was in effect for a number of years. Sal Tarantino didn't like it, but couldn't turn it down. At the time he found himself in need of a greater cash flow to continue his investments in legitimate businesses. He reluctantly agreed to offer whatever physical protection Arena needed in lining up the freight forwarders and trucking companies for their weekly contributions.

Tarantino comforted himself with the thought that he would drop out of this line of business as soon as the Family's finances improved. But it was put off from one year to the next in exchange for other "favors" he was able to extract from Tommy's local of the Teamsters. The Tarantino Family didn't have to work hard for its share of what Arena collected. Its only obligation was to convince a recalcitrant trucker, now and then, to complain less and have his payments in on time.

Arena was in the middle of a transaction at the J.C. Newton warehouse when the beeper went off. He saw that the call was from his office and ignored it. Instead, he continued counting the money handed to him by one of the drivers on his schedule. After the driver entered his initials on the sheet listing the name of his company, Arena scribbled his own "TA" next to it and told his visitor to have a great day.

Arena's secretary had standing instructions not to bother him on Monday, Wednesday or Friday mornings. He told her that he'd always get to the office on those days shortly after noon, and he always did. None of the other business agents in Local 719 knew his beeper number.

"What the fuck does she want?" he said out loud. The words came from deep in his throat and just managed to slip out. He considered whether he should ask the fat girl out front—Marlene, her name was—if there was another office he could use that had a phone. His thoughts were interrupted by a knock on the door. Another paying customer came in.

"Hiya, Gus," Tommy said. "Out on the road today, huh?" He looked for G&G Trucking on the list. They were one of the larger freight carriers that delivered in Rhode Island. Arena's local represented G&G's drivers. He remembered that in the last contract negotiations Gus did a lot of crying about the money his company was losing. Eventually, Arena agreed to let G&G pay its drivers twenty-five cents an hour less than the going rate. He also conceded Gus the right for management personnel to make pickups and deliveries on days that Local 719 drivers missed work. But he absolutely refused to accept anything less for

Teamster pension fund contributions than the amount he received from every owner of a unionized carrier. There were no exceptions, he told Gus, "none, none, none." If anyone had to get hurt, it wasn't going to be the Union. There were too many people in the Teamster hierarchy waiting to carve that pension pie into slices. Tommy wasn't about to start making excuses to any of them.

"Why the hell don't you get another chair in here, Tommy?"

Gus Bagdasarian hated Arena's guts, and having to stand while being forced to pay over money his company couldn't afford made him seethe with anger. "The bastard makes me feel like shit, George," he told his cousin and partner the same day. "I'd kill him if I thought I could get away with it."

"Take your fucking complaints to Jack Newton," Arena answered. "He does all my interior decorating."

The beeper sounded again. He looked at it right away and saw his office number in bright red digits on the screen.

"I gotta go deliver another fucking baby," he said. "Stick your initials right there and I'll see you next Monday."

He followed Bagdasarian out the door and down the hall. Marlene told him he could use her phone but to make it quick. "This better be good," he told his secretary when she apologized for disturbing him.

"Mr. Sileo called," she blurted out. "He said you should get back to him as soon as possible. And you should tell his secretary to interrupt him if he's in a meeting."

She gave him the number in Washington and he hung up. Tommy stood there, wondering whether he had done anything lately that the big boys could consider a screw-up. Armand Sileo was the International Vice President of the Teamsters.

* * *

"The news isn't good, Tommy," Armand Sileo told Arena, "but it isn't necessarily bad. The feds are going to start checking you out, along with a couple of business agents in Albany. You know what they're looking for—just to see if any of you guys are holding hands with organized crime. If you're clean, you've got nothing to worry about and there'll never be any charges. If they find something and want to start digging deeper, you'll have to get your own lawyer. Under the settlement

96 • Bob Weintraub

agreement the International made with the Justice Department, we couldn't pick up a nickel of the cost, you know that. You're okay, aren't you Tommy? No shit in any closets if they open the doors?"

Arena answered without any hesitation. "They got nothing on me, Armand. I don't even know who's running things up on fucking Federal Hill anymore. It'll just be a waste of fucking time and money."

"Good, Tommy, I'm glad to hear it. Call me if you need me." Sileo wasn't interested in hearing anything else.

Arena put down the phone. He walked back to the office and looked outside through the dirt encrusted window. "What a fucking way to start the week," he grunted.

He knew the Teamsters settled the federal case against them to avoid a major trial that could have destroyed the Union if the Government proved its allegations. Since then, at least sixteen officers were brought up on charges and forced to resign as a result of their association with known mobsters. "Billy's blunder" was what most of the locals across the country called the deal their president, William McDevitt, signed with the Justice Department. It started a groundswell to keep him from being reelected at the next Teamster convention.

A judge in New York with an impeccable record of fairness was put in charge of the whole investigation. Anyone found guilty at trial of having mob connections could appeal to that judge and hope to get the local decision reversed and thrown out. But there was a Catch 22 in the appeals process. If the judge upheld the verdict, the Teamster representative not only had to resign from office but forfeit whatever Union pension he had coming.

"Not one fucking cent of retirement income," Arena whispered. He inhaled and let out a long deep breath. *He sure as fuck didn't want to see that happen to him,* he thought. All of a sudden Tommy didn't feel too good about his collection business.

14

WITHIN THE SAME HOUR that Arena was returning the call to Sileo, two other important phone calls were made from exchanges in Providence to numbers in Washington.

Jenna Richardson had contacted a few sources and snooped around in some of the places Jim Callum first brought her, where good alcohol usually loosened a few tongues. But she was unable to find anyone who heard even an inkling of a rumor that Spence Hardiman might not be running to keep his Senate seat. Still, she was convinced that the books she saw on John Sacco's desk weren't just some kind of coincidence. He had to have a reason for reading them, she felt. Finally, with no one else to try and pry information from, Richardson decided to go straight to the horse's mouth.

Senator Hardiman's secretary continued editing a document in her word processor as she listened to Jenna identify herself and ask for just one minute of the Senator's time. She replied, as she always did when someone from the media called, "I'm not sure whether the Senator will be able to interrupt what he's doing and come to the phone, Miss Richardson."

He did. He was bright and cheery. "I hope Walter Mullins is recovering nicely from his operation," he said. Mullins was the *Herald* publisher. "How can I help you?" he asked.

Jenna jumped right in. "I heard someone at the Statehouse say you wouldn't be running for another term, Senator. Can you confirm or deny that for me?"

She timed the pause before he answered her. Five seconds. That told her everything. When Hardiman said, "I have no reason at this time to think that I won't seek reelection," she thanked him for speaking with her. She'd quote him, she said, if her editor thought any kind of a story was necessary.

Richardson hung up the phone and looked around at the other reporters in the newsroom. They were oblivious to everything as their fingers worked the keyboards of their word processors. She couldn't hold back a smile.

* * *

It was an exceptionally raw morning in Washington, DC. Cyril Berman completed one of the many tasks received from Sandy Tarantino and was ready to make his report. When his secretary told him that a Steve Pearson was on the line—Sandy Tarantino said he would always communicate under that name—Berman unlocked the top drawer of the desk in his K Street office and pulled out a piece of lined yellow paper. They exchanged greetings, after which Sandy said he would listen while Cyril gave him the full report he was anxious to hear. Berman rubbed his black mustache several times with his forefinger, a habit he engaged in unconsciously at the start of every phone call.

"There's absolutely nothing in Fiore's family or his wife's family to worry about. They're both lily-white and both blue-collar types. Fiore's old man is a machine shop employee. He's worked at the same place for over thirty years and came close to being disciplined out of there a couple of times. Hers is the head cutter in a garment district shop that makes ladies handbags. Mostly knockoffs of Italian designers. Her family was always involved in activities at the neighborhood level. His folks kept to themselves. Fiore's got one sister, his wife's got a brother. From what I've seen, there aren't any skeletons in their closets.

"Thanks to you, he's been bringing in more client money than anyone else for years. He's their biggest rainmaker by a long shot, and that gives him the power he clearly loves. He could move from managing partner to governor with no sweat. He pushes for what he wants, and gets his partners to go along most of the time. But it doesn't look like he's trying to run roughshod over anyone. All in all, Sandy, I'd have to say he's very fair, and no one in the firm is talking about electing someone to replace him.

"I was impressed by a couple of things he did recently. For one, he successfully represented a judge in Providence who had some wild allegation of unethical conduct thrown at him. Fiore handled that pro bono. And he also convinced his partners that it would be wrong to lay off a bunch of associates at the end of last year just to have more money to spread around for them. He's got a good moral attitude about a lot of things, and he'll have the moral position on gambling in the campaign so he should feel right at home.

"Anyway, everything I've heard sounds like he'll make a good, tough candidate. Most importantly, he can think on his feet. He's a fierce debater and awfully smooth around people when he wants to be. Again, you probably knew all that."

Tarantino interrupted briefly. "He's the best debater I ever heard. I'm sure that's what got him editor-in-chief of his law review."

Berman went on with his report. "The one real negative, from our point of view, is that he has trouble keeping his fly zipped up. That's where his morality takes a breather. He's had three affairs I know about in the past ten years. One of them is going on right now. He was even shtuping his secretary for a while, and that violates the cardinal rule. You know what shtuping is, right?"

Berman laughed at Tarantino's answer and continued. "We may have to give some hard thought to his present romance. He's been sleeping with one of his law partners for about five months. Her name just happens to be Carol Singer, wife of our man Bruce. I'm inclined to leave it alone right now. Singer will probably get the Democratic nomination for governor if he wants it, but we can't be a hundred percent certain of that at the moment. First, we've got to get Fiore through the primary and into the general election. If Singer's his opponent, she might even be willing to help us out during the campaign. She'll probably have access to an awful lot of information. It sounds crazy, I know, but I guess it depends on how she feels about her husband and how she reacts when she sees who he's up against. We know something's awfully wrong between them if she's shacking up with Doug. She may love Singer enough to break off the affair when she finds out what's what. Then again, she may want to keep getting the good stuff Fiore's giving her. We'll just have to wait and see."

15

THE THING THAT THE *Providence Herald* executives liked most about the downtown Holiday Inn was that it was a non-union hotel. At lunch or dinnertime they could choose to go to the Biltmore or the Marriott for more gourmet dining. And if circumstances forced them to stay overnight in the city, they could sleep at those same two hotels without the din of automobile and truck traffic from the highway keeping them awake. That was a critical problem for the Holiday Inn, with its fourteen stories sitting almost on top of Interstate 95. But the *Herald* crowd knew that when they sat in the large windowless dining room, just off the main lobby, they didn't have to worry about union business agents overhearing their conversations. If you worked for a union in Providence, you didn't go near the Holiday Inn.

Terry Reardon was about fifteen minutes early for his meeting with Richie Cardella when he took a table at the far end of the dining room. Experience taught him that people weren't always on time for their lunch or dinner dates. So he made it a habit on such occasions to borrow a magazine from the reception area near his fourth floor office in the *Herald* building.

On his way to the hotel he stopped at the Civic Center to pick up a couple of concert tickets for his oldest son. They were for a band Reardon never heard of that would be in town for just a Saturday night performance the last weekend of the month. But on entering the spacious and unheated lobby, he saw a line of people waiting to make their purchases from the single ticket window that was doing business.

"Why the hell do they have one window open and nine closed?" he grumbled. And then supplied his own answer, still talking under his breath: "Because they probably figure they'll sell out anyway, so they might as well do it as cheaply as possible, the bastards."

Most of those in line were the "long hair and jeans crowd," as he later referred to them in his chat with Cardella. He looked at his watch and timed how long it took for the next two transactions to be completed. That convinced him it was too late to get at the end of the line. *Maybe he'd try again after lunch,* he thought.

"Sorry, sir, no cigar smoking allowed." Reardon heard the words and knew, even before looking up from his *Sports Illustrated*, that it was Cardella he'd find standing there with a big grin on his face.

"Hiya, Rico, have a seat," he said, and waited until Cardella sat down across from him. "I just don't like to see these smoking tables go to waste. Take a look around. There are eighteen tables in the dining room—I've already counted—and you can only light up at four of them. They keep squeezing us down all the time, pushing us into the corners of the room. Pretty soon I may have to buy a table here, like you do a condo, just to be able to come in and enjoy a Garcia Vega with my meal."

Reardon took another puff and then put it out, first flicking off the burnt ash and then carefully tamping the end easily into the ashtray so he could relight it later. "But I know your rule, counselor, so I'll save it for the walk back to work. How you doing, Richie?"

Cardella unbuttoned the jacket of his brown pin-striped suit and smiled. His wasn't a handsome face but it was one that most everyone who met him liked and trusted right away. The large nose couldn't hide the fact that it was broken at least once, and he had the boxing stories to give it credibility. His lips had a soft, spongy look about them, and his smile revealed not only an unfortunate gap between two of his front teeth but an earlier nicotine habit that left its mark in his mouth.

"Really great, Terry," he said. "Busy as a son of a bitch. My theory is that white collar crime just multiplies in a recession. I've had my hands full with a bunch of greedy executives who tried to make money without earning it the old-fashioned way. I've also had some interesting contract negotiations."

Richie Cardella was a big man, "built like a tall fire plug" many people said. The evidence was a solid 230 pounds on a six-foot frame. His shoulders seemed to be in constant motion when he spoke. "We made the *Herald*'s front page when the Teamsters put up the white flag and called off the strike at Coastal Trucking."

"Yeah, I read the story. You really beat up on Tommy Arena in that one."

"He deserved what he got. I don't know what the hell makes him so arrogant. He still thinks it's supposed to work like it did with the Teamsters in the old days. He wants to show up at the first meeting, throw a new contract on the table, tell the company to sign it or else, no matter what kind of shit he puts in there, and then have you take him out to dinner. I kept trying to introduce him to reality but he wouldn't listen."

"How long did that strike last?" Terry asked. "I forget."

Richie moved his fat bottom lip over the top one and looked up at the ceiling for a few moments. "Almost six weeks," he answered. "The company got some hungry independent operators to make its deliveries for a while. They weren't looking to go to war. But Arena cancelled out of two straight meetings without even letting the mediator know he wouldn't be there. That's when Coastal figured he could go fuck himself if he thought he was calling the shots. So they started hiring new employees and replaced almost half the twenty-seven guys on strike."

"Yeah, that was the tough part," Reardon said.

"But that's what it took for Tommy to finally see the light. He made damn sure he was at the next meeting the mediator called and agreed to almost everything in the company's final offer. All he kept saying, over and over, was, 'The International will have my fucking head for signing this.' I didn't know whether to laugh or cry, listening to him.

"But it's really sad, Terry. I'll bet anything the Union couldn't find new jobs for the strikers Coastal replaced. There's almost nothing out there! Gravel drivers, cement drivers, freight, even moving and storage, they're all hurting, laid off all over the place. But I don't think Tommy really gives a shit about what happens to them. He's been at this so long it's all water off a duck's back. If he cared about his members, he'd smarten up and stop acting like Jimmy Hoffa's still running the Union."

"Well, I hope he doesn't try and take it out on the *Herald* in August just because he's pissed off at you."

The waitress came over and put two menus on the table.

Reardon handed his right back to her. "I've got every line memorized, Mary. And it'll probably be another two months before they change it again. Give me the scrod with the cheese sauce, salad, oil and vinegar on the side, and bring a regular coffee as soon as you come back."

He watched Cardella look over the menu. They had eaten numerous meals together in the past, usually during the long negotiating sessions with one of the four unions at the *Herald*. Cardella had been the newspaper's legal counsel on all labor matters for almost eight years, from the time he left politics. Terry was Labor Relations Manager for half that time, handling all the day-to-day problems and employee grievances. He moved up to Vice President for Labor and Employment when his predecessor left the Company to take a similar position in Portland, Maine, his hometown.

"Is the scrod fresh or frozen?" Cardella asked the waitress.

Reardon smiled and thought to himself, *Oh, man, here we go.* He knew Richie could ask a dozen questions and drive any waitress crazy before deciding what to order.

Mary said she thought it was fresh but she would check if he wanted to know for sure.

"Usually it's frozen," Reardon offered.

"And what's the sole stuffed with?"

"A bread stuffing," she answered.

"No seafood in it?"

"No." Mary and Terry answered at the same time.

Cardella hesitated, scanning the menu. "Does the tuna salad have celery?"

"Some," Mary told him, "but not a lot."

Richie frowned. He hated celery. "I'll take the scrod, too, but no broccoli. Do you have a baked potato you can put with it?"

Mary shifted her weight from one leg to the other. "I'm not sure. I know we have French fries and Lyonnais."

"Well, see if they can throw a baked potato in the microwave. But I like it real soft so it mashes up easy. And with some sour cream. If not, I'll take the Lyonnais."

"Yes, sir, anything to drink?"

"Not now. Maybe later . . . or I'll tell you what. Bring me a decaf when the scrod is ready."

Mary left. Reardon chuckled and shook his head back and forth. "I don't believe you. I watch you do it all the time and I don't believe you. Your wife must go nuts at home."

"Never," Cardella replied, and his shoulders provided the exclamation point. "Anita doesn't go for the twenty questions routine I use outside. She just puts the food on the table. Take it or leave it. But she's a fantastic cook so I have no problems. She even hates broccoli herself. Anyhow, did you hear the one about why New Jersey has all the waste dumps and New York has all the lawyers?"

Reardon said he didn't.

"New Jersey got to pick first."

They both laughed.

"So what's the reason for this lunch and should I put it on the clock?" Cardella asked.

"Answer to the first question, the rumor mill has been turning out some stuff I wanted to ask you about. Answer to the second question, bill me if the scrod is fresh, not if it's frozen."

"I think I've been had." They both laughed again.

Reardon picked up his teaspoon and hit it lightly against the tabletop as he spoke. "I'll tell you what I've heard, but it doesn't come directly from anyone I can quote as a source. Like I said, rumors, so don't press me for a name afterwards."

"Okay," Cardella said. "I hear you."

Reardon continued. "Supposedly, Spence Hardiman has decided not to run for his Senate seat again. I know it's hard to imagine him giving it up, but he wouldn't be the first one to make that kind of decision. That freshman senator from Colorado already said he won't be a candidate again. A couple of others have indicated they're still noncommittal.

"Apparently, the great United States Senate isn't as much fun as it used to be. Some politicos who get elected there really expect to introduce new legislation and get things done, I guess. Then they find out what gridlock is all about. Either the Senate talks a bill to death and nothing comes of it, or if they finally get enough votes to pass it, the President vetoes it because his party wasn't the one that pushed it through. Hardiman has only been there one term, but he's a very sensitive guy. He was a good governor because he knew what he wanted for Rhode Island and pretty much forced the legislature to give it to him. Imagine how frustrating the last five years have been for him in Washington."

"No doubt about it," Cardella said, agreeing with him.

"Anyhow, what Hardiman does or doesn't do is the key. That's a no brainer. But if he's decided not to go for another term, that puts Sacco in the race for his job. We both know that John would definitely be odds on to win."

Richie nodded his head. "I can't even imagine who's out there to make it a race against him if that happened. Lindgren, bless his soul, was the best the Democrats had to offer in the race against Hardiman five years ago."

"You're probably right," Reardon continued, "but those who trade in gossip and scuttlebutt, otherwise known as the city's rumor mongers, have more to say. I'm told that if Sacco decides to run for the Senate, one Rico Cardella may be a candidate for governor on the Republican ticket. And that leaves me, in the intellectually rewarding job I hold, to say nothing of the money they pay me, to ask the sixty-four thousand dollar question. Is there anything to what I'm hearing? And if there is, who's going to help me negotiate a new contract with Tommy Arena in August and September?"

The waitress returned to the table with a basket of rolls, their salads and a coffee for Terry. "I didn't ask what kind of dressing you wanted on your salad," she said to Cardella. "Is the oil and vinegar okay?"

"No. I'll take Russian dressing."

She glanced at Reardon, as if to confirm her certainty ahead of time that the oil and vinegar wouldn't satisfy his friend. She saw the quick wink he gave her. "Be right back," she answered.

"And put mine on the side, too," Cardella said as she began walking away.

Reardon put his head down and shook it from side to side in feigned disbelief. He was afraid he might burst out laughing if he made eye contact with Mary again.

Cardella took the neatly folded cloth napkin out of his empty water glass and put it on his lap. "We'll have to be strictly off the record on this, Terry."

"That's what I figured." Reardon leaned forward, knowing Cardella would have to speak softly.

Richie did the same thing, glancing around first to be sure no one else was seated close to them. "The fact is I've been approached," he said. "There are some big wheels in the party who are there just to look down the road and plan for every contingency. They told me not to get myself worked up over it because chances are there won't be an opening for governor anyway. They see no reason for Hardiman not to run for reelection and stay where he is."

"But we know that's probably just their best guess," Terry said.

"That's right, and maybe they're feeling out someone else at the same time. It's definite that Ray Michaels wouldn't try and move up from lieutenant governor. He won't even run for office again, no matter what Sacco does. The heart attack he had a year ago scared the hell out of him and he doesn't want any pressure kind of job. They'll find something easy for him to do. Someone will come up with one of those 10:00 a.m. to 3:00 p.m. committee assignments, with no homework and two hours for lunch. That's his reward."

The two men nodded at each other, and Cardella continued. "If Hardiman stays put and Sacco goes for a second term, would I run on the ticket with him? That's a definite 'No,' even though I might regret it when John's time is up and he moves on. I've already told them that. But if it was the governor's chair this year, I think I'd have to give it my best shot."

Terry stopped long enough to add milk to his coffee and take a first sip. "So let's assume the scenario in which Hardiman quits, Sacco steps up and you're the candidate . . ."

Cardella answered before Reardon finished reframing the question he asked a few minutes earlier. "I've thought about your negotiations with Arena while running all this stuff through my head. If there's nothing unethical about doing it—you know, in case the *Herald* planned to endorse me later on—I think I'd have the time. The contract expires at the end of September. That leaves plenty of time after the primary to meet with Arena. If worse comes to worse, I could get someone else in the office to sit at the table with you and I'd call the plays from the locker room. I'm sure it can be worked out. But the odds are we won't ever get to that bridge, so why don't we relax for now and wait and see what happens."

"That's okay by me," Terry said. "But you're going to know what's happening before I do, so keep me posted."

Richie nodded affirmatively, just as the waitress set down her large server's tray on a nearby stand and got ready to bring their lunches to the table.

"Now we can enjoy the best that the Holiday Inn has to offer," Reardon declared.

As soon as Mary put their plates in front of them, Terry sampled the fish. "Yup, it's frozen," he said, breaking out a smile.

They both laughed out loud.

* * *

Jenna called him in the middle of the afternoon. "Well, was I right?" she asked.

"It'll cost you," Terry said.

"Cost me what?"

"About thirty minutes of your undivided passion tonight." He paused for a moment. "And that's just the foreplay."

Jenna laughed. "No can do, Superman. It's girls' night out tonight. Me and Cindy and Annette."

"Haven't the three of you had enough of 'The Golden Banana' yet?" Terry asked, a chuckle in his voice. "I hate to see a hard-working girl dropping those dollar bills inside a bunch of strange jockstraps. There's no redeemable social value in it. Besides, you can't afford it on what the *Herald* pays you."

She laughed again. "Come on, Terry, tell me. Was I right or not?"

"You were right on the money," he answered. "How'd you do it?"

"Whoopee," Jenna cried, ignoring the question at first. He could picture the huge grin on her face. "I knew it! I am terrific! How did I do it, the vice president wants to know. Wants me to reveal everything, spill all the beans, let the cat out of the bag. Okay, I will. Are you ready?" she asked, but didn't wait for an answer.

"It was a little luck, my own brand of chutzpah and some research, all in that order." She told him how she was able to glimpse just the titles of the two books on Sacco's desk and how she concocted the idea of the supposed rumor she put to Spence Hardiman. "Once I was convinced Hardiman wasn't running and that Sacco would go for his

Senate seat, the rest was research. I just checked to see which republicans held Statewide office in the past ten years who might be attractive to the Party for the governor's race. In my opinion, Cardella's the only one who fits that description."

"That's a hell of a job," Terry said. "I'd love to see you get a scoop out of it, but I had to give Richie my word it was off the record."

"No sweat, lover boy. It's still awfully thin anyway. Sacco could come up with a half-dozen reasons for having those books in his office, even if he didn't deny they were there. And Hardiman said he hasn't made any decision about what he'll do. If I wrote it up, Cardella would be sure you ran back here and fed me the information, regardless of what you promised. If I know McMurphy, he wouldn't want to run something based on what we have so far. Right now I'm just pleased that I got my nose into something political for the first time and my instincts were good. But you know what, Terry?"

"I know, and I don't blame you. You just changed your mind about tonight."

Jenna sparred with him. "Not on your life," she said, slowly and deliberately. "Nothing gets in the way of another night at the 'Banana.'"

It was Terry's turn to laugh. "Okay then, what?"

"If Cardella wasn't contacted by the party, it wouldn't have surprised me."

"Why not?" he asked.

"Because a lot of republicans in Rhode Island might not want to vote for him."

"Same question, Jenna. Why not?"

"Some of the blurbs I read about Richie in the library pointed out that he was very outspoken about the State having a lottery when that first came up as an issue years ago. I mean he was gung ho for the idea. That was the easiest way to raise money, he said. Something that wouldn't get the taxpayers up in arms. He may feel the same way now about the State getting into casino gambling. I've still got a little follow-up to do. I heard something about his law firm being hired to help write some of that legislation for one of the senate committees. If he's in favor of the State opening up casino parlors, I know one big hurdle he'll be facing down the line at election time."

Reardon didn't want to try to figure it out. "I give up again. Tell me."

My Honorable Brother • 109

"No, mister vice president, I'll just give you a clue." Jenna's voice had a triumphant ring to it. "It's a certain newspaper in Providence . . . that signs our paychecks. Big Daddy on Fountain Street has always been dead set against it."

He was silent for a few seconds. He was also amazed at how much Jenna learned so quickly. "So how about tomorrow night, Wonder Woman?"

16

They came close to having an accident when Fiore swung off Interstate 95 and didn't pay attention to the Yield sign at the end of the ramp onto 195 East. He heard the blaring horn of the car whose lane he just entered, and was thankful it had room to swerve to the left. The minivan barely avoided hitting Doug's black, one-year-old Mercedes, and its driver raised his middle finger in a silent salute as he went past.

Grace didn't say a word when it happened. She and Doug weren't speaking to each other at all since the shouting match they had shortly after leaving East Greenwich. It was Saturday night, and they were on their way to the Valentine's Day party at the Hanleys. He informed her, much too nonchalantly she thought, that he'd be spending most of Sunday in the office.

"How come?" she asked.

"Because I've got work to do. That's why I go to the office," he answered sarcastically.

Grace was calm at first. She reminded him that they had tickets for the Providence College performance of *Swan Lake*, and that they were taking Susan and a friend of hers with them.

Doug said that they could go without him. "Susan probably has another girlfriend who'd like to see it. It's not like I really look forward to watching a ballet."

Grace's composure turned quickly to anger. She told him to remember those words when he had to start traveling around the state, making speeches. "If you don't have time for something like this with your daughter, I'll be too busy to go traipsing all over Rhode Island whenever you want."

Before they were through hollering at each other, he said, "Don't be an asshole," and the conversation stopped at that point.

Fiore turned off the highway at Gano Street and followed it to Waterman. He reached inside the pocket of his sports jacket for the directions he took down over the telephone from Brad Hanley. A series of right and left turns finally brought them to the white Victorian at 37 Orchard Avenue.

As they approached the front steps, Doug took hold of Grace's left arm, just below the elbow and squeezed it slightly. "I'm sorry I swore at you," he said. "I've just been in a crappy mood today. I should have gone to the gym and worked it out. Let's be civil in there and talk about tomorrow on the way home." Grace shook her arm so that he would release his hand. She didn't say anything.

Pat Hanley greeted them at the door with a big smile. She chatted with Grace a couple of minutes after being introduced and called Brad over to take their coats. Brad shook hands with each of them. "Glad you could make it," he said.

"He'll put your coats upstairs in the bedroom," Pat said. "It's a night for lovers, so go meet the other guests and maybe you'll get lucky." She smiled broadly at both of them again and hurried off in the direction of the kitchen.

Entering the living room, Fiore saw a table in the far corner with bottles of liquor, soft drinks and mixers. "Let's have a drink," he told Grace. He made his way to the table without speaking to anyone. When he turned around, he discovered that his wife wasn't behind him. He didn't want to risk any kind of scene with her while they were there, and decided to mingle with those around him on his own. He and Grace could always find each other if the Hanleys intended to play any party games that brought couples together.

Fiore mixed some dark rum with orange juice, added a single ice cube and sipped his drink while he took in the scene. A number of huge, white paper Cupids, in different poses, hung by strings from the ceiling in both the living room and dining room. Someone had brushed a little red paint on each of them, calling attention to certain details: the puffy cheeks on one, the arrows held by another, a wing on a third. They were suspended low enough to make them part of the crowd in each room.

Large red valentines were taped onto the walls in the same two rooms. Each had the name of one of the party guests on its top section. Someone used a flair pen to print in poetry form, "Roses are red, Violets are blue" on all of them. Doug noticed one next to the mantle with a completed verse that read, "I've got two nuts, And I need a screw." He laughed and realized that he was supposed to fill in the last two lines of the poem on his own valentine when he found it. An older man standing near him remarked that screwing seemed to be the theme of most of the poetry. The way he said it left no doubt that he wasn't pleased.

Fiore moved around slowly. He introduced himself to different guests and tried to find the appropriate small talk pertaining to what they did or where they lived. He was good at that and got most people to open up to him immediately. He also had a talent for remembering names, associating them with something in his mind and linking the two together through a mental repetitive process. When he mentioned his own occupation, several guests asked him whether he'd heard one or another of the latest anti-lawyer jokes that seemed to be springing up every day. Fiore was mindful of the fact that he might be calling on any of these people in the months ahead for money or other support. He let them have the pleasure of framing the riddle and giving the answer, even if it wasn't new to him. At the punch line, he usually laughed the loudest.

Between some of the conversations, Doug glanced at several other valentines on the wall. He saw one with Pat Hanley's name on it in the dining room and went over to read what it said. "Roses are red, Violets are blue, I'm first mate on, A hanky-panky crew." He smiled and thought that he wouldn't mind at all if she turned that kind of attention on him.

Farther down on the same wall Fiore found his own valentine. He thought for a few minutes, picked up a pen from a nearby table and completed the rhyme with, "I charge by the hour, When I'm servicing you." To make sure everyone understood what he meant, he added an "Esq." after his name at the top of the large red heart.

Just as he finished writing, Pat Hanley was standing beside him. He didn't see her approach. She read the verse out loud and grinned. "Well, they do say some lawyers are forever screwing their clients, and of course they always charge for it. I suppose there's a double entendre there. Am I right, Doug?"

"I hadn't meant it that way," he answered, "but in either case I guess there are clients who consider it time well spent." He lingered, with a slight emphasis, on the last word.

"Touché," she said. They were both pleased with the repartee. "Are you having a good time?" she asked.

"Yes," he replied. "You've got some nice friends. I'm enjoying myself."

"But you're wondering why we invited you." She looked directly into his eyes, still smiling.

Something told him not to deny it. "From the minute I opened your envelope," he answered. There was a pause before he asked, "Are you going to tell me?"

"Of course," she said. "And thank you for being honest. But be patient with me for a little while. I've got to put more food out on the tables right now and start the entertainment going." She took a step away from him and then turned back. "It's probably a good time for you to go and make up with your wife." She spoke the words almost in a whisper. He didn't say anything, and she left. Doug had to admire an unnamed quality in his hostess. He knew that Grace wouldn't have said a word to anyone about their quarrel.

Pat found him again later on while some of her guests were still in hysterics at what was taking place. She had removed all the valentines from the walls and put them in a large straw basket. By lot, each person was asked to pick one and read the verse on it. The other guests scored each verse on a scale of 1 to 10. The authors of the three receiving the most points were given large chocolate hearts as a reward.

Afterwards, each of the men was asked to say whether he'd rather spend some time alone with Princess Diana or Madonna. The women were given a choice between Robert Redford and Joe Montana. When all the answers were submitted, Brad brought out life-sized cardboard-backed photographs of the four celebrities. But the photos had been altered and each of them appeared as a frontal nude. Brad got his camcorder, and one by one the guests were called up to pose with an arm around the personality he or she had chosen. One of the other guests took Polaroid pictures and passed them out.

"You looked great with Madonna," Pat told Doug. She joined him near the liquor table where he went to freshen up his drink.

"Thanks a lot," he chuckled. "I'm sure Joe Montana would like to see that picture with you on his arm. He might find room for you in his trophy case." He offered to fix her a drink, but she declined. The smile she was showing him suddenly vanished.

"Doug, the reason I asked you to come tonight was that I wanted to tell you something in person that I didn't think I could convey over the phone. I suppose I could have made an appointment to see you in your office, but I thought it would be a little easier to talk this way. Besides, it's always nice to get to know people on a more personal level. We probably should have invited you and Grace here years ago."

Fiore saw that she was tensing up as she spoke. He wanted to say something to get her to relax. "I don't see ninety percent of my clients on a social basis. I might take them to dinner once in a while, but that's either to talk about our latest case or see if there's any more business I can scrape up from them or someone they know. One-on-one marketing they call it. Just take a deep breath and tell me what it is."

An outburst of laughter caused Pat to look over at Brad at the other end of the room. One of the men was having his picture taken between Madonna and Princess Di, embracing them both. Brad seemed to be in charge, and was encouraging other guests to come forward for a similar photo.

She smiled and turned back to Doug. "I'm very worried about Brad," she began. "He's been killing himself trying to keep Ocean State Wire going. I'm not sure the owners understand how much he's been doing, the hours he puts in, or what the Company means to him. I know that the union negotiations are coming up soon and Brad's very afraid of what might happen as a result."

Pat reached for a tissue in the pocket of the red silk jacket she was wearing and dabbed at both eyes. Doug saw the tears coming before she tried to stop them. "If that plant shuts down, I'm afraid of what it will do to him," she said. She was crying again, and turned toward the wall so no one else in the room would notice.

"I guess I picked the wrong occasion for this, after all. Here I am crying, with a house full of friends. I'm sorry, Doug. Can we discuss it another time?"

He had moved into a position to hide her from the couple closest to them. "Sure we can," he answered. "Whenever it's good for you. Just let me know a day ahead. Do you want to come into the office?" He hoped she'd reject that idea and choose to meet him somewhere else where they could have more privacy. His gut told him he would like to get to know this woman a lot better.

Pat blew her nose and breathed deeply. "No, I'd rather not. I don't think I'd be comfortable there. We'll find someplace else. I'm really sorry about this."

"Please, don't say a word." He tried to be as reassuring as he could. "I understand what you're probably going through. Maybe I'll be able to help in some way." Pat Hanley was already turning him on.

She recovered enough to give him a modest smile. "Thanks, Doug. I appreciate your feeling. I want you to know I'd do anything in the world for Brad." Pat looked at him for a few seconds and then smiled again, as if signaling that the difficult part of their conversation was over. "I think it's time for me to get the coffee and dessert out here." Turning away, Pat felt relieved and certain that Doug Fiore was the person she could trust to help Brad get both Ocean State Wire and himself through the present crisis.

Fiore watched her as she walked across the room, stopping briefly to say something to Brad and kiss him on the cheek. *Not a bad-looking woman,* he thought to himself.

On the way home from the party Doug apologized to Grace again, said he would go into the office the next morning a couple of hours earlier than he originally planned and would quit work in time to accompany her and Susan to the ballet.

Grace thanked him, and asked, "Do you have any idea now why we were invited tonight?"

"Not a clue," he answered, "not a clue in the world."

17

Rosa Santos was usually among the first people to arrive at the Walters, Cassidy & Breen office each day. Her official hours were from 8:00 a.m. to 4:00 p.m., but invariably she stepped off the elevator each morning about twenty minutes early. Soon she was busy preparing the first of many thermoses of coffee that were consumed each day by the lawyers, paralegals and clerical staff of the firm. During the day she also checked to see that the kitchens and snack areas on each of the three floors were clean and that there were enough cans of soda and cartons of milk in the refrigerators.

Each morning Santos taped a sheet of paper to one of the cabinets in the kitchen on the thirty-first floor. As the day progressed, she learned from Mary Talbot, the receptionist, which conference rooms were reserved by lawyers for the following day and how many people would attend each meeting. She noted the locations and numbers on the sheet so she'd be certain to have sufficient coffee and muffins waiting for the conferees when they arrived.

Santos saw that there would be four people meeting in the private conference room adjacent to Doug Fiore's office at 8:15, and decided to check on the condition of the room. As she headed in that direction, she heard an unusual sound coming from behind the closed door of Frank Scardino's office. She stopped to listen. A few seconds later the noise was repeated several times. Standing there, she realized that what she was hearing were the intermittent sighs and moans of a woman having sex. It was coming from the right side of the room, where she knew Scardino's sofa was located. Rosa smiled, but continued on toward Fiore's office when she heard the muffled sound of Scardino's voice.

At five minutes after eight, Santos again walked from the kitchen to Fiore's office. She was pushing a small cart on which was placed everything needed for the meeting. As she passed through the reception area and into the corridor where Fiore was located, Scardino emerged from his office, a short distance ahead of her, followed by Janice Rossman. They turned in the opposite direction, proceeded to the end of the corridor and turned left. At 9:30 Santos was able to take her first break. She removed her white apron and went over to the reception desk where Mary Talbot was busy fielding incoming telephone calls.

Talbot had a well-deserved reputation for being both difficult to get along with and very demanding. Booking conference rooms was part of her jurisdiction, and she regulated it with an iron hand. Rosa saw her bully young associates on several occasions. She drove them out of a conference room where they were working if protocol wasn't followed and the room reserved with her ahead of time. Talbot didn't concern herself with the fact that the attorney needed a large table on which to spread out a raft of papers or that no one else was signed up to use the room at the time. Incredibly, her victims tolerated such conduct without questioning it.

Santos figured that Talbot was probably about fifty-five years old, perhaps ten or twelve years her senior. She knew Talbot was employed by the firm for almost twenty years, all of it as a receptionist, and that she always had to be aware of everything going on within the confines of Walters, Cassidy & Breen. Santos learned early on that Talbot had no problem reprimanding her if she mixed up one of her assignments. But she felt that her job security was enhanced to the extent that she could pass on any interesting tidbits of information, especially those considered scandalous.

Santos rested her left elbow on the high wooden counter that enclosed the reception desk in the form of a horseshoe. She looked around to be sure no one else was close enough to overhear the conversation. "Mr. Scardino had girlfriend with him this morning," she said.

"Where?" Mary asked.

"In his office. I went by not yet eight o'clock. I think . . ."

A call came in and Talbot put up a finger, indicating that Rosa shouldn't say anything until she answered it. One call followed another for several minutes. As soon as the switchboard was silent, she asked, "Was the door open?"

"No, no, the door closed." Rosa shook her head from side to side.

"Did you see her?"

"Not that time. I just listen."

"You were eavesdropping?"

Santos knew what the word meant. "No, no, they say nothing. I hear them making love when I go by."

Talbot stared at her, a smile forming at the corners of her mouth. The switchboard began to light up again, but she ignored it. "You heard them?"

"Yes, I hear her, you know." Rosa smiled and arched her eyebrows. "She make lot of noise . . . ow, ow, ow."

"Do you know who it was?" Talbot finally raised her finger again, before Santos could reply, and took care of business. When she looked up, Rosa told her of seeing Scardino and Janice Rossman come out of the room a short while later.

"This place is really getting to be something," Talbot said, shaking her head. The sarcasm was as heavy as she could make it. "Don't tell anyone else."

"Oh no, no one else," Rosa hurried to answer. "I tell only you."

Talbot opened the notebook she used to log in room reservations and moved her finger partway down the page. "That conference in Room 9 at two o'clock has been cancelled. There's a box of Danish pastry in the refrigerator upstairs that they were going to have. Leave one with me—I'll eat it on my break—and take the rest home."

Santos understood that the immediate reward, though small, was an indication of the value of the information she delivered.

As soon as Rosa left the area and returned to work, Talbot dialed Helen Barone's exchange. Barone's employment at the firm began exactly one month after her own, and the two were always close friends. Helen was promoted to the office manager position five years earlier, and Scardino was now her immediate boss. "Come down when you have a chance, or meet me at break at 10:30," Talbot said. "I've got some news that may give you something to think about."

18

Light snow was falling, slowing down the evening's rush hour traffic even more than usual. George Ryder had the radio of his '88 Ford station wagon tuned to a sports talk show, but wasn't aware of much that was being said. He was pleased with the fact that for the second consecutive day he was able to bill out a full eight hours, and was thinking about all the potential work ahead of him in negotiating the new Ocean State Wire & Cable contract. *Maybe things were beginning to turn around,* he told himself.

Ryder and Brad Hanley were together all afternoon. They met for lunch at a small Italian restaurant called Abruzzi's, just a block away from the plant, where both ordered the super calzones baked by the owner. Afterwards, they went to discuss strategy for the negotiations with the Machinists Union. Hanley led Ryder to the conference room located a floor above Ocean State's main office area. The space was used for storage before Hanley came to the Company, but he had it remodeled when the plant showed its first profit under his stewardship. It was a place where he could be certain no one overheard his conversation. In his office the previous day, Ryder reviewed his notes from the contract talks that took place three years earlier. In those negotiations the Machinists Union represented the production employees for the first time. He studied the papers carefully and made a list of everything he wanted to share and discuss with Hanley the next day.

The settlement with the Union hurt the Company badly. From a financial point of view it was disastrous, especially since the decreasing demand for Ocean State's wire in the recession made it virtually impossible for the Company to even achieve breakeven status.

Hanley went to the Union after the first year of the agreement, looking for any sort of wage concession he could get. He was turned down flat. The negotiating committee listened attentively to every economic argument he made, but taking its cue from Johnny Morelli, the Machinist business agent, it refused to bring Hanley's proposal to the membership for their consideration and a vote. Countless hours spent on the preparation of detailed graphs and other industry statistics to support his appeal for help were futile, a total waste of time.

The contract settlement also accelerated Hanley's own loss of face with the employees on the production floor. His rash behavior in trimming their wages and benefits too drastically as soon as they threw out the Steelworkers Union caused them to get back at him the only way they could—by voting for representation by another union. Then, when the negotiations reached the critical point, they went eyeball to eyeball with him on the final offers put on the table by each side. With the threat of a strike riding on his next move, Hanley was the one forced to blink. The workforce fittingly took that as a sign of the Company's weakness and celebrated its own strength. In the ensuing three years, whenever they thought that management was violating either the explicit or implicit meaning of any of the forty-seven articles of the labor agreement, they didn't hesitate to file grievance after grievance to retain what they had won.

Ryder knew that he and Hanley had a lot of ground to cover that afternoon. His goal was to find out what Ocean State's president hoped to achieve in the upcoming contract. To try and get a good handle on the Company's economic situation, he looked at a series of profit and loss statements Hanley gave him and reviewed the amount of wire tonnage shipped to Ocean State's twenty largest customers in the past year.

Ryder understood that Hanley's emotional involvement weakened his client's position at the bargaining table. His proposals in search of relief came off sounding more like pleas for mercy than realistic presentations meriting the other side's deliberation. Ryder realized that the burden of trying to soften up the Union negotiating committee at the opening session would be his, not Hanley's. It was important to put together the best statistics available for making a strong initial presentation to the committee. He had to find the right data from Ocean State's recent three-year history that everyone could comprehend and discuss in a rational manner. The most telling set of facts was needed to convince the employees that costs had to be held in check in order for Ocean State to be able to compete with other wire plants while it waited for the recession to end.

By 5:30 that afternoon Ryder had organized a lot of the information given to him, but wasn't ready to discuss any of the details with his client. He wanted to spend the next day in his office reviewing the material—a good start toward another full billing day—and drafting an opening statement to guide him when he addressed the Union at the first meeting. It was already scheduled to take place in two weeks. The statement would be supplemented with the best exhibits he could put together from all the economic information given him by Hanley. He'd have to look confident in his position when the time came to hand out copies of the Company's proposals to John Morelli and all six of the employees on his committee. If nothing else, Ocean State had to be seen as being completely credible in its presentation. If not, whatever proposals it submitted during the negotiations wouldn't stand a chance.

Ryder intended to begin pressing Hanley about his position on taking an employee strike this time around, if necessary. He had no idea whether the Tarantinos would have any input in the discussions or whether the direction on any crucial decisions would be coming from the Platt brothers, still the Company's majority owners. He remembered that neither he nor Hanley knew for certain who called the final shots three years earlier. Whenever Ryder thought about that fiasco, he suspected that Doug Fiore encouraged the Tarantinos to deliver a "no strike" ultimatum to Hanley for purely selfish reasons. He was certain Fiore didn't want to risk losing a client over a strike, whether it was the right strategy for the Company or not. Speaking to Fiore might get him the answer he was looking for, but it might also lead to embarrassing questions about Ryder's billable hours. Better stay away from him for now, he decided.

The meeting with Hanley ended abruptly, however, before Ryder could raise the subject of a strike. Brad suddenly informed him that he had to attend to a few matters with the second shift and that he had a prior engagement that evening. They arranged to meet again the following Monday.

"I've done one smart thing you'll be happy about, George," Brad told him. "We're renting a small suite at the Biltmore on a monthly basis. It's to make sure we have a nice place to meet with customers whenever they come to Providence. If any of our meetings with the Union run late, you'll probably be able to sleep there instead of having to drive home. If you want, you can leave a change of clothes and a toilet kit in the room. I'll get another key made and give it to you when I see you on Monday."

"Yes," Ryder said out loud as he turned off Interstate 95 at the West Warwick exit, "there's going to be a lot of work to do for Ocean State in the next couple of months." His billable hours would look good on the computer printouts for a change, and the partners could stop thinking of him as a problem with whom the firm had to deal. He figured that would take the pressure off him for a while at least.

Maybe there'd be other work coming in too, he thought. Bob Gorman told him that Fiore seemed receptive about speaking to Paul Castillo. That could mean some arbitration cases or other projects Castillo might give him to handle. Ryder had also discussed his free time with Lynn Benedetto, the marketing director. She was enthusiastic and promised to send out letters on his behalf to all the employer associations and chambers of commerce in the State. The firm would offer his services, at no cost, to speak at their meetings on any subject concerning labor relations.

You never know where you'll find your next client, he mused, turning off the radio in the Ford. Maybe I can start getting as lucky as that sonofabitch Fiore.

19

It was the first day all week that any mail was delivered to the Pawtucket Store 24 mailbox rented in the name of Steve Pearson. Sandy Tarantino didn't get to his office on Atwells Avenue until just after eleven that morning. He had already spent two hours speaking to several teachers at the private school in Riverside attended by his son. By the time he sat down at his desk, the two envelopes addressed to "Steve Pearson" were picked up by a messenger and were waiting for him. Neither one showed a return address.

He opened the first and found a handwritten letter, on yellow legal-size paper, from Tommy Arena. Arena wanted Sandy and his father to know that some agents from the Justice Department would be coming to Providence soon to see whether they could discover anything that would connect him with the Tarantino family. They were playing this game with his Union all over the country, Arena wrote. "It's because the fuckers never did like the Teamsters, ever since fucking Bobby Kennedy."

If they asked him any questions, Arena would say that he hadn't spoken to Sal Tarantino once in all the years since Sal became a don, and that he bumped into Sandy occasionally at a restaurant on Federal Hill. If the agents wanted any history, Tommy would let them know that he and Sal worked for the same trucking company when they were younger. Later on, after Arena became a Union officer, Sal called him once in a while for a little help in getting a Teamsters job for one of his friends. Arena even found work for Sandy a couple of summers while he was attending Princeton. That's how the two of them first met. He would deny that he ever set foot in the building where the Tarantinos had their offices. "Make fucking sure that anyone who works there says the same thing," he wrote.

Arena also said he felt he should stop making collections for a while, at least until he heard that the investigation was over. He figured that if government agents started following him, they would see the small army of drivers calling on him at the warehouse and restaurants he used as offices. That could mean trouble for everyone, he said, not just him. All he had to do was notify the three freight warehouses he did business with and they'd get word to the drivers that all collections were being postponed. Arena wrote that when it was safe for him to start up again, he'd push his "clients" to pay everything that was due, retroactively.

"But don't count on getting all of it. Some of these fucking independents don't know how to save shit," he noted. "And some of them drive a truck four days a week only because they found out they can't fucking survive on three." But he would find a way to pick up the summaries from the three warehouses every week, and he'd keep a running tab on what everyone owed.

Sandy knew that Arena was right about postponing his collections for a period of time. He was also well aware that his father didn't trust the Teamster agent at all. If Tommy could use the investigation as a way of putting more than his share of the money received from the drivers and warehousemen into his own pocket, Sal Tarantino was sure he would.

The second envelope had a Washington, DC, postmark. Sandy opened it and took out a small piece of plain white paper. Written on it, in pencil, was "S.H. March 15." That was all. Sandy knew exactly what it meant. He picked up the phone and dialed two numbers.

"Are you busy, Pop? I've got a couple of things to talk to you about."

Sal Tarantino was sitting behind a huge oak desk. The many deep nicks that showed on top evidenced the fact that it was solid throughout, not a veneer over plywood or something just as cheap. Its back and sides displayed intricate floral carvings. It was the same desk that Tony Buscatelli used in running the Family for almost thirty-five years. Word had it that it was surreptitiously removed from the Senate President's office at the Statehouse in the middle of the night and delivered to the senior Buscatelli as payment on a gambling debt.

"Come on in, Salvy," his father said, as Sandy opened the door. He was the only one who called him by that name. For him, Sandy was too effeminate a name for a man. He also disliked "Junior" intensely, and gave his only son a different middle name than his own to avoid it. Still, since he was always "Sal" or "Salvy" himself to his friends, he understood the reason for the nickname.

Sal Tarantino wore a baggy woolen sweater over an open-necked beige shirt. He obviously hadn't shaved for two or three days. A skin rash that worsened within the past year necessitated his washing his face six times a day. The ailment had him on the verge of growing a beard although he was never fond of the one worn by his son.

The man sitting in the large upholstered chair to Sal's left got up. He appeared to Sandy to be about the same age as his father. He was dressed immaculately in a gray, pin-striped suit with a white shirt that looked as if it was being worn for the very first time. His flowered silk tie, in maroon and navy blue, was the perfect accessory. Sandy was quite certain he hadn't seen him before.

"Vito, this is my son, Salvatore." The elder Tarantino didn't get up to make the introduction. "Salvy, I want you to meet Vito Recci. I would not have let him out of here before he got the chance to see you. Vito's an old friend of mine. You would never know from looking at him that he grew up on the same block as me. We used to play ball together all the time. But Vito here got smart and took off for the West Coast after he got out of the Navy. Fell in love with Frisco when his ship got back from the Pacific, and kissed all us poor slobs in Rhode Island goodbye. Went from the smallest state to the biggest one, right Vito?"

Sandy walked over and shook hands with his father's friend. He could tell immediately that the lush black hair on his head was an expensive toupee.

"I wanted Vito to stay and have dinner with us tonight. He could tell you some good stories about when we were kids. But he's catching a flight out at three o'clock."

"Yes, it's important for me to get back to San Francisco," Vito said. "It's a pleasure to meet you, young Salvy. Never hesitate to call on me if I can be of some service. I owe your father a lot of favors." He turned to

Sal. "Thank you for all your time today. We appreciate your help. Take care of yourself, and my regards to Concetta."

Sandy watched as his father put down the cigarette he was smoking, got up from his chair and reached out for Vito's hand. He could see how firmly each gripped the other. "And you send my regards," Sal replied. Vito went over to the closet for his black woolen overcoat and left the room without saying another word.

"What does he do?" Sandy asked.

"Take a guess."

"Okay, a wild guess. He's in San Francisco. I say he's a member of the Raffetto family."

Sal Tarantino smiled. "You're right. Another dividend from all that education I paid for. What did you want to talk to me about?"

"Hold it a second," Sandy said. "What's the help you're giving him?"

"Just a favor between families," Sal told his son. "One of their guys is AWOL. Vito is the one who convinced the Raffettos to give him a job. The kid comes from Woonsocket and went out to California with some local references. He learned a lot about the Family's business and they're afraid he might talk about it if he gets picked up for anything serious. It would help him cut a deal for himself. Vito asked me to just keep my eyes open and have someone fly him back to the coast if he turns up here. Nothing big."

Sandy had no doubt that the Raffetto family would kill the guy if they got their hands on him. But if he said anything, he knew his father would just shrug and tell him that what goes on in other families wasn't his business.

"He came all the way here for that?" Sandy asked.

"Of course not, Salvy. He came here because his mother's still here. It was a chance to do some business and visit her at the same time. How do you think she felt when she saw how good her son looks? He told me he drove up in a limo just so all the old ladies in the neighborhood would have something to talk about. And he made sure she came out to the car when he left so they could see him give her a big kiss. Now she can tell all of them what a success he is in the computer business and they have to believe her. He made her feel like 'Queen for a Day.' Hey, I'm going to lunch in ten minutes. What is it you want?"

My Honorable Brother • 127

Sandy told him about the letter from Arena. "I can't believe that guy writes the same way he talks."

His father thought for a minute. "I told you before, Salvy I don't trust that bastard anymore, not at all. He's gotten too arrogant. Talks like he knows all the answers. Tell Eddie to see where he goes on the mornings he usually does his collections. Arena isn't stupid, so have Eddie use a different car every time. Let's be sure Tommy's not trying to con us out of our share, even for a week. And tell everyone they never saw him here in the building, in case they get asked."

"The other news, Pop, is that Spence Hardiman will be making his announcement on the fifteenth. We got a note in the mail today."

"That's two weeks before the deadline I gave him."

"Right. Eleven days from today."

"Good. You should talk to your friend, Fiore. Make sure he's ready. I'll bet Johnny Sacco already knows. I found out Hardiman has been keeping him up to date for a while. Is that everything?"

"That's it."

"I'm out to lunch. Just be across the street. You're in charge." He winked at his son and went to get his coat.

* * *

Sandy Tarantino left the office at six o'clock. Halfway home he turned into the parking lot of a large mall and went inside. All four telephones along the wall of the entranceway were being used. He waited until he could get one of the end phones so he could turn to the side and not be heard by someone next to him when he spoke. He dialed a number and had three quarters ready in his hand when the operator told him to deposit seventy-five cents. Someone answered and said "Yeah?"

Tarantino spoke softly. "Get hold of Joe Gaudette. Tell him I want my good friend to take the six o'clock Delta flight from Green to LaGuardia next Monday night. He should use the same name as last time. Have him go to the Ramada Inn next to the airport when he gets there and wait in the lobby. Let him know he'll be back in Providence by eleven the same night. You got that? Okay, good."

20

The only other person to whom Brad Hanley gave a key to Room 606 at the Biltmore Hotel, Ocean State's regular suite, was his wife, Pat. He told her she could always use the room to freshen up if she happened to be in downtown Providence for any reason.

Pat asked Doug Fiore to meet her there about seven o'clock on Thursday night. She told him not to eat before coming, that he'd be her guest for dinner. Pat knew that her husband wouldn't be getting home from the plant until sometime close to midnight. That gave her all the time she needed to plead her case with Fiore.

She filled the ice bucket from the dispenser in the hallway and had almost finished her first drink before Fiore arrived. Brad stocked several bottles of liquor along with soda and tonic water in an alcove of the living area's large armoire, just below the television set. At Pat's suggestion, Fiore poured a drink for himself and refilled hers. They raised their glasses and toasted their good health. Hanley sat down at one end of the tuxedo-armed sofa, moving several pillows aside to make room for herself. She expected Doug to join her there, but he chose to sit opposite her, in a large wing chair covered in an attractive lime green fabric.

"Let me tell you a little about Brad and me," Pat began. For the next twenty minutes, uninterrupted, she took Fiore from the morning she first met her husband in a Dayton, Ohio, factory to the Valentine's Day party at their home a week earlier when she started to talk to Fiore about Ocean State Wire. She described the various jobs Brad held in Pittsburgh and how they anguished over the decision of whether to relocate to Rhode Island. The Platt brothers found him running a very successful company, a subsidiary of Bethlehem Steel, and offered him the chance to be president of a wire-making facility. Brad made several trips to Rhode Island before reaching his decision. He spent hours observing the operation of the plant and almost as much time being driven around Providence and a number of other towns to get a feel for the area.

"He was sure from what he saw that he could make Ocean State much more productive than it was," Pat continued. "That was a real challenge to him. And he fell in love with the East Side and the ocean and being so close to everything that Brown University offered. He wanted to come here but was ready to turn it down if I didn't think it was a good time for our three children to move. The oldest was about to start high school at that time. He also was ready to reject the offer if I couldn't be happy this far from my family. I honestly didn't know what to tell him. Brad finally called Irwin Platt and asked if he could bring me to Providence for a few days before he gave them an answer. That was a pretty unusual request in those days. But Mr. Platt agreed, and the rest, as they say, is history." She smiled as she finished telling the story. Then, glancing at her watch, Pat added, "And that's just the short version."

"Sounds like it has the makings of a major motion picture," Fiore countered. He returned her smile. "Anyway, did Brad accomplish what he thought he could get done at the plant?"

"Oh, yes," she said. "For a while he was going like gangbusters. In just over a year they were setting records almost every month for the amount of wire being shipped. My husband was as happy as a pig in doodoo. He changed some of the production methods that didn't come under the union contract, and the Platts let him purchase a few of the new machines he wanted. Brad was sitting on top of the world. Those first two to three years with the Company were some of the best years of his life. He couldn't wait to get out of bed in the morning and go to work."

Fiore got up to get another drink and asked Pat if she wanted one. "I shouldn't," she answered. "Two is really my limit. But if you make sure I don't do anything foolish, I'll join you."

"You're among friends," he said, and they smiled at each other. He put more ice in both glasses and asked, "So what happened?"

"A few things," she answered. "First, a couple of big wire companies in Canada started marketing campaigns to go after business here in the States. Brad said they did it because things had gone sour with their own customers who cut way down on their orders. Their plants are much newer than Ocean State and can produce more on their up-to-date machinery with a lot fewer employees.

"When they brought their prices down, they began picking up orders this plant was handling for years. Brad knew he had to get more production out of his men to stay competitive and hold on to as much business as they could. But the Union—it was the Steelworkers back then—wouldn't let him make any changes that weren't in line with the contract. He warned them that they were cutting their own throats, but they wouldn't listen." Fiore mixed the drinks and was standing behind the wing chair as Pat spoke. As soon as she stopped to take a breath, he returned her glass and sat down again.

"They never do," he said. "That's why union memberships have been going straight downhill for the last twenty years."

"I wish they'd all just disappear forever." Pat almost hissed as she spoke.

"Let me hear the rest of it," Doug said.

Pat took a sip of her drink, and then another. "When the contract expired," she began again, "Brad went after the language he needed to run the plant differently. The Union fought him every step of the way. By that time, the Company was losing money for over a year. Every month things kept getting worse. He knew it could be suicide for Ocean State to sign the new contract the Union wanted, so one day he called everyone into a meeting. He explained to the men how the Union was standing in their way and wouldn't budge, and showed them how their jobs were in danger unless they could turn things around. That got to some of the older employees, the ones who had the most to lose. They went around and spoke to the others, including the second shift. I forget the procedure, but they had some sort of an election and voted to get rid of the Steelworkers Union."

Fiore started to find it very disconcerting to look at Pat as she sat with her legs crossed. He moved from his chair to the other end of the sofa. "That was just about the time the Tarantinos bought into the Company," he said.

"That's right, and that was the worst thing that could have happened to Brad."

"Why do you say that?"

"Because he'd already shown the Platts what he could do. Now he felt he had to prove himself all over again to the new people. He wanted them to see a profit right away and figure they'd made a good investment. He was free to run the plant as he wanted, without any union work rules or interference. That let him get more wire produced with the same number of people as before. The problem was that customer orders kept drying up. It was the first stage of the recession but no one realized it. Brad called everyone he knew in the wire business to find out if they were all seeing the same thing. And he tried to get any leads he could for the kinds of wire Ocean State produces." Pat reached for her glass again.

"That should have been a signal to him to just go with the flow and not try anything drastic," Fiore said.

"You're right," she concurred, "and in hindsight Brad knows that. But he was obsessed at the time. When there was no chance to show a profit from sales, he decided to get there by doing what he could with the wages and benefits. First, he took fifty cents an hour from everyone, across the board. Then your office showed him how much money he could save by switching health plans for the employees. He did that too, moving them from Blue Cross into an HMO. They learned to live with that, I guess, until Brad made everyone start contributing part of the cost—I think it was about fifteen percent. They never had to do that before. And since he already cut their wages once, they saw that as a second cut in pay. They had no idea those things were going to happen to them when they voted out the Steelworkers."

"Do you know who in my office spoke to Brad about changing health plans?" he asked.

"I'm sure it was George Ryder," she replied.

Fiore realized that he most likely would refer any call from Hanley on that subject over to Ryder. He now remembered Ryder showing him how much money the new health coverage would save Ocean State, and his complimenting George on their getting off on the right foot with the client. The fifteen percent contribution by the employees came later, as Pat said, most likely put into effect by Hanley without first consulting Ryder.

"I get the picture," Doug told her, nodding his head up and down. "That's why they went out and brought the Machinists Union in to represent them."

"And forced Brad to give them back a lot of what he took away," Pat added. She was silent for a few moments. "The Union called his bluff at the end of the negotiations. Brad said the owners cut his balls off at the last minute by ordering him to settle the contract without a strike." Pat quickly realized she should have made the same point less crudely, and wondered if that thought caused her to blush at all.

The words titillated Fiore. In the short time he knew her, he never expected to hear her talk like that. "It was an image problem for the new investors," he told her. "They have good friends in most of the labor unions in Providence." He was lying to her, creating an excuse on the spot, but he felt he had no choice. He wasn't going to tell her that he made the decision for the good of Doug Fiore, or even for the good of the firm, that he didn't want to chance losing a good client to a strike. "They were under a lot of pressure not to have a big fight with the Machinists at that particular time, and the Platts went along with it. But understand that it's the Platts who call the shots, not the Tarantinos, and maybe they're ready for a fight now if the Union's demands are ridiculous. I don't know. What does Brad say?"

"I guess that's why I wanted to see you tonight, Doug. What he says scares me. Brad's certain there's going to be a strike this time, and I can see how badly he wants one. He lost the respect of most of the men at the Company three years ago when he cut their wages and benefits and then caved in to their demands. That hasn't changed at all, so he figures he has to start over again with a new workforce. He can only do it if the guys who are there now go out on strike. This is the best chance he'll ever have, he told me, because there are so many unemployed people looking for work. He believes he can find good replacements for most of the production employees in no time at all."

"Brad may be right," Fiore said.

"He seems to be sure of it. He's going to see what the Union wants the most, what issues they're ready to strike for. He's prepared to say 'No' to all of them, no compromises. Brad wants to hold the door open for them if they decide to walk out. How shall I put it, Doug? He wants his manhood back."

Fiore thought it was a great opening and didn't hesitate. "In the locker room they'd say he wants to show he's grown a new pair of balls." He watched Pat's reaction. She nodded her head up and down and then surprised Doug by continuing the conversation in its off-color mode.

"Yes, that's it, but I'm afraid they're getting so big they'll drag the rest of him down. It's hard to do much when you're on your knees." Pat looked at him for a few seconds, smiled coyly, and added, "At least, if you're engaging in war, it is."

But not if you're making love, Doug thought to himself. The smile was still on her lips. He was sure she was thinking the same thing. The conversation was getting him horny.

Pat continued. "From last July to December he was staying at the plant five nights a week and going in part of Saturday. At least eighty hours a week most of the time. He's still working late every Tuesday and Thursday and it's almost impossible for me to keep him home for a whole weekend. He's doing anything and everything he can to get more production for less money without violating the goddam contract. He sends personal letters to every customer that ever bought wire from the Company, trying to get orders from them. I guess I'm the only one who's close enough to see what's happening. Brad's got a love affair going with Ocean State Wire and he doesn't want to let anything come between them."

Fiore felt instinctively that it was the right moment to move over and sit next to Pat on the sofa. He wanted to be able to offer her support, if he could, and thought his closeness to her would send that signal. "What would you like me to do?" he asked softly.

"It's really what I want you to be ready to do," she said. "The owners lost a lot of money last year. Brad was afraid they might decide to call it quits when the auditor's figures came in a month ago. I never saw him in such bad shape as the week after he got the report. He looked like he was falling apart, one day after the next. And believe me, it had nothing to do with what he was losing on his three percent of the business.

"Maybe you already know whether they're planning to close the place or trying to sell it. I probably shouldn't ask about that. But if nothing's been discussed, or at least decided yet, I just hope you can let them know what Brad's been doing to try and keep it alive."

"No problem," Fiore told her. He felt he had to fudge his answer to her so that she wouldn't be questioning him as to the status of the plant every time Brad worried about its future. "Just so you'll know," he continued, "the Tarantino family employs my firm to handle certain matters for them, but there are other things they prefer not to come to us for advice on. Labor relations is one of them, although it wouldn't matter in this case anyway. It's been a while since I heard anything from the Platts. But as soon as Irwin or Sam calls me, I'll make sure they understand the effort Brad's been putting in."

"Thanks, Doug. I really appreciate it."

He wanted to find out more about this woman. "I assume everything's okay between you and Brad?" he asked.

"I'll answer that in a second," Pat responded. "That favor I asked comes in two parts, and I only gave you the first."

"Okay, let's hear the rest."

"I'm afraid Brad might force the employees out on strike even if he could get a fair settlement of the contract without it. His attitude seems to be, 'Give me everything I want or to hell with you.' He's like the *Titanic* looking for an iceberg." Pat took note of the half smile her words brought to Fiore's lips, and went on.

"I'm not sure George Ryder really understands what's going on in Brad's head. If he does, I don't know whether he can control him. That's why I'd like you to keep an eye on what's happening in the negotiations. See if the Union is looking for a settlement that's fair to both sides. If they're going to try and push Brad around again, like last time, that's one thing, and a fight will be inevitable. But if they recognize the problems at the plant and their demands show it, someone else may have to sit down with Brad and talk sense to him."

Pat was beginning to have trouble continuing with what she had to say. She looked down at her hands, folded together, and closed her eyes for several seconds. When she raised her head again, he could see the film of water in her eyes.

"I think you may even have to ask the owners to step in and stop him from doing something foolish. Maybe they'll have to tell him again that they don't want a strike. Is it something you can keep up with, Doug?"

He waited until she was looking directly at him. "I'll make the time. Don't you worry about it. I'll tell Ryder to show me all the proposals that go back and forth in the negotiations, and to update me orally as often as necessary. We won't let Brad jump off the deep end if we can help it."

A few tears began running down the sides of Pat's face. She brushed them away with her finger. Once again she was certain she had a close friend in Doug Fiore, the only person she could trust to help her keep Brad from taking too many missteps and falling off the cliff. She thanked Doug again and then leaned over and kissed him softly on the cheek.

"Back to your question," she said. "Brad and I have been in love for almost twenty-five years. It's been a good marriage. It hasn't been perfect but no one should expect that. I could always tell when some other woman caught his fancy for a while. It happened a handful of times. I never once said a word to him about it because I knew it was just an infatuation, a temporary need for a different sexual outlet, one that would blow over soon enough. A woman has a lot of ways of knowing when that's happening. Men aren't as smart when it comes to that. None of them want to believe that their wives may be getting some much-needed sexual satisfaction somewhere else. The male ego can't handle that. So they ignore the clues that may be sitting right out there in the open."

Fiore was poised to follow up on her last statement but then thought better of it.

"There were times when I was very depressed about something and Brad couldn't be there for me. He was too busy. There were too many things on his mind at work. There was no way he could give me the attention I wanted, the holding and the hugging my body was crying for, even the sex that I hoped would push the depression away, at least for a while.

"I didn't go out looking for other men when that happened. But I'm convinced we send out bright red flashing signals when we feel like that. It seems that every man in the street, or in the restaurant or bar can pick up on it. Sooner or later one of them has the right opening line and you end up in bed. The regrets come later on and hang around longer than you like, but at the time it's a catharsis, a wonderful release."

Pat took one of Doug's hands and worked her fingers into his. He wasn't sure what to make of it. "Brad and I? Like I said, still in love. But for the past nine months Ocean State Wire & Cable has been the only thing on his mind. I'm there for him, but all his energy is aimed in another direction." She hesitated but he could see she wasn't finished. "It's very depressing," she whispered.

Fiore felt the sudden hardening in his crotch. Pat was leaning toward him and he could see that she wanted to be held. He raised his arm and she brought her head and shoulders into his chest. *Where are we going with this?* he asked himself. Doug was comfortable in his relationship with Carol Singer and wasn't looking to get involved in another liaison. Pat raised her head and silently asked for a kiss. He couldn't refuse, and pressed his lips lightly against hers. But she wanted to kiss hard, long and hard.

Pat's intention was clear, and the moment of decision presented itself. Either he had to back off immediately and give her some lame excuse, or take what she was offering and consider it a onetime unexpected bonus. *What the hell,* he thought, as his natural eagerness for sex took over, *it's like I'm doing the client a favor.*

"Don't I know you from somewhere?" he said, when she rested her head back on his chest.

Pat laughed. "That's the best opening line I've heard in a long time. But I invited you here for dinner and we haven't had a thing to eat yet."

"It's okay," Doug answered, all indecision now gone. "I've been thinking about giving up dinners for Lent."

She laughed again, moved away from his arm and got up from the couch. "In that case," she said, reaching down to take one of his hands, "let me show you the rest of my humble dwelling."

Doug followed her into the bedroom. He was thinking that he'd slept with Carol at the Marriott the night before and with Grace at home on Tuesday. This would make it three different women on three consecutive nights. It wasn't quite his favorite fantasy of having two women in bed with him at the same time, but it would do for now.

21

Carol Singer was in a terrible mood by the time her husband got home and came into the family room where she was watching *L.A. Law*. At four-thirty that afternoon Doug Fiore surprised her by coming into her office. It was something he did only on rare occasions since they became lovers six months earlier. He was carrying a briefcase and had his coat over one arm.

"Hi. Got a second?" he asked.

"Sure. What's happening?"

"I'm on my way to the airport. Something urgent just came up with one of my clients in New York. I've got to hold his hand over dinner at LaGuardia."

"Oh."

He could see that his words upset her. "I'm sorry, Carol. I was looking forward to tonight at the Sheraton as much as you were."

"Who's the client?" she asked.

Fiore hadn't anticipated the question and deflected it. "I'm running late. I'll tell you all about it tomorrow, I promise."

Carol got up. "I'm not working on anything that's rush rush. Let me drive you to the terminal."

That was the last thing he wanted. "Thanks anyway," he said. "It would take us almost half an hour to walk over to your garage and get out of there. If I grab a cab now, I can probably beat most of the traffic."

She walked over to him and kissed him on the cheek.

"I really wanted to be with you tonight," he told her. "I've been saving up to make a large deposit."

She returned his smile even though the disappointment was beginning to turn to anger. But she would have been in a rage if she knew that Fiore made his reservation for the flight five days earlier—using the name Paul Rome again—and simply neglected to tell her.

* * *

Carol ate dinner at home alone that same night. She was reviewing a case file at the kitchen table when a woman called on the telephone, asking for Bruce. Carol said that she didn't expect her husband back before ten o'clock. The caller introduced herself as Jenna Richardson from the *Providence Herald* and said she needed some information for a story she was checking out.

"Perhaps you can help, Mrs. Singer. I'm just following up on a rumor going around the Statehouse that your husband plans to run for governor this year. Are you able to confirm that?"

Carol had no idea that Richardson was looking at her watch to see how many seconds passed before she got an answer. The question produced a sudden ache in her stomach. It was as if she was told by her doctor during a routine checkup that she had a life-threatening illness. She had to breathe deeply several times before she could speak.

Jenna was already convinced that the "No" she expected to hear momentarily would be a meaningless denial. She was unprepared for the words that came through the phone: "God, I hope not," Carol answered.

"Thank you, Mrs. Singer. I won't quote you on that. I'll try and reach Mr. Singer at his office tomorrow. Or he can return this call at 241-5000. Goodnight." Jenna hung up the phone and started biting her thumbnail as she considered Carol Singer's answer. It was something she was doing quite often without realizing it.

22

Bruce Singer sat down on one of the leather chairs in the family room. He waited for the next TV commercial before asking his wife how she was and whether there were any messages for him that night. Carol told him about the call from Jenna Richardson at the *Herald* and watched his reaction.

"I've seen her name in the paper on some stories, but not usually on political stuff," Bruce said. "That's Jim Callum's turf." He got up and began walking back toward the kitchen. "She's probably just helping out."

Carol tried to stay calm. "What are you going to tell her?" she asked.

He hesitated slightly. "That I haven't made a decision yet."

"You never mentioned that you were even considering it." She turned down the volume to silence the commercial.

"I didn't think we had to talk about it unless I was first convinced it was something I wanted to do. Cross the bridge when you get there, you know?"

"You know damn well, Bruce, that I don't want to see you getting anywhere near that bridge." She had raised her voice. Once again, she told herself not to get worked up. "Besides, Sacco has done a good job and he's a shoo-in for reelection."

"Are we going to talk about this now, and have it out, or do you want to watch the rest of the show? Just tell me what you want to do," he said.

Carol didn't answer. She reached for the remote again and pushed the power button. Bruce sat down on a side chair, instead of the leather one he was in at first, and leaned slightly forward in her direction.

"Someone has to run against Sacco," he began. "You know that. Even if the polls show that nine out of ten people say they'll vote for him, the Party can't roll over dead and not contest the election. Dave Waller's in a tough position. As Democratic Party Chairman, he's got to come up with a candidate who has some credibility and then run a campaign. He talked to me about it. Remember, I was lieutenant governor for four years. I'm the last democrat who held such a high state position."

She interrupted him. "Ed McGurty ran against Sacco two years ago, not you."

"Right. And he got beat. Clobbered is the word. He came out of his automobile showroom and disappeared back into it when the election was over. He hasn't taken a public stand on anything since then. He's not even in the picture this time."

"He was good enough to beat you in the primary," Carol said.

"You don't have to remind me." He spoke the words slowly. "Believe me, it still hurts. I didn't take McGurty seriously and I paid the price. The public got turned on for a while by a successful businessman who said he could run state government the same way he did a car dealership. He had everyone believing he'd spend less money and be able to lower taxes. People were tired of listening to politicians, and that's what I was at the time, unfortunately. Also, it didn't hurt McGurty to have some wealthy backers and a million dollars of his own money to throw into the campaign. He was running three TV spots for every one of ours.

"John Sacco had the same kind of story to tell. He served a couple of terms as a Republican state rep, but that was twelve years ago. He was the executive director of Rhode Island Blue Cross when the Republicans picked him to run for governor. That made him another outsider who could keep saying it was 'time for a change.' But that was the mood the voters were in and he rode the wave. He killed McGurty in the debates because Ed never understood the issues or how state government works."

"And he's done a good job," Carol said. "There's no reason for people to vote against him."

"Sacco's been fairly successful, I'll admit, but that doesn't mean he's unbeatable. Rhode Island has taken its share of hits in the recession and a lot of people are out of work. Mostly blue-collar jobs, Carol, and those are democrats. Sacco didn't exactly beat up on the banks when the *Herald* broke the story about the redlining that was being done in different towns. He's going to take a lot of heat for that. And the statistics on crime and drugs aren't any better than they were two years ago. I don't know how he feels about casino gambling run by the State. That could become a major issue in November. There are some pretty important things to discuss and debate before the election. Anything can happen."

"There must be someone else in the Democratic Party who wants to run," Carol said.

Bruce laughed. "No question about it. So far three mayors have told Waller they're interested, including Gene D'Amico in Providence. There's still plenty of time for a few more candidates to come out of the woodwork. Spence Hardiman is probably getting ready to announce for another six years in the Senate any day now. Then Sacco will call a press conference and let us know he wants a second term as governor. At that point any democrat who's serious about running against him will have to go public if he wants to start getting some name recognition before the primary."

Carol suddenly began to feel cold. She reached for the afghan on the couch and wrapped it around her. "I don't want you to run, Bruce." There was a hard edge to her voice. "I mean it. Politics has already done enough damage to our marriage. Another campaign could kill it."

They were both silent for several seconds. Carol thought about what she would say from the time her phone conversation with Jenna Richardson ended. Now it all began to spill out. "I went along with you two years ago because you said you owed it to the Party. You told me they would never have supported you for lieutenant governor earlier if they knew you wouldn't go after the governor's chair when it was vacant. I hated every minute of that campaign. It was a blessing to me when McGurty beat you in the primary. I thanked God for that. It gave me back two months of my life that I thought would be thrown away in the general election."

She found an old balled-up tissue in her bathrobe pocket, wiped her nose and sniffled deeply several times before going on. "If you get into this campaign, you know what it means. It's running all around the State every day of the week. You'll be getting home at midnight Monday through Friday, when you don't stay over in a hotel somewhere. On weekends you'll be attending all kinds of stupid functions. The two of us will be like ships passing in the night. You'll shake hundreds of hands a day, but you won't have a minute to hold mine."

She paused again. "We were very happy when you just practiced law. There were always periods when one of us was stressed out with work, but we still managed to find time for each other. That's not how it is when you get into one of those campaigns. The meetings, the phone calls, the fund raisers, the radio and TV shows, everything else . . . they never end. You do it eighteen hours a day and that's only because everyone else is sleeping the other six.

"I'll tell you right now that if you get into this, I won't be out there with you. I mean for anything! Not when you make your announcement, not for any of the fancy dinners, not any place where they want to see what your wife looks like before they consider giving you their vote. So do what you want, but if the loser in this whole thing is our marriage, don't say I didn't warn you."

And yet Carol knew that she already did as much to destroy their marriage as he had. It all started during the primary campaign two years earlier when Bruce simply had no time for her. He was coming home late every night and running around from one event to another on weekends until he was exhausted. As it turned out, he kept delivering the wrong message, and the State's democrats gave Ed McGurty a victory on primary day.

The result left Bruce in a deep depression. He couldn't hide the embarrassment of a two time lieutenant governor losing to a neophyte politician, a car dealer who came out of nowhere. His law practice became his refuge and he began to cut himself off from Carol and their closest friends. He might as well have been off campaigning for President for the amount of time he spent at home. Nothing changed after John Sacco soundly defeated McGurty in the general election, receiving sixty-seven percent of the vote, an unbelievable result in a state where Democrats were the overwhelming majority. Carol began to worry about her husband. When he wouldn't discuss his feelings with her, she urged him on several occasions to see a psychiatrist. But he refused, always intimating that his workload was getting lighter and he'd have more time to be with her.

She recalled that little changed even a year after his unexpected defeat. Carol took several weeks off from work during the summer to

My Honorable Brother • 143

spend as much time as she could with Rachel, their younger daughter, who was starting college at Cornell University the last week in August. They spent long days at the shopping malls, mostly in the Boston area. And there were some wonderful mother-daughter talks when they went out for dinner together on nights when Bruce let her know he'd be home late. Carol wanted him to get in some "quality time" with Rachel also, but his tentative plans to do something with her always fizzled at the last moment.

Their sex life was mostly non-existent after Bruce's failed campaign for governor. Every so often he seemed to break out of his depression for a day or two and appreciate her being there, but then weeks of nothing more than a soft "good night" at bedtime would follow. Carol hoped things would change when Rachel went off to Ithaca and they were alone in the house. She dressed a little more provocatively in the evenings and tried to bring a more romantic setting to the dinners they had together. Even so, her success in stimulating Bruce's passion was very limited.

She felt unloved and unwanted most of the time. Eventually, Carol began to fantasize about a love affair that would make her desirable to someone and let her respond like a woman again. She knew she was ripe for the picking when she first fell into Doug Fiore's arms. Her marriage would come to a crashing end if Bruce ever learned of her infidelity, but he still was far from being the partner she had to have before she could stop seeing Fiore.

Bruce looked at his wife a long time before answering. He noticed the dark shadows under her eyes and the small folds of flesh that were beginning to invade her face on both sides of her jaw. He spoke in a quiet, relaxed tone, the same way he would have tried to persuade one of his children not to drop out of college.

"Look, I don't want anything to happen to our marriage. You know how I feel about you. But I've got to tell you a few things. In the first place, Carol, you're exaggerating the time that goes into a campaign. Maybe it turns into an all consuming thing a few weeks before the primary and for a good part of the general election, but the period from April through July isn't that bad at all."

She cut him off. "So maybe you're home by eleven on those nights. Call me a liar for an hour."

"Wait a minute," he answered quickly. "I listened to everything you had to say. It's my turn, so let me finish." He didn't speak until she sank back into her chair. "I got home late a lot of those nights because I had to go back to the office and do some things for clients after I got through campaigning. Everyone there helped me out as much as they could, but there were some cases I still had to work on myself. I'm pretty sure they'd give me a commitment for more assistance this time if I asked for it. That would let me be here for dinner most nights until the heavy campaigning picked up.

"Secondly, you knew when you married me that I wanted to get into public service at some point. Two of my uncles were in the State Senate for years and that's all I used to hear about when I was a kid. You and I laughed about my being governor some day, remember?" He paused a few moments to see if she would answer, but she didn't.

"I stayed out of politics until Bonnie was twelve and Rachel was ten because it would have been too hard on you before that. I waited until the kids could stay home alone. That way you wouldn't be under any pressure to leave your office by a certain time every day if I couldn't be there. But I always contributed whatever spare time I had to help out in the elections. I networked, Carol, because I felt pretty sure that I'd be looking for those people to support me some day.

"Politics isn't an ego trip for me. You know me better than that. I never wanted power just for the sake of having it. I don't want people fawning over me and I don't need anyone applauding when I speak or telling me what a great man I am. As far as I'm concerned, that stuff is just bullshit.

"All I'm interested in is making this State a better place to live and giving people a chance to grab hold of at least part of what they dream about. I want to help solve problems. Since I think I've got good ideas on how to make that happen, I have to be in a leadership position. Those four years as lieutenant governor don't count. My role was just a ceremonial one. No one was interested in what I thought. I'd hate to look back years from now, knowing that I had a chance to make a difference, but stayed out of it. That would really hurt. Look, Carol, I . . ."

"You've already done your share," she interrupted, not quite in control of her voice. "And you know that you don't stand a chance of beating Sacco, so why drag the both of us through hell for nothing? It doesn't make sense."

"You may be right," he said. "And I haven't told Waller yet that I'd be a candidate. It might be a lot smarter for me to wait until I don't have to go up against an incumbent, assuming the Party would still want me then. Whoever runs this time may be the Party's choice in the next election too. It would depend on the type of campaign it turns out to be and how close the vote is. Look at what happened to Mario Cuomo in New York. He figured it would be better to wait and run against Dan Quayle instead of Bush. He never dreamed that Bush would get beat by Clinton or any other democrat. Now he's looking at maybe eight years of Clinton and eight more years of Gore. At his age, he's probably all washed up as far as ever running for President."

Bruce moved his chair a little closer to Carol and put his hand on her knee. He gave her a smile he hoped would send a message that he was serious about what he was about to say but didn't want it to anger her. "I feel bad for Mrs. Cuomo if Mario decided to stay out of the race because she told him he didn't stand a chance of beating Bush."

Carol didn't react to it in any way. "When do you have to give Waller an answer?" she asked.

"He didn't give me a deadline but the time's getting short."

"How will you make up your mind?"

"The usual way," he said. "There are a number of people I still want to call. I'll see what they think, get their advice. Then I'll just have to weigh it myself and make a decision."

Carol put her hand on his. "Can I add my parents to that list of people you'll speak to before you decide?" She gave him less of a smile than she intended. Her face wasn't cooperating.

Bruce was relieved by her change of mood. "Carol, I started to say before that I don't want anything to hurt our marriage. I really mean that. I may hardly ever come out with the words and say 'I love you,' but I do, I love you very much. I can't imagine what my life would have been like without you in it. You've been a wonderful wife and a great mother.

"But you're a lawyer because it's something you wanted to do and I've had to adjust to that in different ways. I'm not complaining about it. I admire you for what you've achieved. I just want you to understand that public service is a very big thing in my life right now and that it's something you have to find a way of adapting to. Maybe I'll never run for office again, who knows? But if I do, we've got to work out something we can live with during that period. I'll do my best if that time ever comes, I promise. What do you say?"

Carol understood why she chose to marry this man. "I don't know, Bruce. You've got to appreciate the fact that I detest politics as much as you love it. I hate what it takes away from our lives. But for right now, let's wait and see what happens."

Bruce took his wife's hand, stood up and pulled her to her feet. He opened his arms and she moved willingly into his embrace. He held her tight and pressed his cheek against hers. "Are you in the mood?" he whispered.

Carol took his hand again. "To tell you the truth, I was looking forward to some good sex all day long."

23

When Delta flight 458 landed at LaGuardia, Doug Fiore made his way quickly through the terminal and took an escalator to the lower level. He waited at the designated location for the Ramada shuttle bus that brought him to the hotel, a half mile off the airport grounds. Fiore entered the lobby and followed the signs to the men's room where he washed his hands and face in cold water and combed his hair. Returning to the lobby, he found a chair facing the entrance. It was easy to see that the hotel was in need of some serious renovation. Listening carefully to hear a pager call for "Paul Rome," he didn't notice when an older man carrying a briefcase sat down in the chair closest to him. Several minutes later, the man turned to Fiore and said, "We ought to go outside now, Mr. Rome."

He followed the stranger out the door without asking any questions. A black stretch limo, with its lights on, was parked in the road to the left of the entrance, about 200 feet away. As soon as the two men were in its sight, the limo pulled up to where they stood. The rear, passenger side door was opened from the inside.

"Come on in, old buddy."

Fiore recognized Sandy Tarantino's voice, climbed in and sat down next to him. They greeted each other by name and with a half hug.

"Doug, let me introduce you to Cyril Berman," Sandy said. Berman had followed Fiore into the car and took one of the large, padded jump seats opposite them. The two men leaned toward each other and shook hands. "Cyril flew in from Washington. His plane got in just a few minutes after yours."

Fiore looked at the man who was hired to put him into the governor's office. Berman appeared to be about ten years older than Doug, and central casting's answer to a call for a tenured English professor at a small university. His tweed jacket had leather patches at the elbows, and a gray turtleneck sweater overlapped the waistline of his wrinkled khaki pants. A pair of glasses rested on his chest, hanging from a thin leather strap around his neck. Berman's hair was long and black, but with some graying at the temples. A heavy mustache over his lip showed more pepper than salt, while his cheeks and nose were red, as if recently sunburned. Fiore would later find out that Berman's face kept that color all the time. It was the result of a skin disease called rosacea that he constantly aggravated by his regular consumption of hot coffee and alcohol.

"Well, it's time to get our campaign for governor on the road," Tarantino said to them, "both literally and figuratively." He looked at Fiore as the limo pulled away from the hotel and headed for the Expressway. "Providence is four hours away. It's your show, Cyril."

Fiore listened, in awe at times, as Berman laid out the progress of the campaign to date. He told Doug that exactly fifty-five people throughout Rhode Island were contacted and that his impending candidacy was discussed with each of them.

"I spoke with every one of them personally and visited the dozen who I believe have the most influence in the State. They know it's all predicated on some inside information that Spence Hardiman will be stepping down when his term is up and the assumption that John Sacco will want to run for that seat in the US Senate. No, your name wasn't divulged yet, but they were told you're one of the state's finest lawyers and a candidate whose positions on the issues they can wholeheartedly support."

Almost a third of the number Berman talked with were also informed that the Tarantino family endorsed the individual and would contribute heavily to the campaign. Each of the seventeen urged Berman to assure Sal Tarantino that he or she would be committed to the candidate's election.

"Some of the people we're talking about are in the State legislature," Berman said. "Others are well-to-do businessmen and women. A few are socialites we'll count on to throw the big parties where hopefully the heavy hitters get separated from their cash. We probably could have added twenty more names to the list, but we didn't want too much dilution. Down the road, one full page ad in the *Herald* will list the fifty-five of them if they're all still on board at the time. Believe me, with maybe a few exceptions, they'll like being in each other's company."

Berman told him that Spence Hardiman would make his announcement, declining to run again, somewhere between the thirteenth and eighteenth of the month. (Tarantino didn't inform Berman of the exact date. He thought it better for him not to know until a day before the event.) Sacco would probably then take less than a week to get into the race for Hardiman's seat, Berman said. About three weeks after that he would see to it that Fiore's name started to leak to the press as a potential gubernatorial candidate.

"In the meantime, you'll start visiting the fifty-five names on the list at the rate of six a day, in the order I've laid out and according to the appointments I'll set up. You'll be accompanied on all those visits by Russell Walsh, a former chairman of the Republican State Committee, and by Lester Karp, a real estate developer who's serving as your campaign treasurer.

"As soon as the paparazzi get hold of your name," Berman warned, "you can expect calls all day long in the office and at any time of the night at home. In fact, you probably ought to change your telephone number in the house right away and keep it unlisted. It's okay to confirm the rumor that you're thinking about throwing your hat in the ring. Tell them you're trying to gauge what support you could count on, but don't mention any names.

"If your answer to seven out of ten questions isn't 'no comment,' you'll probably be saying too much. We'll tell you exactly when you can make it official, where, and how you'll do it. That's when I'll step out of the shadows and join you as the campaign manager you just hired." After glancing down at his notes again, Berman asked, "Any questions?"

Fiore had a few things he wanted clarified. As he gave the answers, Berman took a videotape out of his briefcase and inserted it into a miniature VCR that he also brought with him. He ran a wire from the VCR to the Sony color TV that was mounted behind the limo driver's seat, and turned it on.

"Sit back and relax, Doug," he said with a smile. "I'm going to introduce you to the fifty-five pillars of your campaign."

24

BY THE TIME THE limo turned off Interstate 95 in Stamford, Connecticut, and pulled into the parking lot of a nearby Friendly's Restaurant, Fiore had seen the faces of all the people he would start to visit in about two weeks. He watched them talk to the camera about themselves, and listened to Berman, on the video, fill in a number of other background facts on each of them. Berman rewound the tape and gave it to him. "Do your homework on these folks," he said. "If you bump into any of them at the Trinity Theatre or the TK Club, you should recognize them and know their names without any hesitation."

Tarantino was silent throughout the tutelage. In the parking area, he jotted down their food orders on a piece of paper and gave it to the driver. Berman declared it an official break time. "I don't want to discuss anything else about the campaign until we're through eating," he said. He got out of the limo to stretch.

"This guy's good, Doug," Sandy said. "I want you to listen to everything he tells you." After a moment's pause, he corrected himself. "I mean I want you to *do* whatever he says. We're paying him good money to get you elected. He's been through the mill on this stuff and he knows his way around. You'd make us very unhappy if you did something Cyril was against and it cost us the election. We've all got to be on the same wavelength. Right, buddy?"

Fiore knew it was time to simply agree. Sandy's voice made it clear he was dead serious about him taking his orders from Berman.

"Right. No debate. I hear what you're saying," he replied.

After that, the two of them took the opportunity to engage in some small talk, inquiring first about each other's family. Fiore asked whether Tarantino had any thoughts about the kind of contract settlement that management was looking for at Ocean State Wire & Cable, whether he was discussing the matter with the Platt brothers. He was surprised to find that Sandy knew all the current wage rates for production employees at the plant, and what it was costing the Company on an hourly basis for employee health insurance and pensions, its major fringe benefits.

"I imagine your negotiator will show the Union how much money Ocean State lost last year," Sandy said. "Hopefully, that will make it a little easier to settle." He gave Doug his view of what changes ought to take place in the most important economic items over the three-year term of a new agreement and waited for Fiore to write them down. "Those are the wage and benefit numbers we're looking at for a settlement, and they should be the only major issues," he concluded. He never said whether the numbers were discussed with the Platts.

"Maybe, maybe not," Fiore replied. "Johnny Morelli gave Hanley a pretty miserable time three years ago. He called his bluff on the final offer Hanley gave him, and won. That was *your* decision, remember. What if Morelli feels like trying to do more of the same and get everything he can?"

"I'm not worried about that, Doug. I couldn't do anything about the situation last time. There was too much emotion involved and it was the Machinists' first contract there. They had to come out of it smelling like roses. This time I'll have a friend of mine take a message to Morelli."

"Will he listen to you?" Doug asked.

"I can't order him around. I can only try and reason with him. But make sure you let your guy—what's his name, Ryder—make sure Ryder knows the numbers I just gave you on the economics. He'll know the Union wants to settle if Morelli shows he's willing to go along with those same numbers."

Fiore nodded affirmatively to confirm that he'd speak to Ryder. After a brief silence he said, "It's not my business, Sandy, so you don't have to say anything, but have you or the Platts given any thought to selling the place or shutting it down?"

Tarantino shifted in his seat before answering. "Irwin Platt is getting a little impatient, I'd say. He's got real deep pockets but he doesn't like it when his hand can almost feel the bottom. I've been encouraging him to give it more time. He says he will, but who knows what he'll do if there's any serious cash squeeze from their other businesses. I think Ocean State will do a lot better if we can ever get out of this goddam recession."

Fiore pressed a little further. "What if Hanley's determined to settle for less than the numbers you gave me and the Union threatens to strike? I mean what if he thinks that to save the plant or just to save face he's got to get back some of the stuff he gave Morelli three years ago?"

Sandy answered without any hesitation. "I figure Ryder has been around the track enough times to know how to rein him in and avoid a fight if Morelli isn't looking for one. The guy is supposed to be a pro at what he does. You told me that yourself. But if there's a real problem, we'll talk about it. See if you can keep up with what's going on over there. Shit, old buddy, you don't have anything else to do, do you?"

They both laughed out loud.

The driver brought the food and Berman returned to the limo. They ate quickly, filling the back of the car with small talk about the Celtics and Knicks and how the fortunes of the two teams had changed dramatically from what they were five years earlier.

"The Knicks could spot the Celtics ten points a game and win nine out of ten times," Berman said.

No one argued with him. "You can't expect the Celts to do much without a big man in the middle," Fiore offered.

"Hold it there," Berman interrupted. "Those words of wisdom you just spoke, Doug, reminded me of something. I don't want to get personal, but I want to make sure you understand that Mr. and Mrs. John Q. Public expect their candidates for high office to have various attributes. High on that list is a very elusive thing called morality. I know for a fact that you have an excellent reputation in that regard. But between us guys, it's that big man in the middle that can cause trouble. Know what I mean, Doug? Let me put it as simply as I can. It's virtually impossible to get elected to public office if you get caught with your pants down. I mean literally. It cost Gary Hart a real shot at the Presidency, no doubt about it. Clinton slid by, with everything he did, because it all happened with him before anyone knew who he was. So don't screw up, and that was no pun intended." Berman and Tarantino had agreed earlier that nothing would be said at that time about Fiore's affair with Carol Singer.

Fiore sat looking at Berman, his eyes riveted on the man who clearly controlled his immediate future. Berman returned the gaze at first but it made him uncomfortable and he turned to get something out of his briefcase.

"Sandy?"

"Yeah Doug."

"Ask Cyril a question for me, will you?"

Tarantino was about to tell him to do it himself, but something in Fiore's eyes, something he could recall from their days together in college, prompted him to go along with the request. He knew whatever was coming would be funny.

"Sure. What do you want me to ask him?"

Berman looked back and forth at the two of them. He didn't know what was going on and felt awkward as he waited.

Fiore hesitated. He kept his eyes on Berman, prolonging the suspense. When he spoke, he let the words come very slowly. "Ask Cyril . . . whether it's okay . . . if I'm only caught with my fly open."

Berman's look of disbelief quickly faded in the wake of the boisterous laughter coming from the two men sitting across from him. He was about to reemphasize how serious he was but was stopped short by a quick wink from Tarantino.

* * *

When they got back on the highway, Berman announced that it was "quiz time." He took out his copy of the notebook containing the policy positions sent to Fiore earlier. Asking questions as if he was the only member of the media who was present at a news conference, Berman took Fiore through every one of the campaign issues he was instructed to study. If Doug said too much, he was cautioned to think like a witness in court.

"Answer only what you've been asked. That's *important*," Berman stressed. "Don't volunteer anything else."

If Fiore's answer deviated at all from the position prepared for him, Cyril scolded him in a professional manner and made him discuss the particular point again.

Berman posed some questions that weren't covered at all in the position papers, knowing they would catch Fiore unawares. He simply wanted to see how Doug reacted under fire to something he knew little or nothing about. After each one, he showed his client how to sidestep the inquiry and discuss something he was familiar with instead. He also instructed him on the correct way to avoid answering a question when he hadn't yet had the opportunity to review all the facts.

"This is very important also," Berman cautioned. "They don't expect you to know everything, even though they ask it. Just don't make up things as you go along for the sake of sounding smart at that moment. Someone there will always check out what you said. If they catch you in a lie or just plain wrong about something, they'll crucify you in the papers."

The limo turned off the highway again shortly after crossing the long span of bridge just beyond New London. Berman continued his persistent grilling until they pulled up in front of the single terminal at the Groton-New London airport.

"You sound very good, Doug," Sandy said. "I'm really impressed. You're going to be a hell of a candidate. But we're getting close to Rhode Island and sometimes the boys in blue like to pull a limo over just to see who's inside. It's probably the easiest way to get themselves free concert tickets if they stop the right car. If they see me in here, they'll want to know who you two are, and that would get reported to a few of the wrong people right away. We don't want that to happen, do we? So you two can get out here and go the rest of the way by yourselves."

Tarantino shook hands with Berman. "I reserved a Buick at Hertz under your name, Cyril. Thanks for meeting us in New York. I'll be in touch." He extended his hand to Fiore. "Talk to you soon, old buddy. Don't forget what I said before about the campaign."

On the way to Providence, the soon to be candidate and his undercover manager talked sports again most of the time. They went back and forth about how the Red Sox and Yankees were doing in spring training, which of the two teams would finish the season higher in the standings and how the new free agents they picked up would help each of them.

As they neared the city, Berman said, "I understand from Sandy that you were delighted with his suggestion you run for governor and with his Family's willingness to back your campaign financially. He said he expected you to need a couple of weeks to think about it, check with your wife, sound out the partners at your firm and call your friends, but that you took just three days to let him know you were gung ho for it. That's a great attitude to have going in to one of these things, but let me assure you there'll be times before it's over when you'll wish you never gave running for office a second thought."

Doug didn't say anything. There was no point in correcting the version of events Berman was given. After all, Sandy was making that scenario look a whole lot better than it was.

"We went over a whole lot of stuff tonight," Berman continued, "but it was all me talking and you listening. Is there anything I should know that you want to tell me before the hard work begins?"

Fiore was pleased with the opportunity the question gave him. "Yes, I guess there is," he began. "I'm new at this game, no one's ever heard of me and chances are I won't get elected. I may not even make it through the primary. That doesn't mean I'm not going to try as hard as I can to win and to justify Sandy's faith in me. But the reality is that I'll probably be going back to my law firm in September if I lose to some other Republican, or in November after the election. So I want to be certain that during this campaign I don't do or say anything I'll regret, that I'll be ashamed of later on or that could hurt my firm. I understand that I may have to say some negative things about my opponent. That's okay if he earned it by something he did that's on the record, but I'm not going to tell any lies, or half truths or whatever you want to call them. We're not going to do anything that anyone can call immoral or unethical. Winning doesn't mean that much to me. I want to go as far as we can on the issues—and I believe we're on the right side of the important ones—not on what throwing dirt at anyone will get us."

"That's fine, Doug. I'm all in favor of a positive campaign. Let's just hope that whoever your opponent is feels the same way."

Berman dropped Fiore at his downtown garage at just after ten o'clock. "I'll stay at the Sheraton overnight and fly back to DC in the morning. Work hard on that videotape."

Fiore assured him he would and said goodnight. As he walked toward the elevator, he remembered that he was scheduled to spend some time at the Sheraton himself that night. But Joe Gaudette's phone call changed his plans. He hoped he could still get Carol to meet him during the week. *I'd better get as much of her as I can,* he thought, *before things start to heat up.*

25

Incredibly, the temperature on March 15th was threatening to reach 60 degrees, and sunshine filled the park in Kennedy Plaza. The homeless who slept there at night and occupied the benches during the day removed their heavy, tattered jackets and overcoats. The out of fashion designs on the sweaters they wore left little mystery as to how old they were, removed at last from a bureau drawer where they had lain untouched for years, or handed down a number of times before being brought to a Salvation Army or Morgan Memorial storefront. People who normally just nodded at acquaintances in the street couldn't pass each other without asking, "Can you believe this weather?" Spring, still officially six days away, was giving a welcome preview of coming attractions.

Carol Singer had already looked down twice on this scene from her office window on the thirty-third floor. She was writing a brief for a case in the State Supreme Court and liked to walk around the room for inspiration whenever it became difficult to translate her thoughts into just the right words. She ignored the telephone when it rang. Her instructions to Kathy Walsh, her secretary, were to tell clients she was in conference and would return their calls later on. The unexpected sound of Kathy's voice on the intercom startled her for an instant.

"Your husband is on line one, Mrs. Singer."

When she answered, Bruce invited her to have lunch with him at the Biltmore. His firm's offices were just two blocks away, on Weybosset.

"What's the occasion?" she asked him.

"I've made a decision about running against Sacco," he told her. "I want to share it with you."

"I wish I could, Bruce, but my department's hosting a lunch for some big wheels from Fleet. We've been after some of their banking business for a long time and I'm one of the speakers." She hesitated a few moments. "Is it what I want to hear?"

"I really think we should be holding a glass in our hands when we talk about it." His voice was playful. Carol knew what he would tell her. She felt relieved and wonderful.

"I'm sorry, honey," she said. "How about a rain check for tomorrow?"

"Not for all the money in the other banks your firm already represents. This is today's decision and today's celebration. I'll tell you what. I haven't had a good Italian dinner in weeks. Let's go to 'Capriccio's' after work. I'll pick you up in your lobby at 6:30 and we can walk over."

Carol didn't know how to respond. She had already promised to meet Fiore at the Hilton, at seven. Her body still tingled when she thought of their lovemaking the week before. She was angry with him about the trip he suddenly made to New York, cancelling their tryst at the last minute. But he was anxious to make it up to her when they got in bed two nights later. She hadn't felt as satisfied in a long time, and thought now of the way he teased her as she kept crying out in pleasure. "That's number five," he chuckled, "or is it number six? I hope no one on this floor is trying to concentrate on anything."

But she understood how much anguish Bruce probably went through to reach this point. He was doing it for her. Losing the election to Sacco wouldn't bother him as long as he had the opportunity to debate the issues with his rival and let the people of Rhode Island know what he wanted to accomplish as governor. His confidants had obviously convinced him that it would be better to wait for the next election, when there wouldn't be an incumbent to go up against. The State Constitution limited any governor to two terms. Bruce was taking their advice, "pulling a Cuomo," as he would put it. She realized that he didn't want to risk seeing their marriage fall apart where the chances of achieving a political victory were remote. She couldn't reject him now.

"Okay, it's a date," she said.

Carol dialed Fiore's number. Dana Briggs answered and told her that he was out of the office for the day but would probably call in for messages. She asked if Carol wanted to leave one for him.

"Yes, I do," she replied, her mind racing furiously to come up with something that would sound innocent. She recalled the stories going around years earlier about Fiore sleeping with Briggs and was sure Dana knew how to read between the lines. "Doug told me he might be going out to dinner tonight with one of his clients. He wanted to bring me along because the client's having some financial problems. I don't know if that's still on, but something else has come up and I can't join them. If he calls, just tell him I'm unavailable tonight. He may want to change the date for the meeting." She tried to sound as nonchalant about it as she could.

"Who's the client?" Dana asked.

"I don't know," she answered. "He never told me."

"I'll give him your message."

Briggs hung up the phone and went into Fiore's office. His calendar was on the desk, open to that day. She looked at it and saw only the initials "C.S." in the space for appointments after 6:00 p.m. She smiled, and thought about what a terrific lover Doug was.

26

Jenna Richardson was bored. Nothing of any interest was happening on the political scene. She had done telephone interviews with Nancy Williston and Michael Droney, the two incumbent members of Congress from Rhode Island. Both indicated earlier through their offices that they would be seeking reelection. They would formally announce their candidacies, they told her, after Spence Hardiman declared his. "Protocol, you know," each said.

She also tried to get some leads on who might be coming forward to try and unseat them. The Republican and Democratic Committees did what they could to be helpful. They gave her the names of those local lawmakers who showed some interest in running statewide for Congress, and she dutifully followed up with phone calls.

But as several contacts in the Statehouse had enlightened her, "Things are different today, Jenna. It's not like before, when you served one or two terms in the House or Senate in Rhode Island, or at least you'd been a mayor for a while before you tried to step up and become a 'US Rep.' Now, anyone who's successful can decide to try and get elected. It doesn't matter whether it's a lawyer or some nobody running a restaurant. All it takes is money to have a shot at the job. Just look at who ran for governor last time. Sacco against McGurty. Neither of those two guys was serving in the legislature when they got in the race."

Richardson was beginning to think that she assumed too much about those books she saw on John Sacco's desk. And since Spence

Hardiman never spoke to her prior to that telephone call, maybe he was just being a little cautious when he took his time before answering her question. She knew McMurphy was right about not speculating in print that Hardiman wouldn't be going for a second term, not without some reliable source for the information. Otherwise, it could have caused a lot of embarrassment in different places. Still, she had always pushed ahead on what her gut told her. She believed in what she saw and what she heard, whether anyone else did or not. If there was a place she could go and put down a few dollars on Hardiman not running again, she would do it.

At two o'clock Jenna phoned the *Herald* newsroom to let McMurphy know what her story would be about that day. There was a surprise waiting.

"Get some background material on Hardiman ready because he's in Providence to make an announcement. They've called a press conference for four o'clock at his office in the Courthouse."

"I'll get right on it," she said.

"Now we'll see what kind of a swami you are, Jen."

"Five dollars says he bows out," she countered quickly. "Even money, Dan."

"Uh, uh, since you're so sure of yourself, my five to your ten," he answered.

"You're on, sucker."

27

Fiore called the office for his messages in the middle of the afternoon. Dana told him about the call from Carol Singer. Anxious to confirm her suspicion that Fiore and Singer were a twosome, she asked whether he wanted her to contact the client and change the dinner date. Doug didn't identify the client and said he'd take care of it himself. Dana had her answer.

"Shit!" he shouted inside the phone booth after slamming down the receiver. He already told Grace that morning not to expect him home before ten. That meant she wouldn't have any dinner waiting for him and might start asking questions if he got there any earlier.

Since his meeting with Pat Hanley at the Biltmore, Fiore had thought about her a lot. She gave him a wonderful time in bed and made it clear to him afterwards that she didn't consider the evening a one night stand. He realized that his situation with Carol was becoming more tentative each day as the race for governor got closer to its start. If, as Sandy Tarantino predicted, Bruce Singer did become the Democratic nominee and Doug was his opponent, he would no longer be able to count on Carol as his playmate. He guessed that she would probably drop him like a hot potato if that contest for governor became a reality. Besides, he wouldn't want to be the cause of her losing her husband to an adultery—one that could cost him his own wife as well—that risked exposure by a news hungry media covering the election. That would be a horrible embarrassment for everyone, and, as Cyril Berman told him in the limo, could well cost him the election.

But he figured that the situation with Pat would be less fraught with danger. She had a suite at the Biltmore where he could meet her whenever his campaign gave him some free time at night in Providence. They could take their meals together in Room 606 and not risk being seen in the hotel's dining room or bar. He was certain Pat would understand the importance of their avoiding the public spotlight. And she made it perfectly clear that she looked forward to more sexual encounters with him. That being the case, Doug had no trouble changing his mind about the continuing nature of his relationship with her.

After hanging up from his call to Dana, he opened the telephone directory, the cover of which was partially torn off, and looked for Brad Hanley's number. Several pages of names starting with the letter "H" were also ripped out of the book. Fortunately, the one containing a listing for the "Hanleys" was still there. As he dialed the number, he couldn't recall whether it was one of the days Pat worked at the lab. When she answered, Fiore told her he had some new information about Ocean State Wire & Cable.

"I've got some free time tonight if you want to meet and talk about it."

Pat was delighted to hear from him. "I'd suggest Room 606 at the Biltmore," she teased, "but then we might forget what we went there for."

The words brought a smile to his face. "I'll write it out ahead of time," he answered, "and you can read it if I forget to bring it up." He already knew he'd score with Pat again.

"Seven o'clock?" she asked.

"Yeah, that's good. I'll be the guy in the gray suit with the big bulge in his pants."

"Maybe we should change it to six," she offered suggestively.

Doug laughed. "Great line. I love it. See you at seven, and you owe me a dinner."

He was very pleased with himself when the call was over. "Screw Carol," he said out loud.

* * *

"It's your husband on line two, Mrs. Singer, and I'll be leaving in about three minutes. Will you be here in the morning?" Kathy Walsh asked.

Carol said she would, pressed the loudspeaker button on the telephone and sat back in her chair. "I've got you on the box, Bruce, so don't say anything sexy."

"Hi."

"You don't have to be *that* careful," she said, a playful tone in her voice. "Let me guess. You're calling to tell me you're too hungry to wait until 6:30."

"That's not it," Bruce answered. "I just didn't know whether you heard the news." There was a short pause. "I guess you didn't," he said.

Words like that always unsettled her. Carol immediately pictured one of her daughters in an overturned automobile or being rushed into a hospital on a stretcher. "What happened?" she asked, raising her voice and leaning forward involuntarily in the direction of the speaker.

"Spence Hardiman announced he's not running to keep his senate seat. He said he'll finish up his term and that's it. He's getting out."

Carol breathed a sigh of relief that Bruce's news had nothing to do with Bonnie or Rachel. Still, she didn't grasp the relevance of it to anything concerning her husband or herself. She was joking when she asked whether Bruce intended to try and succeed him.

"Dave Waller wants to see me, Carol. He's getting as many members of the committee together tonight as he can reach. He insists that I be there."

"I don't understand," she replied. "You pretty much said that you were out of it. Why do you have to go?"

"Don't you see?" he said. "Hardiman has changed everything! I had decided not to run against Sacco. But now Sacco's a sure thing to want to go to Washington. That means the governor's office will be up for grabs and Waller thinks I'm the one who can win it for the Democrats."

Carol was stunned. It was as if she were told in the morning that she was pregnant and then having the doctor call back later to say it was a mistake. In the course of the day she went from uncertainty to happiness and now to despair. She picked up the receiver and switched off the loudspeaker. Singer could hear his wife let out a deep breath.

"You know how I feel about it, Bruce. If you do this, you'll be choosing between politics and me."

"It doesn't have to be that way, Carol. I've thought about it. I can take this on and still be there for you a lot of the time. Let's talk about it when I get home."

"And what time will that be?"

"I can't say. I don't know how long the meeting will last."

"That's just what I mean." She hung up without saying goodbye.

* * *

Carol took the stairway to the firm's main floor and walked down the corridor to Fiore's office. She could tell from the condition of Dana Briggs's workstation that Briggs was gone for the day. The word processor was turned off and there were no papers on her desk. She looked into Fiore's office. No one was there and the lights in the adjoining conference room were off. She didn't hear Frankie Scardino come up behind her, and was momentarily unnerved when he asked if she was looking for Doug.

"Yes," she replied. "I had a client matter to ask him about but it's not all that important. It can wait." Carol was certain she was blushing. "I guess it will have to wait," she said, trying to smile.

"I'll tell Doug you wanted to see him."

As she turned to leave, Scardino asked if she had a minute to answer a question for him.

"Of course. What is it?"

"I was wondering whether you thought Helen Barone was doing a good job as office manager."

Carol considered the question. She immediately felt that he was up to something. "How do you mean, Frankie?" she asked.

He told her that it took in a number of things: whether Helen ever personally made certain that Kathy Walsh was at her desk by 8:30 in the morning, back from lunch at the end of an hour or working right up until five o'clock; whether Carol had any problem finding a secretary available for overtime to type something that had to get done that day; whether the message center was diligent in taking calls for her when Kathy was away from her desk; and whether the work Kathy did and her productivity were as good as the firm had the right to expect for what it was paying her.

"Kathy's not perfect," she told him, "but she does a good job and she's there when she's supposed to be. Helen doesn't have to keep tabs on her. And I've got no complaints about the overall clerical support I get or the calls that come in for me. As far as I'm concerned, the office runs fine."

"I'm glad to hear that," Scardino answered, but he didn't look pleased at all. Carol wondered whether he was laying the groundwork for moving Janice Rossman another rung up the ladder. "I'm not bashful, Frankie. If I have a secretarial problem, I'll speak up." Then she decided to come to Helen Barone's defense for whatever good it might do. "Yes, I think Helen runs a good tight ship," she added.

Carol returned to her office. She called the Hilton and asked if they had a reservation for a Mr. F. Douglas for that night. The clerk put her on hold for a minute. When he came back on the line, he informed her that Mr. Douglas cancelled the room reserved in his name.

"Shit," she said, and slammed the receiver down into its cradle.

28

Fiore couldn't remember the name of the movie. It was the one starring Harrison Ford and Melanie Griffith. They were anxious to get to Ford's apartment in one scene and had each other half undressed before they got through the front door.

He thought of it when Pat Hanley let him into Room 606, planted a kiss on his lips and started to unbutton his shirt in a sort of frenzy. By the time he took off his jacket and tie, she had loosened his belt and was pushing his pants down over his hips. Doug kicked off his tasseled Deerskin loafers and let his pants fall to the floor. He reached for Pat's sweater at the waist and pulled it over her head. She undid her skirt and fell into his arms as it was dropping to her feet. Fiore kissed her neck as he quickly unfastened her bra and helped her step out of her panties.

"Why are you still dressed?" Pat asked in a teasing voice, as she put her hand on the erection still hidden by his shorts.

"Don't squeeze the veggies, lady," he said, as he walked her into the bedroom. She pulled the spread down in one continuous motion, letting most of it fall onto the floor. He took off his underwear, but not his socks.

Pat got into bed, resting on her knees. Doug joined her, laying on his back. "It looks like your big guy is ready to go to work," she said. "In fact, I'll bet he's looking forward to some overtime."

Doug reached up and pulled her toward him. He put the nipple of one breast in his mouth and ran his tongue around it. Pat shuddered and cried out softly, and he did the same thing on her other side. He moved his mouth from one breast to the other several times. Then he pushed her back up and put his hand on her pubic hair, moving his fingers in little circles before letting them rest on the lips of her vagina. She took a long deep breath and her thighs shook back and forth involuntarily.

Doug felt a little wetness on his fingers. "You must have been getting ready since I called you this afternoon," he said, smiling at her.

"Do you want a bite?" she asked quietly.

"Only if you promise not to leave any tooth marks. Go easy, okay?"

He moved onto his side. Pat bent over and began wetting the tip of his penis with her tongue, stroking the rest of it with her fingers.

"You don't know how good that feels," he told her, moving his hand over her body.

She continued doing the same thing for several minutes. Suddenly she felt the massive shiver that went through him and let go. He groaned several times and his hand pressed tightly on her thigh. Neither of them moved or spoke until Doug rubbed his hand over her nipples and whispered, "I owe you one tremendous fuck."

Pat lay down on her side, facing him. "Which I will collect after a brief intermission," she said. She smiled at him and caressed his face with her fingers. "But while we're waiting for the south to rise again, tell me what you found out about Ocean State."

Fiore told her what he knew but lied about where he'd gotten the information.

"From what Irwin Platt tells me, the Tarantino family thinks its investment will start to pay off once the economy straightens out. The Platts respect their opinion because they know that other Tarantino business investments have done very well. I'd say the brothers Platt will be as patient as they can with Ocean State, but Brad has to hope their cash flow overall stays manageable."

"What if there's a strike?" she asked. "Wouldn't that make things worse?"

"It would, and nobody wants one," he said. "The Company feels it has to show the Union what kind of financial trouble it's in and get a fair settlement. The Platts are looking for the right person in Providence to put some pressure on Johnny Morelli, the business agent, to make sure he doesn't ask for too much. And we've got to be certain Brad doesn't try to paint Morelli into a corner with contract demands he doesn't like and could never sell to his membership. If your husband doesn't start a war, I don't think there's going to be one."

He leaned over and kissed her on the cheek. "Don't you worry about it," he said softly. "I'll stay on top of Ryder so I know what's going on all the time."

Pat smiled at him. "Thanks, Doug, I feel a lot better." She ran her fingers through the hair on his chest and then quickly moved her hand down to his groin. "Speaking of staying on top of people, I do believe there's something you owe me."

29

At eleven o'clock that night Carol turned on the radio next to her side of the bed. She listened to a report of Spence Hardiman's news conference, followed by speculation that John Sacco would most likely seek to fill the Senate opening. "If that happens," the announcer went on, "there's sure to be a wide open race for governor, but former lieutenant governor Bruce Singer is already being rumored to be the man who would get the endorsement on the Democratic ticket."

She moved the dial to the station that carried "oldies" music and left it on for half an hour. When she set the alarm for 6:30 in the morning and closed her eyes, Bruce still wasn't home.

"Rotten fucking politics," she hissed into her pillow.

30

ONCE SPENCE HARDIMAN INAUGURATED the election season with his unexpected announcement, it was as if a huge industrial machine was activated. As soon as the main gear started functioning, the smaller gears surrounding it began turning in sync, as they were designed to do.

The *Herald*'s headline the next morning read, "HARDIMAN DROPS BOMB." A week later John Sacco made separate appearances in Providence, Newport and Lincoln to inform the electorate that he was a candidate for the United States Senate. Two days after that, on a Friday, Richie Cardella met with the media in the Bounty Room of the Marriott Hotel and declared himself in the running for the governor's office. Surrounded by a noisy group of supporters, he delivered a twenty-minute speech in which he conveyed his view of the issues facing Rhode Island in the immediate future. "I'm confident that I'll be endorsed by the Republican State Committee," he said.

On that same Friday night, Doug Fiore received a call from Russell Walsh at home. It was the first time he spoke to Walsh, who would be travelling with him throughout the campaign. Walsh informed him that the friends he still had on the Republican State Committee confirmed Cardella's boast that he would receive its official endorsement for governor. "But don't let that discourage you," he added quickly. "By primary day, most republicans won't even remember who the Committee came out for. They'll vote for whichever candidate has the message that turns them on."

Walsh said that Cyril Berman had faxed him a copy of the schedule Fiore was to follow the coming week. On Tuesday he would begin courting the fifty-five "pillars" of his campaign. They arranged to meet at Fiore's office at ten o'clock the next morning for Walsh to give him an up-to-date briefing about the people they would be seeing. He also said he would bring along a tape of Cardella's news conference since Doug didn't watch it.

By late Sunday night, Fiore had memorized all the information he was given by Berman and Walsh. He knew everything there was to know about the twenty-four Fiore supporters on that week's schedule. If their pictures were on a deck of cards, he could have turned over any one, identified the particular VIP instantly and recited everything he was told to learn about that individual. He felt confident of what lay ahead.

On Monday morning, Fiore called a meeting of the firm's Executive Committee in his conference room. He kept them waiting almost half an hour before informing them that he would be out of the office for the remainder of that week and all of the next. "I can't discuss the reason for my absence. All I can tell you is that I'll be close enough to call in and discuss the operation of the firm if any problems come up while I'm gone." He was amused by the looks of concern that showed on their faces. He flirted with the idea of keeping them completely in suspense, but decided against it.

"Let me assure you that there's nothing wrong with my health, and I'm not trying to avoid being served with a subpoena," he told them, smiling at the end. Doug informed the Committee that he was appointing Ed Jackson, its senior member, acting managing partner while he was away, and adjourned the meeting before any questions were raised.

Fiore tried to reach George Ryder on the phone. Ryder's secretary said that he was working outside the office on the Ocean State Wire case. She explained that he wanted to avoid the normal interruptions he faced at his desk. Fiore assumed she meant he was at home, in West Warwick. He instructed her to call and inform Ryder that the managing partner wanted him to come in and discuss the status of the negotiations early that afternoon. "Let me know when he gets here," he said.

31

Whenever he wanted to go to Carol Singer's office, Fiore always spent time elsewhere on her floor first. Sometimes he sat in the lounge, drinking coffee and schmoozing with the lawyers who came in. Or he contrived excuses to walk in on one or two of the attorneys whose offices were close to Singer's before finally stopping at hers. He often addressed her from the doorway, asking questions that others could overhear about loans or other financial matters she was negotiating with the banks on behalf of his clients. Doug was convinced that anyone seeing him close her office door behind him suspected nothing, assuming those visits to be business related also, only more confidential.

Toward midafternoon, Fiore went upstairs and into the library. He sat there for a while, reading back copies of the *Wall Street Journal* and greeting anyone who approached his table. He took two of the newspapers with him when he left. Instead of heading directly down the corridor to Singer's office from that end of the library, he took the longer route, around the perimeter of the floor, to where she was located.

Fiore had spent two evenings with Carol since their aborted date on the night she cancelled out at the last minute. The first was a difficult time for him and was over in less than an hour. Carol was obviously crying before he arrived at the hotel room, and she continued, almost incessantly, while he was there. She told him about Bruce's waffling in regard to the governor's race and his decision to go forward with it despite her warning that another political campaign could ruin their marriage.

"I've been through the long, grueling election process too many times, Doug," she said. "I won't do it again, no matter how much Bruce feels he needs me along the way." Carol punched her fist into the mattress several times for emphasis and cried out that the marriage obviously meant more to her than it did to her husband.

"I hate politics and I hate politicians," she hollered. "He's willing to give me up for the next seven months just for his goddam idealism about public service. I keep hearing about the wonderful things he's going to do for the great people of Rhode Island. As if he's the only person who can do it. And do you know what happens if he gets elected? Do you know what happens, Doug?"

Fiore shook his head from side to side in response, without saying a word. He knew that anything he said would only stoke the fire.

"It means he'll be home late half the nights in the week. He'll have parties, or meetings, or strategy sessions, or fund-raisers, or conventions of one sort or another to go to three weekends out of four. There'll be governors' conferences for a week at a time and trips to Europe and Asia to try and bring business into the State. His inside people will always be calling at night to let him know who his latest friends and enemies are, or what he has to promise this one or that one to get some law passed. We'll have to give dinners for a bunch of dumb State representatives and senators, and fancy parties for his financial backers.

"I'll be expected to be the gracious hostess at every event. To hell with my own career, put it on hold if I have to. I saw all those things happen when he was lieutenant governor, and it would be even worse if he's governor. Our privacy would be shot. We'd have hardly any real time together or time to spend with our daughters. We'd grow further and further apart, I know it." When she finished, Carol threw her head down on the bedspread covering the pillow and sobbed.

Fiore comforted her, but what could he say? This wasn't the time to let her know he was about to get involved in the thing she hated so much. Would she feel better if he told her he intended to do everything he could to win? It seemed ridiculous to say, "Look, Carol, I'm going to be a Republican candidate for governor, and if I make it through the primary I'll do whatever it takes to beat your husband in November. You might as well relax and stop worrying about being the governor's wife because hopefully it will never happen."

My Honorable Brother • 175

He had no idea how she would react to hearing that. Besides, he still couldn't reveal to anyone else what was going on. But he told himself that if campaigning successfully meant having to sleep on the road so he could give a speech somewhere early the next morning, it was a price his wife would have to pay. He decided that women like Carol didn't understand that when a man has a driving ambition to do something, you don't get in his way. When he was convinced that Carol's mood wasn't going to change, Doug told her that it was probably better for her to be by herself, and he left.

They met again the following week and the sex was great. Fiore knew before seeing her that he'd be hearing from Cyril Berman any day about meetings with his fifty-five backers. He assumed that the politicking would keep him going until late each night, too late at least for any early evening twosomes with Carol. He found himself getting horny whenever he thought about her, and wanted everything to go just right.

Carol was feeling good about herself that night. She made up her mind that if Bruce didn't care enough about her to stay out of politics, she would do whatever she pleased for her personal satisfaction. That meant she could probably see Doug more than the one night a week they usually scheduled for their affair.

As soon as they were alone, each of them wanted to make love right away. There was almost a wildness about it as they held and fondled each other and found positions that brought pleasure and delight to both of them. They napped between their amorous periods, Carol lying in his arms. When she felt his penis pushing hard against her, she awakened him by whispering his name.

He opened his eyes and laughed. "Guess what I was just dreaming?"

"I hope it was me you were doing it with," she answered, and rose to get on top of him.

* * *

"Can I come in?" Doug asked from the doorway.

Carol was looking the other way, concentrating on some numbers she was entering into her calculator.

"Hi, Doug. Sure." She was obviously pleased to see him. "Let me just write down this last item before I lose it."

He closed the door and sat down on the dark oak chair that bore the Wellesley College emblem. Carol received it as a graduation present from a favorite aunt and used it for many years before switching to a leather executive chair that gave her more comfort. She and Fiore hadn't talked to each other since being together the previous Thursday night.

He spoke softly. "You were really great the other night."

She smiled. "You weren't so bad yourself."

"I wish we could have had about three more hours. We were both on a high."

Her smile broadened. "My rates for the first hour are expensive, but they drop significantly the longer you're there. By hour number six, I'm practically free."

"We'll have to find a way sometime to get a whole night together," Doug said. "Shall I take out my appointment book?" Carol teased.

He became serious. "Actually, I came by to tell you that I probably won't be able to see you for a couple of weeks." He watched as Carol immediately sank deeper into her chair. Her reaction told him that despite the compliments he gave her moments earlier, she worried that something was now wrong with the relationship.

"Everything's fine," he assured her. "I'm just not going to be around at all this week or next. I'll be away from the office altogether."

She rested her hands on top of the desk. "Why, what's up?"

"I got a telephone call Friday night, out of the blue, that may change some things for me. I can't tell you what it is now, and there's a good chance it won't amount to anything. Just something I've got to look into. It will take a little time to find out what I have to know. It has absolutely nothing to do with you. But I was told I have to keep all my days and nights open, and I'm not even sure where I'll be on any particular one. I wanted to tell you in person so you wouldn't start getting concerned."

He said it pretty much the way it was rehearsed. It was all a lie, he knew, and the day of reckoning was probably just three weeks away, at the most. But he wanted to hold on to Carol as long as he could. He wasn't going to worry now about how she would react later on.

"Will you be able to call?" she asked.

"I think so. I will if I can," he answered, and got up to leave.

Carol came around the desk and stood next to him. "Good luck with whatever it is, Doug. I hope it works out if you want it to."

He wondered what she'd be hoping if she knew the truth. "Thanks. I'll know better when I see what it's all about."

"In the meantime, is there a convent you can recommend that takes nice Jewish girls?" She assumed the question made her blush.

He touched her jacket at her breast lightly with his fingers. "Forget the convent," he said. "Just remember that 'Jesus saves.' For the next two weeks we'll both save too, and then we'll go on a spending spree at your favorite hotel. Okay?"

Carol knew she was going to miss him. A tear started falling from one eye as she nodded her head up and down.

32

George Ryder was talking to Dana Briggs when Fiore got back to his office. Ryder drove in from home after his secretary called that morning, but Fiore postponed the meeting for a couple of hours. Later, after lunch, he apologized for the delay and led Ryder into the adjoining conference room. Since the earlier visit from Bob Gorman when he urged Doug to find work for Ryder that would make his billable hours more respectable, Fiore arranged for Paul Castillo to parcel out small amounts of work to him, but nothing that had the potential to turn into a major matter or that involved any of the firm's important clients.

"Throw him an employee handbook to draft or some arbitration case you'd just as soon not handle yourself, especially if you think it's a loser. Just stuff like that," he told Castillo. The younger labor attorney sensed what was going on and was smart enough not to ask any questions.

Following the night he discussed the negotiations with Sandy Tarantino in the limousine on the way back from New York, Fiore twice asked Ryder for updates on Ocean State Wire & Cable. But he didn't say a word to him about the guidelines he received from Tarantino as to how the contract could be amicably settled. At that point in time he didn't want Ryder questioning him as to where the guidelines came from. He realized that the sooner the Ocean State Wire contract was settled, the fewer opportunities he would have to initiate more meetings with Pat in Room 606 to discuss the progress of the talks and Brad Hanley's positions while making love to her.

Fiore closed the door to the conference room behind him. "What's happening in the negotiations?" he asked, even before sitting down. "Let me see the latest proposals."

Ryder untied the string that was holding the bulky case file together, opened it and combed through a number of documents inside before finding what he was looking for. He placed several sheets of legal paper on the table. "I'll have to read where we are from my notes," he said, and proceeded to do so when Doug gave him a silent affirmative nod. Ryder updated him on the proposals and counterproposals offered by each side at the most recent meeting. When he finished, Fiore said it sounded as if the Union made more of an attempt than the Company to move closer to a settlement position.

"It all depends on your view of what that position should be," Ryder answered. "Hanley is pretty damn firm about getting a two-year freeze in wages. He also wants the employees to contribute more to the cost of their medical insurance. In his mind, there's absolutely no reason for the Company to put one cent in new money on the table for anything in the first year of the contract after what it lost last year."

"Has the Union seen Ocean State's financials for last year?" Fiore asked. "Do you think Morelli gives a damn about its problems or not?"

"Yup, I mentioned that before," Ryder said. "We gave him a copy of the profit and loss statement at the first meeting. We also gave the committee the production invoices that show the drop in tonnage sold to the companies that were Ocean State's ten biggest customers when we negotiated the first contract three years ago. It was pretty significant in some cases. I think those things made an impression on him. When they came out of their caucus, Morelli wasn't belligerent at all. He said something about it being important for both sides to work things out. He's listening carefully to whatever we say."

"When's the next meeting?" Fiore asked.

"We're scheduled for this Thursday afternoon," Ryder told him, "and then two full days next week." As he spoke, he took a small, leather bound calendar out of the inside pocket of his suit jacket and opened it. "Next Thursday and Friday."

"How about those dozen other issues you read off? Some of them are economic, too."

Ryder thought that Fiore's tone of voice seemed to imply that he was trying to avoid discussing them. He wasn't sure whether something was bothering Fiore and couldn't understand why Doug had any trouble with the negotiations at the stage they were at. He tried to stay calm.

"We'll do some trading on those," he answered. "Hanley wants certain language that he thinks he needs for better production. I know he's willing to move on a number of these things to get it. I think it will all fall in line. The only potential strike issues I see are in the wages and medical insurance."

Fiore got up and paced halfway down the length of the conference room and back. He thought again about the potential consequences of letting Ryder operate in the dark as to Tarantino's view of the right settlement, and concluded that there was still sufficient time for Hanley and Ryder to find the "magic" numbers on their own. But he also wanted them to be certain not to provoke an employee strike. "I'm sure the owners don't want to see a strike in this economy, George. If Hanley loses customers because he can't deliver on the orders coming in, that would make things a lot worse. A long work stoppage could even send Ocean State down the tubes. It's up to you to see that he doesn't go overboard on those concessions he's looking for. He'd better have a damn good handle on what kind of settlement Morelli and the rest of the negotiating committee can sell to the employees in the plant."

"I assume Brad's position on these things are all based on some guidelines he got from the ownership," Ryder said. He waited a few seconds for Fiore to correct him if he was wrong, but Doug was silent. Ryder concluded that Fiore wasn't brought in on the desired settlement package by either the Platts or the Tarantinos. If that was the case, Fiore would only be guessing as to ownership's position on a strike.

"He seems pretty confident that they'll back him up if he gets in a fight with the Union," Ryder continued. "I'll tell you this. He's certainly not afraid of hiring permanent replacements right away if there's a strike. He knows how many people are looking for jobs these days. Hanley figures it's the best chance he'll ever get to bring in a new workforce and get rid of the Machinists. That's why he's taking a tough line, and it's hard to blame him for it."

Fiore placed his palms on the table and leaned toward Ryder. "When you go to war, George, you suffer casualties. You've handled enough strikes to know that. And you know the economics Hanley's dealing with. Ocean State can't take a lot of casualties. Remember that when you're advising him."

He opened the door to his office. "I can't give this any more time today. From now on I'd like a typed copy of your negotiating notes on my desk the day after you meet. And I want to see each side's latest position on every issue. Line it up on the sheet one opposite the other so I have no trouble reading it. Okay?"

"Sure, Doug."

Fiore didn't wait for Ryder to return the papers to his file. He walked out of the conference room, through his office and down the hallway. Watching him leave, Ryder thought, *Thanks, asshole, I've got nothing better to do.* Minutes later, as he headed toward his office, he began to wonder why Fiore was getting so involved in the negotiations.

33

The "road show," as Russell Walsh called it, went beautifully. Each morning Fiore parked his car in the Biltmore garage and waited in the hotel lobby until he saw Lester Karp's light green Lincoln Continental pull up in front. Karp always drove, while Fiore and Walsh shared the back seat.

Doug marveled at the physical contrast between the two men. Karp, who was at least seventy years old, was about an inch taller than Fiore but couldn't have weighed more than 135 pounds. There was a certain herky-jerkiness to his walk that made his companions tend to hold on to one of his arms when the wind blew, afraid he'd be unable to withstand its force. The sunglasses he wore most of the time hid the deep sockets in which a pair of dark squinty eyes were located. Although freshly shaved each morning, a very noticeable five o'clock shadow would settle in by early afternoon. Almost everything about him seemed to impart a feeling of sadness.

Walsh, on the other hand, stood several inches over six feet and carried about 225 pounds very well. In his early sixties, he still had most of his hair, which was rapidly turning gray and which he wore cut short. There was a constant gleam in his green eyes, as if he was about to spring the punch line of a dirty joke. His square jaw, the envy of any Hollywood leading man, was even more attractive for the small cleft it featured. He moved with the assurance of a man who was an athlete for many years, and knew when he smiled that others couldn't avoid its infectious quality.

As they went from meeting to meeting, Walsh continuously refreshed Fiore's recollection about the next one of the "pillars" they were about to visit.

"Remember, Doug, Ted Morris is anti-abortion. He hates John Sacco with a passion because he gave a lot of money to the campaign two years ago but Sacco didn't find a job for his son-in-law. If he brings it up, tell him you sympathize with his position on 'right-to-life' but you may have to support 'choice' to get elected. He spent a fortune for the art work in his house, so go ga-ga over every piece you see."

Back on the road an hour or so later, Walsh's prepping picked up again.

"Don't forget, Jane Hoyt had a nephew killed by some kid who was whacked out on cocaine. The drug and crime issues are the only things that really count with her. She's been on the Portsmouth School Committee for a hundred years. Don't waste time with her husband, just the formalities. She calls all the shots and she can bring in a lot of votes. She thinks the slot machine parlor on the main drag is the worst thing that ever happened to Newport. Tear into it if she brings it up."

Whenever Walsh thought Fiore was getting a little nervous about the next person on the schedule, he told war stories from his own years in politics. His tales evoked smoke-filled rooms, last minute deals and money being passed under the table. He had a story to tell about every former politician whose name Karp threw over his shoulder from the front seat. Each one seemed to begin the same way: "Jimmy Dwyer, huh, Lester? Let me tell you a little something about Jimmy Dwyer you never heard before." Invariably, the anecdotes he recited and the history he chronicled, full of the zaniest of characters, brought on gales of laughter from his companions in the Lincoln. They succeeded each time in putting Fiore in a relaxed frame of mind.

The three men played a game throughout the road show. After each meeting with one of Fiore's supporters, they would grade his performance in their separate notebooks, from a low of fifty points to a high of one hundred. On the way to their next stop, they compared scores, while dissecting the pros and cons of the meeting itself. Doug never gave himself a mark below ninety.

The lowest grade came from Walsh, who hit him with a seventy-five after one visit during the first week. He was incensed that Doug forgot to discuss his pro-Israel position in a meeting with a wealthy Jewish couple who lived on Providence's East Side. Walsh was certain the Shapiros were waiting for Fiore to bring it up, but he was afraid it would look phony if he tried to prod Doug into mentioning it. Fiore couldn't attempt to excuse the lapse by telling Walsh that his mind was wandering during the conversation. He didn't want to confess that he kept thinking about Pat Hanley who lived just a block away on the same street.

Three of Fiore's "pillars" were State senators, including the second and third most powerful republicans in that chamber. Five others were State representatives and eleven were either mayors or selectmen in various cities and towns. Fiore noticed that it was his supporters from the political arena who were most vocal about the need to keep State government out of casino gambling. He assumed that the Tarantino family contributed significant financial assistance toward getting them elected to office and ensconced in their positions.

Doug spent the weekend between meetings catching up on his sleep and studying the tape of the thirty-three people he would be seeing in the next five days. The schedule underwent minor alterations by Berman when two of the supporters on the first list had to rule out their availability at the last minute for different reasons.

On Saturday morning, Federal Express delivered an audio cassette to Fiore's home. On it, Berman let him know that he made a great impression all around. "I've followed up every visit you made during the week with a phone call," he related. "Everyone's much more enthusiastic about the campaign now that they had the chance to meet you. Lester won't have any trouble raising funds once all the meetings are over and he turns his attention in that direction."

Fiore recalled that the last words spoken when they left the homes of his prime supporters were always those in Karp's high-pitched voice saying, "Thanks for your trust and encouragement. We'll be back in touch soon." Berman's message succeeded in bolstering Doug's confidence even more. It sent him into the second week of meetings determined to be able to grade himself no lower than a ninety-five at any time.

The first three days flew by. Fiore was exhausted after the last of the supporters they saw each day listened to his views on the issues that concerned him or her the most. Walsh usually fell asleep in the car as

My Honorable Brother • 185

soon as they scored Doug on the final performance of the evening, and they made the return to the Biltmore mostly in silence. Fiore preferred to take a room there overnight instead of driving back to East Greenwich, but he didn't want to upset Grace at this early stage of the campaign.

On Thursday, with all of their appointments in the neighboring towns of Warren and Bristol, Walsh was able to schedule them closer together. Shortly after five o'clock, they left the home of a software manufacturer who lived about half a mile from Roger Williams College. When they returned to the Lincoln, Berman contacted them on the car phone. He told them that the State representative from Bristol, who was scheduled to be their last visit that night, was going to join them instead at their six o'clock meeting in Warren. That was at the home of Don Avila, the general manager of the Raytheon plant located across the Mount Hope Bridge, in Portsmouth.

"It should be okay," Berman said. "Sousa, the rep, has been trying to get a few jobs from Raytheon for some engineers in his district who have supported him for a long time. He wants the chance to lean on Avila a little tonight. He figures it will be easier to do with you guys there because they're both in our corner. He may even stick around after you leave. Just don't let him put you in the middle of his problem."

Berman finished his message, wished them good luck and cut off. They decided to kill a little time and have another cup of coffee before crossing into Warren and looking for Avila's house.

Fiore realized that the change in schedule would have him back in Providence by eight o'clock that night. When Karp pulled into the parking lot of the Jade Tree Restaurant on Main Street, Doug went to the pay phone and called Carol in the office. The receptionist said that no one was answering that line but that she would have her paged.

It took a couple of minutes before Carol came on the phone. When she heard his voice, she responded icily, as if the name meant nothing to her.

He picked up on it right away. "Hey, give me a break. I know you're upset but you can't believe how busy I've been. The last ten days have shot by like a bat out of hell."

"You could have called."

"If I could have, I would have. I apologize, but there was just never the time. I've missed you very much."

She melted quickly. "I missed you too."

That's what he was waiting for. It was the prelude for the invitation to follow.

"I'll be through with what I'm doing in a couple of hours. I can be in Providence early enough for us to get together at whatever hotel you work best in."

"I can't, Doug. It's out of the question." Her voice revealed the regret she felt over having to say it. "I'm in a three million dollar closing with Twentieth Century Windfarm," she explained. "Spalding Bank is putting up the loan. We were supposed to start at noon but one of the lawyers was tied up in bankruptcy court until three. There are piles and piles of documents on this one. You wouldn't believe what the large conference room looks like. I think it may take six hours to get through this if everything goes smoothly, and how often does that happen? I'll be ready to collapse when it's over." There was a pause before Carol asked, "Are you going to be back in the office on Monday?"

He said he would, and she told him she'd see him then.

"Is anything new with Bruce and his campaign?"

"We don't talk about it," she answered quickly.

When the conversation was over, Carol hurried back to the conference room from the office where she took Fiore's call. She wondered why he asked her that last question. She couldn't remember his ever inquiring about Bruce before.

Doug phoned Pat Hanley. He informed her that he was away from the office for two weeks and didn't speak to George Ryder in that time. "Is anything new on Ocean State?" he asked.

"I'm more worried about it than before, Doug. Is there a time we can get together to talk about it?"

"I'm coming into Providence from Warren tonight to pick up my car. I'll be there about eight o'clock. If you want to do it then, it's okay."

"Yes, let's. Brad's in negotiations with the Union today and warned me that he'd probably be home quite late. It's very nice of you, Doug."

"My pleasure. Where will we meet?"

"I'll be waiting for you in Room 606."

Doug smiled. "Definitely, my pleasure," he said.

My Honorable Brother • 187

34

CONTRACT NEGOTIATIONS WITH THE Machinists Union began at 10:00 a.m. in the Ocean State Wire conference room on the floor above the office. The Company provided coffee and donuts for the Union committeemen when they convened by themselves before the scheduled meeting. That gave rise to some friendly conversation when Hanley and Ryder first entered the room. But it didn't take long for Johnny Morelli to begin losing his temper and periodically ranting at the bargaining positions being voiced for the Company by Ryder.

Morelli knew what direction he was supposed to be moving in to arrive at a settlement. Tommy Arena had met him in a bar near the Machinists' office building before the negotiations with Ocean State got under way. He came with a message for Morelli from Sandy Tarantino. Arena pulled a small piece of paper out of the pocket of his gray silk shirt and looked at it as he spoke. "The Company wants a wage freeze in the first year. It will go along with small increases in the second and third, but nothing over two percent. And it will agree that employee contributions to the health plan can stay where they are now.

"I'm telling you this from one fucking business agent to another," he continued. "Tarantino said the Company's hurting and a settlement along these lines is set in stone as far as he's fucking concerned. He also wants you to know the Tarantino family will pull the plug and let the fucking plant close if the economics of the new contract don't make sense. Tarantino says the rest of the issues are up to you and Hanley," Arena told his friend. "He figures you two can trade off on some and drop the others. But that's his fucking bottom line on the two strike makers."

At the first meeting, when Ryder gave Morelli and his committee the package of economic information he put together with Hanley, the Machinist business agent looked it over very carefully. The Union took a long caucus to review the documents. Morelli used the time to ask the members of the committee a lot of questions about Ocean State's operation. He was interested in finding out why many of the past customers no longer showed up as current ones. He reviewed the accuracy of monthly tonnage figures on shipments with them and inquired about the amount of overtime being worked. He also sought out information on supervisory staffing, returns of defective product, second shift efficiency and inventory problems.

When the caucus was over, Morelli told Brad Hanley he needed more information and more time to review it. Hanley bristled at the request, as if being accused of not telling the whole truth.

"Let's hear it," he said in a surly voice. "What do you want?"

As Morelli read off the four items on his list, Ryder jotted them down and Hanley agreed to send the data to the Union office in a day or two.

Once he was able to study all the facts and figures supplied by the Company, Morelli realized that the Tarantinos were justified in presenting the contract position he was given by Arena at their meeting. He was convinced that no one was trying to jerk him around. If anything, the Union membership at Ocean State was even getting away pretty good on the medical, he concluded. It was no secret that health insurance premiums were going up about fifteen percent a year. He knew it was costing the Company a bundle.

Morelli got his negotiating committee together at the Union hall the day before the next scheduled meeting with the Company. He explained to them that all the data they received from Hanley added up to a company in deep trouble.

"Hear me good," he told them. "Right now, the most important thing for you to be concerned about over the next three years is keeping your jobs. Unemployment's up more than eight percent in Rhode Island. I'm sure you all know what that means. Ocean State's gonna have a much easier time finding permanent replacements to take your jobs if you ever go on strike.

"We ain't gonna have no strike unless Hanley really tries to stick it to us," he told the committee. "He ain't gonna get no two-year freeze, no way. But we'll let him have it for one and we'll take whatever we can get in the second and third years. It might not be no more than two percent, but if we can push it up to that, we'll be doing great. Him and his lawyer are pissing in the wind if they think you're gonna pay more for your medical. We'll hit the bricks on that one if Hanley won't wise up and tell us to forget it." He paused, and looked at each of the committee members sitting around the table. "Everyone here see it the same way as me?"

Morelli knew the response would be unanimous. He gave this same speech more times than he could remember. Once the other side let you know, off the record of course, what you could expect to get for a final offer at the end of the negotiations, and that they were ready to go to war if you didn't like it, the rest was easy. You'd just use those same numbers to tell the employee committee what your side would insist on being given if the other side wanted to stay out of trouble. That way, the committee could start getting used to the idea that the new contract wasn't going to give the bargaining unit a lot of what it wanted. At the same time, the business agent could set himself up as a hero to the employees for eventually "forcing" the company to agree to his bottom line proposal. Most of those off-the-record meetings took place over a nice dinner, with plenty to drink, in some fancy restaurant, with the company picking up the tab. You could find a quiet corner in back, or even a private room if anyone was worried about being seen socializing together. Morelli was unhappy about the fact that he didn't get a dinner out of this one from the Tarantinos or anyone else, but he understood the circumstances.

As long as both sides in the negotiations knew pretty much where they were going in order to reach a new agreement, Morelli didn't want to waste a lot of time getting there. He told himself that he had much better things to do, especially after five o'clock, than sit for hours on end with a guy like Hanley. He knew that Hanley hated his guts anyway because he called his bluff three years ago and came out of it with a tremendous contract. Morelli felt the same way about this stuffy asshole of a lawyer who wrote down every word that was said, talked in circles and wanted to caucus for a half hour every fifteen minutes. Ryder was handling things like he wanted to go on meeting forever, he thought.

Morelli already made major changes in the proposal he gave the Company when the bargaining first started. His demands were lowered considerably, and now, five meetings later, Ocean State was still dragging its feet. Well, he'd let Hanley and Ryder know today what he thought of their positions. Depending on what they said, he'd decide whether to get together with Tommy Arena again and send a message back to Arena's friend on Federal Hill.

The two committees broke for lunch at one o'clock. On the way out, Morelli said that his people were sick and tired of what was going on. "The Company better show some movement in the proposals when you come back to the table." As he opened the door to leave, he added, "Because if you don't, the Union's gonna have to reassess the concessions we've already given you." He was throwing his opponents a signal they couldn't fail to understand.

When he and Ryder returned to his office, Hanley told his secretary to phone out for some sandwiches. Ryder was hoping they would get out of the plant for a hot lunch, but didn't want to push it. "Whatever you like," he said, when Hanley asked him what he'd prefer as they walked downstairs from the conference room.

Hanley was actually pleased with the way the meeting went. "I think we've come that much closer to forcing the Union to strike when the contract expires. What we have to do now in our next proposal is give Morelli something to really rattle him." His face lit up as he predicted that his nemesis would either jam all his papers into his briefcase in dramatic fashion and lead the committee out of the room, or request a short caucus.

"If they caucus," Hanley added, "he'll have to follow through on his threat by raising their demands, probably wiping out most of the progress we've made to this point." In either case, he viewed the Company's move as the way to send a strong signal to Morelli and the committee that he was dead serious about wanting a two-year freeze in wages and more money from the employees toward their medical plan.

Ryder was becoming concerned. There were still over three weeks left in which to reach a settlement, but he was having trouble figuring out exactly what Hanley was willing to do to get a contract. After years of negotiating on behalf of employers, Ryder took it with a grain of salt when a company's chief executive tried to show his masculinity by expressing no fear of a strike. It was no different even when the CEO talked as if he relished one.

He was used to seeing that macho attitude go up in smoke as the last day of the contract approached. As always, he began, of necessity, to put together a strike plan for the company he was representing at the time. He knew how swiftly the bravado could disappear, especially when he stressed the need to hire expensive security personnel on an around-the-clock basis to protect the plant from overzealous strikers. And he could predict the fear he was used to seeing in the eyes of management when he urged the presence of a police detail in front of the premises twice a day.

"It's the only way we can restrict the amount of violence we've got to expect when the replacement employees enter and leave the plant," he told them. The guts of the strike plan awakened the company to the kind of fight it could be getting into.

But Hanley was different. He went into the negotiations with a vendetta. Ryder recognized it and feared that his client might not be satisfied with anything less than a contract he regarded as giving him back his manhood. Hanley was clearly looking for a victory, not a compromise. The question was how short a leash the Platts had him on and how close to that precipice called a strike they would let him venture. Ryder figured that Hanley received settlement guidelines from the Platts that he was keeping from him. Brad was probably afraid that his chief negotiator would "give away the store" once he learned how much money was available to work with. So he wasn't going to tell him what settlement would make the Platts happy, at least not yet. It forced Ryder to conclude that a lot of what Hanley said was just bluffing.

Still, Ryder had to assert himself and make sure the negotiations didn't go off track. He admonished Hanley on several occasions to forget what happened three years earlier and simply find the best economic solution for the Company's present problems. His client never directly rejected that advice, but answered each time with an affirmative nod of his head. Now Ryder was wondering whether the message in those nods meant something completely different to Hanley than it did to him.

He explained all the difficulties contained in the position Brad insisted on pushing. "It's hard enough to get a group of employees to accept a one-year wage freeze, let alone two. But you don't have to do it that way. If the wage increase in the second year is minimal, you accomplish essentially the same purpose," Ryder advised. There was no sense making it doubly insulting, he said. "That's how a freeze is regarded. I'm sure the Platts know that," he added, hoping to get Hanley to reveal their position. Again, a nod of the head was his only reply.

Morelli called Hanley's office at just after three o'clock. "How much longer do you expect to take before you're ready?" he asked.

Brad repeated the question out loud and Ryder put up both hands to signal ten minutes. Hanley hung up the phone. "I think we ought to go back in with essentially the same proposal we gave the Union earlier," he said.

Ryder disagreed. He felt they had to discuss the primary money issues further among themselves before risking the consequences of answering the committee with a "no change" position.

"I've got to analyze the numbers again, Brad. If you just go in there and offer them the same thing, these guys will march right onto the factory floor with it and production will grind to a halt." It was the only thing he said that day that made an impression on Hanley.

When they returned to the conference room, Ryder made a short speech about the fact that the two sides were obviously having a lot of trouble coming together on the main issues. "Let's put those aside for the time being," he suggested, "and try and get rid of all the other stuff first. I think it will help to do it that way."

Morelli wasn't happy. It was clear to him that Ryder was stalling. He considered ending the meeting with another tirade, but decided he'd only be hurting himself if he did. He wanted to get the negotiations over with as soon as possible. The other issues needed to be resolved sooner or later anyway, so they might as well get started with them now. Still, he had to say something about the other stuff.

"You two seem to think that coming together means we crawl on the floor and give you everything you want just for the privilege of working here. Well, that ain't the way we see it. Let me introduce you to reality. If you expect to get this deal wrapped up without a fight, you'd better think hard about what these guys need to live on." Morelli dropped his pen on the table in front of him. "Give us ten minutes to talk," he said. "Then we'll be ready."

When negotiations resumed, the two sides went back and forth. Each took long, relaxed caucuses over the next four hours before submitting its proposals and counterproposals. The Union withdrew a number of its demands in return for the Company taking several of its own off the table. At 7:15, just as Ryder was starting to explain the Company's position on another matter, Morelli interrupted him.

"We've had enough," he said. "These guys want to go home and eat dinner. We'll be ready to pick up from here at ten o'clock tomorrow."

Hanley and Ryder returned to the office area. It was deserted, except for the accountant who was working overtime to meet the deadline on all the important numbers for March. They sat down on two well-worn vinyl chairs in the room where job applicants waited when they came to the plant for interviews. Ryder remembered Fiore's warning about guiding Hanley to an acceptable new agreement. He figured that pressure from the Platts would bring Brad in line as the expiration date got closer. At the moment, he was more concerned about appearing weak to his difficult client at this point in the negotiations. Time was still on their side. Ryder was sure there would be four to six more meetings before all the issues were resolved. And every billable hour was a godsend. But he still felt somewhat apprehensive about the completely intractable stance Hanley showed all along. He would have to bet that if Brad was calling the shots himself, he wouldn't back down from his position on the big money items, even if the contract terminated the next day.

They talked for almost an hour. At one point Hanley left the room and returned with a bottle of vodka and two paper cups. He poured until Ryder told him to stop. When the conversation resumed, Hanley surprised him by asking, "Have any of the owners of Ocean State called to discuss the negotiations with you?"

Ryder assumed that Hanley wanted to find out whether the Platts were looking for a second opinion on how things were going. Or maybe his client wondered whether the Tarantinos had a different view from the Platts of what the ultimate settlement should be. "No, no one's contacted me, but Doug Fiore wants me to keep him up to date on everything." The reply pleased Hanley. He figured he had the support of the Platt brothers if their Connecticut office wasn't ordering him to negotiate differently. He guessed that Fiore was reporting back to the Tarantinos who were most certainly keeping the Platts advised. Since no one in either camp told him to drop any of his economic demands, they must think he was doing the right thing.

Ryder interrupted his thinking. "I'm going to figure out what it would cost the Company if the freeze was limited to one year and the wage increases in the two remaining years were no more than two percent."

"Okay," Hanley replied. He knew it wouldn't hurt to have the information in case any of the owners raised the question. His response was reassuring to Ryder, and made him more hopeful for the meetings still to come.

When they finished working, Brad suggested they meet for breakfast the next morning at a coffee shop located three blocks from the plant. Ryder agreed. "If the Company's suite at the Biltmore isn't being used tonight, I'll stay there again," he said. "That will give me more time to prepare for tomorrow's session."

"Good idea," Hanley said. "It's all yours."

At last, George Ryder's long and difficult twelve hours were at an end.

35

Opening the door to Room 606, Ryder was surprised by what he saw. He took an immediate step backwards and looked again at the number on the door to be sure he was in the right place. Lights were on in both the living and bedroom areas of the suite, and in the bathroom as well.

He closed the door quietly behind him and walked in. A man's black raincoat was thrown over one of the wing chairs in the living room, close to the large armoire in which the TV was located. Ryder unfolded it just enough to see a Burberry label on its plaid lining. The initials "DF" were inscribed in heavy black ink on the bottom of the label. Two glasses, both empty, were on the coffee table, and an open bucket of ice, half melted, sat on the lower shelf of the armoire. A dark brown briefcase rested on the floor next to the chair holding the raincoat. The initials "D.A.F." were embossed in gold lettering on its side. Ryder recognized it immediately as belonging to Doug Fiore.

In the bedroom, the bed was unmade. Both the blanket and bedspread were lying on the floor, at the foot of the king-size bed. The top sheet was pulled back on both sides.

Ryder walked into the bathroom. He saw two used bath towels on the side of the tub and a tube of lipstick, its cap off, on the vanity. One face towel, still wet, was on the edge of the sink. His eye caught a piece of paper that was thrown into the wastebasket next to the toilet. It stayed near the top where it landed on the plastic liner that was placed inside the receptacle. He picked it up and saw that it was the wrapper from a package of Trojan brand condoms. He bent down again and put it back exactly where he found it.

When he used the room on an earlier occasion, Ryder left a suit hanging in the hall closet. It was still there. Next to it he saw a woman's beige raincoat. It had a Saks Fifth Avenue label but no other identification. The toilet kit he put on the closet shelf was there also.

Ryder was suddenly concerned that Fiore might return to the suite while he was still there. He hurried out and walked to the stairway at the end of the hall. It was closer to Room 606 than the elevator. He opened the fire door, went down two flights of stairs, entered the main corridor on the fourth floor and took the elevator to the lobby.

When Brad Hanley gave Ryder a key to the suite, he told him to be sure to notify someone at the front desk when he stayed there overnight. "That's the only way a maid will get instructions to clean up the next day," Hanley said. "I sure as heck don't want to bring a customer into a dirty room."

Ryder showed his key at the desk and asked if anyone checked into the room that day. The clerk was an athletic-looking young man who appeared to be close to six and a half feet tall. Ryder was tempted to ask him whether he played basketball at one of the area colleges, but didn't. He watched as the clerk went over to a stack of cards that were inserted into separate slots on a rotating column behind him.

"Yes, sir," he said, after fingering several of the cards. "Mrs. Hanley is occupying the suite right now." Ryder thanked him, walked up the lobby staircase to the hotel mezzanine where he could take the crosswalk to the garage, and drove back to West Warwick. His short stay at the Biltmore gave him a lot to think about.

* * *

Doug Fiore and Pat Hanley sat in a booth on the far side of the L'Apogee Restaurant. It was across the room from the picturesque view out the eighteenth floor windows of the Biltmore Hotel. Pat's face was still somewhat flushed, a sign of lovemaking that always stayed with her for at least an hour afterwards, sometimes to her severe embarrassment. They had each finished a cocktail and were sharing a Caesar salad. Doug ordered a small steak while she decided that a cup of clam chowder would be enough for her at that time of night.

Pat told him what Brad was saying in the past week about the negotiations. She related how pleased he sounded that afternoon when she called him at the plant and learned that the Union committee was probably getting ready to walk out of the meeting. "He's definitely thinking in terms of a strike, Doug. The deadline is just a few weeks away, but nothing has changed. Brad has programmed himself to win this fight at all costs, and he seems to be getting even further out of control. When I ask him what George Ryder thinks about the Company's proposals, he says that it makes no difference. Brad's convinced that Ryder doesn't have the same feel for Ocean State's problems that he does."

"That doesn't tell us much," Fiore said. "Did you try and pin him down on what exactly Ryder was advising?"

"Yes," she answered. "Once after last week's meeting and again when I talked to him today. As far as I can tell, Ryder hasn't warned him that anything he's pushing for is either outright ridiculous or something the Union would never agree to. He's only told Brad that what he wants to come out of the negotiations with may be very hard to get. But for God's sake, that's just a challenge to Brad in the frame of mind he's in. If anything, that's egging him on."

Fiore poked at the salad with his fork. "You're right," he said.

"Has Ryder told you what he thinks the Company will have to do for the Union to keep the employees from striking?" she asked.

"No, Pat, but I haven't seen him since a week ago Monday. That's the last time I was in the office. He knows damn well he's supposed to be keeping a lid on this thing. I told him that I expect him to use his expertise and let Brad know if he's asking for too much or risking a strike on some proposal the Union would never buy. As soon as I get back in there next week, I'll find out what the hell's going on."

Pat started to reach for his hand, but remembered where they were, and stopped. Doug caught the movement and they smiled at each other.

"Trust me," he said. He was already looking forward to seeing Ryder on Monday.

36

"If nothing changes, Richie, this campaign could be a breeze."

Richie Cardella reached for some nachos and cheese from the large platter sitting on the table. He was sharing the food with Jack Lucas, his campaign manager, and Phil Witts, his best friend, who agreed to handle publicity and media relations. Witts and Cardella were the starting guards on the basketball team for Barrington High School in both their junior and senior years—that's when his name was still Witkowicz—and they grew closer as the years went by. Their wives became good friends also, as if that were a condition of the two marriages.

"Murphy's Law says that something bad will happen, Jack," Cardella answered.

They were sitting in Chi-Chi's Bar & Grille in downtown Providence. It was the same Friday night that Doug Fiore was bringing his two-week road show to a close with several meetings in Woonsocket. Located just two blocks from City Hall, the bar had a fairly regular clientele for the three hours between five and eight o'clock at night. The customers enjoyed the food prepared by Maria Gonsalez, wife of Luis, the owner and bartender. The drinks were honest and priced at the lower end of the scale. Maria chose the name when they purchased the business seven years earlier. She never even hinted to her husband that her first lover, Carlos, was known as Chi-Chi by everyone in their San Juan suburb. By now, Gonsalez was used to everyone calling him by that name.

It was Cardella's favorite after-hours watering hole, a place he frequented about twice a week when he needed some transition time between the problems he worked on in the office and the ones he had at home. He and his wife, Anita, weren't sure whether they had outgrown each other or were both going through a midlife crisis. They had been at each other's throats for a long time, arguing repeatedly over everything and nothing. Neither of them seemed able to muster enough control to let the things that displeased them just pass without comment. When a truce was declared, they agreed that it would have a better chance of taking hold if, for a while at least, they spoke to each other only when it was necessary.

The situation was made worse by the fact that Anita's mother lived with them. She was there more than three years already, ever since her own husband suffered a heart attack shoveling snow and died a week later. He was warned by his doctor at the HMO, as well as by Richie, that it was dangerous for him to be doing that sort of thing at his age. But he continued convincing himself that he had better things to do with twenty-five dollars than pay it to a plow every time snow filled his driveway. Anita's mother had an advanced form of multiple sclerosis, requiring help from one of them with almost everything she did. Whenever Richie fought with his wife, her mother came into it on Anita's side. Inevitably, he found himself standing over her wheelchair, telling her to mind her own business and keep out of it.

At least four months had gone by since Cardella and his wife had sex. Despite the tension, they slept in the same bedroom, in the queen-size bed they purchased at an estate sale just before they got married. It was big enough to let them lie on their own sides, facing away from each other, their bodies not touching. They did it because they knew that if one of them moved into the spare bedroom, Anita's mother would blab it out to everyone in the family and anyone who came to visit her.

But it couldn't continue much longer the way it was. They both knew they had to either get counseling and try to pull the marriage together, or they might as well go their separate ways. He was still virile and was sure Anita missed the sex as much as he did.

Cardella realized that trying to pick up women in bars was fraught with danger for several reasons. And he was certain that his wife's strong Catholic upbringing would never let her sleep with any man to whom she wasn't married. It was ridiculous for them to be wasting away sexually, he thought. But the rift had grown wide enough so that it was still going to take some time, if it happened, before they turned toward each other in bed. Richie could live with the fact that he was going to campaign without Anita at his side. He knew Phil Witts was right when he took the position that there was no sense bringing the matter to a head right now. It wouldn't help to have word of an impending divorce get into the newspapers just before the election.

Lucas finished his beer and called out to the waitress who was standing at the end of the bar, across from their table. He held up the empty bottle for her to see.

"You want a round?" she asked.

Lucas didn't bother to check with the others. "You got it," he answered. He smiled at Cardella and Witts. "I can't think of anyone I'd rather see going up against Bruce Singer in the primary than June Bates," he said. "She's perfect. She won't beat him, but she'll cut him to ribbons in the next five months. Singer will bleed, believe me when I say that. Then, when it's you against him, the women's vote will go to you, Richie. I love it."

Bates announced her candidacy that morning, and used the occasion in front of the TV cameras to lob her first bomb against Singer. She was serving her sixth term as a State representative from Warwick. Her name was invariably in the forefront on legislation that involved the rights of women and other minorities. She and Singer won their seats in the House as democrats in the same year, but were never particularly friendly toward each other. They served together on a few committees, and she thought of him as a humorless lawyer who couldn't restrain himself from lecturing everyone whenever he spoke. For his part, Singer saw this former real estate broker as a woman with much more vim than vision.

During the years in which Singer was lieutenant governor, Bates had several run-ins with him. She felt that he ignored her calls to speak in support of certain issues—both to the governor, whose ear she assumed he had, and in public appearances—because he refused to take her seriously. "That hypocrite keeps putting me down," she told her husband a number of times. "As far as he's concerned, nothing's important unless he's all for it. Some day I'm going to get even with him."

As soon as Singer declared his intention to run for governor, Bates began soliciting her colleagues in the House to see how much support she could get if she opposed him. She also did a lot of telephoning to find out what kind of financial help to expect from women's groups throughout the State. The results in each case weren't overwhelming. Still, they were good enough to persuade her that she could put up a decent fight against him. The bonus was in having a terrific forum in which to get attention for the issues she championed. The exposure would give her a golden opportunity to move them into the public's awareness.

Bates knew that elections were unpredictable events. Thousands of votes could ride on one wrong answer, one impolite remark, or a single inexplicable goof. *Who knows?* she told herself, *maybe Singer will do something stupid and hand me a victory. After all,* she thought, *if a nobody like McGurty who sold automobiles could beat him in a primary, Singer was far from invincible.*

The hardest part she faced was the phone call from Dave Waller, the Democratic Committee Chairman. Someone told him that she was canvassing for support around the State, he said. So he wanted her to know how passionately the Committee felt about her staying out of the race. "We can win the governor's seat with Singer," he told her, "and we're endorsing him. You'll only take votes away from him in November if you run in the primary. You don't have a snowball's chance in hell of beating him, June, and you know it. If you make things difficult for us, you'll never see another dime in financial support from the Committee when you're up for reelection in the House or if you run for the Senate. Think about it and do the right thing."

She thought about it into the early morning hours and decided it would be hypocritical for her to back off. With the media following her, she knew she'd get more publicity for minority rights during a primary campaign than in ten more years of speeches to a mostly empty House chamber that saw its members leave in droves when she took the podium to protest against gender and racial inequality.

Bates did some meaningful research before her Friday news conference. Checking the payroll records and staff photographs for the four years that Singer occupied the lieutenant governor's office, she discovered that every one of his aides and assistants during that time was a white male. The only females he employed were his secretary and two receptionist/clerks, one of whom was black. Characterizing Singer's support for women and minorities as "dismal" and "disgraceful," she castigated him for it in the speech in which she declared herself a candidate. She emphasized the need for more representation of those groups in state government, and promised that at least half her appointments within the governor's office would be either female or "people of color."

"To hell with Singer and Bates," Witts said to Cardella as he poured what was left in his bottle of Sam Adams beer into the long narrow glass in front of him. "You won't give a damn who wins that one unless you finish first in our own primary. I just can't believe no one else is going to run against you."

"I'm with you, Phil," Cardella answered, "except I've thought about it and I can't put my finger on who it'll be. There are plenty of ambitious guys up at the Statehouse, but my contacts there tell me they don't hear any names getting tossed around." He turned to Lucas. "But he's right, Jack. Wait and see. Someone's going to come out of the woodwork one of these days with his running shoes on. I can't see me getting a free ride through the primary."

Lucas lit up a cigarette. Before he inhaled once, Witts told him not to blow any smoke in his direction. "You have to be stupid to still be smoking today," he said.

Lucas ignored the remark, but exhaled straight up into the air. "You don't give yourself enough credit, Richie," he said. "How many guys do you think are out there who figure they'd stand a chance to beat you in the primary? I can't think of more than two or three up on the Hill, and it looks to me like none of them want to get into it if we haven't heard anything by now. No one expected there'd be a contest for governor this year, so they weren't gearing up for a campaign. The Hardiman thing and Sacco leaving office caught them all with their pants down." Lucas paused to take a long drag on his cigarette. This time he turned to his left and blew the smoke at the wall. "Who else has the name recognition in Rhode Island you've got, and who else can match the money the Party will be putting up for you?" he asked.

Cardella didn't answer. He knew Lucas was right but that didn't allay his apprehension. He looked pensive and shook his head from side to side several times.

"Wait and see," Lucas said. He wagged his finger in the air. "Let's ask Chi-Chi. He knows everyone in town and hears everything that's going on." He called to the short, dark-skinned man behind the bar.

Chi-Chi came over to their table. Cardella introduced him to Witts who was in the bar for the first time. Chi-Chi's broad smile revealed a small fortune in gold crowns in his mouth.

Lucas spoke. "I've been telling our mutual friend here, the esteemed former attorney general, that no one's going to run against him in the primary. We figure that if anyone knows whether I'm right or wrong, Chi-Chi, it has to be you. We come to you for guidance, oh guru of the underworld." Everyone at the table smiled.

Chi-Chi looked at them one by one, as if trying to decide who should be the recipient of his wisdom. He leaned over, his fingers resting lightly on the table. "Of course someone's running," he answered, with certainty in his voice. The smiles on the three faces watching him quickly disappeared. "And I can tell you everything you have to know about him," he added.

There was silence in the group. Lucas appeared hesitant, like a lawyer afraid to ask the witness one more question, the answer to which could win or lose the case for his client. Witts and Cardella looked at each other. Their eyes affirmed the correctness of what they predicted earlier.

"Okay, Chi-Chi," Cardella said finally, "let's hear who it is."

Again, he took his time to eyeball each of them before speaking. "Here's everything," he said. "He's an asshole. That's it." Chi-Chi laughed and walked back toward the bar.

Lucas laughed the hardest. "Well, if Mr. Asshole does show up, we'll kick his butt, or something like that." Forgetting himself, he exhaled some smoke directly at Witts.

37

George Ryder got home early on Friday afternoon. In the negotiations that day, some grudging progress was made on a few small items. The Union committee took a two and a half hour caucus over lunch, only to announce on returning that they were quitting for the day. Brad Hanley urged them to go back to work in the plant for the remaining ninety minutes of the shift, but John Morelli rejected the request on their behalf.

"No way," he said. His voice was hardly able to contain the anger he felt. "The Union's paying them for the day and they're all done."

Ryder opened the liquor cabinet in his den, hesitated, and took out a bottle of vodka. He returned to the kitchen and added some tonic water to the glass that was filled halfway. After several sips, he telephoned Amos Woodrow, president of Woodrow Associates, a financial investment firm in West Warwick. Ryder attended a free seminar given by Woodrow a number of years earlier, and the two men became friendly. Occasionally, Woodrow called to see if he was interested in some new public offering coming on the market.

"Amos, is your brother still in the private investigator business?" Ryder asked. He had successfully represented the younger Woodrow in a discriminatory discharge case referred to him by Amos. The back pay Ellison Woodrow received in the settlement was large enough to encourage him to open his own office.

"He sure is, George. And he's got another investigator working for him full time. Business is great."

Ryder got the address in North Providence and the telephone number. He called Ellison Woodrow, chatted for a few minutes and arranged to meet with him the following morning. Satisfied, he continued working on the glass of vodka.

38

THE TELEPHONE CALL FROM Cyril Berman came just minutes after Federal Express dropped off the package at his home. Fiore was eating a late breakfast and reading the *Herald*'s Saturday sports page when the front door bell rang. He brought the package inside, looked at the return address on the small bubble envelope that was sent by overnight delivery and put it down on the dining room table. When he answered the phone and heard Cyril's voice, he had a mental picture of the Fed Ex driver returning to his truck, dialing Berman's number in Washington and saying, "Okay, he's got it."

Fiore's campaign manager was just short of ecstatic. "Everything I'm hearing is terrific, Doug. Those 'pillars' of ours loved what you had to say and how you said it. Lester will follow up soon with phone calls to all of them, and I'm sure the money will start rolling in. We'll ask everyone you met to give us lists of friends who can be counted on to make a contribution, and we'll invite them to small parties to hear you speak. But none of that will start until after you're officially in the race. In the meantime, we'll do what's necessary right now with some of the funds coming through you know who."

Berman explained that Fiore's name would begin to leak out as a possible candidate for governor in about a week. He reminded him to keep his answers to the press and other media short when they began contacting him. It was best, Berman said, to stay with the line that he was tremendously interested in serving Rhode Island but still evaluating the extent of those promoting his candidacy.

"Someone will probably ask what makes you think you're qualified to start at the top since you've never held political office before. Don't let a question like that rattle you. Just tell them the same thing is happening all over the country. Stress the fact that Reagan's first political campaign was for Governor of California. Point out that if you're elected, you can come in with a clean slate. You won't owe anything to anyone, especially other politicians in the Statehouse.

"Later on, once you're officially in the race, you can say that your Republican opponent didn't serve in the legislature either. By the way, never mention Cardella's name if you don't have to. Tell them that whatever experience he picked up as attorney general means nothing as far as having the vision Rhode Islanders want to see in their next governor. You got that?"

Fiore assured him that he did, and Berman continued talking. "I don't know whether the Republican State Committee will try to put any pressure on you to stay out of the race. They're definitely going to have to endorse Cardella. But they may think it's better for him to get his feet wet in a fight with you instead of just sitting around waiting for the democrats to choose their candidate.

"Not only that," Berman went on, "but who's going to pay attention to what Cardella has to say between now and September if he can't tell the voters his opponent is full of crap? The Committee has to worry about that. I'm guessing they'll decide it's better to have you around, even if they think you may land a few punches before the primary. I've already spoken to Russ Walsh about it, Doug. He agrees with me, but he's going to stay tuned in to what those folks have to say. And just in case anyone on the Committee calls you a traitor to the Party or tries to buy you off, you get hold of Russ right away. He knows all the players over there and he's the best one to handle it, okay?"

Fiore was just swallowing some coffee and had to wait for it to go down.

"Okay, Doug?" Berman asked again.

"Yes, I heard you, Cyril," he replied. His curiosity suddenly was aroused. "What's in the package you sent me?"

"My next point," Berman said. "Unless there's some good reason to change it, I'm planning on your making the big announcement three weeks from today. I want to let some suspense build up after the public first hears about you. We'll milk that for what it's worth. Then I want your picture on the front page of the *Sunday Herald*. Decide where you want to give the speech and we'll book the room. The Holiday Inn is the only place off limits. It's non-union. Not that we'd expect much support from labor, but there's no sense starting off with enemies. Let Lester know by Tuesday at the latest and he'll do the rest. Still okay so far?"

"I'm with you, Cyril."

"The package has a tape in it, Doug. It's a draft of the speech I want you to make. In this case, draft doesn't mean rough draft. A few people worked on it before we were all satisfied. I recorded it so you could hear how it sounds. There's a transcript there too. It's important for you to be comfortable with the whole thing. You can reword anything you see there—say it the way you like—but don't change the substance. That's going to be your basic speech all through the campaign. A lot of hard work went into it and we think we've got it right. For the time being, at least, your views on the issues are written in stone. So, you got any questions?"

"None on that," Fiore said. "At least not until I hear the speech myself. But when are you coming to Providence and when do you plan to get involved full time?"

"Good point," Berman answered. "I meant to tell you that. I'll be there two days before you announce, on Thursday of that week. We'll spend some time together, you, me, Russ and Lester. The four of us can polish up the speech if it needs it. Between now and then, I'll find a place for a campaign headquarters in Providence and put down some deposits on locations in a few other towns around the State.

"We've already ordered the signs and buttons from a union printer we can trust to keep his mouth shut. We're going with blue and green, by the way, the same shades that BayBank uses. I like those colors together. The phone company promised to install all the lines we need on one week's notice. We'll handle that on a tight schedule, even if we have to go without for a day or two.

"I'm taking a look at some old computer printouts to see who gave money to John Sacco two years ago. We ought to know something about every republican and independent in the State. I've contacted a PR firm that will start setting up some focus groups in about a week. We'll see how they react to the different issues once you and Cardella start hitting the stump. There's a bunch of other things to get done that I won't even bother telling you about. The short answer to your question is that I've been involved full time for a while already."

"Will Walsh or Karp know where you'll be staying when you get here?" Doug asked.

"Oh, that's already arranged," Berman replied. "I've rented a room by the month at the Biltmore."

39

THE PLAYER'S CORNER PUB on Washington Street was always Terry Reardon's restaurant of first choice. The food was simple, blue collar American cooking, large portions on large plates, just the way it always was when he grew up in Narragansett. He never trusted restaurants that spent a lot of money on atmosphere, and no one would ever accuse Player's of doing that. Besides, for someone who liked kidding around with waitresses who knew how to dish it out themselves, Reardon was right at home. He often felt that the women who worked there were hired for having that special quality.

Terry was looking forward to spending some time at Richardson's place that Monday night, but Jenna suddenly begged off. She told him she devoted almost the entire weekend to research in the *Herald* library after Jane Bates's announcement of her candidacy on Friday. Her time was spent reviewing a lot of the political history involving both Bates and Bruce Singer. Now that there was a contest for governor among the Democrats, she wanted to learn as much as she could about the backgrounds of both candidates. Monday was another hectic day for her, Jenna told him, and she figured she'd be worn out by the time she got home.

Reardon didn't press her to change her mind. He said she was probably doing the right thing, but that she ought to join him for an early dinner in town. That way, she could avoid shopping and cooking and just fall into bed when she returned to her apartment. Jenna accepted the invitation. She was pleased that he wanted to spend some time with her without sex being on the menu.

They sat opposite each other in a booth along the wall farthest from the entrance. When the cocktail waitress brought their drinks, they reached out and clicked glasses.

"To sleeping alone," Terry said. He smiled.

"But not too often," Jenna replied, and nudged his leg with her foot under the table.

"So what do you know today that you didn't know before you locked yourself in the library?" he asked.

"If I tell you now, you won't have to buy a paper every day, and I'm supposed to help sell them." She was being coy. "At least that's what McMurphy keeps banging into my head."

"But I'll send whatever I save to a charity of your choice," he told her. "Swear to God."

"Okay, I'll hold you to that. I don't even have to think about it. Make the check out to Jenna Richardson." She paused for only a second, cutting into his laugh. "Seriously, Terry, this whole election campaign is beginning to show some promise. I'm getting excited about it."

"You haven't started drafting an acceptance speech for the Pulitzer Prize yet, have you?"

"Of course not." She hesitated just a beat. "My PR agency is handling that."

"Touché," he said, tipping his invisible cap to her. "So tell me what's happening out there."

Jenna took a deep breath before answering. "First of all, I think the Bates-Singer fight will be a beauty. He is not going to just walk away with it. That woman is one terrific legislator who hasn't been wasting her time in the House. Most of the civil rights statutes that have been passed in the last ten years or so have her name on them. She's a hell of a street fighter when it comes to getting what she wants.

"I'm really looking forward to whatever debates she has with Singer. He's Harvard Law and she took five years to get through New England Law at night after she won her House seat. But she's a heavyweight in my opinion. Just look at what she did to Singer in her speech on Friday. If he's got any brains, he'd better take her seriously from day one."

"Are you on the women's bandwagon on this one, Jenna?"

"Nope. I'll just call 'em as I see 'em. Bruce Singer has a pretty good record and he feels strongly about a commitment to public service. That comes through loud and clear in the speeches he made over the years. But he's had an easy life and may not be in touch with the average guy in the street. He won going away in both his campaigns for lieutenant governor, but look what happened to him in the primary for governor two years ago. He got whipped by a nobody, a real nobody. Maybe there's a message there. Still, despite what Bates says about him, the statistics show he's always been popular with the women voters."

"How about my boy Richie? Will he have a chance against either of them in the general election?"

"Cardella's no slouch," Jenna responded immediately. "He had four good years as AG. He's handsome, he's been a successful lawyer and he'll have Sacco's republican coattails to hang onto. That's assuming he wins the primary."

Reardon looked somewhat startled. "It's hard to lose when you're the only one on the ballot," he said. "Or are you trying to tell me something?"

"Don't bet the family jewels, Terry, but if my gut and intuition are as good as they've always been, we're going to see some competition for Cardella pretty soon. I've asked a lot of people if they expect someone else to get in the race. Too many of their answers are like, 'It's still early,' or 'You never can tell.' I'm hearing that from powerful people in the State. By now, they should be able to say 'Yes' or 'No' definitely. It's almost like there's a conspiracy out there to spring a surprise at the last minute. I'm just about ready to offer McMurphy the usual two to one odds."

The waitress came over to take their orders.

"Hiya, Pauline," Terry greeted her. "Any chance of getting tomorrow night's special tonight?" he asked.

"You sure are lucky, Mr. Reardon," she answered. "They moved it up a day."

"Great. What is it?"

"The same as last week."

"Sounds good. I'll take it."

"I'm sorry. We just sold the last one."

Reardon burst out laughing. "That was beautiful, Pauline. We ought to put together a routine. We'll be the next Abbott and Costello."

Pauline grinned broadly, revealing several missing teeth. She was about fifteen years older than him. "You're a devil, Mr. Reardon."

Jenna listened to their fast paced repartee in amazement. She smiled for a few seconds and then looked serious. "If that's gone, is it a good time to order the Wednesday night special?" she asked.

Pauline winked at Terry. "I like your daughter," she said.

He laughed first, followed by Jenna. Pauline waited a few seconds before joining in.

40

Doug Fiore's working lunch with the Executive Committee on his first day back in the office lasted until after 2:30 p.m. As soon as it concluded, and while Rosa Santos was still clearing off the conference table, he told Dana Briggs to call George Ryder.

"Tell him to come to my office for a meeting. He'll know what it's about," he said.

Dana buzzed him a few minutes later. She reported that Ryder took some personal time off for the afternoon.

That's why I hate this guy, Fiore thought. *He knew I'd be back today and I'd want to see him, but he's going to do things his way.* A moment passed. "Okay, tell his secretary to bring me a copy of the notes from his negotiations last Thursday and Friday at Ocean State Wire & Cable."

Briggs was back to him again quickly, opening his office door this time. "Myra says he didn't give her any notes to type yet."

"Okay, leave him a message to see me as soon as he gets here tomorrow." Dana started to leave. "And tell Paul Castillo to come in." Fiore was upset at the contempt Ryder was showing him, but it had a good side to it. *The fat bastard is killing himself,* he thought. *He's making it easier on me all the time to show him the door.*

Fiore thought about phoning Carol Singer while he was waiting, but decided that he didn't want to see her after work. His penis suddenly went limp as he started making love to Grace on Saturday night, and they had to forget about it when he couldn't recover. He tried again on

Sunday, but was unable to induce an erection after they got into bed and lay there for a while. He hoped to get hard by picturing Marilyn Monroe sitting on top of him, high enough that he could watch his penis enter and leave her time after time. It did no good, and he said nothing to Grace about the problem. She was unaware of his efforts and afraid to bring up the subject. After a while she turned away from him with a quiet "Good night."

Fiore assumed that the impotence was a sign of his growing anxiety about what the coming week would bring, the spotlight he would suddenly find himself in. It never occurred to him that his sex drive might be affected this way. He decided to watch some TV with Grace that night, go to bed early and try again. But if it wasn't going to happen, he didn't want to embarrass himself with Carol. There was no sense talking to her, he figured, if they weren't going to sleep together. He'd wait until he was over the problem.

His thoughts were interrupted by a knock on the door, and Paul Castillo entered.

"Hello, Paul. This will only take a minute." Fiore turned his chair halfway around to the credenza behind him and picked up his briefcase from the floor. He took out a thick file, turned back and handed it to Castillo. "Do me a favor, Paul. This has to do with Ocean State Wire & Cable, a good client of ours. Most of the papers in here are copies of stuff that Ryder has in the main file. Read over everything tonight and let's talk about it tomorrow. I may need your help. What time do you get in?"

"What time do you want me?" Castillo asked. His tone sent a clear message that anytime would be all right.

"Is 7:30 too early?"

"No sweat. I'll stop for coffee. Do you want one?"

"Yeah, a large black with one sugar." Fiore got up to walk him to the door. "I really appreciate this. By the way," he inquired, resting his hand on Castillo's shoulder, "have you been giving George any of your own cases?"

Castillo was again anxious to show he was a team player, ready to do whatever the managing partner asked of him. "Whatever I could, Doug, within the guidelines you gave me. Nothing big and no work for a major client. Different small stuff."

"Good," Fiore said. "I knew I could count on you." They reached the door. He turned toward Castillo and looked directly at him. "But as of right now, I want you to stop feeding him anything." It was a decision he had reached just before Castillo entered his office, and now he felt he had to support it in some way. "For all we know," he said, pointing a finger in Castillo's direction, "George may be looking to move to another firm. He doesn't seem to be too happy here anymore, and I think he may be losing control of the negotiations in this Ocean State case. If he does want to go somewhere else, we sure as hell don't want him taking any of our work with him."

"No sweat. What do I say if he asks me for something?"

"Just tell him things have slowed down and you've got everything under control," Fiore answered. It suddenly occurred to him that Ryder would be able to track Castillo's hours on the weekly computer printouts. "Don't show more than thirty-two hours a week of billables. If that puts you in a bind at any time, let me know right away. I'll find an associate who can give you whatever help you need without Ryder knowing about it. And I'll keep track of all the hours you could have done the work yourself."

41

"Dana, tell Frankie I'm ready to look at the numbers." Fiore called out the instructions to his secretary through his open office door as he headed for the conference room. Scardino joined him there a few minutes later, wearing his usual silly grin. Early on, Fiore used to think that Scardino was ready to tell a funny story that brought a premature smile to his face. After a while he learned that it was the look Frankie carried around most of the day.

"The financials will take us a couple of hours," Scardino said. "Can we talk about something else first?"

"Go ahead." Fiore sat back in his chair. He figured it would involve Frankie's private life in some way.

"Doug, we've got to do something about Helen Barone." The words came out almost in a whine.

He immediately sensed what Scardino had in mind. "What's the problem?" he asked. His tone implied that it was difficult for him to believe Barone could be the source of any concern.

Scardino picked up on the inflection in Fiore's voice and realized he might have a difficult selling job. He decided to inject more emotion into his answer. "The problem is that she's always ready to give me a hard time. She resents my keeping after her to make sure she's doing the job right. I guess I must be the first person who ever checked up on her—you know, ask around to see if the lawyers and secretaries are happy with the way she runs things, how she treats everyone.

"When I get complaints, I speak to Helen about how to correct things or do them differently. The trouble is that she doesn't want to hear it from me. She thinks she's doing a perfect job. And I'll tell you something, Doug, it's even worse when you're away. Like it was the past two weeks. She figures the managing partner is the only one who can tell her what to do. She just ignores anything I say. How am I supposed to do my job that way?"

Fiore didn't respond immediately. He stared at Scardino during the pause, then leaned back in his chair when he spoke. "Frankie, do you know how long Helen's been here?" He dragged out the word "long."

"Twenty-three years," Scardino replied. "I checked it out in case you asked."

"That's right. And how do you think it would look if we just let her go?"

"We don't have to fire her."

"What then?"

"Put someone in over her with a new title, like 'Senior Administrator.' Let Helen report to her."

"She'd never accept that, Frankie," Fiore said. "It would be too embarrassing after all that time. She'd quit first."

Scardino was ready for that one also. "If she quits, that's her decision," he answered, as if rendering a solemn judgment. "We're only doing what's best for the office."

Fiore decided to play the game with Scardino a little longer. "Besides, it would cost us money to go to a headhunter and find someone new to bring in," he offered.

"No, it wouldn't, Doug. We could promote from within."

He kept it going. "How can we do that, Frankie? We don't have an assistant office manager now. We never needed one with the way Helen handled things."

"You're right. I know that. But we've got one or two people who could step right in and do the job."

"Who do you have in mind?" Fiore asked. He knew for sure who one of the two would be.

"I think Janice Rossman would be good," Scardino said. "She's been doing a fantastic job supervising the mail room. Things have improved a hundred percent down there since we moved her into that slot."

My Honorable Brother • 219

Fiore smiled to himself, recalling his being informed by Dana Briggs earlier that morning that Manny Puleo gave the firm his two weeks' notice the previous Friday afternoon. He had worked in the mail room for almost three years and everyone complimented him on the job he did. He didn't just walk, he danced through his chores there every day to the rhythm of whatever Latin song was playing on his stereo. But Puleo told Dana that too many things in the mail room changed after Rossman was put in charge.

"He spoke to me because Helen left early on Friday for a dental appointment," Dana told Fiore. "He said it's not a fun place any more, that Rossman doesn't know how to treat people. He told me she always blames someone else for anything she messes up herself. Manny expects that a couple of the others will quit too," Dana reported.

As he thought more about what Dana told him, Fiore began to get angry. Frankie must think I don't know what's going on around here, he said to himself. I don't like his trying to bullshit me like this. Maybe it's time for me to tell him that Rossman's gone as far as she's going to go. He decided to hear the rest of what Scardino had to say.

"Who else could you recommend?" he asked.

The question caught Scardino off guard. He didn't have another candidate for the position because the whole idea was to put Rossman in a situation where she could make more money and keep her dependent on him. He stared at Fiore blankly for several seconds before getting a sudden inspiration.

"I think Dana could handle it, but I know you'd hate to lose her."

Fiore didn't confirm that supposition. "Janice or Dana, huh? Let me think about it. Maybe I ought to speak to Helen first and see if I can straighten her out."

"I really think it's too late for that," Scardino said quickly. "She'll know I spoke to you and resent me for it. Then she'll always be looking for a way to undermine me."

Fiore was impressed with the answer. *Frankie's put some time into this,* he thought. *He really wants it bad.* Doug had already considered the various things he would be asking Scardino to do for him in the months ahead when he'd be spending so much time out of the office. He knew he'd have to step down as managing partner temporarily once the campaigning began. It was important to have someone like Frankie around to watch everything that was going on and report to him on a regular basis. He realized that Frankie would be aware of things that might never catch Dana's attention. If he wasn't going to be the next governor, Fiore wanted to be sure that no palace revolts were taking place in his absence, and that the power he now had would still be there when he returned to practice law. If all it took to guarantee Scardino's loyalty to him was a decision making it easier for his comptroller to keep getting a piece of ass in the office, it was a cheap price to pay. When he was through campaigning, he could move Rossman to some other job, or even terminate her if she wasn't performing well as office manager. And he would do his best to convince Helen Barone to take another position, with the same pay. In fact, he might be able to create something new for her, something she'd be happy doing. *It could work out well for everyone,* he thought.

"You're probably right," he said, lifting Scardino's spirits instantly. "I'll think about it. Okay, let's get off that and see if we're making any money around here."

As Fiore turned to the spreadsheets placed in front of him, he was sure that Frankie's shit-eating grin had gotten even bigger. There was a strong temptation for him to say that maybe Dana *would* be great for that job. But for the sake of getting through the work in front of them, he resisted it.

42

When he thought about it afterwards, George Ryder realized that he was ill prepared for the meeting. He was remiss in not suspecting what Doug Fiore would say and do. But if he was ever to learn all the facts he was unaware of that day, he'd understand that there was nothing he could have done to change things.

Ryder was barely seated in the chair across from Fiore's desk on Tuesday morning when Doug began to show his outrage. "I thought we had an understanding that you'd have a copy of the Ocean State Wire negotiating notes and the latest proposals on my desk the day after you met with them. There was nothing here yesterday from either your last Thursday or Friday sessions. Your secretary told Dana you didn't give her any notes to type."

Ryder reached for the folder he set down moments earlier next to his chair and began opening it. "I didn't give Myra anything because I wanted to type them up myself at home on Friday night while everything was still fresh in my mind." He pulled several papers from the file and put them on the desk when Fiore didn't reach out to take them.

Ryder continued. "I came by here yesterday morning at about 9:15 to give them to you and explain a few things in the notes I hadn't spelled out in detail. Dana said you'd be in meetings most of the day. I figured you probably wouldn't have time to read them anyway, and that you might get concerned about what's in there if I didn't clear up a few things for you ahead of time."

Fiore was trying to keep his displeasure under control. He didn't comment on what Ryder said. The answer took some of the wind out of his sails. "Are you any closer to a settlement than you were the last time we spoke?" he asked.

"We've gotten a number of things off the table," Ryder answered.

"Do you mean the small stuff, the language changes, sick leave, those kinds of things?"

"That's right. It all takes time, Doug. I thought getting those items out of the way on Friday might help break the logjam on the big issues when we get back together again."

"Are you and the Union any closer on wages?"

"No, there was no movement there." Ryder bit his lip slightly and shook his head back and forth.

"What's the Company's last proposal on wages?" Fiore skipped through the notes as he asked questions.

"A freeze for the first two years and a one percent increase in the third."

"Isn't that the same thing it was two weeks ago?"

"That's right," Ryder said. "Hanley doesn't want to move yet. He's convinced the Company needs a two-year freeze. I think the Platts may have told him last week that they don't want a strike on that issue because he gave me the OK to figure out the cost for small raises in the second and third years. But I'm not sure because he never mentioned having talked to either one of them. He may just be buying time before the contract runs out, hoping he can somehow persuade the Union to go along with what he's looking for."

Fiore turned his chair so that it was facing a side wall and continued reading the notes. Ryder started looking inside the bulky file folder for his own copy. Doug spoke without looking over toward him.

"At the Thursday meeting—the one the week before last—the Union lowered its demands in half, for the second and third years, from a buck more an hour down to half a buck, right?"

"That's right."

"And you guys stood pat."

"Right."

"Then this past Thursday they moved again, cutting the increase to a quarter an hour."

"Yes. On Thursday morning."

"And after that you gave them the same two-year freeze proposal all over again?"

"On wages, yes, but we changed it slightly on medical."

"Goddammit," Fiore hissed, ignoring the last comment. He returned to the notes. Ryder began reviewing his copy also. Suddenly, Fiore was out of his chair and standing by the door to the conference room. The anger about to be unleashed was foreshadowed by the rapid flush appearing on his face. Fiore had already concluded that it was too late to give Ryder the settlement guidelines he received from Sandy Tarantino. He thought that since Ryder wasn't certain whether the Platts had communicated any instructions to Hanley on what they wanted to see in a new contract, Ryder might figure that Fiore was calling the shots. He might also conclude, as Fiore was aware he had during the negotiations three years earlier, that Doug was ready to force a settlement favorable to the Union in order not to risk losing the client through a work stoppage regardless of what Hanley thought he had to have in the contract. It was better, Fiore decided, to handle the situation in a way that wouldn't prompt Ryder to have those thoughts.

"You're supposed to be guiding Brad Hanley to a settlement, George. But you guys are bogged down in the mud. The Union makes two big moves in a row, dropping from a buck down to a quarter, and Ocean State pisses all over them. I don't understand what's going on."

Ryder tried to stay calm, but he could see that Fiore was loaded for bear. "I explained in the notes that I had a talk with Hanley afterwards. I let him know he's being unrealistic at this stage of the negotiations. As I just told you . . ."

Fiore cut him off. Ryder gave him just the opening he was looking for, the chance to act as if he was incensed by the lack of progress in the negotiations. He took full advantage of it. "Are we going to watch this company go on strike just because Hanley says he doesn't give a shit? Strikes cost money, for Chrissake. You know that. What if the Platts decide they don't need the aggravation or the rotten publicity and shut it down? Where does that leave us? It leaves us without a client that pays its big bills on time, that's where. And I'm not about to let that happen because Brad Hanley wants to act like an asshole. Maybe you're ready to just sit by his side and watch him steer the damn boat onto the rocks, but I'm not. Someone else is going to handle the tiller."

43

Fiore was getting increasingly uptight as the week moved along. He was waiting for that first telephone call from the *Providence Herald* or some other newspaper in the State inquiring about the rumor that he'd be a Republican candidate for governor.

"Screen all my calls," he told Briggs. "Don't put anything through to me from the *Herald* or anyone else in the media unless I'm alone in my office." Her look told him that she wondered what was going on. "Be patient," was all he said.

On Friday morning Dana buzzed and let him know that Carol Singer called while he was talking to a client. Doug had spoken to her only once since returning to work that week. Standing in the doorway of her office, he asked several questions about the loan she obtained from Spalding Bank for his client, Twentieth Century Windfarm. He wanted to close the door and arrange a time they could get together, but it was still touch and go with his sexual apparatus. He could see the humor in that phrase, remembering that until recently it took only a female touch and he was ready to go.

Fiore was sure that Carol's phone call meant she wanted to pin him down to a date. They hadn't made love in over three weeks, and from what she told him, the nights of passion at home were few and far between. He would agree to meet her, he decided, during the following week. He counted on being confident by then about his ability to perform, especially once word got out concerning his possible political ambitions. If things didn't improve, he could always cancel it that day. And there was also the possibility that his on-again, off-again impotency—he saw the comic twist in those words also—was only with Grace, not anyone else.

Fiore checked his calendar for the following week before dialing the four numbers of Carol's direct line. When she answered, he said, "It's the managing partner, Mrs. Singer, but don't let that make you nervous."

"Doug, you have to tell me it's not true." The words seemed to burst from her mouth. They caught him off guard.

"What do you mean?" he asked

"Bruce said last night that there's talk about your entering the Republican primary for governor. I told him I couldn't believe it." He waited for a question to follow, but she stopped there, saying nothing else.

He was too flustered to ad-lib. Without thinking, he fell back on the answer he rehearsed all week for the press. "I'm not in a position to say that I will or won't be a candidate. A number of people in the State have spoken to me about running for office. Right now I'm in the process of making other contacts and considering my decision. I'll probably have an answer very shortly."

This time there was a long pause before Carol answered him. Her disappointment was evident in her voice. "I'm married to a politician, Doug. I know exactly what that pap means. Don't expect me to wish you good luck, now or when you make your formal announcement later on. I'm sure you'll regret what you're doing. Good-bye."

He put the receiver down and exhaled a long breath. Carol's words meant that he wouldn't be seeing her soon—which didn't bother him that much in his present circumstances—but he didn't want to lose her on account of this. No woman ever made him look forward to an hour of sex as much as she did. No one else could stimulate him the same way. *She's too good to let get away,* he thought to himself, *at least until this race gets started.*

A half hour later, Dana informed him that a John Robbins was on the line, a reporter from the *Pawtucket Evening Times*. "Here we go," he said out loud as he picked up the receiver and spoke his name.

"This is John Robbins, Mr. Fiore. Just checking out a story. We heard something about the possibility of your law firm merging with a firm in Boston. Can you tell me if there's anything to that?"

Fiore was getting agitated. It was as if some unknown force was trying to rattle him this morning, sneaking up on him in unexpected ways. Expect "A" and you get "B" was the message. It reminded him of playing three card monte and having the ace of spades turn up everywhere but where you were certain you saw the dealer put it. It was true that a committee from the firm was doing some preliminary investigation in Boston. Walters, Cassidy & Breen was considering some form of expansion into Massachusetts. It didn't want to risk losing the business of several clients who already announced plans to build new facilities near Route 128, the Bay State's technology highway. The committee was assigned the task of checking out potential Boston law firms for a merger. But it began its work only within the past month, and any possible action was at least a year away.

"I don't know where you heard that, but there's no truth to it at all, Mr. Robbins."

He waited, as if expecting Robbins to now ask the question he anticipated. But the reporter merely thanked him and hung up.

44

"Terry, does the *Herald* use Walters, Cassidy & Breen for any legal work?" Jenna asked, as soon as he picked up the phone and said "Hello."

"Hey, where are your manners? You're supposed to say 'Good morning' before you start in with the questions."

"Come on, this is rush, rush . . . but for you, good morning."

"And you should really let a guy know how terrific he was the night before. By the way, did your engine ever shut off after I left?"

"Stop asking embarrassing questions." He could envision the smile on her face as she said it. "You were very very good. Now tell me the answer."

"Yes, my love. The answer is that we use one of their litigators whenever we get sued on First Amendment stuff. That's all I'm aware of. Why do you ask?"

"Do you know a Douglas Fiore over there?"

"I've heard the name," he said, "but that's it. I never met the guy. I think he's the managing partner or the CEO or whatever they have. Oh, oh, what's he been charged with?"

"A couple of sources tell me he may run against Richie Cardella. I'm going to try and contact Fiore at work right now. If I get him, I'll let you know what he says. You may want to tell Richie. But don't say anything to Dan McMurphy. If the rumor's true, I want to break his heart with the news myself. That man really hates to lose a bet."

"Listen, Jenna, if you do speak to him, ask him if he knows why the sharks didn't bother that lawyer who fell off the boat into Narragansett Bay."

Jenna knew what was coming. "Okay, I give up," she said quickly. "Let's have it."

"Professional courtesy."

She laughed. "Not bad, Superman. Have a good weekend."

"You too. Good luck."

45

THE NEXT TWO WEEKS passed very quickly for Fiore.

The feisty reporter for the *Providence Herald* was the first one to ask him if he was running against Cardella for the Republican nomination for governor. After he read her the prepared answer, she fired off several questions. Among other things, she asked what special qualities he thought he'd bring to the race. But he gave her a "no comment at this time" on all of them. To end the conversation, he finally told her there was a call from a client waiting for him. By the time he gave the same boilerplate response to press, radio and TV reporters from all over the State during the ensuing days, he knew it by heart. Several national magazines contacted him also, along with *USA Today*, *The New York Times* and *The Boston Globe*. After that, he told Dana to say he was unavailable and to read the prepared statement in response to any other inquiries about his candidacy.

As soon as the news about him became public, Fiore called a meeting of the firm's partners in the large conference room. He confirmed what they read in the papers and told them he was having a difficult time reaching a decision. He was honored by the fact that so many important people in Rhode Island saw fit to ask him to run, he said.

"This same kind of opportunity might never be there again. Still," he continued, "I have to take into consideration the strong feeling I have for WC&B and my responsibility as managing partner. I'd be here about half the time through July and could keep an eye on most things," he explained. "After that, I'm confident there's nothing the Executive Committee wouldn't be able to handle in my absence. Frankie would do all the numbers, as usual, and make sure that copies of everything get delivered to me, wherever I am. I'd have enough time between campaigning to review his printouts and anything else that was important for me to see. Running doesn't mean that I'd necessarily win, even in the primary, so I might be back here full time by mid-September. I'd work as hard as I could to get the votes, but if it's not in the cards for me to be the next governor, I'd want everyone to say I ran a clean campaign all the way through. Still, win or lose, we all know that the publicity can only help the firm. Anyway, as soon as I decide whether or not it's a 'go,' I'll let you know first."

When Fiore finished, everyone applauded politely and then quickly dispersed. He noticed that Carol did not attend the meeting.

The following day he met with the associates at noon and told them pretty much the same thing. Afterwards, Dana Briggs asked him whether she'd be assigned to work for someone else since there would be so much less to do for him. Fiore said that he wanted her to stay where she was and pay attention to everything going on in the office during that time.

"Keep your eyes and ears open while I'm gone," he told her. "Earn your salary that way, and there'll be a bonus there too." Listening to him, there was no doubt in Dana's mind that his decision was already made.

"By the way, how would you feel about being the office manager?" he asked. Fiore knew Briggs well enough to be certain of her response before she gave it. He also realized that it was the politically correct thing for him to do. If she ever had reason to turn against him or the firm in the future, he didn't want her to be able to claim she was bypassed for a promotion.

Dana reacted as if on cue, not hesitating for a moment. "Not me, Doug. I don't like telling people what to do, and I'd have a terrible time letting someone go if I had to. But why did you ask? Is Helen leaving?"

He decided to play "Mickey the Dunce" for now. There was no sense getting into an argument about it before Scardino cut Barone loose. "Not that I know of," he answered, figuring that his intention to find Barone another job in the firm kept his denial from being a lie. "But you

My Honorable Brother • 233

can never be sure what will happen next. Two weeks ago I had no idea I might be going into politics. The only thing I'd bet on right now is that I'm going to lunch." He gave her a mock salute. "See you in an hour," he said, and headed toward the elevators.

Dana watched him walk down the corridor. *The only thing I'd bet on right now is that Helen Barone is in big trouble,* she told herself. *But we haven't advertised for anyone and there's no one else in the office who can replace her . . . unless . . .* Dana closed her eyes for several seconds. "Oh, no," she muttered, "not her!" She went back to her word processor and resumed work on a report she started earlier. She didn't want to think about the change in personnel.

46

Paul Castillo came to see Fiore the day after Ocean State's most recent negotiating session with the Union. Using the numbers Ryder worked up just before the matter was taken away from him, Castillo persuaded Brad Hanley to give up the idea of getting a freeze in wages beyond the first year of the contract. Still, he was having difficulty convincing him to make a more reasonable offer for increases in the second and third years.

"At least you've made some progress," Fiore said. "It's a beginning."

"Yeah, but the bad news is on the medical. Hanley is dug in at having the employees contribute five percent more of the cost. The Union says the ten percent they're already paying is too much. Morelli told us they'll walk before they agree to anything higher. He blew his cool on this one a couple of times during the meeting. The guys on the committee say that if they agreed to a higher contribution and tried to sell it to the membership at the ratification meeting, they'd get thrown out of the room. I believe them, and I think they're probably right. But Hanley just doesn't want to hear it. Anyhow, that's where it stands. There are still a few small items, but they'll all settle or go away. We've got meetings scheduled this Thursday and the last two days of the contract next week."

"It sounds like you've got a good handle on the situation, Paul," Fiore told him. "You got Hanley to do more on economics in one session than Ryder could do in all the time he was there. I did the right thing in getting him out of the picture."

Fiore pulled a paper out of the top drawer of his desk and held it up in front of him. It contained the notes he made after Sandy Tarantino laid out the guts of the settlement position for him in the limo coming back from New York. He knew that what he shared with Castillo had to be consistent with the story he told Ryder. "The owners have looked over all of Ocean State's numbers, Paul, and I passed along everything Hanley said about what the final settlement should be. One thing I know for goddam sure is that the owners don't want a strike. They think that if you offer the Union a two percent wage increase in the second and third years of the contract, they'll go for that along with a first-year freeze."

Fiore waited while Castillo took a yellow pad out of his briefcase and started making notes. "On the medical, keep telling Hanley that Morelli's right and that this isn't the time to fight about pushing their contribution above ten percent. Try to make him understand that it will be easier to do when he can offer more in wages. Tell him it'll kill morale if they have to pay more, and that production will drop way down. Use every argument you can think of. Push him as hard as you can, and don't worry about anything he has to say. Between you and me, the owners are ready to drop that proposal because they're not going to let Hanley's personal vendetta put Ocean State out of business. But if possible, they'd rather see you and Hanley get that done at the table so they don't have to push it down his throat. If he keeps holding out on either the wages or the medical, let me know right away. But come see me Friday about Thursday's meeting, okay?"

After Castillo left the office, Fiore decided to try and give him a little help in bringing Brad Hanley to where he wanted him. He called Pat at home and arranged to meet with her on Wednesday night.

47

"I can't stay long," Pat Hanley told him when Fiore entered the Ocean State suite at the Biltmore just before seven o'clock. "Brad will probably be home by nine. This is one of his on-time nights. He'd be there now except he has a meeting with Paul what's his name."

"Paul Castillo," he said.

"Would you like a drink?" she asked.

"Just a little white wine," he answered.

Pat found the bottle in the armoire and poured the drink for him. "It's a Chablis," she told him, handing him the glass and moving toward the sofa. Doug followed her.

"Brad's not too happy with Castillo, I can tell you that," Pat said. "He swore up and down at you for taking Ryder away at this point in the negotiations. He thinks your law firm considers Ocean State a second-class client. I gather you told him that Ryder was swamped with other work and wouldn't be able to devote all the time he'd need if the Company has a strike. Brad figures that was a bridge they could cross if they came to it. Now, from what he tells me, it sounds like Castillo's saying he's wrong about everything."

Fiore was sitting at the other end of the sofa. He got up and brought over one of the chairs to rest his feet on.

"Let me make this short and sweet, Pat," he began. "No, wait a second. That sounded kind of rough, and I didn't mean it that way. But you don't want to see the employees walk out of that plant, and I sure as hell don't either. The thing is that you're right about what you said before. The Platts are *absolutely* opposed to any labor trouble. They *won't* let a war start. Maybe they're negotiating to sell the Company and want a peaceful settlement to make sure the deal goes through. If that's the case, they're not letting me in on it. It's certainly a possibility, but I don't think that's the reason. From everything that's been said, they just feel that better times are on the way. They don't want to risk losing customers to all the vulture wire companies out there who'd go after them with fantastic deals and sale prices as soon as word got out that Ocean State was on strike. It's not worth it to them.

"What I'm telling you is that Brad better negotiate a deal in the three meetings that are left with the Union. If he doesn't, he's going to get a phone call telling him exactly what to put on the table in the Company's final offer. And if that happens, he'll come out feeling about as low to the ground as he did three years ago when the Union called his bluff."

"But what if . . ." Pat started to ask a question.

Fiore didn't give her a chance to continue. "Hold on. Let me get it all out. The Platts had a conversation with Castillo about what they're willing to do for a new agreement, and he's trying like hell to steer your husband in that direction. I'm not worried about wages at this point. Both sides are coming together there. But Brad is being a stubborn prick on the medical. He wants the employees to contribute five percent more of the cost, and the Union isn't going to let it happen, not unless hell freezes over.

"That's the thing you've got to help us with. Get him to talk to you about it and tell him you think he's wrong. He *is* wrong, so you won't be saying anything you'd have a reason to regret. The cost of the medical plan will be going up every year. The ten percent they pay now is going to cost his guys a bigger piece of their wages each year of the contract. The owners are prepared to keep putting up ninety percent of the total cost, whatever it is. They'll live with it, and they've made it perfectly clear to us that it's more palatable to them than a strike."

Fiore stared at her in silence for several seconds. "That's it in a nutshell." He reached over for his glass of wine. "Any questions from the audience?" he asked.

Pat looked overwhelmed, and had nothing to say on Brad's behalf. "I understand," she whispered. "I'll do what I can. I don't want to see him get hurt again." She was silent a few moments before asking, "Do you think there's any concession he can get from the Union that will make him feel better about it if he does what you say?"

"Maybe yes, maybe no," Doug answered. He realized that Pat raised a good point, one he hadn't thought of. "Brad may be able to get Morelli to agree to a little less money in the last year of the contract, even if it was just half a percent, in return for dropping his demand for a hike in the medical payments. It would be a good tradeoff, and hopefully leave him with his manhood intact. I'll talk to Castillo and see what we can come up with."

Pat stood up. She smiled, and walked around the coffee table to Doug's end of the sofa. "Well, we got the business over within fifteen minutes. That leaves us an hour for pleasure. I was excited to read about you in the *Herald*, Doug. I hope you decide to run. I think you'd make a wonderful governor."

Fiore sat where he was. He knew she wanted to go to bed. He'd have loved to accommodate her, and was in the mood. But speaking of stubborn pricks, that's what he had in his pants. He met with his urologist about it on Monday, after being just partially successful in making love that weekend.

It was all related to stress, the doctor told him, after discussing the things happening in Doug's life. "What you're going through in trying to make the right decision about running for office is what's giving you so much anxiety. As soon as you figure out whether or not to cross that Rubicon, you'll straighten out, Doug, if you'll forgive the pun." They both laughed at that, a good locker room laugh.

"Thanks for the compliment, Pat," he said. "If I throw my hat in the ring, your job will be to get Brad to vote for me too." He got off the couch. "But that's probably a mission impossible after these negotiations." He moved closer and embraced her. "Listen, I hate to be a killjoy, but there's a PTA meeting at the high school and I promised Grace I'd go with her. It's a fatherly duty, one of the things I've got to show up for while I've still got the time. Maybe we can find a night next week." He kissed her on the cheek.

"Okay," she answered softly, as they pressed against each other.

Doug didn't want her to think that politics would put an end to their liaisons. "You know," he said, "if I jump into this thing, there are going to be nights when I'll just be hanging around, waiting to go make a speech or put in an appearance at some affair in the Providence area. We could meet here and have dinner in the room . . . or whatever the time allows. How does that sound?" He released his embrace so he could look at her.

"I'll come whenever I can," she said. She smiled, recognizing the double entendre in her words, not knowing whether it registered with him. "But there may be times I can't get here, so why don't I give you a key to the room. That way, at least you'll have a place to relax before you have to go out and make them love you."

She went over to the table by the door where she left her pocketbook. The key lay beside it. "Here, take this one, I've got a spare at home. I won't need it when I leave tonight. Anytime you stay here, just tell the front desk to have the maid straighten up the room the next day. Enjoy it."

"Thanks," he said, "this is really great." He squeezed her hand. "Work Brad over good tonight."

"I promise, Doug. And if there's time," she said with a wink, "I'll speak to him about the negotiations, too."

They smiled at each other and he left.

48

FIORE WAS BACK AT the Biltmore the following night, meeting in Cyril Berman's room with Berman, Walsh, and Karp. The ninth floor suite was about the same size as Ocean State's, but it was on a list of those waiting to be refurbished. Instead of overlooking Kennedy Plaza, it gave its occupants a very unglamorous view of the roof of the hotel's garage in back.

The first order of business was Doug's speech. His advisors spent almost two hours listening to him read it, patiently pointing out lines that needed more emphasis and those that had to be slowed down for a better effect. Everyone was pleased with the changes Fiore made to what Berman drafted several weeks earlier. The editing gave it a more intimate and comfortable sound.

After that, it was Fiore's turn to listen as his campaign manager, personal advisor and chief fund-raiser discussed the pieces of the puzzle already in place. They talked about the various things that would begin to happen as soon as Doug became an official contender in two days. Up for review also was some of the strategy that would carry them through the primary.

Karp had a number of fund-raising events penciled in over the next few weeks. He bragged that the financial support already coming in from the 55 "pillars" was everything they hoped it would be. "They love you, kid," he said to Doug, raising a fist in the air as if victory was already theirs. Berman gave Fiore a copy of the schedule they would follow for the immediate future, and carefully went over the issues to be emphasized at each gathering.

Their work was interrupted by a telephone call. Berman answered the phone. He spoke a few words the others couldn't hear and then indicated by a nod of his head to Fiore that it was for him. Doug moved toward the desk in the corner of the room. He wondered who else knew he was there. As soon as he heard the voice, he scolded himself mentally for not guessing who it was.

"Hey, good buddy," Sandy Tarantino greeted him, "I hear my horse is getting ready to move into the starting gate. I just want you to know we all think you're the best looking runner on the track."

Fiore tried to make a joke out of it. "You mean my handicapper doesn't think I've got any handicaps?"

"You're not perfect," Sandy answered. "We know you prefer stud to mud, but we like you in this field."

"That was pretty good," he chuckled. "Thanks, Sandy. I'll give it my best shot."

"Nervous?" Tarantino asked.

"I was a couple of weeks ago, but not anymore. Anxious to get going is more like it."

"Sounds good to me. The guys treating you okay?"

"No complaints."

"Well, just remember, if you and Cyril don't always see eye to eye and you need my input, you know how to reach me." There was a momentary pause. "But that doesn't mean I'll agree with you. Like I told you before, he's the one with the experience in these things."

"I understand." Fiore didn't want Berman to pick up on what Sandy was telling him, although the three men seemed to be ignoring him, continuing their own conversation.

"By the way," Tarantino said, sounding more serious, "congratulations on the new Ocean State contract. You guys had Morelli wondering what the hell was going on for a while, but he told me Hanley did a bang-up job at the last two sessions. First he scared the shit out of John's committee with all that talk about permanent replacements ready to come to work five minutes after any strike started. Then he gave them a tough take it or leave it package at the end. He dropped his demand on the medical but cut half a percent off the wages Morelli was looking for in the third year. Johnny wasn't thrilled with that, but went along with it. He did what he was supposed to do and told the committee they'd be crazy not to accept the deal. So everyone shook hands and walked away happy. But how come you pulled Ryder out of the negotiations?"

Fiore could lie again without any fear of Sandy ever finding out that he never discussed Sandy's settlement numbers with Ryder. "I didn't have any choice. He let Hanley convince him that the Company had to have a two-year freeze and a better split on the cost of the health plan. He stopped listening to what I told him the new contract settlement had to look like." Again, Fiore considered the lie all part of what he had to do to rid himself of the partner most likely to cause trouble, to want to take down the king of the hill.

"That explains a lot. Good man, Doug. Okay, I've got things to do, so go out there, old buddy, and give 'em hell. Don't forget everything we've got riding on you."

Fiore heard the click on the other end of the line. He hung up the phone and returned to the group.

"We were just talking about the casino gambling issue," Berman said, looking at him. "That's one of the major points of difference between you and Cardella. Everyone in this room knows you're here today because of it. That means you've got to bang away at that issue every goddam chance you get."

Berman got up and began pacing the floor. He kept his head turned toward Fiore as he continued talking. "Richie Cardella's going to be a tough opponent to beat. He's got a lot going for him. I figure the first poll that comes out will give him the lead with between 60 and 65 percent of the vote. If we lose this thing, I'm sure we all want certain parties in Providence to know we gave it the good fight. That means everyone in Rhode Island must be told over and over again why State-controlled casino gambling would be the worst thing that could ever happen. By election day, they should know it as well as they know their names. Are you with us on that, Doug?"

"I hear you loud and clear," he replied, emphasizing the last three words.

"Okay then." Cyril returned to his seat. For Fiore's sake, he wanted to wind up the meeting on an optimistic note. "We should have about twelve hundred people on Saturday. I want to see the Grand Ballroom here at the Biltmore jammed, and Doug, you should bring your parents as well as your wife and daughter. They'll all be behind you, on the dais. We'll make sure the *Herald* photographer gets a picture of the whole family. Give the crowd plenty of time to cheer whatever you say. Just keep smiling and waving your hand until they run out of applause.

"When you finish the speech, kiss your wife, your mother and your daughter, and shake hands with everyone else on the platform. All your good friends from the House and Senate will be there. I'm not sure how many of the mayors supporting you will show up, but I think you know them all by sight. Watch the tape again if you've forgotten any of their names. That suit you're wearing now is a good color. I like it, but get it pressed for Saturday. Wear a tie with a red background, something classical, with stripes or polka dots, not the crazy stuff that's popular today." Berman looked at Walsh and Karp but they had nothing to add. "I guess that's everything," he said, finishing up with a smile. "So let's have a toast and call it quits for tonight."

They retrieved the glasses from which they were sipping Scotch that evening. Berman poured a few drops into Walsh's, the only empty one. "To a great campaign," he said.

"To a great campaign," they repeated, and drank up.

"And a clean one," Fiore said, as they put their glasses on the coffee table.

* * *

On Sunday morning Fiore was out of bed as soon as he heard the sound of the route driver's station wagon entering the cul-de-sac on which he lived and the *thunk* of that day's paper landing on his front walk. He put on a pair of pants over his pajamas but didn't bother tying his sneakers before opening the door and going outside.

There he was on the front page of the *Herald*. It was a four-color photograph taken while he delivered his speech at the Biltmore the night before. He looked very good. Inside, page eleven carried the official campaign photo given to all the newspapers on Saturday. There was some unexpected trouble before Berman succeeded in getting the bearded and slovenly looking *Herald* photographer to accept it. Below it was a picture of the Fiore family, all saying "cheese."

Fiore sat down at the kitchen table and read the article from beginning to end. He was more than satisfied with it. The byline belonged to Jenna Richardson. He recalled that she was the first media person to contact him and ask whether he intended to be a candidate, as rumor had it. He hadn't spoken to her since then, either before or after his rally at the Biltmore. That meant she received a lot of her information from Berman or Walsh. Whoever it was did a good job.

He went to the refrigerator, took out the carton of orange juice and poured himself a glass. Reading on, he found an unexpected bonus on the editorial page. The lead commentary welcomed his entry into the race and said that voters in both parties should be pleased to have such excellent candidates from which to choose. The *Herald* would listen to all four of them carefully, it went on, and would make its endorsements shortly before the primary.

"Certainly," the editorial concluded, "the people of Rhode Island want to hear what plan each of the candidates may have for revitalizing the economy of the State and getting those on unemployment back to work, as well as their views on whether State government should allow the introduction of casino gambling under its auspices and control."

Fiore was ready to go on the campaign trail and let them know what he thought. "Hey," he said out loud as he put the news aside and looked for the sports section, "what's good for the Tarantinos should be good for everyone else."

49

ON THE FIRST DAY of summer, the longest day of the year, the temperature climbed into the low seventies, the sky was a cloudless blue and sunshine was everywhere. It was the wrong kind of a day for Tommy Arena to receive some very bad news. He was sitting in his North Providence office early in the afternoon, swapping war stories with another business agent. The telephone call was from Teamster headquarters, the "marble palace," in Washington. The Union's general counsel was relaying the information he received from the Justice Department in that same hour. Its investigation of Arena uncovered sufficient evidence to conduct a hearing under the terms of the Teamsters' national settlement agreement with the US government.

Arena was devastated by what he was told. The probe into whether he had any ongoing relationship with the "Mob" in Rhode Island dragged on for over two months. Specifically, the federal agents were trying to determine whether Arena and anyone they considered part of the State's criminal establishment were doing business with each other for their individual or mutual benefit. During that entire period of time, Tommy kept his hands clean. He stayed away from all three of the freight forwarding warehouses and the restaurants where he normally made his collections. And just in case the agents tapped the telephones at those locations, he made no calls to any of them while he waited for the investigation to come to an end.

The freight forwarders, like Jack Newton, knew what they had to do. Arena made that perfectly clear to each of them a day after he got word that the Justice Department lawyers were coming to Providence. "There ain't gonna be no collections for a while," he told them. "But that don't mean you don't keep producing the fucking paperwork. When we start up again, I gotta know everyone's assessment for every week."

He gave each of them the number of a post office box he rented in Cumberland so they could send the information to him weekly. "I don't know if anyone will have to pay the whole retroactive," he said. "We'll see. But don't skip no fucking weeks on me. If it ain't all there later on, someone will come by to see you and find out why not."

Arena said that they should pass the word to each of the drivers who came in to pick up freight. "Every fucking one of youse had better understand if you get asked any questions about collections, you don't know what they're fucking talking about, and Tommy Arena never asked no one to give him anything that wasn't in the contract."

The three freight forwarders assured him they understood and that they'd be certain the drivers got the message. But Arena didn't let up. He had another warning to pass along.

"If any one of youse says the wrong fucking thing to these shitheads who come nosing around and they charge me with breaking the law somehow, you'll get called to testify in court about what you said. And you'll have to go because they'll stick a subpoena on you. Then I'll know who mouthed off. They may get something on me, but my partners will make sure whichever one of youse puts his fucking foot in it will get fitted for a pair of cement sneakers."

Arena knew they understood him clearly. He could read the fear in their eyes. Every transaction between them was always on a cash basis. But they were giving him his percentage from the gross, not the net, so there were no missing funds for the feds to go looking for. Whatever they paid Tommy one week became part of their expenses under a bunch of legitimate looking headings the next. Whatever showed up as the figure on the bottom line was the amount that got deposited in the bank.

There was nothing else the federal agents could trip him up on. Arena never fooled around with the money the employers paid in under the terms of the labor contracts for health and welfare or pension fund contributions. He knew how many other Teamster agents and officers hustled themselves into trouble that way.

The Justice investigators spent almost every day of their four-day weeks in Arena's office. They were there for a month and a half, but never on Monday. He kidded them about having a day off every week. After a while he learned that they flew back to Washington on Friday afternoons, caught up with everything else at work on Monday and returned to Providence on the 7:00 a.m. Delta shuttle Tuesday mornings.

The agents had a right to go through every file and record they wanted to see, and Arena figured they did just about that. They had little to say to him personally except when there seemed to be something missing from a file that they thought ought to be there.

The feds made copies of every check he signed for the Local in the past five years. All the invoices that were received from the Union's vendors were reviewed. They requested his own income tax returns for the same period along with statements from any bank that paid him interest during that time. Arena chuckled to himself at all the work they were going through for nothing. All his illegal transactions were in cash, not on paper, and that money sat in several places he was certain the government would never be able to find. His wife was the only person who knew where it was all hidden.

Arena was asked, of course, whether he knew anyone from the Tarantino family. It was a question he was ready for. He said that Sal Tarantino drove a truck and was a member of Local 719 years ago, when Tommy was still driving himself. "I had some beers with him back then," he told them, "and I got Sal's kid a summer job once or twice while he was in college. But I swear I ain't spoken to no one in the Family for maybe fifteen years unless you count the two or three times I bumped into young Sal at a restaurant."

"How about the Tarantino office building on Atwells Avenue. You ever been in there?" one of them asked.

"No way. I ain't never set foot in the place. In fact, I ain't even sure where it's at." They sat him down just that one time and questioned him for almost three hours. They never came back and asked him if he wanted to reconsider certain answers he gave them.

"So what the fuck went wrong?" Arena kept asking himself out loud after the phone call from Washington. His collections had resumed the

Monday before the call. He gave everything a chance to cool off for two unbearably long weeks after learning that the agents checked out of their motel and left town.

Arena asked every one of his collection accounts whether they were spoken to by the investigators. Most gave him a flat "No." Some told him that the government agents asked general questions about him, like whether Tommy ever bragged about knowing anyone in the Tarantino family or whether they ever saw him with anyone in Rhode Island who had a criminal record. According to what they told him, their answers to all those questions were in the negative.

All three of the freight forwarders had their books examined by the federal agents. That part of the probe took one day in two cases and two days in the third. Some records were copied at all three locations, but very few, they said.

"So what the fuck went wrong?" he kept muttering. "Think, asshole, think!"

Exactly four weeks from the day he got the crushing phone call from Washington, Arena received a registered letter from the Department of Justice. It informed him that the hearing in his case would begin on November seventh in the US District Courthouse in Providence. He had the right to hire a lawyer to defend himself and to present whatever witnesses he chose. But he knew it would have to be at his own expense, not the Union's.

50

His first six weeks as acting managing partner of Walters, Cassidy & Breen were not exactly a bowl of cherries for Ed Jackson. And today, what he had to do with George Ryder didn't make his life any easier.

If asked under oath whether he wanted the job, he would have said "No," immediately and emphatically. The problem was that he didn't have the nerve to refuse it on the morning that Fiore called him in, just a half hour before the Executive Committee meeting, and told him what he had in mind.

Some people in the firm called him "Big Ed." He was six feet five and a half inches tall and was on the basketball team at Rhode Island College. In fact, he played very little during his three varsity years. Saddled with a team that could claim only a few players good enough to compete in their small college league, the coach lived with the hope that Jackson's clumsiness on the court would give way to at least marginal talent at some point. That wish was never fulfilled.

Fiore was sipping a cup of coffee as he spoke. "I don't know how much of my time I'll be able to spend on office business, Ed. It's not fair to the firm for me to stay on as managing partner under those conditions. I'm going to tell the Committee that I want you to fill the job temporarily. You've got more seniority on the Committee than anyone else. We'll take a vote on it. The rules allow you to vote too—I checked it out—so it will carry with you, me, and Rubin. Then we'll take it to the partners with an Executive Committee recommendation. Some of them will probably fight it, but we'll have the numbers on our side. I've already spoken to the right people about it."

Jackson got a less than welcome insight into his unpopularity at the partners' meeting two weeks later. Listening to the discussion and the arguments, he concluded that about half of those in the room strongly opposed his right to be in the firm's primary position of leadership, even for a short period of time.

Someone contended that Jackson didn't have the right to vote for himself when Fiore submitted his name to the Executive Committee. That being the case, he argued, there had really been a 2-2 vote by the Committee, not enough for a recommendation. Fiore anticipated the objection and answered by reading from the section of the partnership agreement he reviewed earlier. While not definitive, it lent enough support to his position to keep the vote from being successfully challenged.

Another partner raised a related issue. His respect for Jackson's veracity was lost years earlier in the course of a debate at the firm about the propriety of targeting a rival firm's client, and he avoided contact with him to the extent possible ever since. He maintained that even if Fiore was right on the point he just defended, the Executive Committee shouldn't have come that far. "The rules governing the Committee's conduct allow a managing partner to recommend his own replacement only when his absence is going to be temporary," he said. He then pointed out that Fiore would be giving up that office for four and a half months if he was away from the firm through the primary, and for almost six months if he was still a candidate in the general election.

"That's longer than what's reasonably thought of as temporary for a managing partner," he argued. "A lot of pretty important things can come up in that kind of time period, problems that someone may have to resolve right away to keep the firm out of trouble. And of course the possibility exists that Doug won't be back at all if he's elected governor. You're calling it temporary, but it's more than temporary in any case and could very well become permanent."

That generated a buzz among the partners in the room. In the ensuing forty minutes of debate a number of them offered their own views on the point, pro and con. It was finally agreed that the group was unable to resolve the intent when the word "temporary" was written into the specific clause. Fiore had the final say. He reminded everyone that the firm traditionally gave the strongest weight to an Executive Committee recommendation. Ballots were passed around the room and Jackson's elevation to acting managing partner was approved by a scant two votes, much closer than Fiore anticipated.

After a short break, Jackson was asked when he intended to submit the name of a nominee for the fifth member of the Committee. Someone was now required to serve until Fiore resumed his position or, if he became governor, until approved by a vote of the partners for a full term. Jackson's reply was scripted by Fiore who knew the question would be raised. "Big Ed" said that he would look into it, propose someone to the Executive Committee, and most probably have a candidate for the partners to consider at the next month's meeting.

Fiore's preference, already made clear to Jackson, was to fill the vacancy with Mark Zappala, one of the younger partners. He knew he could count on Zappala's loyalty to him. It was Doug who successfully lobbied the hiring committee to offer Zappala a position with the firm ten years earlier, even though his grades from Suffolk Law School in Boston were far from spectacular. No one else was aware that Zappala's stepfather owned the automobile dealership in East Greenwich where Fiore purchased four cars over the years, including the Mercedes 300SL he now drove.

A second plus going for Zappala was that he did a large amount of work for Margaret Cardoo, and at times she praised him ecstatically. Fiore felt that Cardoo would be hard pressed to vote against his being put on the Executive Committee, even though she might suspect he was Doug's ally.

Fiore gave Jackson a quick education on firm politics. "I want Zappala on the Committee," he told him. "But if you try and get it done at the same meeting you're elected acting managing partner, it won't fly. Some of the partners are going to be pissed off good, at me more than you, once you get the votes to take my place. They'll be dead set against anyone else they think I'm supporting. Instead of doing anything about Mark right now, hold off until the next Executive Committee meeting. I think you'll get the votes you need for a recommendation to the partners. Rubin will be with you, I'll make sure of that. Deveraux will vote against, so we've got to hope Cardoo sees it the way I figure she will."

Cardoo proved Fiore right. Later, despite some heated opposition, a majority of the partners were again reluctant to vote down someone who had the Committee's endorsement. Still, many of them were aware that Jackson had virtually no relationship with Zappala, and he easily read the disbelief on their faces when he told them, before the vote, that more young blood was needed on the Executive Committee. Jackson's opponents knew that Fiore was behind the recommendation, and he knew that they knew it.

51

IN THE PERIOD BETWEEN those two partners meetings, Fiore gave Jackson an ugly task to perform. In revealing what had to be done, he said it was his intention to take care of it himself when various complaints about Helen Barone's performance as office manager were brought to him, but that the political situation didn't let him get around to it. Fiore felt extremely uncomfortable all along about removing Barone from her position—he knew this should never happen to an employee who has performed her job competently—but reasoned that for the good of the firm as well as himself, it was necessary for Scardino to know whether anyone was eager to stir up trouble in his absence. He also took reassurance in the fact that Barone would be offered another job at her same salary. Still, he knew he had to lay it on thick to get Jackson to act without questioning the decision.

"If her performance continues going downhill, it will affect how the lawyers and staff feel about you, Ed. When she screws things up, you'll be blamed for it. Helen probably figures that the crap she's pulled up to this point will be forgotten about because I'm not in charge any more. She must think it's a new ballgame and that she's got a lot more rope before anything gets back to you.

"But there's no reason for you to get hurt by her. Just call her in and tell her you've decided to make a change. A new broom can sweep away whatever it wants. Offer her a job in accounts receivable instead. If I know Helen, there's a good chance she'll take it and I think she'll be happy there." Fiore wasn't certain at all that Barone would agree to the new job assignment, but according to Scardino there was no opening to offer her and no new position was being created at that time. "Tell her she'll keep her same salary and benefits," he said.

Jackson couldn't think of anything negative he heard about Barone. In fact it was his impression that she was well liked by the office staff she hired and the lawyers who needed her assistance once in a while. But he felt that Fiore had a better handle on what was going on and that he wouldn't react well to being questioned about specifics.

"Who's going to replace her?" he asked.

"Give Janice Rossman the job," Doug said. Again, feeling guilty in what he was doing, he had to create a new set of facts for Jackson. "She proved she could handle things in the mail room. I understand she's made a big difference in there, gets along with everyone and knows how to use her authority when she has to. It will be a good move for both you and the firm." Fiore suspected that Jackson was unaware of the turnover in the mail room since Rossman was put in charge. He was right.

At 4:30 on the following Friday afternoon Jackson spoke to Barone. He gave her the weekend to decide whether to accept a transfer and work as an accounts receivable clerk. Sitting across from him, she cried and said she always thought seniority and good performance were worth something. "I've never been demoted before in my life," she sobbed, blowing her nose several times. "This is like a slap in the face. If someone didn't like the way I was doing my job, why wasn't I told about it? This isn't right. Mr. Fiore would never do this to me."

Jackson didn't know how to answer her. He wished now that he'd asked Fiore for some of the details, at least the highlights of how she had supposedly screwed up. But Fiore spoke of many complaints about her work, so he felt certain there were good reasons for the termination and was sure Doug wouldn't risk having an age discrimination suit filed against the firm. Jackson waited until Barone composed herself and then walked partway down the corridor with her.

"Think about it," he said.

On the following Monday morning he learned from Frankie Scardino that Barone had quit. Scardino reported, "She said she's not interested in working in accounts receivable. I told her I'd let you know." But he failed to tell Jackson that Barone asked to be considered for the opening as an assistant marketing director she knew Scardino was in the process of creating and would soon fill. Scardino had risked not telling Fiore about the position, correctly assuming that Doug would be too engaged in the race for governor to have office employment matters on his mind. Barone wanted Jackson to know she would wait at home several days for him to contact her.

Before the end of the week, Scardino circulated a memo about Helen Barone's decision to retire from Walters, Cassidy & Breen after almost twenty-five years of service. There was no attempt to explain her sudden departure. "We all thank Helen for her many contributions to the firm and wish her well in the new career challenges she's looking forward to," the memo concluded.

Jackson certainly didn't know that Janice Rossman celebrated her latest promotion in Room 118 of the Econo Motel that night. When she came out of the bathroom and got into bed next to Scardino, he put his arm around her and said, "I never had a blow job from an office manager before. I'm really looking forward to it."

She sat up and looked at him lying there before moving down in the bed. "You're gonna love it, Frankie, but I'm still saving a few tricks until you get me the top job in marketing."

* * *

Now today Jackson had to meet with George Ryder and let him know where he stood. Fiore went over the latest computer printouts with Ed the day before, and called his attention to Ryder's numbers. The first five months of the year showed 359 billable hours against the firm's target number of 700 hours. He pointed out that in the prior year Ryder put in 1042 billables, just 61 percent of what was expected from him.

Fiore fully intended to have Jackson plunge the dagger into Ryder's heart and force his resignation, but in such a way that Jackson would believe Doug did everything he could to keep Ryder from suffering that fate.

"At the rate he's going now, he'll finish with a max of 860 hours. I may be wrong, Ed, but I don't think the partners feel we can afford to keep him on board with that kind of production. He got a wake-up call in January when we lowered his percentage share of the profits for this year. Either he doesn't care, which I doubt, or he's run dry on work. I

256 • Bob Weintraub

know he lost some of his good clients, but that's not just his problem, it's the firm's. The consultants I talk to emphasize that the recession has changed the way most law firms operate today, and that when business is bad you've got to take steps to make sure your financial picture stays in good order."

Jackson was unaware of Ryder's low billables. When he scanned the computer printouts, it was usually just to see who the top producers were and to verify that his own billable hours remained among the highest in the firm. His only concern was the bonus he'd receive for the hours he billed. "What should I tell him?" Jackson wanted to know.

Fiore got up, stuffed his hands in his pockets as he did so often and began pacing around the office as he spoke. "First of all, ask him what's wrong. But do it in a nice way because he's probably very depressed right now. See how much you can find out about the clients he's got left and what work he's absolutely sure will be coming in the rest of the year. If we think it's not too late to save him, we just won't make any recommendation to the Executive Committee about his situation. Tell George you know he's not the first lawyer at WC&B to have this kind of setback. But be sure not to commit the firm either way in the event his billings force the partners to take some action."

"That's it?" Jackson asked. His voice indicated that he hoped the answer would be "Yes."

"Not quite. I'd tell him you feel ridiculous doing it to a senior partner, but that your conversation with him is putting him on notice about his billables and that you'll have to stick something in his file. You probably ought to make a little speech about the fact that life is different in law firms these days. George knows that many of the older partners don't want to have to take home less money than what they're used to. He felt the same way I did when a number of them proposed laying off a bunch of associates right after Christmas so there'd be more money available for bonuses and partner shares this year. We won that fight and kept every associate on the payroll, but we may not win every fight over money. Blame the younger partners too. They're looking to make more every year and they resent carrying someone with a big salary who doesn't produce at the same level. We can't afford not to give them what they should get or we risk losing them to other firms. Make sure you give him the whole picture. At the end, of course, be sure he understands you'll do everything you can to help."

Jackson never heard of any lawyer at the firm being disciplined for low production, but, as usual, he figured that the managing partner knew more about it than he did. "What about Castillo?" Jackson asked. He was aware from his quick scan of the computer sheets that Castillo now ranked among the top six producers for the year. "He'll be 300 hours over target this year at the rate he's been going. Is he giving Ryder any work?"

"He does when he can," Fiore lied. "I've talked to him about it a few times. A lot of his work is litigation oriented, and Ryder's weak in that area. George told me he's not confident in a courtroom because someone in the litigation department always handled that for him if the case got that far. Castillo likes to do the trial work himself."

Fiore suddenly thought of another way to press the point. An old lie was coming to the aid of a new one. "Also, Paul's a little afraid of letting Ryder get too close to some of his best clients. He told me he heard talk in the street that George was sending out resumes to other firms. That really disappoints me but it doesn't surprise me if he thinks he sees the handwriting on the wall here. So I can't blame Castillo for wanting to protect himself and hold on to what's his. But he knows I want him to pass along any work he can. Listen, I can't tell Castillo it's his fault that Ryder is sitting on his hands all day. I'm sure he's looking forward to a healthy bonus with the billables he's putting in." Fiore knew that Jackson would be very sympathetic to that kind of scenario.

From the moment he arrived at work that morning, Jackson felt uncomfortable about the pending conversation with Ryder. He sat at his desk, puffing away at his pipe. *Dammit,* he thought to himself, *I've known George for thirty years. Being a guy's partner used to mean something. There was a bond. If somebody got in trouble, the other partners did whatever it took to help him out. The main thing was for everyone to survive, not to leave anyone out in the cold. Even if Fiore's right, that other big law firms don't work that way anymore, why do we have to go along with it? To hell with what the goddam consultants say, why can't we stay the way we've always been?* He opened his top drawer and pulled out a pouch of tobacco. Before filling his pipe, he dialed his secretary and told her to ask Mr. Ryder to come to his office.

Dammit, he thought again, and then said it out loud.

52

Fiore absolutely loved the campaigning. Thus far, approaching the July Fourth holiday, Berman had him out meeting voters most afternoons, three or four nights a week and the better part of both Saturday and Sunday. It was important to establish name recognition as early as possible, Cyril told him. Doug never questioned the scheduling. Their Fountain Street headquarters was located almost directly across the street from the *Herald* building. One of the volunteers there was charged with notifying the local media in each town of Fiore's presence in their community whenever the speech he was scheduled to give was not considered closed to "outsiders."

Fiore had every message he wanted to deliver down pat, and already dispensed with the 3x5 cards he partially relied on at the start. He felt equally at ease talking to a small group of supporters in someone's living room, addressing the members of an association in a hotel function room, or telling whoever came to listen to him at a local mall what his plans were for the State of Rhode Island. The excitement that suddenly filled the air when he arrived to make an address buoyed him. He shook hands incessantly when he finished speaking, stopping only when Lester Karp or Russell Walsh warned that they'd be late for their next appointment if they didn't get going.

At the beginning, Doug found himself thinking only in terms of contacts. He might lose the primary, he reflected, but when he returned to practicing law there would be a slew of people he could call about giving their work to Walters, Cassidy & Breen. His appearances had all the trappings of a fight to become governor, but he really saw it as a fantastic opportunity to advertise for himself professionally. And better yet, other people were financing his chance to present his credentials to everyone as a lawyer. All he had to do was show the public how well-spoken he could be, while avoiding an appearance of superficiality and emphasizing the fact that the interests of the State came before his own.

Of course, the polling numbers in those early days had a lot to do with his attitude. Initially, as Berman predicted, they showed him trailing Richie Cardella by about 65 to 35 percent. It was discouraging at first, but both Berman and Walsh assured him that the polls didn't mean a thing until they got to September.

Still, they were quick to fortify his ego when the *Herald*'s three day poll in early June of almost 500 registered republican voters throughout the State gave him 39 percent of their support. And as they sat around in Berman's suite one night just two weeks later, Lester Karp insisted on their joining in a toast when the Channel 6 news anchor reported that Cardella's lead over Fiore was even narrower, sitting at 58 to 42 percent. They agreed that just two months of campaigning produced great progress. At that point in time, Fiore began a pivotal readjustment of his thinking. Making contacts for the future started to become secondary to winning the election. Returning to his office at WC&B seemed less of an attraction than occupying the large corner one at the Statehouse.

The Fiore campaign got a huge lift from the *Providence Herald* on Independence Day. About a week earlier, Doug met with Jenna Richardson in one of the law firm's conference rooms and gave her a long interview. She came well prepared, and sounded him out carefully on all the positions he advocated in his speeches.

Richardson seemed primarily intent on following up the editorial that appeared in her paper the day after Fiore announced his candidacy. She wanted to know what he would do as governor to rejuvenate Rhode Island's economy, and why he so strongly opposed the introduction of casino gambling in the State.

Fiore was fully briefed early on by Cyril Berman as to both issues. He took the time to study some of the reference material Berman cited in his position papers, and practiced his answers several times with his campaign handlers. When discussing the economy, Doug borrowed heavily from the terms of the Greenhouse Compact that was defeated in a Statewide referendum in 1984. It was too large a dose of medicine for the voters to swallow back then. Fiore realized, however, that most of it made sense. Best of all, it sounded like exactly the right message to thousands of people now on unemployment who were becoming desperate to find any kind of work.

He looked directly at Richardson as he spoke, turning on all the sincerity he could bring to the conversation. "The key to our revival is to bring new industry into Rhode Island. The key to doing *that*, as the Greenhouse Compact emphasized, is to give favorable tax considerations to the companies that accept our offer. All of the high tech industry on the East Coast used to be located along ten miles of Route 128, outside of Boston. You would have thought it was a crime to try and set up shop somewhere else if you wanted to write software, build computers or manufacture any kind of electronic parts."

He began talking a little slower to be sure she could write it all down. "But look at what New Hampshire did. They made land available in the Nashua area for a good price. They advertised tax concessions for technology companies to move in over the border and get away from unfavorable financial conditions in Massachusetts. Now you've got the so-called Golden Triangle up there, and that's what saved the state's economy in the last few years. They were probably hit harder than we were by the recession, but they're thankful they attracted all that new technology business before the bottom started falling out of things.

"That's what we've got to do in Rhode Island right now," he continued, quickly lowering his fist toward the table but stopping just before it made contact. "There's plenty of skilled labor here just waiting for jobs to open up. We could create a high tech highway on Interstate 95, from Warwick all the way down to Westerly. The land is there. We've just got to make it available at the right price. And we've got to let every company that takes the time to listen to our sales pitch know we'll do everything we can to help them get successfully established. That includes tax breaks for the first five or ten years of operation, depending on how well they do. Over and above that, we could give them a one thousand dollar reward for every high-paying job that gets filled by a Rhode Island resident.

"I can see technology companies in Silicon Valley setting up their East Coast plants right here. Others would move in from Massachusetts. A lot of the industry in Connecticut, down around Bridgeport and New Haven, could be persuaded to come north, cut their costs and be more competitive. Maybe some of the insurance industry giants in Hartford would like to get out of a crowded city and build new offices along a quiet stretch of 95. If we're only partly successful in doing all that, we could still have one hell of a building boom going on."

"Sounds impressive," Jenna replied, looking up at him just seconds after he stopped talking. He hoped she was able to get it all into her notebook. "I write fast," she added, as if reading his thoughts.

"Rich Cardella says there's no way we can avoid a tax hike if casino gambling isn't allowed to become law," Jenna said. "He says the money the State will pull in from it will help pay for a lot of services. What's your take on that?"

Fiore explained all the reasons why he disagreed with his opponent. He probably overstated the size of the new bureaucracy they would need to set up to supervise gambling operations throughout the State. He emphasized the danger it presented to attracting the new industry he just spoke about because of how adversely businessmen viewed the presence of a temptation like gambling for their employees.

"Tell me, Ms. Richardson, how much industry have you got in the State of Nevada, or even in Atlantic City? Essentially nothing," Doug said, answering his own question. "And don't tell me about Connecticut," he added, "because the Indian reservations where they have gambling are hidden away in the woods."

He wrapped up his position on the issue by arguing that gambling on that scale was morally untenable because most of the money the State collected would come from those who could least afford to be throwing it away. "We'll take their gambling losses and then give it back to them in welfare, Medicaid, food stamps and whatever else we have to do for the homeless."

Fiore was pleased at seeing Richardson nod her head up and down as she took notes. "If anyone needs craps or roulette or blackjack so bad," he continued, "let them go where it's legal and get it out of their systems. But let's not take money from the poor people in this State with the idea of providing services for everyone else. That's just not going to happen."

Jenna closed her notebook. "Well, I'm sure the folks on Federal Hill who run their private gambling houses agree with you. You can probably count on their support."

Fiore hesitated before answering. He wanted to be sure her remark was made innocently, that she wasn't throwing out a signal to show she knew or suspected something about his relationship with the Tarantinos. Her smile convinced him that was the case. "I guess I can only hope they're republicans," he answered, smiling back.

Richardson included most of the interview in her holiday column. She succeeded in convincing Dan McMurphy to let it start at the bottom of the front page and continue for more than half of page eight. As if that weren't enough, the editorial page writer made reference to her column in one of his items that day. Previewing the primary, he encouraged the other candidates to share their best ideas with the electorate, "as Mr. Fiore has done."

Berman called Fiore at home at eight o'clock in the morning to give him the good news. He was optimistic that their numbers would continue to rise in the polls as a result of the interview and the editorial. Doug rewarded himself with another half hour in bed. When he finally went downstairs for breakfast and read the paper, he was pleased with how far he'd come in just over two months. He was halfway home, he figured, halfway to victory in the primary.

Some hours later, as he marched down Hope Street in the traditional Independence Day parade through the town of Bristol, Fiore was a picture of confidence. He waved at the crowds, stopped to shake hands with people all along the route and kissed at least three babies in each block. He loved every minute of it.

53

IT WAS DEFINITELY FATE, Carol Singer told herself as she lay in bed, annoyed by Bruce's heavy breathing. She hoped he would soon turn over in his sleep and face the opposite direction. The several hours that just passed were vivid in her memory.

Carol customarily had a second cup of coffee after dinner, especially when she dined alone in a restaurant. But for some unknown reason that evening she didn't ask the waiter to refill her cup. Instead, she signed the credit card charge in Stanford's, on the first floor of the Biltmore, and left the table. As the newsstand in the lobby was still open, she went over and purchased a package of sugarless gum. Turning around, she came face to face with Doug Fiore who saw her standing there as he was leaving the hotel.

They hadn't been together since just before the night she learned from Bruce that rumors had Fiore running for governor. Doug didn't deny it when she called him in the office the next day. The news devastated her, and she reacted like a victim. She convinced herself that he owed her an explanation if their relationship was to have any chance of continuing.

From Fiore's point of view, Carol had pretty much brought the curtain down on their affair the way she spoke to him that morning on the telephone. Her words and tone of voice left him certain she'd reject him if he asked to see her again, so he never did. He spoke to her a few times, but only when necessary in connection with work she was doing for his clients. The conversations were cold and as brief as possible.

Carol waited a month for Doug to come to her office and explain the circumstances that had him plunging into politics out of the blue. After that, she decided it was too late to call him and suggest they talk about it. One month became two, and then quickly stretched to three since she verbally confronted him about the rumor.

They greeted each other cordially. In response to her question, he told her he thought his campaign was going well and that he had a shot at defeating Cardella. "How's Bruce doing?" he asked.

Fiore knew that June Bates trailed Singer badly in the polls. Despite a series of mailings to registered democrats throughout the State, she was unable to raise the kind of money that allowed her bid for a primary victory to get the publicity she needed.

Thus far, her biggest ally was Jenna Richardson. Several columns by Richardson in the *Herald* detailed the meaningful legislation that Bates was instrumental in getting passed during her tenure in the House. They favorably portrayed the representative from Warwick as being a no-nonsense type of person who understood the plight of minorities and women and worked to end discrimination against them. "She has not only fought against economic disadvantage for those whose cause has few other champions," one of her columns asserted, "but Bates has also stressed the need for members of the community to understand the serious harm inflicted by acts that bring pain and anguish to those they are directed against."

"He's doing well, unfortunately," Carol answered, flashing a quick smile. "Hopefully what June Bates is putting him through will make him a better person. He suddenly realizes the things he neglected—didn't even *try* to do—when he was lieutenant governor. Bruce has a lot of respect for her now, but he still wants every vote he can get."

Carol looked very nice, Doug thought, and didn't seem anxious to leave. He invited her to sit down with him in the lobby for a few minutes.

"I don't think that would look too good," she answered. "Bruce Singer's wife and Doug Fiore. We could make tomorrow's *Herald* in the same column."

He realized she was right, of course. He was about to say that he'd speak to her in the office the next day concerning a more appropriate time and place. At least he'd be able to get her reaction to meeting with him. Then he remembered the key to Room 606 in his briefcase.

Fiore had spent about half a dozen evenings there with Pat Hanley since she gave him the key. He also stayed over one Saturday night with Grace after she complained again about becoming a widow to his new career. He knew he'd need his wife's presence more often at different functions as the primary campaign wound down. So they had done it all—dinner, a comedy club and overnight in Providence. Grace became much more understanding of his late hours after that occasion.

Fiore recalled the lecture he gave himself about the danger of meeting with Carol during the campaign. The potential consequences of being seen with her in the wrong place at the wrong time were significant. Berman's warning to him about the public's reaction to what was or even appeared unseemly by a candidate was still fresh in his mind. He knew that if he enticed Carol to be with him that night, they would end up in bed. His desire to be with her again was strong and growing stronger as he detected a sadness about her. He was at a crossroads, trying to decide what to do next. "Are you in a hurry, Carol . . . I mean, are you on your way somewhere?"

She tried to smile at him, but couldn't. He saw the tears come suddenly into her eyes. "I just had dinner in Stanford's," she said. "Today's my birthday, and I ate alone because Bruce is out somewhere making a speech. He didn't say anything to me this morning or call during the day. I'm sure he's forgotten. I'm on the way home to spend another night by myself."

Fiore wanted to take Carol's hand or put an arm on her shoulder to comfort her, but knew he couldn't do that where they were standing. His caution gave way to desire. He leaned closer to her and spoke softly. "Carol, listen, do me a favor. I've got a room in the hotel that I'm using during the campaign. Room 606. Let's talk for a little while. I don't want to see you go home feeling like this."

She took out a tissue and dabbed at her eyes without answering him.

Fiore took advantage of the silence. "I'm going to go out the front door, around to the garage and then use the walk ramp on the second floor to get back into the hotel. Give me ten minutes and I'll be there. You can wait in the lobby or go freshen up, okay?"

Carol nodded affirmatively, without speaking, her eyes still moist.

He extended his arm and they shook hands politely, as if parting company. It was for the benefit of anyone who was watching. "See you soon," he whispered. "606."

After he left she went to the Ladies room and repaired her makeup. Ten minutes later Carol knocked gently at the door to Room 606. Fiore embraced her as soon as he closed the door, and she held him tightly around the waist. He kissed her ear several times and spoke very softly, telling her how much he had missed her.

"I would have called about meeting somewhere, but I didn't think you wanted to be with me," he said. He moved his lips around the top of her head.

"For a while I didn't know what I wanted," she answered. Her head remained flat against his chest. "I was so confused and frustrated by what was happening. Everything seemed turned upside down. It's like you became another Bruce overnight, and I felt there'd be no room for me in your life either."

"Don't blame yourself for what happened. You had every right to think that way. You've been through it a few times." He moved his hands to her face and gently pushed her head away from his chest. He kissed her eyelashes and then her nose. "But I'm not like Bruce. I'd always find time to be with you."

Carol pressed her face against his chest again. He heard her sniffle several times. "I'm so sorry, Doug."

"It's okay, it's okay," he said. He brushed his lips along the side of her neck, blowing a little air in the same motion. Her whole body trembled for a brief second. He reached for the zipper at the back of her blouse and pulled it down slowly, unsure of how she would react. The movement sent a wave of anticipation through Carol's body and she bit lightly on her lower lip. She felt him pull the ends of the blouse out of her skirt and released her arms from his waist so that he could slip it off. He folded it once and went to place it on the back of the tall chair closest to them.

Carol moved her hands toward the buttons of her skirt but then pulled them away. She could feel the desire coming alive in her groin. At the same time, she felt a shaking feeling in her knees and hoped Doug would hurry.

My Honorable Brother

He came back to her. He put his hands on her bare shoulders and kissed her lips. Carol kissed back hard and kept his lips on hers longer than she thought he intended them to stay. She expected to feel his fingers at the snaps of her bra. Instead, he bent over and began kissing whatever flesh his lips could reach on her breasts. Pushing a finger underneath the cups on each side, he ran them around her nipples. Carol took deep breaths, and let them out noisily, feeling the sensation inside her race from her breasts to her hips.

She watched as Fiore got down on one knee. "Your shoes, madam," he said, smiling up at her. She noticed the tiny bald spot in the middle of his head as he removed one, then the other, and flipped them in the direction of the same chair. When he stood up, he reached for the buttons of her skirt and easily pushed each of them through the opening.

The skirt fell to the floor and again he stopped undressing her long enough to pick it up and lay it on the chair. Carol suddenly felt self-conscious, standing in the middle of the well lit room in her underwear. But the feeling quickly passed when he was close to her again. She began unbuttoning his shirt, her fingers working clumsily in their haste. She took hold of the wide end of his tie and pulled it around his collar until it was off. At the same time, he undid the clasps of her bra and sent it flying through the air toward the chair.

Carol shuddered as Doug kissed each nipple and then pulled as much of each breast into his mouth as he could. She had to dig her fingers into his shoulders as he let his teeth come together easily at each nipple before running his tongue over it. Her heavy breathing gave way to soft but uncontrollable moans as he kept his tongue busy, moving it down her stomach, around her navel and toward the top of her panties.

Carol reached down and released the garters holding her stockings. His fingers tickled her when they touched her thighs as he took the top of her stockings and pulled each one down carefully until it was off. His lips returned to her navel, kissing all around it as his hands massaged her buttocks, on top of her panties. She smiled as she noticed the position of her hands, pushed out to either side, palms down, fingers spread wide apart, as if she were trying to keep something on the floor from rising any higher.

"Hurry, Doug," she whispered, already anxious to have his body become part of hers again after so long. But he kept covering her with kisses below the waist, tiny little ones that filled her with flashes of energy and desire. She knew she was soaked inside already.

"Let's do this right," he said. When he picked her up and walked to the bedroom, she felt the strength of his grip. He dropped her easily on the bedspread. She hurried to pull it down, along with the blanket, as he got undressed.

"You get on top," Carol said when they were both ready, and he slipped inside her as soon as he was in position. She was filled with pleasure instantly and moved her head back and forth on the pillow as sounds of gratification escaped her lips. She cried out each time he pushed into her and breathed in deeply as he pulled back. They kept a regular rhythm for a while until Doug changed it by leaving just the tip of his penis at the opening of her canal for a few seconds each time before completing the stroke. Carol loved the timing of it, but soon found herself pushing toward him, wanting all of him back in her as soon as possible.

"I hope Noah got the animals out before the flood," he teased.

She knew how wet she was but could still feel every bit of him each time he was extended inside. "It hasn't rained like this in a long time," she answered. "Pretty much of a drought since late spring."

Fiore was moving again with the timing she liked. One of his hands was under her buttocks and he squeezed them each time he pushed all the way in. It let her feel him even better than before.

"I think the cobwebs are all gone," she said.

He smiled. "The cobweb busters have come through again."

Suddenly Carol felt the beginning of the tide that couldn't be stopped. She threw her arms around his backside and pulled him closer to her. Her pelvis thrust up and down in time with his forward and backward movements. Her passion reached a state of pure bliss as he rubbed hard against her with each stroke, in rhythm with her pelvic swing. The long moan came from deep within her throat and continued until she felt the huge wave pound ashore, break over her and then finally begin to recede. Only then did she become aware of the sound from Doug. It was a softer echo of her own, as he lay on her, his face pressed into the end of the pillow.

Carol waited for his heavy breathing to subside. She teased him. "Frankly, I think I'd prefer this to running for governor."

"Both are good," he answered. "Take my word for it." Eventually, he pushed himself up, climbed over Carol's leg and lay down on his side of the bed. They were silent for several minutes. "I had an uncle who used to say something like, 'A woman is only a woman but a good cigar is a smoke,'" Fiore said. "He must have been out of his mind."

Carol pulled the sheet up to her shoulders and turned away from him. She started to cry but didn't want Doug to know it.

* * *

Now, as Bruce's snoring continued, Carol lay there, thinking how confusing the whole situation had become. She was certain that if her husband won the election, she would lose him to politics, to something she despised. And perhaps their marriage was over anyway, even if he lost, because he made it clear by his choice that she came second in his life.

Fiore was the only other man who ever took her to bed. At the time, she wasn't looking for an affair, for a lover. But Bruce had let his work take over his existence and continually ignored her needs. Carol knew she did everything she could to make herself attractive to him, to try and "recapture the rapture" as some terrible old song put it. It just didn't work.

So she was vulnerable that night when Fiore took her to dinner with one of his clients for whom she was writing a brief. The evening went well, with much laughter and wine. When the client left, Doug suggested they go back to the office for a few minutes. It never occurred to her that he had something in mind other than the assignment of more work for one of the many companies that competed for his services.

They saw no one as they entered the main reception area from the elevator and walked down the corridor to his office. Fiore locked the door behind him and unbuttoned the jacket of Carol's suit before she even thought of protesting. He kissed her once on the lips and fondled her breasts. It was enough to stimulate the desire building in her for a long time as a result of Bruce's neglect. She offered no resistance. They undressed quickly and had intercourse on the floor without any foreplay or additional kissing. He ejaculated quickly, in the early stage of her pleasure and before she barely made a sound.

Carol was angry with herself at first. She was convinced that Fiore thought of it as a "one night stand." It surprised her when he came to her office several days later and spoke of meeting with her again. "I think you owe me at least a second chance," he told her. "I'd hate to have my lovemaking judged by what you'd probably say about me now."

She returned his smile and accepted the proposition. When they saw each other again, he showed her how great a lover he could be.

The affair was good for her, she knew. It was easier to fall asleep in the king-size bed at home without wondering why Bruce didn't reach over and pull her next to him. The tension she felt in her body for so long began to abate. Carol turned her interest to other things at night. She no longer resented preparing a light dinner for her husband when he got home late, as he so often did.

On the evenings she met with Fiore, Carol was confident that Bruce would still be out campaigning when she returned home. If, by chance, he was there before her, he readily accepted whatever explanation she offered for being late. In the morning, she left for work after he did. On her scheduled nights out with her lover, she put instructions for dinner on the refrigerator, explaining that she might be home late.

Then Fiore ruined everything for her by getting into politics himself. When she first learned of it, Carol realized that at best she was going to see a lot less of him in the months ahead. She knew all the demands the campaign would make on his time. At worst, she was going to lose him altogether if he became governor. There was no way the two of them would ever be able to be alone at night, even at some small out-of-the-way motel, without the wrong people finding out about it. The risk would be too great for him to take, especially if he wanted to be in position to run for the United States Senate someday. The romance would be finished, she understood, and she probably would lose both of the men she had loved.

Carol knew all along that her outburst to Doug on the telephone regarding his political future was stupid. But she was unable to find a way of apologizing for what she said without again forcing him to hear her true feelings about what he was doing.

They weren't intimate again for three months, not until that night. Doug fell asleep quickly after they had sex and didn't respond when Carol whispered his name a half hour later. She showered, dressed, and called him again softly, but he was still dead to the world. She left a note under his watch on the night table and set the alarm clock to go off thirty minutes after she left the room.

Bruce was home and already sleeping when she got there. There was no indication that he made any dinner for himself. The message on the refrigerator read, "Exhausted. See you tomorrow." Nothing about her birthday. Carol went through the mail and took the latest *Newsweek* magazine into the living room with her. An hour later, before going upstairs, she stopped in the kitchen for half a Toll House cookie. She thought of putting a lit candle in it and making a wish, but let it go.

Lying in bed, Carol called to mind what happened earlier that evening and realized she still tingled inside.

Yes, it was definitely fate, she said to herself, closing her eyes.

54

Richie Cardella was sitting with Terry Reardon in the latter's fourth floor office. There were five days to go before August 1st and the *Herald*'s initial negotiating session with Tommy Arena whose local union represented its delivery drivers. It was shortly after ten o'clock in the morning. Their work began two hours earlier with a review of the new contract proposals Arena sent to Reardon in the mail. The current agreement didn't expire until the last day of September, but Reardon decided early on to take advantage of the full sixty days in which the contract was open for modification. He was concerned about the possible difficulty of having Cardella available for meetings with the union when his campaigning heated up and took him on the road for days at a time. Reardon fully expected his lawyer to win the September primary, and was fearful that Richie would have little time for labor contracts after that.

Cardella said he intended to bring Mike Donlan, one of his younger partners, to all of the early meetings. He expressed confidence that Donlan, sitting with Terry, could handle the negotiations anytime he couldn't be there himself. "Don't worry about Mike," he said. "He's very bright, and has already been through a few contracts on his own."

"Any with the Teamsters?" Reardon asked.

"No, but I've told him all about Arena. He'll know how to keep it moving when I'm not around, and he'll make sure I'm up to the minute on everything that happens."

Cardella's eye caught the red digital reading on his calculator and he reached over to push the "off" button before continuing. "Arena will have the usual two-man committee of drivers with him at the meetings. As always, he'll be looking to get together and agree to things ahead of time. I'm convinced he does it just for the dinner and the booze. I've never seen him pick up a tab. But we'll only set it up when I can be there with you. I don't trust Tommy for a second, and he knows it. Even when we're off the record, I take notes. I do it so he won't try to pull any shit later on and say we reached an understanding on something if we didn't."

Reardon took a muffin out of the Dunkin' Donuts box, broke it roughly in half and put one piece back. "I've been wondering, Richie, what do you think's going to happen to Arena at that trial in November?" Word of the impending trial was published in the *Herald* just several days after Arena received his notification in the mail.

Cardella shook his head. "I don't know. It depends on the evidence. If they've got enough on him, they could get him thrown out of the Union."

"Could he appeal it, or what?"

"Yeah. He's entitled to an appeal. There's a judge in New York who's got jurisdiction over the whole deal between the Teamsters and the Justice Department. But his chances of getting the decision reversed would be pretty thin."

"I know the guy's a bastard, but do you think he has connections with Federal Hill? As I get it from the grapevine, the government's accusing him of playing footsy with the Tarantino family. He's either supposed to be on their payroll for something he does for them, or he's moving money from the Union into their pockets for some reason. That's what they've got to prove, right?"

Cardella chose his words carefully. "I guess that's the case they're going to try to make."

Reardon wasn't put off that easily. "You didn't answer my question, counselor. Or let me make it a little clearer. Do you think they'll prove it? You've known him for years."

Cardella got up to stretch his legs. "Tommy brags a lot, you know that. He likes people to think he's a big man on campus, can do anything he wants, that he's got good connections. Sometimes what he says is true, but usually he's full of shit. He makes most of it up as he goes along, I think, just to sound tough, just for the effect. It might depend on whether he ever talked about stuff that really was true just to get a rise out of the people he was with. Maybe he wished later on he kept his mouth shut. That's why I said it'll depend on the evidence."

Reardon turned his chair partway around so he could face Cardella who had walked to the other end of the room. "His trial is a week after the election in November," he said. "I don't see it having any effect on our negotiations, do you?"

Richie moved slowly back toward the table. "None, none at all," he answered. There was a certainty in his voice. "I figure Tommy, you and I will probably be sitting down for breakfast on September 30th, working out the final settlement before the last meeting starts later that morning. Just like we've done it the other times, Terry. And if Arena's satisfied, he'll sell the package to the committee and jam it home at the ratification meeting. It's good to know exactly what his routine is all the time. If the feds make an ex-Teamster out of him, I think I'll miss the guy."

55

George Ryder wasn't surprised when his secretary informed him that Ed Jackson wanted to see him at three o'clock that afternoon. The latest computer printouts told the whole story. His billable hours for June, which he and Jackson discussed earlier, were up slightly, at ninety-one. But July was a total disaster for him.

There was no doubt in Ryder's mind that favorable settlements he worked out for two of the firm's clients that month cost him over a hundred billable hours. His skill and experience had moved the cases off the litigation track on which they were headed. Each case would have required lengthy hearings, one with a Federal agency, the other before an arbitrator. The chances of being forced to pay out large sums of money in both, by way of back pay or damages, were quite high. Ryder engineered settlements that let both employers off cheaply, but the result, in terms of his billables, was anything but good. Production records for the month showed only seventy hours of his time for which Walters, Cassidy & Breen would be paid. Paul Castillo did not give him work of any sort in that period, although Castillo continued to show a full billing schedule for the month.

What upset Ryder the most was finding out from Alan Deveraux, who invited him to lunch, that Deveraux was already aware of the fate in store for his good friend George that afternoon. Before the deli sandwiches they ordered were brought to the table, Deveraux took out a copy of a memo addressed to Ryder from Ed Jackson. The memo first outlined the history of his billable hours over the past two years. After that came the terms the firm was prepared to offer him in exchange for a voluntary resignation. Deveraux informed him that his secretary found the document in the copy machine that morning when she went to use it.

"I think it's a goddam insult for them to be offering you three months' severance, George. You've got about thirty years with the firm, right?"

"A little over thirty-two, but it doesn't surprise me. We've been going in this direction ever since Fiore became managing partner. Everything is strictly bottom line now. What you've done for the firm in the past doesn't mean diddly-squat."

"Do you think he's behind this?" Deveraux asked.

"Of course he is," Ryder replied. "He's been after my ass for years, ever since he succeeded me as managing partner. He didn't want me to run against him that year. Said he had all the votes he needed to win at the partners meeting, and I should recommend his election unanimously. I told him I didn't think he was the right person to lead the firm at that time and that he'd have to beat me on the ballot. That pissed him off real good and he warned me I'd regret it someday. I guess I handed him the opportunity and today's the day."

"Then you figure Jackson's just doing what he's been told?"

"Absolutely. He's just a wimp. He knows it, and so does everyone else. He's a workaholic with no balls. Big smile, friendly guy, but principles don't mean a thing to Ed if he has to worry about his own rear end. That's why Fiore put him where he is."

"You know, George, if you don't resign, Ed's recommendation will have to go to a vote of the partners, and he may be worried about whether a majority would support him. He barely won his own election. If he gets voted down on this, it's a big slap in the face. He'd definitely lose most of his power and he might have to step down himself. Maybe you can negotiate a better severance package out of him for that reason, unless you intend to fight it altogether. You'd have plenty of support."

"I'm not sure, Alan. I'll have to think it over. Practicing with this firm isn't the fun it used to be. This may be the right time to get out and go somewhere else, or even start a new career. The best thing that could happen to WC&B is for Doug Fiore to be elected governor. And I don't mean because it would bring in business."

* * *

At a few minutes after three, Ryder picked up the paper Ed Jackson pushed across his desk. He took less than ten seconds to scan it, to make sure it was the same one he was shown at lunch by Deveraux.

"Make it nine months' severance and I'll resign today," he said. He was prepared to accept a counterproposal extending the package through the end of the year, making it a five-month deal.

Jackson was shocked at the speed with which Ryder reviewed the memo and responded to it. He hardly had time to turn his chair toward the window and puff away at his pipe. "I'm not sure we can do that," he said.

Ryder feigned surprise. "Come on Ed, I've been here thirty-two years, a little more than you. You don't think I'm asking for too much, do you?" He made it sound as caustic as he could. "Make believe no one was going bankrupt anymore, and your undertaker services weren't needed. You wouldn't think severance pay from August through April was excessive after all that time in the firm, would you?" He looked hard at Jackson who had a blank look in his eyes while he continued blowing smoke in the air.

"And I'm not so sure the partners of this firm are willing to sit back and watch someone with my seniority get booted out just because sales happen to be down for a while. Maybe they'd rather see my billables for the past thirty years and then vote on this kind of a policy."

Jackson held the pipe away from his mouth and pursed his lips several times. He seemed to suddenly realize that Ryder was waiting for an answer. He had no idea how to respond to the proposal. "What you do is up to you, George. I'm not prepared to change the offer today. Let me think about it and I'll get back to you in a day or two."

"Do you mean you want to discuss it with Fiore?" Ryder paused for just a second. "I mean with the Executive Committee?"

"Maybe yes, maybe no. That's up to me to decide."

"Have you already gone through this with the Committee?"

"That's confidential. The partnership agreement says I can handle this kind of thing myself or bring the Committee in on it. You know that."

"Right. And I also remember that while I was managing partner anything this serious had to get a majority vote at the Committee to get off the ground."

"Don't make a big deal out of it, George. If I needed three votes, I'd have Rubin's and Zappala's."

Ryder stood up. "That's right, I forgot that the court has been packed." He dropped the memo on Jackson's desk.

"That's your copy," Jackson said. "Hold on to it."

Ryder turned to leave. "I don't need this one. I'll wait until it gets changed."

* * *

But there was no change. Fiore laughed to himself at Ryder's request for extended severance pay. He knew he could successfully help Jackson bully enough partners into upholding a termination if it came to that. The vote would be close but he counted heads and knew which partners would be afraid to oppose him.

"Listen, Ed, I'm not happy about it but I think you'll just have to tell Ryder the three months you offered him is all he's going to get for his resignation. He knows that the firm's been overpaying him for almost the last two years. His salary has been higher than his billables for all that time. I like George as much as anyone, but times are tough right now and we've treated him well. If this was a year ago, I could see giving him five or six months' severance, but we've more than made up for that in the pay he's received while WC&B was losing money on him. To give him the severance he's asking for now wouldn't be fair to the partners who have been doing the work and bringing in our revenue. I think George knows that. I don't blame him for asking for more, but if he doesn't want to go along with the fair offer we've given him, be sure he understands that you'll submit a motion for his termination at next week's partners' meeting, supported by a recommendation from the Executive Committee. Tell him you're well aware that he could fight it but that you're not worried about getting a majority of the partners to support the Committee. If he wants to force a vote, we'll respect his decision but there'll be no severance pay for him at all if he loses."

Jackson didn't look forward to another face-to-face meeting with Ryder. He began dialing his number, intending to communicate the decision over the phone and to support it with some of the thoughts Fiore laid out for him, but then decided he didn't want to speak to Ryder at all. He took out a copy of the memorandum, updated it with a hand-written note in which he said that the Executive Committee had decided not to change its severance offer, and asked for an immediate reply. He had the mail room send a clerk to his office and instructed him to deliver the sealed envelope to Ryder. When the messenger arrived, Ryder told him to wait. He read the memo and figured that Fiore had the votes he needed to support Jackson. Without hesitating, he wrote "OK" at the bottom of the page, initialed it and sent it back.

Almost immediately he experienced an unexpected surge of relief. In one sense Ryder felt defeated, saddened by the fact that a distinguished career was coming to an end in such a shabby manner. He always looked forward to a kind of "Goodbye, Mr. Chips" farewell when he left the firm, with everyone applauding his final words about friendship and loyalty. He never imagined that his departure would be forced on him. Worse yet, that it would come on the heels of an argument with some gutless partner over the length of his severance pay. At the same time, there was a rush of pleasure at what was happening. He realized that he wouldn't have to have anything more to do with the likes of Fiore and Jackson and those partners whose cowardly conduct, in his estimation, reflected the knowledge that it was in the best interest of their careers to go along with whatever Fiore wanted to do.

Ryder was no longer obligated to give WC&B a single billable hour. It was up to him whether he cleaned out his office and left the next day, or chose to use it for the entire three months while he made telephone calls, received secretarial assistance and looked for other employment in town. He knew that a letter of resignation, approved by Jackson, could be circulated to the firm anytime he desired. That's when he could announce his date of departure and go out a gentleman, not someone who seemed bent on revenge. It was understood that the office manager would arrange a party for him on his last afternoon unless he notified her to the contrary ahead of time. Coffee and cake would be served to those who came around for a final handshake. He circled the date on the calendar that would be his last day in the office. Ironically, he saw that his three-month severance would officially end on the day before the general election in November. If Fiore was the Republican candidate, Ryder wouldn't be showing any disloyalty to his "employer" when he voted Democratic.

56

IN THE FIRST WEEK of August the *Providence Herald* reported that Richie Cardella's lead over Doug Fiore now stood at 55 to 45 percent. The Fiore campaign team was delighted with the numbers. They told anyone who would listen that their candidate was climbing steadily in the polls as more and more people got to hear his message. They were confident he would be peaking at just the right time for the September 13th primary.

Two weeks later, Fiore stood in the middle of the living room in Cyril Berman's suite, fielding questions from Berman, Walsh, and Karp in preparation for another open forum that evening. Cardella's margin over him had moved back up to twelve points.

"I think we've hit a brick wall," Russell Walsh told the others before the session began. "The positive campaigning brought us to one level. We're going to have to bring out all of Cardella's negatives to get beyond where we are."

"Russ's right," Lester Karp said. "I could see contributions begin slowing down when we stopped gaining ground in the polls. This past week was the worst we've had. We need something to give us a jump start and wake up our supporters. What do you say, Cyril?"

Berman didn't look ruffled. He sat at one end of the long sofa, leaning back into the corner where several small pillows were placed for support. He held a drink in his hand. "I say it's easier said than done," he answered. "Cardella had four good years as Attorney General, I told you that before. We read every editorial the *Herald* wrote about the guy during that time. You'd think he was the publisher's nephew for Chrissake. They loved him, which is why I can't help feeling they'll endorse him before the primary."

The others said nothing, waiting for Berman to continue.

"I think what we ought to do is take a closer look at his law firm and see what kind of connections it has with State government. Maybe we can find something that will let us accuse Cardella of wanting to funnel money from the State coffers to his fellow partners. That would be hitting the jackpot. We should also put a private eye on him. It might help to know where he goes and who he's with when he leaves his office. With a little luck we may find out he's fooling around somewhere."

Berman turned toward Fiore who was thumbing through the latest issue of *Rhode Island Monthly Magazine*. "How about you, Doug? If we can dig up some dirt on Cardella, do you have any problem using it?"

Fiore looked up from the magazine and was silent just briefly. The things he said earlier about running a clean campaign and not doing anything that would cost him his self-respect flashed through his mind. They weren't asking him to tell lies. They simply wanted him to reveal Cardella's negatives, if they found any, in his speeches. He had said earlier that if Richie's past conduct included anything he now may regret having said or done, it was fair game to remind the public about it. Fiore believed that doing what Cyril suggested did not turn a clean campaign into a dirty one because it was not being dishonest. He looked and sounded very serious when he answered Berman's question. "We've done a lot of work to get where we are, and if that will help us win, I'll do it."

Berman smiled at him. "Good. Then we're all together on this, because Sandy Tarantino thinks we ought to start digging."

57

The sixth negotiating session between the *Herald* and the Teamsters wasn't going well at all. Terry Reardon wanted to get as many issues as possible out of the way before the primary. Despite Cardella's assurances, Reardon feared there would be tremendous pressure on the candidate to drop everything after his primary victory and spend all his time campaigning for the general election. It would be difficult to get him to a meeting for at least a week after the primary, leaving just ten days before the contract expired.

Reardon wasn't worried about the apparent conflict of interest that saw Cardella running for public office and still working for the *Herald*. Jenna convinced him that the paper would never endorse Richie over Doug Fiore in the primary.

"There's no way this newspaper will support a candidate that's pushing for State-operated gambling parlors," she told him. So Reardon insisted on more meetings in August than Tommy Arena and his committee were ready to handle. The two sides were seeing too much of each other too soon, and tempers were beginning to flare.

Cardella was present for the first two hours of bargaining on the last Tuesday of August. When the parties reconvened after lunch, Arena learned that Richie had left for some campaign work.

"Then let's just quit for the day," he said.

"But I wanted to present some counterproposals and get the Union's response before we adjourned," Reardon said. "That's why Mike Donlon's here."

"You give us whatever you want," Arena shot back, "but don't tell us when we have to fucking answer you. We may wait until fucking September thirtieth to let you know what we think." Tommy wanted his two committee members to tell the other drivers how tough he was. Now they could report how he pretty much told Terry Reardon and his lawyer to go fuck themselves.

Donlan opened his notebook and read the Company's newest proposals. When he finished, he tried to set the mood for some concessions by the Union, repeating several of the statements Cardella made at earlier meetings about the poor economic climate. "Richie already stressed the importance of the *Herald* not being pushed into a situation where it would have to save money by requiring some drivers to double up on routes at the same time it laid off some others. The drivers have never struck the Company, and we look forward to another peaceful settlement this time around. But I'd be remiss in not making it perfectly clear that if the drivers did engage in a work stoppage, the *Herald* would hire other personnel to make the deliveries."

Arena didn't interrupt Donlan's delivery. He kept busy doodling on a paper in front of him without looking up. Reardon could see the Teamster boss's cheeks begin to flush. He anticipated the worst. When Donlan stopped talking, Arena politely asked if he was through. As soon as the young lawyer said he was, Tommy proved Reardon's apprehensions correct.

The verbal tirade lasted almost ten minutes. Arena stood up and walked back and forth on his side of the table as he shouted and swore at the *Herald* representatives. He removed his sport jacket early into his diatribe and threw it against the wall behind him to emphasize a point. After a while, Terry saw patches of sweat staining the armpits of Arena's silk shirt. Still, he continued to wave his arms wildly while denouncing his negotiating opponents in every way.

Reardon was afraid he'd witness a heart attack before it was over. The two Union committeemen obviously enjoyed Arena's remarks when he began his wordy assault, unable to hold back their smiles at the start. Now they showed signs of concern as their spokesman continued to hurl invective and criticism across the table.

"Take it easy, Tommy, take it easy," Reardon said at several points, trying to get Arena to lower his voice and bring himself under control.

But his calls for restraint fell on deaf ears. The sound of Arena's "fucking this" and "fucking that" continued to reverberate around the room.

"We don't need a fucking contract with you guys. We don't *want* a fucking contract with this fucking newspaper. You want to try and fucking replace us, huh? Go ahead and try. You won't get a single fucking paper onto a truck and out of this building. Anyone who tries to take a fucking job away from one of my men will have his goddam head broken. I got friends up on Federal Hill who'll do whatever I ask, do you fucking understand me? I do favors for them and they'll do whatever the fuck I want. One fucking hand washes the other. All I have to do is make one goddam phone call and I'll have whatever help I need to keep your fucking papers off the streets. Don't forget that."

When he finished, Arena slammed his notebook shut and picked his jacket up off the floor. "Let's get the fuck out of here," he said to the two drivers who had put their papers away and were ready to leave. As the group reached the door, Arena turned toward Reardon, who hadn't moved from his chair. He spoke in his normal voice, as if the dressing down he just administered never happened. "Call me when you want another fucking meeting," he said, and winked.

* * *

Terry Reardon believed that if you got thrown from a horse, you got up off the ground and back in the saddle right away. He preached that to his children so they'd understand that it wasn't a good idea to postpone the inevitable and worry about what would happen the next time. The following morning he telephoned Tommy Arena to schedule another bargaining session. Arena said that he wanted to meet with him and Cardella off the record.

"Leave your kid lawyer home," he told Terry.

They arranged to have dinner at seven o'clock the following Monday night, if Cardella was available. Arena suggested Chi-Chi's, convenient to everyone, and Reardon agreed. Later that day he called back and confirmed the time and place with Arena's secretary. He told her to let her boss know that Richie Cardella could stay for just an hour.

58

On Sunday morning, nine days before the primary, the *Woonsocket Star* and the *Newport Record* endorsed Cardella for governor on the Republican ticket. They split on the Democratic side. The *Star* came out in favor of Bruce Singer, while the largest newspaper on Aquidneck Island supported June Bates with a strong editorial.

Cyril Berman called Fiore at home that morning with the news, but told him not to worry about it. "I've already spoken to some key people about it. They assured me it won't make any difference at the ballot box. There was a lot of infighting at both papers and you had your share of editors pushing for you. The mayors in those towns are strong backers of casino gambling. Someone has deluded them into believing they'll see big bucks flowing back into their treasuries from a State operation. So they lobbied the papers not to support you. It would be good to have them on our side, but you'll get endorsements from others. Wait and see, it will pretty much balance out."

"What about the *Herald*?" Fiore asked. "Does anyone know what they're going to do?"

"Not yet," Berman answered, "but I'm getting good vibes from what I'm reading there." He knew the paper sided with them on the gambling issue but didn't have any idea whether that was enough to get its endorsement. "I know they're publishing their choices in all the races next Sunday. That means the forums on Tuesday and Thursday night will be real important, especially the first one. The Providence

Organization of Women has a lot of clout. P.O.W.? really stands for pow." He smiled at his own joke.

"I'll be ready," Doug assured him.

"Of course you will. See you at 2:30 at the Biltmore."

59

LATER THAT MORNING, AS Fiore was getting dressed to play tennis at a local outdoor court, he received a call from Joe Gaudette. His friend wanted to talk to him, Gaudette said, and would be at a certain pay phone at noon. He gave Doug the telephone number and told him to use a pay phone himself.

Fiore made the call at the appointed time. Sandy Tarantino answered after four rings. "Sorry for that delay, old buddy, but the sun is really beating down on this AT&T oasis I'm at. I was waiting in the car with the air conditioning on. Where are you calling from?"

"A wash and dry right next to Walgreen's."

"Good," Sandy said. He asked a few questions about the campaign and expressed confidence that Doug would win. "Don't tell Cyril—he'll think it's bad luck—but take it from me, you can start writing your victory speech." Then he inquired as to whether Fiore had any recent contact with Brad Hanley.

"No, I haven't. Why do you ask?" As soon as he raised the question, he tensed up, afraid he might hear that Hanley was aware of the ongoing relationship between Doug and his wife.

Tarantino's answer came as a relief. "He's been a regular at one of our clubs for quite a while, Doug, maybe close to a year already. Comes alone, has dinner, and spends some time at the tables. Always had a certain downside limit when he played. If he reached it, he left a tip, said 'Good night' and took off. Same thing when he was winning. Didn't push his luck. Just cashed in his chips and left. In case you're wondering, he lost more times than he won."

The recorded voice of the operator broke into the conversation. Fiore deposited two more coins in the box before she completed her message.

Sandy continued talking as soon as he heard the money drop. "Anyway, maybe six weeks ago he began betting a little heavier and staying later. I had my guys there keeping an eye on him for me. His luck was about the same so he was losing more money than usual.

"First he applied for check writing privileges. I had no trouble approving it, just based on what Ocean State pays him. He cashed a couple of checks—one for two thousand, one for three—and they cleared okay, no problem.

"Then he asked to play on credit. I checked out his bank account and the equity in his house. It was a close call, but there was enough breathing room to let it go through. That was just a couple of weeks ago. The problem is his luck's been running bad and right now he's into us for eight grand. I thought you might know if there's something going on in his life."

Fiore recalled that Pat Hanley hadn't mentioned Brad to him in quite a while. He was with her at the Biltmore a week earlier and she was in terrific spirits the entire time. She apparently had no reason to talk about her husband anymore now that the contract with the Union was ratified.

"No, I haven't talked to him at all, Sandy," he said. "Is he okay at work? Any problems there?"

"Hang on a second. I just want to get a good look at the guy who got in the phone booth next to me." After a short pause, he was back on the line, focused on Hanley again. "Not that I can tell, but that's just from looking at Ocean State's monthly P&Ls. Business hasn't improved much over last year. I don't have any good contacts at the plant. I always figured you could find out what I wanted to know."

Neither of them spoke for a few seconds. Fiore felt the tension return again. He wasn't sure whether Sandy was about to bring Pat's name into the conversation.

"Let's leave it at that," Sandy said. "I won't get worried as long as he starts paying back what he owes. If he doesn't, that's another story. If you hear anything, let me know." There was another pause before Sandy asked, "Are you on the campaign trail today?"

"Why not?" Doug wanted to sound facetious. "Two coffee klatches and a dinner, starting at three o'clock in Cranston. This was my big R&R day. Cyril says next weekend will be a killer."

"You'll do fine, old buddy. You're almost halfway to the Statehouse. Believe me, you've got it made. Get that victory speech in shape."

60

It was ten minutes after seven when Richie Cardella heard his name being called from the back end of Chi-Chi's bar.

"Cardella, hey, Richie Cardella, you got a phone call."

Just a minute earlier he looked at his watch and wondered why Terry Reardon and Tommy Arena hadn't shown up yet. Reardon knew that Richie had to get out of there by eight and drive out to the Quidnessett Country Club in North Kingstown for a speech. As it was, he was cutting it a little close. *Maybe that's him now,* he thought. *I wouldn't mind hearing the meeting's been put off.*

Cardella walked toward the back, where a pay phone hung from the wall between the doors to the men's and ladies' rooms. He passed a number of booths on his left, most of which were occupied. Several people, whose faces he recognized without knowing their names, greeted him as he went by. Al Niro, a bookie who took football bets at Chi-Chi's, was sitting by himself in the last booth, almost directly across from the telephone.

Cardella nodded at Niro. "Thanks, Al," he said, and reached down for the receiver. "Hello," he said. There was no answer. "Hello," he repeated, and was startled by a *thump, thump* sound he heard behind him. He turned slightly, just enough to see the gun pointing at him before he felt his chest begin to explode.

* * *

Terry Reardon was about half the three block distance between the *Herald* building and Chi-Chi's when he heard the sound of sirens coming from two directions. Police cars were moving his way from Lasalle Square, diagonally across from the Civic Center, where their headquarters were located. And ambulances, their sirens wailing like the sound of a sickly person's heavy breathing, were heading toward him from the left, where City Hall sat facing one end of Kennedy Plaza.

Arena called him just before 6:45 to say he'd be about fifteen or twenty minutes late for their meeting. Reardon tried to reach Cardella at his office, but the lawyer who answered the phone said that Richie was already gone. Now he asked himself why he didn't call Chi-Chi's instead and leave a message for Cardella.

As soon as he began making his way across the intersection at Westminster and Mattewson Streets, Reardon saw the scene ahead of him in front of Chi-Chi's. Half a dozen police cars, red and blue lights flashing from their roofs, were parked at different angles, blocking the one-way street. An ambulance was backed up onto the sidewalk, close to the entrance to the bar, while two others waited a little farther away. The rear doors of all three were thrown open.

A crowd of at least fifty people was gathered in the street. They stood in a semicircle facing Chi-Chi's. Others watched from the opposite sidewalk, in front of Saul's Delicatessen. The deli was a favorite downtown location because it stayed open every night until midnight and provided delivery service for hungry legislators working late at City Hall or the Statehouse. As he approached, Reardon could hear several police pleading with the onlookers to stand back.

"What happened?" he asked a young man walking toward him.

"Someone said two guys got shot in there and one of 'em's dead."

"Anyone know the reason?"

"Somethin' to do with gamblin' is all I heard."

Reardon began to walk around the perimeter of the crowd, toward the side nearer the bar. He pulled his *Herald* ID card out of his wallet as he got closer to one of the police cars. Just then he heard his name called and turned around. Tommy Arena was coming toward him.

"What the fuck's going on?" Arena asked, almost shouting. "Were you in there?"

"No, I just got here," Reardon answered. "A kid told me two guys were shot and that one got killed. I'm going to see what I can find out."

"Shit, Terry," Arena said, "we could've been right in the fucking middle of it. Are you gonna look for Cardella?"

"Yeah, Tommy. But Richie said he could only stay until eight. By the time we find another place and sit down, he may have to take off. He might even be a witness if he was there when it happened. Wait here. I'll be back."

Reardon showed his ID to a husky young officer, still wearing his sunglasses in the dusk, who was standing next to one of the cruisers. "What's the story?" he asked.

"Best I know, some crazy bastard walked in the front door, killed one or two guys inside and kept going out the back. He got away in a car waiting for him in the alley."

"Any chance of my going in? I'd be covering the story."

"Uh, uh. The place is already crawling with paramedics and news guys. A few of them came running over from something going on at City Hall. The Lieutenant said everyone else stays out."

Several minutes later Reardon looked toward the door of the bar just as it opened and four police officers came out. They waved their arms and shouted at everyone between themselves and the ambulance to make room. Two paramedics in white uniforms followed, carrying a stretcher. Terry could see that the sheet covering the body was pulled up only as far as its shoulders. The medics quickly loaded the stretcher onto a bed inside the ambulance. One of them began administering to the victim while his partner ran to the front of the vehicle and climbed into the driver's seat. A police officer closed the rear door. Two others got into a cruiser to escort the ambulance. Their sirens began sending signals of distress into the air almost simultaneously.

The scene was repeated several minutes later when two more paramedics emerged from Chi-Chi's. This time the body on the stretcher was entirely covered except for a pair of dark colored socks that could be seen sticking out at one end. The ambulance crew was slower in transferring the victim to their vehicle.

Reardon saw Nate Cohen, one of the *Herald*'s crime reporters, come out of the bar. He was followed by a young assistant carrying several cameras. Cohen took a quick look around to find the path of least resistance through those gathered outside to watch. Terry was forced to run three quarters of the way around the crowd perimeter to catch up with them. The ranks of onlookers had almost doubled since he first arrived.

He shouted at Cohen to get his attention. "Nate, hold up a second."

The aging reporter was dressed in rumpled khaki slacks and a non-designer long-sleeved red golf shirt. He bent his head slightly forward and looked down over his bifocals before recognizing Reardon. "Oh, Terry. Hi."

"What's the story?" Reardon asked.

Cohen shook his head from side to side several times and gave a look of disgust.

"Another sicko," he said. "It was a bad scene in there. The cops figure the killer was a pro the way he pulled it off. He had a silencer on his gun, probably a nine millimeter. He went in after Al Niro, a bookie who hangs out there a lot, and gave him two holes right above the eyes. Richie probably got a good look at him. He was just a few feet away talking on the phone. So the guy shot him too, point blank in the chest. It was a bloody mess."

Reardon's heart began racing as soon as he heard the name.

"Richie Cardella?" he asked, in the same loud voice.

"Yeah, Cardella. Poor bastard. Talk about being in the wrong place at the wrong time. Hey, I got to go back and start typing, and Avedon here has some shots to develop."

Cohen turned away from Reardon but then turned back again. "This was my night off. Jason and I had dinner at the Holiday and then went across the street to police headquarters to see Gerry Quinn. I wanted to find out if there was anything new on that shooting in Olneyville the other day. We were talking when the call came in on this one. Gerry let us ride over here with two of his guys. Now I've got to go to work for a few hours. Just my luck."

"Wait a second, Nate," Terry hollered. "Richie's the one still alive . . . ?" It was half statement, half question.

"Yeah. But one of the medics said it looked like he was just hanging on by a thread."

Reardon watched Cohen and the young cameraman hurry toward Mathewson Street in the direction of the *Herald* building. He took several deep breaths before going the opposite way. He found Arena where he left him and gave him the news.

"Oh, my fucking Jesus," Tommy said, bringing the palm of his hand up against his temple. "Why the fuck did we have to pick Chi-Chi's?"

They talked for a few minutes and agreed to be in touch with each other within a week or so to see how they'd proceed.

"Don't worry, Terry, if we gotta go past September thirtieth on account of this. I'll see to it the boys don't do nothing stupid, not unless they want to get their fucking heads broke."

61

THE FIORE CAMPAIGN STARTED the day in Wakefield where Doug spoke to a group of local businessmen and women over coffee and Danish pastry at 10:00 a.m. He kept his prepared remarks short so that most of the time could be devoted to questions and answers. He learned early in the game that an audience was usually more accepting of what he told them if it was in response to something they asked.

Later, he attended a noon meeting of the town's Rotary Club. The restaurant could seat forty people around a series of tables pushed together, end to end, in a narrow, oblong-shaped private room. There he made what they all referred to as "The Speech," covering all the major points of his candidacy.

Both events went well. Neither, however, offered the right opportunity for Fiore to introduce several of the negatives his team had pieced together on Cardella. None of it was sensational. Still, a few cases from the past that gave the State a black eye would help dampen the popular feeling that Cardella was an outstanding attorney general during his entire time in office. And the sizable fees that Cardella's law firm had already received in connection with its drafting of prospective casino gaming legislation were a significant issue. It would help Fiore bang home the point that his opponent's view on that major controversy was already colored, as he would say . . . "by the color of money, my friends."

Berman suggested that the new material be introduced that night, in Westerly. Doug was scheduled to address a 25-dollar a plate dinner of mostly blue collar Republicans. The others agreed. They were anxious to see how it would go over in a town that already had one-armed bandits operating around the clock.

Karp and Walsh split the driving that afternoon as their party made its way slowly along Route 1 South from Wakefield. The first stop was in Charlestown where Fiore met with many of the hotel, motel and resort owners from the nearby beach areas. There was standing room only in the lobby of the Starlight Hotel to hear him speak. Later, at Dunns Corners, he gave an interview to the local weekly newspaper. The photographer posed him, holding a triple scoop ice cream cone, on the steps of the town's general store.

At five o'clock they pulled into the Sea Gull Motel in Westerly. Karp had reserved two rooms they could use to rest in for up to three hours at half the daily corporate rate. Fiore took one of them for himself so he could telephone Susan, his daughter, and talk to her about her first day of high school, using the time left to nap without being disturbed. The others shared the adjoining room. Berman and Karp played pinochle while Walsh sat up in bed, reading a Tom Clancy novel.

At 7:40 they were back in the Lincoln and on the way to the Shelter Harbor Inn for dinner and Fiore's major speech. Karp turned on the radio just in time for them to hear that Cardella was shot in a Providence bar approximately thirty minutes earlier. According to unconfirmed reports, he was clinging to life at Miriam Hospital. The announcer gave out the few details that were available.

"Jesus Christ," Walsh said, turning to Berman in the back seat. "What's that going to do to the election?"

"Let me think about it for a minute," Berman answered. "I've never had anything like this happen to me before."

After a short silence, Karp spoke. "Don't you think it would be better to leave out that negative stuff, Cyril?" He looked in the rearview mirror to see if Berman showed any reaction to the question. "Seems to me this would be the worst time to bring it up," he added.

Berman remained silent. Fiore fielded the question instead. "Why should we drop it, Les? It's all true, so it shouldn't matter that he won't be able to deny it."

"There's going to be a lot of sympathy for him out there, Doug, hoping the guy pulls through." Walsh spoke quietly, as if trying to impart a valuable lesson. "You wouldn't look good throwing mud at Cardella while everyone else is praying for him."

"I'm not sure I buy that, Russ," Fiore challenged. "What about, 'All's fair in love and war?'"

"That goes out the window to 'Don't kick the bastard when he's down,'" Walsh replied. His tone of voice this time didn't conceal the fact that he was becoming irritated with Fiore's judgment and sentiments. "And I don't think calling Cardella names right now fits in with your idea of running a clean campaign. The names are okay, but the timing is dirty."

"I vote with Russ," Karp said. "But you'd better make up your minds because we'll be there in five minutes."

They all waited for Berman to come up with the answer.

"Here's what we'll do," Cyril said finally, looking across the back seat at Fiore as he spoke. "Russ and Lester are absolutely right. You never know how sympathy can affect what people do. I was just thinking about how Nixon pulled it off in '52. Most people in the country didn't think much of him, even back then when he was running on the ticket as Eisenhower's vice president. His reputation was that he'd do anything to win and couldn't be trusted. Then word got out that some California businessmen had him in their pocket. The press jumped on it and played it up big. They always hated the guy anyway, and this gave them a chance to destroy him politically. That made Eisenhower think out loud about replacing him with someone else.

"But tricky Dicky went on TV and denied the whole thing. Before he was through, he whined about the fact that his wife could only afford to buy an inexpensive coat for herself. He told everyone how much they loved their two little girls and the family dog. The media called it 'the Checkers speech' because that was the dog's name. The point is that he got the little old ladies to cry and people all over to feel sorry for him. That forced Ike to take his finger off the trigger."

"Too bad," Walsh interrupted. "It would have saved the country a lot of grief later on."

"Anyhow," Berman continued, "we've got to avoid doing anything that might build even more pity or sympathy—call it what you want—for Cardella. In other words, Doug, you've got to act like you feel just as bad about what happened to him as everyone else.

"What I think is that it would be a big mistake for you to make any more speeches while Cardella's in this condition. If you do, and you lose the primary, you'll never know how many people out there voted against you because they figured you took advantage of his not being able to fight back. Richie just became the underdog through no fault of his own, and nobody likes to see an underdog get beat up unfairly."

Fiore was not pleased with Berman's advice. "Yeah, but if I lose the primary without making any more speeches and don't let the people know that Richie was far from the world's greatest attorney general, I'll never know how many of them voted against me simply because they figure a good AG will make a good governor. It works both ways, Cyril. Am I the only one in this car who understands what 55 to 45 percent means when we're the 45?" It was difficult for him to stay calm. "You're saying that we do nothing, just the same as them. We just shift into neutral for the next eight days. Great. The voters think I'm a nice guy, sweet as maple syrup, but how does that get me from 45 to 51 percent? Have you all forgotten that we need that much to win?" Doug's voice became progressively louder as he spoke.

"I'll explain it," Berman answered, maintaining the calm he showed all along. "First, like I said, if you don't make speeches, you don't lose the sympathy vote. Second, people aren't stupid. They know that being governor is a full-time job. You can't handle it from a bed in the hospital or a rehab center. If Cardella lives through this, it sounds to me like he's going to be in tough shape for a real, long time.

"The voters have a week or so to come to grips with that, and I think they will. They'll understand that Richie's not going to be in any position to handle the job until who knows when, if at all. They won't want to put him under any pressure to start getting it done because that would hurt his recovery. Some of his support will go to you for that reason. Some of it will sit home and not vote at all. Right now, I think that's the only way you'll win this primary."

Fiore didn't let on whether he concurred with Berman's conclusions or not. His gut told him that the voters needed his continued guidance on the issues, especially the obligation to reject State-sponsored casinos on a moral basis for the benefit of Rhode Island's poorest citizens and to keep them from undermining his economic agenda. His silence now, he felt, would undercut the momentum he had going with the people.

Fiore recognized, however, that Berman, Walsh and Karp were in total disagreement with him and that Sandy Tarantino would know it. If he insisted on making a speech, he'd put himself in the position of being criticized by Sandy for not following Berman's instructions. That left him no choice but to listen to the rest of Berman's plan. "So what do I do tonight?" he asked.

Berman had already thought it through. "When we get there, I'll call Providence and try to get all the facts I can. I'm sure most of these folks won't know much about what happened. You'll give them whatever details we've got and then announce that you've decided not to make any more speeches before the primary. Tell them that it wouldn't be fair to Cardella and you're certain your supporters wouldn't want you to do it under these circumstances. Be quiet for a while but let them see you're not through. Then say that above all you couldn't find it in your heart to keep campaigning while he's fighting for his life."

Berman took a long pause himself at that point. "I'll bet there'll be heavy applause when you finish, probably a standing ovation. Let it go for ten or fifteen seconds, then motion for everyone to be quiet. As soon as they are, tell them you want to have a minute of silence so they can all pray for Cardella. When the time's up, just say 'Thank you' and go sit down. If he has any savvy, the MC will tell the audience that everyone has to have great respect for the decision you've made. After he thanks them all for coming, you make your way out of the room slowly. Shake all the hands you want, but no big smiles. Look serious, like you're at a funeral. That should get us home tonight at least an hour earlier than we planned."

"I go along with you a hundred percent, Cyril," Walsh said. "It's a great plan. Follow his advice, Doug."

Fiore's mind was made up. He wouldn't let Sandy blame a loss in the primary on his ignoring Berman's counsel. "I'll do it," he said, "but I hope you're right. What a goddam time for this to happen."

Berman didn't answer. He was thinking that it probably was the best thing that could have happened for his client. He realized that Fiore was now less reluctant to abandon his "clean campaign" pledge in what was becoming an overriding quest to win the election, and that it was up to him to monitor Doug closely the rest of the way. He wondered whether he should tell Sandy Tarantino how he felt when he heard from him.

62

The headline of Tuesday morning's *Herald* read, "GAMBLER SLAIN, CARDELLA NEAR DEATH IN BAR SHOOTING." The story took up a large section of the front page and continued inside on page six. Nate Cohen's column was full of accounts and descriptions from different people in the bar at the time of the incident. The basic facts, as summarized, were these:

Rico (Richie) Cardella entered the establishment, a place he frequented once or twice a week, at about ten minutes before seven o'clock in the evening. He told the proprietor, Felipe Gonsalez, age 51, who goes under the name of Chi-Chi, that he was expecting a couple of friends shortly and wanted a booth when they arrived. Cardella sat down at the bar and ordered a light beer. About half an hour later, Gonsalez and several patrons heard Al Niro, age 41, shout to Cardella from the back of the establishment that he had a telephone call.

Niro was a bookie who took bets only on football games. He occupied the same booth five nights a week, Thursday through Monday, from about six to nine o'clock. On Thursday and Friday nights, most of his incoming action was for the Saturday college games. The professional contests played on Sunday kept him busy with gamblers on Saturday night. He spent the other two nights handling whatever business there was for the Monday night NFL games.

Niro made himself a regular in the bar and grille in late July when the professional exhibition season started. He always had a drink up front at the bar before leaving for the night, and asked Gonsalez to call a taxi for him when he was ready to go. Niro often told others he befriended there that business was good and that he liked operating on his own. He suspected that his activity didn't please the professionals on Federal Hill, but figured they had enough work to keep them busy without getting overly concerned about him.

Just after Cardella got up to take his phone call, Gonsalez got a quick glimpse of a white male who just then entered the establishment. He was about thirty years old, slim, and no more than five feet, ten inches tall. The individual walked past the bar area toward the rear of the building at a quick pace. His right hand was moving around his head and face, making it difficult for Gonsalez to see his features when he glanced in that direction for a moment. The proprietor's immediate thought was that the individual seemed to be in a hurry to get to the men's room in back.

Other patrons sitting in the booths along the way were equally at a loss to describe the killer in much detail. They agreed that he moved past them quickly and used his hand and arm to hide his face, although not in an obvious manner. All concurred that he was wearing a black polo shirt with gray slacks and had on an unzipped tri-colored (black/blue/green) windbreaker.

Raymond McHugh, age 47, was sitting in the booth ahead of Niro's. He came in a half hour earlier with his wife, Elizabeth, who was in the ladies room when the shooting took place. McHugh was facing the front of the bar and looked up from his newspaper for an instant as the killer hurried by. A second later he heard the words, "We warned you," spoken behind him. That was followed by two muffled sounds. He looked around in time to see the assailant point his gun at Cardella and fire a single shot. Cardella started to reach for his chest, but then fell to the floor. McHugh threw himself down on his seat. Seconds passed before he heard some of the customers shouting and running toward the rear of the building. When he looked up again, the killer was gone and the door in back was closing.

Mary Bennett, a City Hall employee who did some shopping in town after work, was at Chi-Chi's for dinner. She heard some noise in the rear from her booth and saw Cardella fall down. She hesitated momentarily, thinking he might be drunk, and watched as the killer pushed open the rear door of the establishment and ran out. As she began to get up from her seat, several male patrons ran past her toward Cardella. She followed and saw Niro slumped down in the booth, blood running over his face.

One of the men, Bok Lee, age 28, stopped briefly to look at Cardella before exiting the rear door. He saw a dark colored automobile moving very fast down the alley, toward Weybosset Street. Lee did not wait to see which way it turned when it got there. He dialed 911 from the telephone Cardella was using and informed the police of what just occurred. Gonsalez was in the act of calling the police on another 911 line at the same time.

Police cruisers and several ambulances arrived at Chi-Chi's within minutes of being notified. Niro was examined and pronounced dead at the scene. Paramedics worked on Cardella about ten minutes, attempting to stanch the flow of blood and giving him oxygen before rushing him to Miriam Hospital. The emergency room there was alerted to his imminent arrival. As of midnight, doctors at the hospital would say only that Cardella's condition was extremely grave, and he was still in the intensive care unit. As yet, no one has described the extent of the injuries inflicted on him by the gunshot.

Cohen's column raised the strong probability that Niro was slain as a result of his bookmaking activities. "Everyone knows that the Tarantino family has a stranglehold on gambling in Providence and most of Rhode Island," it read. "It remains for the police to find out whether or not the order for Niro's murder came from Federal Hill."

Cohen indicated that everyone in Chi-Chi's at the time was being questioned to see if they could come up with a more complete description of the assailant. His final comments referred to "Cardella's bad luck in having been called to the telephone just before the executioner passed through the bar, intent on ending Niro's life."

63

Five days later, on the last Sunday before the primaries, the *Herald* endorsed Bruce Singer as the Democratic nominee for governor. The editorial listed the accomplishments to which June Bates could point with pride during her years in the House. It also commented favorably on the continuing trend that was seeing more women attempt to move into the highest positions of leadership throughout the country. But it gave seven different reasons for supporting Singer's candidacy, including his years of experience as lieutenant governor.

The *Herald* did not endorse either Richie Cardella or Doug Fiore on the Republican side. "This is the first time in our newspaper's history, since we began supporting one candidate over another that we have failed to take a position. The unusual circumstances facing us demand such a result."

Still, the editorial felt the need to point out that Cardella's condition remained critical. "His doctors will not even venture a guess as to when he might be released from intensive care. Obviously, any recovery will take an unknown and indefinite amount of time. It's a foregone conclusion that he'd be unable to campaign any further, were he to win the primary. Moreover, were Cardella somehow to be successful in both the primary and general elections, the citizens of Rhode Island must realize that whoever is elected to the office of lieutenant governor might well be at the helm of State government for an extended period of time."

The fairness and statesmanship Fiore showed by essentially terminating his own campaign as soon as Cardella was struck down was remarked upon in the piece. The editorial also emphasized that based on Fiore's stated positions, there was no issue of prime importance to the people of the State on which the *Herald* editors would speak against his election.

Cyril Berman was elated when he finished reading the commentary. The polls had tightened up in the last few days, as they normally did. News analysts on both radio and television, referring to the margin of error in the different results, were saying that the race was virtually a dead heat. Berman felt that the substance of the *Herald*'s non-endorsement was an effort to encourage Republicans to throw their support behind Fiore in the primary. The newspaper clearly hoped to have a candidate who was in a position to wage an all-out battle against Bruce Singer for the governorship of the State. He expected it to be enough to tip the election their way.

Berman started to dial Fiore's telephone number, to let him know how good he felt about the latest development. Halfway through he stopped, realizing that Doug would probably respond by saying that he hoped Cyril was right. Despite the praise heaped on Fiore in the editorial for discontinuing the campaign when he did, there would be no recognition of the good advice Cyril gave him. Instead, Doug was sure to say that if he lost, they would have only Berman to blame for not taking advantage of Cardella's disability. It was too nice a day to let it get spoiled that way, Berman thought. He hung up the phone and got ready to go to breakfast.

64

It rained hard throughout the State on primary day, and the turnout of voters was affected to a greater degree than usual. All of the candidates had their sign carriers out in force. They stood in raincoats and other foul weather gear on the sidewalks in front of the polling places. They were spotted at any number of strategic locations, including highway overpasses, bridge crossings and main street intersections. There, they waved at passing automobiles and solicited votes for the candidates they supported from anyone within earshot.

The media did whatever exit polling it could. Its members discovered, however, that few voters were willing to take the time to discuss their choices once outside the election site. Instead, they ran off to their cars or the closest place they could find to stay dry. The limited response was deemed insufficient by radio and TV reporters to risk predicting the primary results of the governor's race prior to the closing of the polls.

Berman and Walsh spent the morning putting the final touches on the victory speech they drafted for Fiore after the *Herald* published its Sunday edition. They knew they had to include a short prayer for Cardella, and finally made up their minds to insert it at the end.

Berman decided not to spend any time working on a full-blown concession statement. But he noted a number of items he would want Fiore to mention if it unexpectedly came to that. He knew that in a certain number of key precincts the votes would be counted within an hour of the poll closings at 8:00 p.m. If Cardella bested Fiore in those locations, Cyril would still have time to put together an appropriate statement for Doug to read to his disappointed campaign workers and supporters.

The critical factors in the election turned out to be those that Berman had predicted. They were the uncertainty of Cardella's physical condition and the "good guy" image Fiore picked up by refusing to campaign after his rival was hospitalized. The inclement weather that lasted throughout the day also aided their cause. Fiore's organization made thousands of phone calls and drove hundreds of his supporters to local school buildings, veterans' halls and senior citizen centers where the election machinery was set up. They did whatever it took to get out the vote.

By 9:30 at night, the TV election coverage on several networks showed Fiore ahead by just 51 to 49 percent. Political analysts were telling viewers that the outcome was still "too close to call." But Berman knew they had won. The entire last hour was spent taking telephone calls from campaign representatives around the State. He compared the vote counts he was being given from the most important precincts with the numbers he and Walsh worked out much earlier—numbers that spelled triumph or disaster, depending on the support the candidate was receiving. A blackboard was set up in Berman's suite, and Walsh constantly updated the figures as Cyril called out the reports he was given on the phone.

While that was taking place, Lester Karp handled the barrage of telephone calls from supporters and news agencies that came in on the other line in the suite. Karp's wife was there also, and when not joining Grace Fiore on the sofa to watch the news, she stayed busy serving drinks and snacks to everyone there.

As the euphoria built, Berman became anxious. "We may have to wait until close to midnight for a concession," he told Walsh. "I suspect Cardella's wife will be at their headquarters at the Marriott to handle it."

Walsh was more optimistic. "If they're getting the same information from their polling place spotters that we are, they know it's all over. It makes no sense for them to drag it out for hours."

Fiore was too excited to sit still. He walked back and forth across the living area of the Biltmore suite like a tiger in a cage, his head turned to the TV from wherever he stood. Occasionally, he shouted out a "Yahoo" or slapped Berman's shoulder when a particularly gratifying vote count was announced. He stopped a few times behind the sofa where Grace was sitting, resting his hands on her shoulders and rooting himself on. As the percentages began to increase in his favor, he massaged his wife's neck with his fingers. "You're halfway to becoming the 'First Lady' of Rhode Island," he told her. At Berman's suggestion, he went into the bedroom shortly after ten o'clock and practiced delivering his victory speech.

An hour later, Fiore finally got to direct his remarks to a Biltmore ballroom jammed with his family, friends and campaign workers. What required just twelve minutes to get through each time he rehearsed it, took more than twice as long when he stood in front of the cheering throng. At times it seemed as if the young volunteers hollering "Fi-o-re, Fi-o-re" over and over again would never let him reach the end. At the completion of his speech, he told the audience that he wanted everyone to be silent while he said a prayer for Richie Cardella. When he asked God's blessing for his opponent, there wasn't a dry eye in the room, and probably the same in any home throughout the State still tuned in to the coverage on TV.

The final election figures, excluding about two thousand mail ballots that would take several days to count, were tabulated by three o'clock Wednesday afternoon. They showed that Fiore received almost 54 percent of the vote. The negative side was that only 18,000 registered Republicans cast ballots. That was almost 17 percent less than the number that was predicted on the basis of the usual turnout.

On the Democratic side, Bruce Singer picked up a very comfortable 58 percent of the vote in defeating June Bates. Thanking the voters and his campaign workers for their support, Singer got a resounding applause when he announced that his campaign for governor wasn't taking a single day off. He promised to be out greeting the busloads of commuters as they arrived in Kennedy Plaza early the next morning.

In the post-election-day study of all the returns that he made on Wednesday, Berman noted that the drop-off among registered Democrats from the number expected to vote was only four percent. He felt certain that a similar result among Republicans would have meant defeat for Fiore. The conclusion he reached was that the huge number of Republicans who stayed home preferred to see Cardella represent their party in the general election. They were smart enough, however, to know that the fates had conspired against his being able to do so.

Berman complimented himself on managing a good campaign to that point. Walsh and Karp came by his room and praised him for a job well done. Each brought a bottle of Cyril's favorite Scotch. Sandy Tarantino called to congratulate him and offer continued support in the weeks ahead. By the time Berman pulled the drapes closed in his bedroom in midafternoon and lay down for a nap, he still hadn't heard a word from Fiore.

* * *

When the people of Rhode Island woke up on Thursday morning and turned on their radios and TV sets as they got ready for work, they learned that Richie Cardella passed away during the night. Only then did the doctors who treated him reveal the full extent of the bullet wounds to his chest. The general consensus among them was that only a miracle let him survive for over nine days.

Saddened by the news, Berman had two thoughts when he heard the announcement. The second one was that legislation of some sort should be introduced to require a candidate's physician to submit a written report of the status of that individual's health when the candidate entered a race for any statewide or federal office; that such a report should leave out nothing that was even potentially life threatening and be made available to the public through the media; and that it be immediately updated in the event of any accident or illness suffered by the candidate that came to the doctor's attention prior to the election.

His first thought was that he should arrange for Fiore to be a pallbearer at Cardella's funeral.

65

The police investigation into the shooting of Al Niro at Chi-Chi's was going nowhere. Since Niro was just a bookie, that fact was not of much concern in the City of Providence until the same incident also claimed the life of Richie Cardella. Suddenly, it became an "outrageous crime," as the nearby *Woonsocket Star* began calling it.

About a dozen people who were in the bar at the time were brought to police headquarters and shown mug shots of hundreds of ex-convicts. None, however, saw a face that made them believe, even for a moment, that they were looking at a photograph of the killer. Each of the potential witnesses sat down with a police artist and described what he or she remembered from a quick glimpse of the young man as he strode past their booths. The composite drawing that resulted from the information was all that Providence's finest had to go on.

Jenna Richardson spoke to Dan McMurphy about working on the story on the very first day. He was quick to refuse. "You're writing political stuff, Jenna, you're not on the crime beat. It's Cohen's jurisdiction. One reporter on the story is enough."

She was back in McMurphy's office the day Cardella died, pressing her case again. "You've got to let me chase down this story, Dan. Cardella was running for governor. That puts it in my territory."

"I don't see it that way," he said. "It's just an accidental connection, not a political story on its own."

"Not so," she shot back. "His death affects the whole race. There's going to be a lot of 'what ifs' right through the election and even after it's over." Jenna got up and stood next to Dan's desk. "I'll make a deal with you," she said.

"What is it?"

"If the police don't come up with a substantial lead in one more week, and if Nate Cohen can't produce any new information to justify keeping the story in the paper, I get a crack at it."

McMurphy sat back in his chair, clasped his hands behind his neck and stared up at the ceiling. The time seemed like an eternity to her. When he agreed, the proviso he extracted was that she continue giving him a good column, three days a week, on the general election.

66

AT FIRST CYRIL BERMAN gave Fiore three days to rest up after the primary. He intended to revise their schedule, he said, and indicated that they would plunge into the general election campaign on Saturday. But when Cardella succumbed and his funeral mass was scheduled to take place the following Monday, Berman called on the telephone and informed Fiore that they wouldn't get started until Cardella was laid to rest.

It was the first time they spoke to each other since Doug left Cyril's suite at 1:30 a.m. Wednesday morning, after shaking hundreds of hands in the Biltmore ballroom.

"We'll have exactly six weeks to go to the election. Expect to work very hard, and don't do anything you might regret afterwards."

Fiore laughed. "Didn't I hear that once before in a big black limousine?" he asked.

"I have a tendency to repeat myself," Berman answered. "I'll try and avoid that when I write my 'How to Run for Governor and Win' book. Meanwhile, Doug, you're going to be a pallbearer at the funeral and I'd like you to spend as much time as you can at the wake both days. A lot of important people are going to be passing through that funeral parlor. We want Cardella's supporters to be there for you in November, not sitting on the sidelines again. Remember, they feel cheated because they're sure he'd have won if nothing happened to him. It's going to be harder than usual to get them interested in coming over to your side, as much as they might hate Singer. So shake as many hands as you can, but be diplomatic. Don't say anything about the election unless they bring it up."

"I'll do whatever you say, Cyril. In case it hasn't hit you yet, I want to win this thing. As of Tuesday night, Bruce Singer became the biggest sonofabitch in the world." A moment later he asked, "Will you be there Monday?"

"Probably not. I'm not too comfortable in a church."

"Then maybe you ought to make sure ahead of time that I get to hold the casket up front, preferably with my left hand. The photographers usually start shooting as soon as the pallbearers come out the front door. That way, everyone who reads about it will know I was there."

"Good thought," Berman said. "I'll make a call." He waited a few seconds, giving Fiore a chance to remember to thank him for the ideas that won the primary for them. But there was nothing more said. He hung up and smiled. At least his ungrateful student was beginning to understand the course.

* * *

Despite Berman's warning, Fiore used some of the time off to socialize.

On Friday night, after spending almost two hours alone in his office working on a speech, he drove to the Hilton near Green Airport to meet Carol. He parked at the rear of the building, entered by the side door and walked up the stairs to the third floor. Carol reserved the room under a false name, paid for it in cash when she checked in, and informed him earlier where she would be. When he hung up his jacket in the closet, Doug took four 20-dollar bills out of his wallet and slipped them into the pocket of her raincoat.

He learned during the course of their affair that her mood was usually unpredictable. "How do you feel?" he asked. It struck him that the question was beginning to sound like a broken record.

"Like maybe killing myself," Carol said. But her words weren't followed by the burst of tears normally expected after an answer of that kind. In fact, seeing that she was in complete control of herself, he tested the waters to see whether her disposition was unalterably gloomy and sex was out of the question. "I think that if you've made up your mind to stop seeing me, it would be a shame not to make love one last time."

Doug was sitting on the side of the bed, Carol in the chair farthest from him. Her answer came as a welcome relief. "I didn't say anything about not having sex. But I've been asking myself all week how I could possibly be in this stupid predicament. I'm married to one man running for governor and having an affair with his opponent. It's ridiculous, Doug. It's like something you'd read in a trashy romance novel and never believe. But here it is happening to me. I just don't know if I can cope with it. Maybe I ought to take a leave of absence from the firm and go live on the Cape until the election's over."

Carol turned toward the window as she finished speaking. Fiore waited for her to look back at him. "How are things going at home?" he asked.

"A little worse every day," she said. "Sometimes it's his fault, usually it's mine. Bruce thinks everything will get back to normal between us after the election, whether he wins or loses. He's convinced that he can keep our marriage from going on the rocks. He never thinks about holding my hand, only shaking every other one in Rhode Island. I'm sure he doesn't even let himself consider the idea of a divorce. Do you think he'd believe me if I told him I was sleeping with someone else?"

If the mood were lighter he would have said, "Only if you don't shower before you go home." But Fiore had thought about what would happen to their relationship if he became governor, and knew that this part of it would be over. He hoped that in that case she'd be able to straighten things out with Bruce.

"This is Bruce's mountain, Carol," he said. "You can't just turn him around and point him in another direction."

She understood the analogy. "I know I can't, but I don't have to stay with a man who's ready to risk my happiness every time he feels he has to go climbing. If he ever gets to the top, he can stay there alone as far as I'm concerned. I can't breathe the air up there."

It was getting late. "I have an important question to ask you," he said.

"What is it?"

"Come over here first."

Carol sat down next to him on the bed. "Well?"

"You'll have to kiss me," Doug said, keeping a serious face. "I need strength to come out with it."

Carol leaned her head toward his and started to kiss his lips softly. But he pushed hard against hers, and in seconds their arms were around each other. They kissed for a long time until she pulled away from him. "You don't have anything to ask me, do you?"

"Of course I do. I just needed that kiss."

She had no idea what to expect. It even scared her a little. "Then ask," she said softly.

"Okay," he said, but took a deep breath first and let it out loudly through his mouth. "Have you decided which of us you're going to vote for?"

She smiled slowly, watching his eyes. Then he smiled and they laughed at the same time. For several minutes their laughter was uncontrollable. When it finally came to a stop, they were both ready to get started with what they came for.

67

On sunday afternoon Fiore took his wife apple picking. He felt he owed Grace a good time, and knew he'd need her help even more when the campaign got into high gear. Two or three televised debates with Singer were being arranged, and Doug wanted Grace to be present at all of them to project a warm family image He wondered if Carol would show up with Bruce. Probably not, he decided. *Still,* he thought, *it wouldn't hurt to find a way to convince her to stay home, just in case. Do whatever it takes to win,* he told himself. That was his watchword now, although still in the context of waging a clean campaign. He reasoned that it was in Carol's best interest for her husband to lose, but he certainly wasn't going to say or do anything that would put pressure on her to avoid being there.

"How come you're so relaxed when you know Singer is out there working today?" Grace asked. They were driving along a country road, about twenty miles south of East Greenwich. The oaks and maples were just beginning to show their fall colors.

Doug took his right hand off the wheel of the Camry, Grace's car, and put it on her knee. "I don't care what Singer's doing today," he answered. "I'm with you and I'm happy, so let's not talk any politics today." He ran his hand along her thigh. She put her own hand on top of his briefly, but then pushed his away when she began to get aroused.

Fiore noticed a sign pointing toward a church fair and pulled off the road. They bought and shared a homemade brownie before perusing the merchandise laid out on long tables in the church vestry. Doug checked out some old 78 RPM record albums and wandered around the used clothing tables that were in an adjoining room. He found a white corduroy baseball cap with a University of Southern California football logo on it, and purchased it for a quarter. Grace caught up with him, looked at the cap and said she didn't think the rust colored stains on the brim would wash off.

They stopped for a light dinner back in East Greenwich. Fiore was beginning to feel the effect of the three Macintosh apples he ate while they filled a 10-pound bag in the Sunny Farm orchard that afternoon. Grace saw a number of people in the restaurant glancing their way during the meal, and several of the diners stopped by their table on the way out to wish him good luck.

"Too bad about Richie Cardella," one of them remarked.

Doug shook his head in agreement. "Yeah," was all he replied. *That's probably what Cyril was talking about,* he thought to himself. *I've got to put on my sad face whenever someone mentions poor Richie's name. Just make believe he was my good friend. Do anything to win the election.*

Grace went into the den to watch television just after they got home. A few minutes later she called Doug to join her. He said he'd be there shortly, that he just wanted to rest for a while. He went to the bedroom and got under the covers without taking off his jeans or his shirt.

Fiore remembered later that in his dream he was making a movie with Miss October, whose nude pictures he saw recently in the latest issue of *Playboy*. They were filming a love scene in bed. The director was standing just a few feet away, next to a cameraman, telling them what to do second by second. The klieg lights were bringing out tiny pebbles of sweat on both of them. He recalled the director whispering to his bedmate to look suggestively toward Doug's groin and to start moving her body in that direction. "Don't worry, the camera won't follow you," he told her. Just then, Doug's ejaculation woke him up. Almost an hour had passed. He could feel the wetness in his shorts and on the inside of his thigh.

"Damn it!" He said the words out loud. He knew Grace would be coming to bed soon, and now he wasn't sure whether he could get hard again. The last thing he wanted was a repeat of those nights when he tried to make love to her but couldn't. He dreaded going through the same embarrassment again.

Doug washed up and put on his pajamas. He sat down next to Grace in the den and put his arm around her. He let several minutes go by before telling her he wasn't feeling well, that it must be the apples. "I was tossing and turning the whole time," he said, "and sweating a little. I took a couple of aspirins and think I'd better try to get a good night's sleep." He kissed his wife on the cheek. "I'll take a rain check and promise to use it tomorrow or Tuesday."

Grace nodded, without looking away from the TV. "Okay," was all she said.

He got up and started to leave the room. Turning around for a moment, he told her, "I sure as hell don't want to look sick for the photographers at Richie's funeral tomorrow."

68

Pat Hanley met him in Room 606 on Monday night. Fiore first took the elevator to the bar at L'Apogee on the top floor of the Biltmore. He sipped a Grand Marnier over ice while talking baseball to the bartender and a stranger who recognized him.

"I just seen you on the news in my room an hour ago," the man said. "At Cardella's funeral, I mean. You look better in person than on TV."

Fiore thanked him, asked where he was from, and said he needed his vote on election day. He finished his drink, left a 10-dollar bill on the bar and took a few more peanuts from the bowl on his way out.

Pat was in great spirits. Her afternoon was spent in town, shopping at the mall and then joining a friend for an early dinner at "Cafe Prov," in the lobby of the Patriot National Bank Building. Afterwards, she returned to the Biltmore for a leisurely bath. When Doug arrived, she was just pouring herself a second drink.

"Brad flew to Ohio this morning to see some customers," she said. "He'll be away overnight."

"How's he doing?"

"He's still putting in too many evening hours at the plant."

Fiore remembered what he learned from Sandy Tarantino about Hanley's regular visits to one of the Family's clubs. It wasn't the right time to mention it to Pat.

"I'm so happy that business is much better this year than last," she said. "Brad used to worry about how it would be almost impossible for him to find a job with another wire or steel company if Ocean State ever shut down. That would be a disaster for us."

"Why such a disaster?" he asked. "You could sell that big house, move into something a lot smaller in the burbs and Brad would have plenty of time to look around."

Pat sipped from her drink and pushed the bottle on the coffee table closer to Doug. "It's not what it all seems, my love. Some guy said that in a book I read. At least I think he did . . . Actually, I'm not really sure if I read it or heard it." They both laughed. "The truth is, Doug, we've got hardly any equity in that place. There's a second mortgage with a finance company, and a large part of the deposit we put down was money borrowed from my parents. If we had to sell it right now, we'd have very little left for ourselves. Besides, it's probably worth only eighty percent of what we paid for it nine years ago. The market was moving toward its peak back then. So buddy, can you spare a dime?"

She flashed a smile at him. "But now isn't the time to worry," she continued. "Not when the wire machines at Ocean State are running two full shifts a day and the numbers on the bottom line are changing color. Things are looking better every month, thanks to Brad."

Fiore considered telling her what was really going on, how poorly Ocean State was still doing, but he knew that would kill the evening. He felt quite certain that Pat wouldn't expect him to be aware of the Company's monthly profit and loss statements. Besides, if the Platt brothers did decide to give up on the business, he knew she'd be too busy blaming Brad for lying to her to start wondering whether Doug knew enough about it to warn her when they were together. He'd let her know the truth when the time was right.

"Here's to Brad," he said, and reached over toward Pat so they could let their glasses touch and clink.

"Well, Mr. Fiore, now that the odds of my sleeping with the next governor of Rhode Island have gone from one in three to one in two, I think it's time for me to place another bet."

"Sure thing," Doug said. He got up and began taking off his tie. Then he smiled at his choice of words. "You're betting on a sure thing."

69

On the night of the second day after Richardson began her own investigation of the murders by talking to Felipe Gonsalez at Chi-Chi's, she was in bed with Terry Reardon. Their room at the Holiday Inn was rented by the *Herald* on an annual basis. They were last together a couple of weeks before the primary. Jenna's energy level was jumping off the chart. She didn't want to meet Terry at her apartment that night because she intended to do more work in the *Herald* library on the Chi-Chi killing—as she referred to it—after he left to go home.

The room was dark, unlike Jenna's own bedroom where one of the shades could not be pulled more than halfway down and let in the light from a street lamp. Lying on her side, she pulled herself close to him, her face just a few inches from his as they talked. "The cops think it's all cut and dried," she said. "They figure the Tarantino family didn't want Niro horning in on any of their business and gave someone the word to put him away."

"That's just about the way I see it," he answered.

"Wait a minute. Don't interrupt until I've told you everything." She waited until he nodded his head and gave her an okay. "The first thing I found out from Gonsalez is that this is the fourth year in a row Al Niro has come into the place and set up shop in that booth across from the pay phone. He was always there for about six months at a stretch. It started when the NFL exhibition games got under way, sometime late in July, and went to the Super Bowl in February. That was always his last day in the place, Gonsalez said. He never took bets on the Pro Bowl because he knew the players didn't care who won.

"The second thing is that Niro was just a small time operator. He used to schmooze with the customers sitting at the bar before he went home. Once in a while he bought drinks for whoever was there, Gonsalez said. He told them he never took a bet over a hundred dollars from one person. He had a bunch of people who called him every week, mostly with 20-dollar bets, or even less, on one or two games. That was the kind of situation he felt comfortable handling. Niro didn't lay off any of the bets he took with other bookies because he never handled the kind of wagers he had to worry about. Both Gonsalez and Niro's wife told me that. He just wanted to run a small independent business without having to go to someone else for help."

Jenna had picked up a head of steam. "Mrs. Niro—her name is Camille, by the way, and she's a beautiful woman—said that it was like a part-time job for him. It let him earn a few extra dollars during the football season. His main business was doing landscape maintenance with the truck he owned. He mowed lawns in the summer, picked up leaves in the fall, plowed snow out of driveways during the winter and went back to lawn work in the spring. There were one or two kids in his neighborhood who used to help him out.

"Another thing his wife told me is that Niro had a few friends in the city who've been booking bets the same way he did for years. It's usually out of a bar, just the way he operated. She didn't want to come right out with any names, but she mentioned a few places I could go have a drink and look around. They do it the same five nights her husband used to be at Chi-Chi's. She says none of them have stopped since he was killed."

"But maybe none of them were ever warned, the way Niro was," Terry said.

"That's another thing," Jenna answered, changing her position to lean on her elbow while she still looked at him. "Camille insisted that he never said a word about receiving any kind of warning, and she's positive he wouldn't keep it from her if he did. She told me he was the type who'd say, 'If anything happens to me while I'm out, tell the cops that so and so threatened me on such and such a date.' After I spoke to her, I checked it out with Gonsalez. He never heard Niro talk about a threat from anyone either."

Reardon didn't think much of Jenna's last point. "Niro probably never got around to telling her. Maybe he thought it was a joke. I can't see why the killer would have said it if it never happened."

"I don't want to argue with you," Jenna replied. "Let me just summarize."

"Okay, okay, but don't take all night."

"We have a small-time bookie, handling peanuts every week, and he's been doing it for four years. He gets shot one night in a downtown bar. This is a place where anything could have suddenly gone wrong for whoever did it. Another car, for example, could have blocked the back alley at the last minute. So there's a big risk there. The cops don't have anyone in their books who looks like the guy the artist drew up from the witnesses' descriptions. The Tarantino family doesn't have to say a word because the police haven't come up with any evidence against them and haven't made any arrests. But they do. They send a letter to the Chief of Police telling him they didn't know about Niro's little operation and couldn't have cared less if they did. According to them, the Family had nothing to do with what happened at Chi-Chi's."

"That's the first I heard about the letter. Was that in the paper?"

"No, but trust me. No one's supposed to know about it."

"Do you believe what it says?" Terry asked.

"I have trouble not believing it," she answered. "I mean if they wanted the guy out of the way for booking football bets, they could have done it at any time. Wouldn't you figure they'd pick a spot where no one was around? Why take that chance in a bar? What was suddenly the big hurry after four years?"

"I don't know," he answered. "What you say makes sense. But I'm suddenly in a big hurry myself, after four weeks. If you don't want to do something right away, *you* may be taking a chance. Know what I mean?"

"Hold on, big fella," she said, lying back so that he could move onto her. "No shooting wildly in the dark, not while I'm around."

70

On the following morning, Richardson called Chief Quinn at Police Headquarters in Providence and asked if she could see him. (She told Terry sometime later that the idea of talking to Quinn had come to her just as she had an orgasm at the Holiday Inn the night before.) He checked his calendar and offered her a choice of eleven o'clock that morning or four in the afternoon. Jenna said she was in the middle of some research and took the second option.

Eight hours later, she was in his office. "Hi, Gerry," she said, when a young police officer ushered her into the big room overlooking Lasalle Square.

"Hiya, Jenna, good to see ya. How do ya like the bullshit circuit they've gotcha on? I'll bet ya bored to tears with all these pols. Always talking outta both sides of their mouths. Oh, excuse me, I want ya to meet Joe Gaudette."

Quinn continued talking as Richardson and Gaudette approached each other and shook hands. "Joe here is from the State Police. I called over to get some help on this Al Niro case, ya know, figuring the Tarantinos run gambling all over Rhode Island, and we could sure use some help in trying to find the killer. I was just telling Joe about ya before ya came in, how ya've got one helluva talent for putting the pieces of a puzzle together. So, is what ya wanna see me about private, or can Joe stick around?"

She explained that she was there about the Niro case herself, and invited Gaudette to stay and listen. Quinn leaned back in his big chair, ready to hear what she had to say. Jenna told him that for openers she wanted to read the letter he received from the Tarantino family. "What letter?" Quinn demanded, sitting straight up immediately.

"Sorry, Gerry, but I heard about it from an old friend who works in the post office. He said he stamped it himself." She winked at him.

Quinn shook his head in frustration, saying nothing. It upset him to learn that someone already leaked news of the letter.

Jenna waited for him to sit back and relax again before saying that she hoped he could help her speak to one of the Tarantinos herself. This time, Quinn showed no reaction at all.

"Let me tell you why," she said, and proceeded to lay out everything she told Reardon while they were in bed the night before. When she finished informing them of what she uncovered in her investigation to that point, both men were silent. Jenna glanced from one to the other and continued. "Last night I started some research in the *Herald* library and just about wrapped it up before walking over here."

"I hope they're paying ya overtime," Quinn cut in.

"From your lips to God's ears," Jenna said.

The two men smiled at her.

"Think about this, Gerry. You can go back twenty years, almost to the day that Sal Tarantino took over on the Hill, and you won't find a single homicide that the Family was ever charged with committing, directly or indirectly. That's not the way it was when Tony Buscatelli ran things. A number of his guys were convicted over the years. Tony himself stood trial twice for allegedly giving the order that got two of his enemies tossed into Narragansett Bay wearing heavy overshoes. He got a hung jury both times and the DA didn't want to try for a third. The papers said he was lucky. Later on there were stories that one of the jurors in each trial was bribed to hold out for an acquittal."

"I remember both them trials like it was yesterday," Quinn said. "Don't remind me. I was right there in the courtroom both times. I can still see the shit-eating grin Buscatelli had on his face when the judge told him he was free to go. You remember that, Joe?"

Gaudette, sitting almost erect in a straight-backed wooden chair, nodded affirmatively. "Wish I didn't, but I do," he answered.

"In fact, Gerry," Jenna continued, "what comes out of the *Herald*'s files is that the Tarantinos have gotten away from the kinds of things

Buscatelli had a big hand in. I'm talking drugs and prostitution, mainly. You'd know that better than anyone. It looks like now they concentrate all their efforts on gambling and want nothing to do with street crime. Is it okay to say that the Mob has cleaned up its act?" She smiled at him.

Quinn didn't answer directly. "So what's this getting us to?" he wanted to know.

"I don't think the Tarantinos had anything to do with Niro's death." She spoke the words in a matter of fact tone. "What happened doesn't fit their pattern at all. But like that old saying goes, 'It takes a thief to know one.' I want the chance to go over this case with them. They may have a feeling about what happened. They could say something that means nothing to them but gives me a lead to go on. My guess is that they'd love to see this Chi-Chi killing get solved A-S-A-P. That's the only way the bad publicity they're getting will go away." Jenna paused. "What do you say, can I read the letter?"

"Ya welcome to look at it, provided I don't see one word about it in ya paper."

"Agreed," she said.

That was good enough for Quinn. He picked up the telephone, dialed a single digit and instructed someone to bring in the Niro file. "And I gotta figure out who coulda leaked it," he said, hanging up the phone. Quinn got up, stretched his arms above his head and sat down again. "But," he continued, "getting Sal Tarantino or his son to talk to ya may be impossible. The only talking they've ever done in the years I've been in this chair is through a lawyer. Maybe if I mention getting their letter it would help. What the hell, I'll give it a shot and let ya know."

A police sergeant came in with the large file. Quinn removed the two heavy elastics from either end, opened it and picked up the document sitting on top. He handed it to Jenna. She read it carefully and saw it was signed by Sandy Tarantino.

"How old is the son, and what does he do?" she asked.

"Mid-forties. Sorta the general manager over there from what I hear," Quinn replied.

She returned the letter and thanked Quinn for his time. She gave him a *Herald* card with her extension at work and her home telephone number. "Just in case you threw away the last one," she said.

"Do ya have enough left for the guys at the singles bar?" he asked her. "I can just copy these numbers down, ya know." Quinn smiled at her and looked over at Gaudette. The State Police officer got up from his chair, but looked serious.

"I'm very impressed with your analysis of this case," he told Jenna, approaching her again for a farewell handshake. "If I were Sal Tarantino and heard about what you told us today, I'd want to meet you. Good luck, Miss Richardson."

* * *

Jenna's horoscope that Friday morning said she would be meeting an interesting stranger. A sometime believer in the stars, she gave it two hours to happen in the Twin Oaks lounge on the way home from work. Back in her car, she consoled herself with the thought that the would-be object of her affections was there, but that they simply missed each other. Arriving home at nine o'clock, she looked through the mail, turned on the radio and put a package of frozen broccoli in the tiny microwave before remembering to check for telephone messages.

There was only one, but it made up for her earlier disappointment.

"Hiya Jenna, it's Gerry Quinn. Would ya believe it? Some guy called me back today for young Tarantino, just when I'd given up hearing from them. Said he'd meet with ya but it has to be off the record. He can do it Tuesday morning, nine o'clock, if ya get outta the sack that early. His place is at 241 Atwells Avenue, next door to the Abruzzi Bakery. Ya gotta walk up a long flight of stairs. There's a parking lot further down that block and around the corner. Ya owe me one for this." There was a short pause before Quinn continued. "As they say on Federal Hill, 'Ciao, baby.'"

Jenna called Dan McMurphy at the *Herald*. He always stayed late on Friday night, as if unwilling to let the job get away from him for the weekend.

"It's a good thing you're seeing him when you are," McMurphy said. "I just got through assigning you full-time, starting Wednesday, to hit the road with the major campaigns. That's Wednesday through Monday, the fifth through the tenth."

He wanted her to follow the two US Senate candidates, Sacco and Whitley, for a day each and do the same with Singer and Fiore right after that. She'd finish the job by getting a look at the incumbents and challengers for the two seats in the House of Representatives over the last two days of her road trip. He didn't care about the fact that Tarantino might give her something to go on in the Niro case when she visited the Family's headquarters on Tuesday.

"There's an old saying about 'a bird in the hand,' Jenna. Maybe you heard it. I think Dolph Jameson, my predecessor, was the one who first made it up." Then he got serious. "Listen, we've got to run some in-depth stories about these campaigns. I'm talking at least a full page for each one, and I need all of it in a couple of weeks. After that, you'll have more time to shoot for the Pulitzer Prize on the Niro business. That's the deal, and it's final." McMurphy let a couple of seconds pass before he added, "Agreed?"

"Thanks for the choice, Dan," she answered. She hoped her good-natured sarcasm struck the right chord. "But as long as you brought it up, do you want to give any odds on my getting that Pulitzer?"

"If I lose, can I pay it off over a year?"

"Six months."

"Sorry, I can't afford it."

71

At the top of the stairway, twenty-four steps up, another door greeted her. A foot above it, a security camera pointed down toward the street entrance. Richardson assumed she was being watched on a monitor since first ringing the bell and gaining entrance from Atwells Avenue. Once again, when a buzzer responded to her ring, she pushed the door open and went inside.

Her first reaction was one of surprise to how old and uninviting a reception area it was. There was just one small window in the room, facing the street. A plain walnut desk, somewhat beat up, sat a few feet away from the window, a matching chair behind it. The top of the desk was bare except for an old black rotary telephone, an empty plastic tray with a paper In label taped to its front and a magazine, entitled *NFL Football*. No rug or carpeting was there to hide the well-worn hardwood floor. Several other wooden chairs, each with a cheap gray vinyl seat pad tied to it, were placed along the wall that continued forward from the entrance. The pale green walls of the room were entirely bare, although some discoloring in several places indicated the size of a picture or poster that once occupied the space. Richardson sat down in the chair farthest from where she entered. She could see several offices off a hallway to the right and realized they were located directly above the Abruzzi Bakery and its adjoining cafe.

Just then, Sandy Tarantino walked into the waiting room and introduced himself, adding, "Most everyone calls me Sandy," as he shook hands with her. He led Jenna back to his office, the closest one to the waiting room. The contrast with the area in which they met startled her. A large oriental rug covered most of the floor space. Its deep pile made her wish she could take her shoes off and experience the luxury. Matching bookcases, made of a dark lacquered wood, lined the walls of the room except for the space behind Tarantino's desk. There, a single large venetian blind covered the only window in the office. Its slats were tightly shut to keep the light out. A lamp, with a Tiffany style glass shade, sat on the corner of Tarantino's busy desk, providing the work area of the room with sufficient illumination. A table, several feet from the desk, held a computer, a printer and a fax machine. Jenna noticed that two of the bookcases near Tarantino were filled with numbered volumes containing the cases decided by the Supreme Court of Rhode Island.

Once inside the office, he opened a door to the adjoining room. "Jenna Richardson is here, Pop," he said. She noticed that the son waited in the doorway until his father came in, then closed the door behind him.

"I'm Sal Tarantino," the older man said as he approached her, not offering his hand in greeting. Again, Sandy waited to see where his father sat before pointing to a chair for Jenna. She sensed that it would have been perfectly natural for Sal to make himself at home behind his son's desk, establishing his authority in that manner. But he chose a side chair instead, and Sandy did the same. The two of them sat facing her, just a few feet away.

Jenna was struck by the differences in their appearance. Sal Tarantino, probably close to seventy she guessed, was tall and almost slim. A Pendleton style shirt and a pair of khaki pants with a large silver belt buckle lent a cowboy's masculinity to his appearance. He walked erectly and sat the same way. His hair, receding at the forehead but gray only at the fringes, was slicked down with pomade. He was clean shaven, despite the fact that a beard would have hidden a series of unsightly red splotches that ran along the lower edges of his cheeks. But it was the senior Tarantino's eyes that riveted Jenna's attention to him. They were coal black, reflecting no light whatsoever, and seemed overly protected under almost semicircular thick hairy eyebrows.

The younger Tarantino, on the other hand, was both shorter and heavier than his father. He had a neat beard and mustache, but a bald spot in the middle of his head appeared to be advancing steadily toward the curly black hairline in front. He wore eyeglasses whose tinted lenses hid the true color of his eyes. Jenna wondered whether those eyes would have the same effect on her as his father's. Sandy countered Sal's casual look by being dressed in a traditional businesslike manner, his well-tailored suit receiving her unspoken admiration.

"Is it agreed that this discussion is off the record, that you won't report meeting with us?" Sal asked.

"Of course," Jenna answered. She felt as if he was staring right through her.

"Chief Quinn says you have a view of the Niro murder he thought we'd be interested in hearing," Sandy said, to open the conversation.

Jenna said that was right, and when both men answered her with silence she proceeded to tell them everything she related to Quinn and Gaudette a week earlier.

"Since then," she continued, "I also found out that Niro was using two all-night self-service gas stations in Providence for his pickups and deliveries. If you lost, you put your name and the cash you owed inside a sealed envelope and left it with someone at the station within two days. Whoever was on duty gave you a receipt for the envelope with his initials and that day's date on it. Niro did the same thing with a payoff, except he just wrote the customer's name on the outside of the envelope. I spoke to the attendants at each place. They told me the cars pulling in for that business were usually Chevys and Toyotas, not Lincolns and Lexuses. To me, that confirms the fact he was dealing with small bettors."

"I congratulate you on that entire analysis, Miss Richardson," Sandy said, when she finished. "We agree with your conclusion and are pleased to know we've got someone like you on our side." He looked toward his father at that moment. "I'm sure my father is especially happy to hear that the direction in which he's brought the Family over the past twenty years can now be seen very clearly by anyone taking a good look at the record." As Sandy spoke, Sal Tarantino nodded his head up and down. "Since we're on the same side in this matter, what is it we can do for you?"

Jenna looked straight at each of them, Sandy first, before answering. "I'm not sure there's a right way to say this, but I was hoping that from the different view you have of these kinds of things—seeing them from the inside, so to speak—you might be able to tell me something that could help with my investigation. I'd like to find out who killed Niro and why. Someone must have been upset at his taking bets. But if it wasn't you, who was it? I just feel there's something here I'm missing."

Sal Tarantino answered. "She wants our professional advice, Salvy. If we can help her, maybe we could go into a business of giving this kind of advice to the police. After all, there's more and more crime every year. We could charge as much as the lawyers." He laughed when he finished, breaking the tension Jenna was beginning to feel. Sandy smiled at his father.

"I'll tell you this, Miss . . ." Sal had forgotten her name.

"Richardson," she offered.

"Miss Richardson," he continued. "Niro was shot by a pro. That whole scene was strictly by the numbers, except for Cardella getting hit too. But that don't mean it was because Niro was booking football games. All we know is whoever did it wanted him dead for some reason or other. Or whoever paid someone else to do the job wanted to see him out of the way. He's got a helluva good-looking wife. Maybe the man you're after is nuts about her, whether she knows it or not. Maybe he decided that's the only way he's got a chance. See who she starts going out with in another month or so. But it could be some other reason. I don't know. That's what you or Gerry Quinn's got to figure out."

"I guess you're right," Jenna said. She hesitated momentarily before asking her next question. "Is there anyone in Providence who *would* be upset by the business Niro was doing?"

Sal answered her again. "Sure. Maybe one of those other barroom bookies thought Niro had the best place to operate out of and was jealous. Maybe this guy, whoever he is, wanted to grow his own operation. Look, I thought about that, but I can't see any of them getting a professional hit man to do the job." He frowned as he spoke and shook his head from side to side. "I can't figure it out. And my son here, the Princeton graduate, doesn't have the answer yet either. So it won't be easy."

Jenna realized that there was nothing more to discuss. She got up and thanked them for letting her come.

"You left out one thing before, Miss Richardson," Sal said on their way to the door. "Of course, you wouldn't know about it. Al Niro used to bet with us every week. Usually he came to the club over on Academy

Avenue, just a few blocks from here. Right, Salvy?" Sandy nodded in agreement. "And he probably left us a good chunk of what he made on the telephone. So we didn't have to go after his business. We got it indirectly, through him, without putting in the work. I don't know who all the other local books are, but it's probably the same story with them. Know what I mean? Bookies like to gamble. Easy come, easy go."

"And I guess Rhode Island wants to make it easy for everyone to do all sorts of gambling," Jenna said.

"Singer does," Sal answered, "but Doug Fiore don't. You should vote for Fiore." He opened the door for her. "My Salvy and I thank you for coming," he said. "And good luck." As soon as Jenna started down the long flight of stairs, Sal smiled at his only son, followed it up with a wink and headed back to his office.

72

On the six days that followed her meeting with the Tarantinos, Richardson did the job McMurphy laid out for her. She spoke earlier to the press secretaries for each of the candidates and obtained their itineraries for the days she would cover their campaigns. She then made arrangements to travel with each candidate and his or her core group of advisors so she could interview them as they moved from one speaking engagement to the next.

Jenna listened to all the speeches the various office seekers made. The essential message each sought to deliver was referred to as "The Speech" by the TV crews and print media that recorded each event. She was quickly able to separate the core points of their deliveries from the glut of issues they felt obliged to sift through and mention in some way or other before different audiences. She watched everyone and everything very carefully, listened to the banter that took place between a candidate and his "brain trust," and made notes of all her impressions.

Character traits were important to Jenna. It was the reason she observed how each of the candidates treated staff and the media. She noted whether they reacted calmly or with some degree of panic to poor audiences or unexpected events. Something bizarre occurred often enough, as when a heckler stood up in the middle of a David Whitley speech to a Catholic organization and asked if it was true that Whitley's daughter had an abortion. Jenna was also curious as to how they spoke about their opponents, both to the voters and in private conversations.

McMurphy warned Jenna that her stories about each of the candidates were only part of the assignment. He said that, later on, when it came time for the *Herald* to make its endorsements, she would be called in by the senior editors and asked a multitude of questions. They would want to know how the candidates either responded to, or evaded the important issues. She'd be told to rate each of them on aptitude, character and sincerity. And the executives would be especially interested in her impressions of whether the candidates' egos seemed more important to them than the welfare of the citizens of Rhode Island.

Other than the half day in which she observed Kate Williston, who was running to keep her seat in Congress, Richardson moved in a man's world during this intense period. Each evening, before going to bed, she assembled the notes she made during the day and used them to draft a rough outline of the stories to be handed in to McMurphy after she returned. At the same time, she reviewed all the background material about each candidate that was contained in the press kit given to her. She was often able to weave pieces of that individual's personal history into what audiences were promised would get done if he or she was elected.

Jenna regarded her day with the Fiore campaign as the most interesting and enjoyable. When she interviewed him the first time, early in the primary battle, she found him stiff and very defensive. It was what could be expected from someone making his first foray into politics, she thought back then. Now he was quite at ease with himself. His "speech" was fine-tuned, and he made an effort to insert a little humor into every appearance, regardless of the size of his audience. Fiore discovered early on, as he recognized at the Hanleys' Valentine's Day party, that those who came to listen to him loved hearing anti-lawyer jokes. They were especially appreciated when coming from a member of that profession, and he alternated the dozen or so he knew as he spoke to the different groups.

Richardson felt that Fiore's handlers were also more knowledgeable and entertaining than any of the others. Russ Walsh had story upon story, some of them side splitters, to tell about politics in "the good old days." There was never a long pause in the conversation when she rode in the same car with him.

Cyril Berman had joined Walsh and Karp that day to assess crowd reaction to Fiore's speeches, and there were some things he didn't want to talk about while Jenna was present. That definitely included ongoing campaign strategy. He said enough, however, to convince her that he knew how to juggle every piece of their program in his head. A real pro, she told herself, realizing it was a term the impressionable young media people threw around far too often.

"How did you get involved with the Fiore campaign?" she asked him.

Berman stared at her in silence for several seconds before shrugging his shoulders. "I never asked who it was that knew my reputation and suggested using me."

"Who contacted you about taking on the job?"

"It was one of Fiore's supporters, a guy I'd never met."

Of course, as Jenna understood, the recent polling results had a lot to do with the good feeling in the Fiore camp. She didn't know that Cyril Berman would have been satisfied to see his candidate even with Singer in the polls at this stage of the campaign, or even running two to three percentage points behind. But Fiore jumped out to a 52–48 lead in the first numbers published in the *Herald* after the primaries. And now, in the second week of October, the name recognition he received as a result of the Cardella tragedy pushed him ten points ahead of Singer, at 53–43, with four percent undecided. Berman knew they would never hold on to that kind of a margin. Still, the election was only twenty-four days away, and he began crossing each day off the calendar before going to bed, telling himself that they were one day closer to victory. He felt confident, but in a shaky sort of way, that if Fiore avoided a major blunder in the time remaining, he'd be the new governor of Rhode Island.

That night, as Jenna familiarized herself with Fiore's background and career before outlining her story, she noticed that he graduated from Princeton University in 1968. She racked her brain for several minutes in an effort to recall where she saw or heard a reference to Princeton recently. Finally, the image of Sal Tarantino, bragging in his own way that his son was a Princeton alum, came to her. The two men were about the same age, she thought, and wondered if they knew each other during their college days. She made a note to call the registrar's office at the University the next day and see if she could get any information.

* * *

"Thank you for holding, Ms. Richardson. I have the record for Mr. Tarantino here. That was Salvatore Michael, correct?"

"Yes, that's right."

"And what is it you wish to know?"

"What year did he graduate?"

"Let's see. Mr. Tarantino graduated in 1968. He entered the University in September of '64 and matriculated the four years without any interruptions."

Jenna felt a small surge of excitement. "How about roommates, Mrs. Thompson, do your records show who they were?"

"I'm afraid not, Ms. Richardson. That would be something the Housing Office may be able to help you with. If Mr. Tarantino lived on campus, I believe his card would show the name of anyone else who occupied the same room. If he was off campus, they'd probably have no record of him for that period of time."

"Well, if he did live off campus, who would have the address? Wouldn't your office need it to make sure he got his grades?"

"It all depends on where he asked to have them sent. In those days, most of the students' grades were mailed out to their parents' home addresses. In fact that was done automatically unless the student submitted a form with different instructions. Today, with the privacy laws, we don't do that anymore. It goes straight into the student's mailbox on campus."

"Is there anything in that file you're looking at that shows an off-campus address?" Jenna asked.

"No, I'm afraid not. This just contains some essential information. Everything else would be on microfilm. You're talking twenty-five years ago."

"How would I be able to get that information?" Jenna was trying to keep her mounting frustration under control.

"Unfortunately, you'd have to come here and look through it yourself. We're not staffed to do that kind of thing."

"Do I need an appointment?"

"No, Ms. Richardson, but I'd advise against coming on a Friday."

"Fine. Thank you, Mrs. Thompson. You've been a great help. I'll see you next week."

73

She just barely caught the 6:05 p.m. commuter flight out of Trenton to LaGuardia. There, Jenna had to wait over an hour in the Delta terminal for the plane, late coming in from Syracuse, that would return her to Providence. She had a lot of time to think about the ordeal she went through that day.

The registrar's office at Princeton was her first stop. Mrs. Thompson, a lovely energetic woman in her fifties, was as polite and helpful in person as she was on the phone. "The microfilm records are kept in the basement of the main library. Let me get you a map of the campus and show you how to find your way there." It took only a minute before she returned with an 8½ x 11-inch map with an index and numbering system for the University buildings. "I suggest you begin your search at the Housing Office, Ms. Richardson. While you're doing that, I'll call the librarian and have her locate the records for Mr. Tarantino and Mr. Fiore. That should save you some time."

Jenna's gratitude for that bit of guidance grew by leaps and bounds later in the morning. While waiting for one of the librarians to bring her the material, she heard the frustration expressed by someone who was just told that the search for microfilm records would take approximately an hour.

"Follow me, and watch your step," the gentleman in the Housing Office said. He took her to a large room filled with cardboard boxes piled about five feet high. The boxes were strategically spaced so that he had easy access to every pile, with room on the floor to stack cartons while he looked for the right one.

The room was laid out by matriculation years. Once he found the location of the 1964–1965 records, he pulled down two cartons. One contained the A-M files while the other held the N-Zs. He then did the same thing for the following three years. He opened one of the boxes and showed Jenna how to look for the information she wanted. "I'll be in my office if you need any help," he said.

The record in Fiore's file noted the room he lived in on campus in his freshman year, along with the names of his roommates. One of them was there for the first semester only, but left and was replaced by another. The file also contained a couple of bills for minor damage done to some furniture and an overhead light.

Sandy Tarantino's first-year record revealed that he also had a dormitory room which he shared with the same roommate both semesters. A parking permit authorized him to have a car on campus.

Jenna wrote down the names of each of their freshman roommates. Later, when she returned to the registrar's office, she was given the currently listed addresses for two of them. She also learned that the first student who lived with Fiore that year dropped out of touch with Princeton shortly after graduating. Jenna couldn't help wondering whether he went off to fight in Vietnam and never returned. Half an hour after she began her search, she knew there were no campus housing records for either Fiore or Tarantino in their sophomore, junior or senior years.

At the library, she sat down in a cubicle containing a microfilm machine. Page by page, starting with Tarantino, she went through everything in the two files the clerk had handed her. The course grades they received were sent to their parents' homes. There wasn't a single entry that disclosed where they lived after their freshman year. All matriculation statements, including separate bills for their use of the campus bookstore, were mailed to Rhode Island and paid for from there. Copies of those checks were in the file. Richardson noted that Tarantino was issued a campus parking sticker every year, but that Fiore never had one. The permit was suspended for one month, starting on February 11, 1966, due to an accident in front of the administration building. There was a memo that the complete accident record could be

My Honorable Brother • 339

found in the files at the Campus Security Office. She jotted down the ID number of Tarantino's parking sticker for that year.

Before leaving the library, Richardson asked to see the 1968 Princeton Senior Yearbook. She was surprised to see it called the "Nassau *Herald*," but didn't ask where the name came from. She turned first to the graduation pictures of the two men and saw how handsome each of them was at that time. Aside from Tarantino's baldness, his face has aged less than Fiore's, she told herself, and wondered why Sandy wanted to hide his good looks behind a beard.

Jenna went through the yearbook meticulously, looking to see whether they played on any of the same sports teams or engaged in any of the same extracurricular activities. She studied all the informal photographs to see if Tarantino and Fiore appeared in any of the pictures together. Every approach came up empty. As far as the records of Princeton University were concerned, Douglas Fiore and Salvatore Tarantino spent the same four years there in classes but had nothing else to do with each other.

Frustrated, she made a list of the names of every twenty-fifth student in the graduating class of 1968 before returning the volume. She figured that if nothing else turned up, she could get current phone numbers from the registrar's office and make cold calls back in Providence.

Jenna was hungry, but didn't stop for lunch. She asked a passing student where she could get a cab and was directed to a taxi hot line phone in the lobby of the theatre arts building. Ten minutes later she was on her way to the downtown office of the Bell Atlantic Telephone Company.

That was where her luck began to change. She was first told that there were no phone records at all during the years in question for Fiore. Minutes later, however, the clerk emerged from behind another file cabinet with a folder on Tarantino in her hands. The contents revealed that he paid for phone service from September 1965 through May 1968. The connection for the entire period was at the same address in town, 2308 Wyoming Avenue.

Richardson found another cab and gave the driver the address on what turned out to be Princeton's east side. When they got there, she told him to wait. A college age female came to the door after she rang the bell.

"Hi," Jenna said. "I'm looking for the owner."

"I don't know who that is," the girl answered. "Do you know the name?"

"No, I don't. Is this a rooming house?"

"Yes. Some Princeton students live here."

"Do you live here too?"

"No, I'm a freshman. I room in the dorm, though I sometimes sleep over here."

"Is anyone who lives here home now?"

"Yes, I'll get him for you."

As she watched from the open door, the girl went to a narrow uncarpeted staircase a short distance away, looked up and shouted for someone named "Roger." In seconds, Roger came running down the stairs. After listening to what Jenna had to say, he told her that he certainly did have the name and address of the owner. He disappeared into another room off to the left, returned shortly with the information on a Rolodex card, and waited as Jenna gratefully copied it down.

Murphy's Law made things a little more difficult. Andrew Coolidge, the building's landlord, lived only three blocks from the Bell Atlantic office, back on the other side of town. Although Jenna had no trouble hearing him holler, "I'm coming, I'm coming" after she rang, it took him several minutes to get to the front door. When he finally opened it, she saw that one hand was holding on to a walker.

"Mr. Coolidge?"

"Yes, that's me."

Richardson introduced herself and said that she wanted to ask him a few questions.

"Questions about what?"

"About the property I understand you own on Wyoming Avenue."

"Do you have any ID," he asked.

When she gave him her *Herald* card, Coolidge held it up in front of him so he could see the photograph and Jenna at the same time.

"I guess that's you," he said. "Come on inside."

She followed him down a short hallway into the kitchen. Looking around, Jenna noted how tidy it was but felt that something hinted at the absence of a woman in the house. When they were settled at the kitchen table, Jenna asked Coolidge if he owned the house at 2308 Wyoming Avenue during the sixties.

"Well, it depends," he replied. "My wife and I—she passed away just three years ago—we bought the place in the summer of 1965. It needed some fixing up, but not too much, fortunately, because I was never too good at that. We started renting it to kids from the college that September."

Jenna felt that wonderful tingle again, almost like an electrical charge that so often told her a hunch was about to pay off. "Do you remember your first tenant?" she asked.

"Of course I do. He took the place for three years. Why he even paid for the summer months in order to hold onto it. Of course, we charged him a lot less when he wasn't in school. The wife and I couldn't believe our good luck with that first rental. After that we never had anyone else stay longer than one year. We got to hate the bother of drawing up leases every fall and then all the phone calls whenever something leaked or didn't work right. We finally got smart and gave it over to an agent about ten years ago. One of the best things I ever did. Stopped being bothered with it. Now I just cash that check about the fifth of every month."

Jenna listened patiently. She figured that Coolidge had few people he could talk to about anything. Letting him go on was like giving charity. *To hell with the cab bill,* she thought. "Do you remember anything about that tenant? I mean, can you picture his . . ."

Coolidge answered before she finished her question. "I sure do. First name was Sandy, like a girl's name. Last name ended in an 'o,' an Italian name . . . like 'Politano' or something."

"I believe it was Sandy Tarantino," she said.

"That was it," Coolidge affirmed, and then showed surprise that she knew it.

"I'm sorry, Mr. Coolidge, I just wanted to be sure you knew who I was talking about before I asked you the next question."

"Yes, that's who it was. A good young man, dependable."

"Do you remember whether he had someone else living there with him?"

"Sure he did. The same fellow all the time. I liked him too."

"Do you remember *his* name, Mr. Coolidge?"

He stared at Jenna and then down at his feet. "No, I don't," he finally answered. "The fact is I'm not sure I ever knew it. Sandy sent the rent checks with his name on them so I got to see it all the time."

"Does Sandy calling him Doug ring a bell? His name may have been Doug Fiore."

He thought about it again. "No, the name doesn't mean anything. All I remember about him is that he was good with tools. He used to fix up some of the things at the house that I couldn't do. He was good with his hands."

She tried to jog Coolidge's memory by describing Fiore's looks to him. He thought most of it fit. "I couldn't swear to it, though. There's been a lot of water under the bridge since then. You're talking roughly twenty-five years ago. That house has seen plenty of students in that time."

Jenna was angry at herself. She realized that she could have brought one of Fiore's campaign brochures with her to Princeton and shown Coolidge his picture. A moment later it dawned on her that she could also have copied the page with Fiore's photograph from the 1968 Yearbook she was looking at earlier. "I found out at the Bell Atlantic office that it was Sandy Tarantino who paid the phone bill all the time," she said. "I wondered if perhaps his roommate was responsible for the gas or electric."

Coolidge shook his head from side to side. "No, I always paid those myself and then added the amount to the next month's rent. We didn't want to end up with some frozen pipes because the tenant forgot to pay the bills on time."

Jenna thanked him for talking to her and said she was ready to leave. He insisted on pushing his walker and accompanying her back to the door. As they shook hands, Coolidge said he was sorry he couldn't remember the other boy's name. "Like I told you, he was good with tools. That's probably why the Sears store had him working in that department all the time," he added.

His last words were music to her ears. Jenna told the cab driver, who by then she was calling by name, to take her to Sears, wherever it was. "From there, Monte, I'll be going to the airport in Trenton. Figure out the fastest route and start praying that I find what I'm looking for."

And she did. They still had the records filed away in the store. The manager confirmed that Doug Fiore lived at 2308 Wyoming Avenue while he was employed there on a part-time basis. "That's where his checks and W-2 forms were sent," he told her. He saw no reason why she couldn't have copies of some of the documents from each of the three years. "I probably should have cleaned out these file cabinets twelve years ago when I took this job."

Bingo, Jenna thought, and asked the manager if she could use his phone. It was just a loose end she didn't like leaving behind. She called the University and was transferred to the security office. A pleasant voice, belonging to Sergeant Clark, offered to help her if he could. She asked if he was able to check the records of an auto accident that took place on campus in 1966 if she gave him the owner's name and the car's parking permit number. Clark thought that was no problem and had an answer for her quicker than she expected. The driver of the car responsible for the accident was a student named Douglas A. Fiore.

The taxi raced to the Trenton airport. When Jenna mentioned that she hadn't eaten since breakfast, Monte handed her a Hershey bar that was under his newspaper on the front seat. At the terminal, with just a few minutes to spare before her scheduled departure time, she owed him thirty-five dollars and change. Jenna gave him two twenties and a ten. "I like the way you drive, Monte," she said, "and I love the way you pray. Keep the change."

74

George Ryder had landed on his feet. Walters, Cassidy & Breen agreed to pay him his regular salary through the first week of November regardless of whether he put in any billable hours for them. It was to his advantage to find employment elsewhere as quickly as he could, bring his remaining clients to the new firm, and augment his income.

Barrows and LeBlanc offered him a good opportunity. They were a fifteen lawyer firm that was started by the two name partners eight years earlier, specializing in corporate and environmental law. Their first office was in a faux brick building on Westminster Street, next to a parking garage. But as they added lawyers and ran out of space, they moved to a renovated building on South Main Street. Their third floor suite overlooked the Providence River. Up until now, the firm had farmed out the various discrimination matters involving its clients, but several well-publicized decisions made the partners more aware of the heavy trial work and billing those kinds of cases could produce.

"I haven't done a lot of trial work in the past," Ryder told Ted Barrows as he sat in the latter's office. "But I'm sure I could pick it up quickly with a little help at the outset. I'm right up to last week on the law itself and the cases," he assured him.

Ted Barrows, more than twenty years younger than Ryder, was a little embarrassed about interviewing him. But he was impressed with his background at WC&B and with the clients Ryder would bring to their growing practice. Both Barrows and LeBlanc liked the idea of having an experienced senior person around the office whose brain they could pick with questions about client relations, ethical problems and practical solutions for difficult cases. A financial arrangement was worked out that was beneficial to both parties. Ryder reported to his new office on the third Monday in September, the week following the Rhode Island primary.

By and large, the departure from Walters, Cassidy & Breen went smoothly. He gave Ed Jackson a list of the clients he expected to take with him, and was somewhat surprised that no questions were raised about any of them. By agreement, Ryder let Jackson have a copy of the letter he was mailing to his clients. It informed them of his move to Barrows and LeBlanc and his hope of being able to service them from there. In return, he received a copy of the notification WC&B intended to send to those same companies and individuals. It acknowledged Ryder's departure and advised them, without actually soliciting their business, that they were welcome to have any future labor or discrimination-related problems handled by other competent attorneys in the firm.

On his last afternoon, there was a "Good Luck George" cake for him in the main lounge. He stood behind a table, cutting pieces of it for those who came in to say good-bye in the hour he was there.

Ryder couldn't help notice that Frankie Scardino remained in the lounge the entire time. He suspected that Scardino's presence was meant to discourage anyone from pressing him to give a farewell speech. He put something together a week earlier in the event that happened, but then decided to leave without making any formal remarks. It disappointed him to see that a number of the lawyers, partners especially, were no-shows at the reception. But he accepted the fact that those who wouldn't have supported him had he fought his termination were too embarrassed to attend, and he guessed that it probably wasn't a good idea for some to be seen shaking his hand or paying him even minimal public tribute.

The only glitch came on that last Friday morning. Ryder met with Scardino to review what he would be receiving from the firm in paychecks after he left. One item confused him. "What's this entry on the list that says, 'Contribution-$100.'" he asked.

"That's what all the partners are being assessed for a firm contribution to Doug Fiore's election campaign," Scardino answered.

Ryder responded with a mild explosion. "Well, goddammit I'm not!" he said. "Don't ask me to shell out a hundred bucks for the guy who pushed me out of here. I'm not a masochist."

Scardino acted as if he couldn't understand where Ryder was coming from. "It applies to all the partners, George, and the firm's paying you for the next seven weeks. I don't see why you should be an exception."

He felt his blood starting to boil. "I'm not sure I expect you to see why, Frankie, or that you'd even have the guts to admit this shouldn't apply to me. I'm not going to give the managing partner one goddam nickel without a fight. And let me remind you that I'm going to have the chance to make a speech this afternoon if I want."

Scardino was obviously flustered. He hesitated and then sat back in his chair, away from the table. "Ed Jackson is the managing partner," he said, "not Doug Fiore."

"If you and Ed want to believe that, good luck to both of you. Just tell me that I'm not making a contribution and let's sign off on the rest of this."

"I'll have to speak to Ed about it."

"I know better, Frankie. I've been around here over thirty-two years. But if you want to go through that charade, be my guest. Just have an answer for me before I walk into the lounge this afternoon."

Scardino moved forward and reached for the paper. "Let's do it this way. I'll cross it out for now. We can initial the other items, and I'll recommend to Ed that the contribution gets dropped. If he won't go along with it, you'll find out by two o'clock."

And, as Ryder knew at that moment, that was the end of it.

75

They arranged to meet at Bruce Singer's law office, in the Fairfax Building, early on Saturday morning.

"Good to see you, George," Bruce said, welcoming him with a smile and a strong handshake. "Carol told me all about the screwing you got at WC&B, except she seemed to let it go pretty quickly. If a woman was given that kind of treatment, my wife would be going through the roof non-stop. How's it working out for you with Teddy Barrows?"

"I like it there, Bruce," he answered, accepting the cup of coffee Singer poured for him. "It's only been four weeks, but I've enjoyed it. They've put together a nice bunch of lawyers. So far I haven't seen any office politics and I don't find a new memo from management on my desk every twenty minutes. Believe it or not, no one has said a word to me yet about going out and doing some marketing with another firm's clients. It's a whole new world."

"I'm glad it's a good situation. You deserve it. It was hard to believe what Ed Jackson did to you."

"It was Fiore, Bruce, not Jackson. Ed doesn't have the balls to do it. He just does what he's told. If you win the election next month, Fiore will be right back in the driver's seat. In the meantime, 'Big Ed' doesn't want to make any waves. He thinks people look up to him because he's on the Executive Committee, and he's afraid Fiore will bounce him off if he's a bad boy while he holds down the fort. Fiore was just settling an old score he had against me, and used Jackson to do it."

Singer noticed the sun hitting Ryder in the face and went over to the window to close the blinds. "It's scary," he said. "Things have gone so far downhill in this business. Some of our honorable brothers will use any chance they get to stick a knife in your back. They'll steal clients from you the minute you turn around, or hold back critical documents in a case when they know they should be turning them over. Some of them will even make a deal with you, shake hands on it and then break it a day or a week later if they suddenly decide it's not as good for their clients as they thought it was at the time. It's hard to trust anyone in this profession anymore. I have no trouble seeing why the average person in the street hates lawyers so much."

Ryder nodded his head in agreement. "You're right," he answered. "And maybe what I came to see you about isn't the most noble thing in the world for a lawyer, either. I thought about it a long time before I called."

Singer waved his arm, a sign that he was giving George the floor. "Okay, let's hear what you've got."

Ryder took a small package out of his briefcase and placed it on Singer's desk. It was wrapped in brown paper and held together by a few strategically placed pieces of duct tape.

"There are eleven audio cassettes in here," he began. "They're numbered in order. Every minute of what you hear on these tapes was recorded in Room 606 at the Biltmore, from late in May through September of this year. You'll recognize the man's voice. It's on sound bites on radio and TV every day, something to do with the race for governor in Rhode Island."

Singer mouthed his opponent's name. "Fiore?"

Ryder shook his head affirmatively. "Yup." He continued. "The woman is the wife of one of his clients. No, I take that back, she's the wife of the president and general manager of his client's plant. Between you and me, it's Ocean State Wire & Cable and her name is Pat Hanley. I used to help her husband Brad negotiate their labor contracts.

"I don't know if there's anything you can do with these, but I don't trust your worthy opponent for a second. In case he tries to pull any bad shit on you before the election, anything personal, I thought you should have some ammunition of your own."

Singer looked stunned, like a man who was just awakened and told to choose either a gun or a sword in a duel to the death that was about to begin. His hands didn't move. "George, I've got to ask you. How did you get these?"

"By conduct unbecoming a man of our profession," Ryder answered. "You listen, and I'll try to make a long story short." He waited for Singer to sit back before he began. "Ocean State has Room 606 on sort of a permanent basis. I think they pay for it by the month. Brad Hanley, the Company president I mentioned, gave me a key so I could sleep there instead of having to drive home if we were up real late negotiating with the union. I went to use it one night and it was easy to see what was going on. Fiore's briefcase and raincoat were there, and the bed was all messed up. I found out from the desk clerk that Pat Hanley had the room for that day.

"Not long after that, Fiore got Jackson to start sitting on me about my billables. It was obvious that he was greasing the skids for my departure. I figured it couldn't hurt to have something on him when the showdown came. I didn't know if I'd use it, being what it is, but I sure as hell couldn't use it if I didn't have it.

"Anyway, I spoke to a private investigator who owed me a favor. I took him to the Biltmore on a Sunday morning and he installed a tape recorder under the bed in that room. Then he put microphones in the lamps on the night tables. I got another key made for him and he changed the tapes every so often. The results are what's sitting on your desk."

"Have you listened to all of these?" Singer asked.

"No, just the first one and part of the second. They get repetitious, if you know what I mean."

Singer nodded. "I don't know what to say, George. I gather you decided against using them yourself."

"Yes, but that's only because I caught on with Barrows and LeBlanc. Before that, I was sick about the fact that a majority of my partners were ready to back Fiore if I refused to resign and took it to a vote. They knew that meant all I'd get is three months' severance after thirty-two years. I know I was a special case, that Fiore had it in for me for a long time, but no one else that I can remember ever had to resign because his billables turned sour. I was told by some of the partners that Fiore has always been fair, even though they knew he wanted as much control as he could get. But when I pointed out that what was happening to me could only happen when the managing partner felt he could do whatever he pleased, and that made it a dictatorship, not a democracy, most of them just said, 'Sorry, George,' and turned away. At that point I didn't have much choice, but I'd already lost my taste for staying there and having to think of those guys as my friends. But I'll tell you, Bruce, that if I didn't have another place to go by the deadline they gave me to get out, I might have mailed one of these to Fiore and let him guess what I was thinking of doing with the rest. I'm sure that would have convinced him to open his heart and improve my severance package. Three months, after thirty-two years."

Ryder got up from his chair. "Hard to believe someone could do something like that," he said. Singer shook his head, but without speaking, and Ryder pointed to the tapes. "Look, do what you want with them. They're yours. I don't need them anymore. Like I said, I think Fiore will do anything in the world to beat you, clean or dirty. That's who he is, in my estimation. Right now, he's way ahead in the polls, and he can act like a statesman. But anything can happen between now and the election, so if it tightens up, watch out." He zipped up his windbreaker. "I'd hate to see that bastard become my governor."

Singer walked out to the reception area with him. "I appreciate your good intentions," he said, and held out his hand.

Ryder shook it. "Say 'hello' to Carol for me."

"I will, George, and thanks again."

Singer watched him walk part of the way toward the elevator. Then he hurried back to his office, opened the credenza behind his desk and took out the Sony tape recorder.

76

When he finished reading the story Richardson gave him, Dan McMurphy had a big smile on his face. "Great stuff, Jenna," he said. "This is going to sell some papers. And it will cut into that big lead Fiore has in the polls. How much, remains to be seen. But now you'll have everyone wondering whether Fiore got into this campaign because he believes in the issues he's talking about or whether he's just a shill for the Tarantinos to stop casino gambling. Yup, you've got a winner here, but we're not quite ready to run with it yet."

His last words put Jenna on her feet, and she reached for the story he was handing back to her. "Why not, Dan?" she asked. Her voice reflected her exasperation.

McMurphy just smiled. He understood how anxious a good reporter was to get a dynamite story into print. But he got paid to make sure it was the best it could be before it went to press. "Because I think you ought to take a day and see if there are any more loose ends out there," he told her. "We know Fiore went to law school, and I seem to remember hearing that young Tarantino is also a lawyer. Take a look. See if it leads to anything else. Today's Thursday. Let's shoot for Saturday or Sunday."

* * *

The first new connection came easy. Richardson put a call into the Rhode Island Bar Association. She learned from that office that

Tarantino graduated from Boston University Law School in 1971 and became a member of the bar later that year. A call to the registrar's office at BU elicited the information that Sandy entered as a second-year student, transferring from Columbia Law School.

As soon as she heard that, Jenna recalled that Fiore's campaign literature included the fact that he obtained his law degree at Columbia. Within the hour, having to work her way from the clerk who answered her call, to the assistant registrar, and finally to the law school registrar himself, she confirmed what she already suspected: that the two of them resided at the same off-campus address during their only year together at Columbia.

Logic immediately took her to the next step, causing Jenna to wonder whether the Tarantino family used Walters, Cassidy & Breen as their lawyers. She assumed it was probably information the firm wouldn't give out—the lawyer-client relationship thing—although she couldn't see any harm in a law firm just answering "Yes" or "No" to that kind of question. Jenna remembered that lawyers often boasted in public or in their marketing brochures about particular clients they represented, especially if they were well-known industry leaders.

"If I don't ask, I'll never find out," she whispered out loud. Moments later, she obtained the firm's number from a local telephone operator and dialed it.

The receptionist who answered put her through to the billing department, as she requested. A clerk there listened to Richardson's question and said she would transfer her to Janice Rossman, the office manager. When the connection was made, Jenna repeated what it was she was looking for.

"Let me check," Rossman said, and called up the master client listing on her computer. "No, we've never represented anyone by the name of Salvatore Tarantino or any other Tarantino."

"Do you have a listing under '241 Atwells Avenue Associates?'" Jenna asked.

"No, we don't," Rossman said moments later.

"Do you have anything at all that begins with the numbers '241' or with 'Atwells Avenue?'"

Again, after a long pause, the answer was negative. Richardson thanked her for looking.

"You know, it just occurred to me that I probably shouldn't have given out that information without asking the managing partner if it was okay. Oh, well," Rossman said, "have a nice day," and hung up.

Jenna was disappointed but continued her search. She recalled that the *Herald* periodically published the names of all individuals or companies that contributed one hundred dollars or more to the candidates for the various offices. She tracked down the dates on which the financial supporters of the gubernatorial contenders were listed, and picked up copies of those papers in the library.

The Tarantinos, father and son, each sent $250 to the Fiore campaign during the primary, she discovered, and supplemented those donations with an additional $300 each before the end of September. Richardson was forced to conclude that their contributions were relatively small compared to the amounts received from many persons and businesses all over the State. She figured it was a dead end.

At that point she decided to forget Fiore for a while and spend some time fleshing out her story on Bruce Singer. Jenna liked him, and remembered vividly how his sincerity came through in each of the speeches she watched him give. Clearly though, he was far less charismatic than Fiore. She suspected that a number of voters would want to take a closer look at Singer once they read her article about the past connection between Fiore and Sandy Tarantino and considered its implications. She resolved to carefully consider and report everything she learned about the Democratic candidate and his campaign.

The personal aspects of Singer's life were sprinkled throughout Richardson's draft of his campaign style and oratory. It wasn't until she almost finished writing it that the two years he spent in Vietnam after graduating from Brown University in 1970 suddenly meant a lot more to her. She wondered how Fiore and Tarantino managed to go directly on to law school after finishing their studies at Princeton in 1968 while Singer's matriculation at Harvard Law was postponed by the draft until after his wartime service.

It was worth looking into, Jenna thought. *Maybe I've got a draft dodger or two on my hands.*

* * *

The Providence and Narragansett draft boards no longer existed, but their records and logs were available for inspection. At Providence City Hall, an unattractive granite building facing Kennedy Plaza, Richardson discovered that Sandy Tarantino was classified 1-A after graduating from college in 1968. She also learned that most other young men his age sharing that classification were inducted into the Army between June and December of that year.

Tarantino's status, however, was changed to "Continue student deferment." Jenna could find no letters addressed to the draft board from family, friends or clergy urging the deferment. But there were two notes of interest to explain what happened. The first, written in longhand on the bottom of the agency form, indicated that his father had no regular income, and that on becoming a lawyer Tarantino would be able to support his parents. Someone also wrote the words, "Defer, per A. B." in the margin of the log next to Sandy's name.

Jenna copied the documents she needed. Her follow-up search to locate the three men who were the draft board officials in Providence at the time took her back to the *Herald* library. She discovered their names in a book containing a series of legal appeals from some of the board's decisions.

It took two hours of frustrating research on the telephone before she finally learned their status. One of the officials was dead. A second had moved to West Palm Beach, Florida, in 1979. She located the Florida phone number and spoke to a housekeeper who was caring for the former official's wife. The housekeeper informed her that the woman's husband resided in an institution for Alzheimer's patients. The status of the third draft board member offered some hope. He was in a nursing home in North Scituate, a 20-minute drive from the *Herald*.

77

The Hawthorne Hill Home for the Aged was located on Route 6, about fifteen miles west of downtown Providence, in what was mostly a commercial area of North Scituate. Richardson spotted the nursing home sign at the foot of a driveway that was just beyond the last of the business establishments in that block. She turned off the main road and followed the driveway for about 300 feet as it climbed a gentle hill behind the stores. The Home was an uninviting two-story red brick building. When she got out of her car, she realized that the facility was set far enough back from the road so that the sound of heavy traffic down below was only a muffled hum at that level. Inside, a receptionist fingered through a card file and directed her to the second floor. There, a nurse at the desk led her to John Darling's room for her appointment with him.

Jenna had worked for several weeks on a nursing industry story just over a year earlier. Her digging uncovered the facts of how a chain of homes owned by one prosperous businessman systematically deprived its patients of various services for which they were being billed. Breaking the story required her to spend hours at a time with some patients, masquerading as a relative. That allowed her to sit alone with them in their rooms and observe the total care administered by nurses and aides. But Jenna still found it very difficult to walk through another facility and witness the vegetative state in which some of the residents were surviving.

She was relieved to find that Darling was remarkably vigorous and healthy-looking for a man in his eighties. He was sitting in a wheelchair, reading a magazine when Jenna entered. Despite her protestations, he lifted himself partway out of the chair to shake hands when she introduced herself.

They engaged in some small talk for a while. Darling got an obvious kick out of describing to her what downtown Providence looked like in the forties, during the war years. It seemed to please him to name many of the current buildings that weren't there at that time. Jenna likened it to an old man letting his grandchild know what kinds of toys they had to amuse themselves with in "the good old days." Then, while discussing the difficult traffic patterns that existed before Interstate 95 split the city in half, Darling suddenly stopped short.

"You'd better get down to business," he said, "or I'll be ranting and raving until it's time to go eat."

Richardson showed him the Tarantino draft records she picked up at City Hall. "Do you have any recollection of the circumstances surrounding this deferment?" she asked.

Darling took his time looking at the documents. "I can tell you that what it says there in the margin with the initials 'A.B.' is my handwriting. That note on there about him becoming a lawyer and supporting his parents, that's not mine, and I don't remember seeing it at the time." He was silent for a couple of minutes while he stared straight up at the ceiling, his eyes closed most of the time. Jenna waited patiently. Finally, he looked back at her.

"I'll tell you everything I remember," he said. But then he remained silent for a while longer, clasping his hands in front of him before continuing. "The man who came to see us about the Tarantino boy was very powerful in some way or another, but I can't recall what it was. He was insistent that the young man be given a deferment. I know that Henry and Dip—that's what everyone called Dillard—had both heard a lot about this fellow, but his name meant nothing to me. Of course I was a scientist most of my life and that's all I ever cared to read about. I never bothered with the newspapers or most magazines. My wife always said I was a one-dimensional man.

"They were afraid of him for some reason, I remember that. And after he left, we took a vote on it right away. It was two to one to grant the deferment, but we never entered the numbers when we voted. We always left every decision looking like it was unanimous."

My Honorable Brother • 357

Once again Darling studied the ceiling for a minute or so. "You can ask me more questions if you want," he told her, "but whatever I say about anything the first time is most always all that'll come to mind. That's how it works with me." Jenna tried to jog his memory about a couple of things, but he was right.

* * *

The draft board records in Narragansett were less revealing. Richardson learned that Fiore was given two consecutive deferments. The first allowed him to continue college after his sophomore year at Princeton, the second to go on to law school. The town clerk couldn't understand why anything that old could be important, and didn't hide her annoyance at having to search for the records in a damp basement storage room. Jenna had come on a bad day, the clerk told her, and then only reluctantly entered the names of the three board officials on her computer to see if any of them paid a property tax to the town in the past year.

"That's the only way of finding out whether they still live in Narragansett, other than just looking them up in the phone book. If they're not listed, I can't help you. We have no reason to keep tabs on them."

It turned out that one of them, a Vincent Curcuruto, resided on Shore Road. Richardson wrote down his address, along with the names of the two other officials, and drove to the white frame house with no shutters that was located on a cul-de-sac a block in from Narragansett Bay.

Virginia Curcuruto let her in and called her husband from the den where he was watching TV. The small living room was furnished entirely in colonial style. As they sat there, Jenna noticed that the stitching in several areas of the brown-toned braided rug were pulled loose. She suspected that the Curcurutos owned a cat at some time. The two of them were probably in their mid-eighties, she figured, but both were full of energy and it wouldn't have surprised Jenna if they told her they were about to go square dancing. She explained the reason she was there.

"I was actually the oldest of the three of us who sat on the board," Curcuruto told her, "but I'm the only one who's still alive and kicking. Neal Wilson died in a boating accident out on Narragansett Bay the same week Nixon resigned as President. And Bobby Silvers had an aneurysm in Bermuda about five years ago. Imagine dying like that while you're on vacation, being someplace you've wanted to see for so long. It was a shame.

"Anyway, let me answer your question. We tried to take care of the kids here and keep them away from Vietnam as long as we could. There was a fair amount of feeling in this town against the war, even in the early days. So if a youngster graduated college and was going to do something else aside from just getting a job, we wanted to do what we could for him.

"Naturally, we couldn't give everyone a deferment or we'd never meet even the minimum quotas that were set for us. Keep in mind that a high percentage of our boys were going on to graduate school for law or business or something or other. But we checked to see how big a family it was, whether any other sons were already in the service, different things like that. Besides, each of us had close friends who called and asked us to do what we could for their kids, so sometimes we sort of swapped favors among ourselves on the board."

"That wasn't very often," his wife interjected protectively, and Jenna smiled in response.

"Now I'll get to the point," Curcuruto continued. "You can see from the record here that only Bobby and I signed off on Fiore's second deferment. What happened is that just the two of us were in the office that afternoon when who walks in but Anthony Buscatelli. Do you know who he was?"

Jenna assured him that she knew all about Buscatelli.

"Well, anyways, there was him and two other guys, they must have been bodyguards. I'd seen his picture in the papers and I'm Italian too, so I knew who he was even before he said a word. He told us why he was there and the fact that Fiore was going to the same law school as the son of a very close friend of his. The two boys already arranged to live together, and the other one was getting a deferment in Providence. He knew that for sure, he said.

"Then he asked me in Italian if I spoke the language. When I told him I did, almost everything else he said was just to me. Bobby didn't know what was going on. I won't say Buscatelli threatened me, but he let me know just who he was. He said that Italians had to stick together because everyone else wanted to crap on us. Here was an Italian boy

My Honorable Brother • 359

from a good family who deserved the chance to go on and be a lawyer. After law school he was going to be partners with the son of that best friend he told me about, also Italian. By the time he was through talking, I had nothing to say."

Jenna now understood what the notation "Defer, Per A. B." meant on Sandy Tarantino's draft board record in Providence.

"Bobby saw what I looked like. As soon as Buscatelli and his boys left, he asked me what we were talking about. He got the picture right away and said if I wanted to approve Fiore's deferment for any reason, he'd go along with me right then and there.

"That's what we did, and the next day we told Neal about it. I don't know anything about Fiore, except it looks like he's got a good shot to be governor. I'm not saying he had anything to do with what happened or even knew about it. He filed the papers asking for another deferment to go to law school, and we approved it. End of story."

Maybe, Jenna thought to herself, *or maybe there's more to come.*

78

Richardson's account of the close bond that existed between Doug Fiore and Sandy Tarantino in the years from 1965 through 1969 ran in the *Sunday Herald*. Although the story appeared on page four of the front section, it was given an attention-catching preview with a headline above the paper's masthead that read, "FIORE'S PAST LINK TO TARANTINOS REVEALED."

McMurphy allowed Jenna to go partway out on a limb. She wrote that " . . . while there's no evidence of an ongoing relationship between them since 1969, it's difficult to accept the fact that two men who shared the same apartment for four consecutive years and live only a few miles from each other in Rhode Island did not continue to have contact after that date." She attempted to put that exact question to Fiore and Tarantino two days earlier, the story indicated, but neither of them was available for comment.

Jenna asserted in the article that "Even the voters of Rhode Island who are pleased with Fiore's stand on the issues, especially his strong position against State-run casinos, have to ask themselves whether this candidate has an undisclosed reason for telling them what his old friend wants him to say. The electorate has to be concerned with whether Fiore is returning past favors to help preserve the Tarantinos' firm grip on gambling. "Furthermore," she continued, "not knowing the intensity of the relationship, the citizens of our State have to wonder whether

Fiore, as governor, would ever be willing to position himself against the interests of the Tarantino family."

* * *

Cyril Berman made a number of phone calls after reading Richardson's story that morning. It didn't have quite enough in it to be a "bombshell," he concluded, but it came awfully close. He was certain that its being out there would eat into their lead.

On the positive side, he realized, no one could blame Fiore for trying to get a deferment to go to law school. He knew, from the way people now felt about Vietnam, that a lot of them would shrug their shoulders at what Richardson revealed in her column. They probably wished that someone with a little influence had been able to keep their own sons or husbands or friends from having to go over there and get killed or wounded for what amounted to nothing as they saw it. Furthermore, there was no indication that Fiore was aware at the time of any intervention on his behalf by Anthony Buscatelli, whom he apparently never even met.

On the downside, the story underscored the fact that Singer risked his life for his country while Fiore stayed home. And Berman understood that anyone who read what Richardson wrote would now link Fiore with the Tarantinos whenever they spoke of him. That meant that any bad feeling against the Family that ruled on Federal Hill, like the suspicion that the Tarantinos were involved in the murder of Niro and Cardella, would inevitably rub off on his candidate.

Richardson's less than subtle intimation that Sandy Tarantino and his father were now exerting influence over Fiore because of a past friendship and a wartime deferment raised a separate issue for Berman. He wanted all the major players in the Fiore campaign to be on the same wavelength in case they were interrogated by someone in the media. He got on the telephone before going down for breakfast and made sure every one of them knew what to say and how to answer questions along that line. In the meantime, he assured them, he would call the *Herald* himself and charge that Richardson's insinuations bordered on libel.

79

It was an example of what Terry Reardon always called, "One of my Irish days."

At midmorning, on Tuesday, he had a visit from Tommy Arena who came to let him know that the *Herald* delivery drivers ratified the new contract. The pressure was off.

Arena had spoken to Reardon again a few days after Cardella was shot. "Like I told you, don't worry about having no new contract by the end of the month," he said. "There's no way I'll let these fucking drivers strike under the circumstances we got now. We can finish up negotiations later on. If you want that Donlan kid sitting at the table with you, that's okay. Or you and me can meet by ourselves and work something out."

Terry thanked him for his consideration.

"Take whatever time you need and get back to me. These fucking guys ain't going nowheres without my say-so."

A couple of weeks later Reardon called Arena and told him he'd like to see if the two of them could put a deal together. They agreed to meet for lunch on the following Tuesday at the Old Grist Mill Tavern in Seekonk, just across the line in Massachusetts. Reardon worked out all his final offer positions on the various economic proposals submitted by the Union. Still, applying one of the lessons Cardella taught him, he held back a little on each when he read the numbers to Tommy as they had their dessert.

Arena wrote them down in a small notebook he carried in the inside pocket of his jacket. He repeated them out loud and asked the question Reardon anticipated: "Are you telling me you got no fucking room to move on any of these?"

Terry responded first with some body English, stretching his arms and shoulders in the chair and looking off into space for a few seconds. "This is the deal my boss said we need to have, Tommy. It's the same thing you'd get across the table." He should have stopped right there, leaving Arena without an opening. Instead, his next words telegraphed the fact that the *Herald* was prepared to do better, to spend more money, if necessary, on settling the contract. "What's your biggest concern?" he asked.

The cocky Teamster business agent had negotiated too many agreements not to pick up the signal Reardon unwittingly sent. He answered in a suitably strident manner, raising his voice enough to remind Terry of the temper tantrum he'd probably be having if they were in a private room somewhere instead of the middle of a crowded restaurant.

"I gotta get enough in wages to make these fucking guys happy, Terry. This last contract gave them shit, you know that. No one wanted a strike three years ago, so you and Richie got away with fucking murder. You probably earned yourself a big fucking bonus on that one. My guys tell me they want more in the paycheck, that's what's fucking bugging them right now. All I keep hearing from them is how much more they've got to shell out for their fucking groceries."

Arena looked down again at the numbers he'd written in the notebook. "I can sell them on this not being the time for another holiday or more sick days or life insurance, but you gotta beef up the fucking wages. This here won't do it. It ain't gonna be easy getting a majority to buy the whole package, but I'll do my fucking best if you give me something to work with. Tell that to your boss."

"I'll speak to him, Tommy, but don't get your hopes up." Then Reardon made his second mistake. "I've still got your word there won't be a strike, right?"

Arena jumped on that one just as quickly. "I told you I don't want to see these fucking guys do something stupid. But we ain't gonna lay down for the *Herald* to walk all over us. If you can't give me what I gotta have to push it through, then we could have a fucking problem."

"I'll do what I can," Terry said, "but it's not up to me. Whatever happens, I'm still going to hold you to a two-week written notice before they walk. We signed off on that one."

"No problem. Now just go back and get me some more fucking money." Arena didn't doubt for a second that it was coming. He felt good enough about it to consider picking up the check, but resisted the temptation.

* * *

Reardon had to make sure he dragged the negotiations on long enough to get through the election. The executives on the *Herald*'s fourth floor made it clear they didn't want to see any labor problems breaking out while all the big races were reaching a climax. Trouble with the Teamsters meant newspapers not getting delivered. Reardon knew he had to keep his tit from getting caught in a ringer for at least the next three weeks.

Arena called a week later to find out what was happening. Terry had a phony excuse all worked out.

"Look, Tommy, my boss told me to make a complete analysis of the Union's outstanding money proposals and the Company's last offer. He's not going to do anything until the publisher and the managing editor review everything and see where we stand. But I had a few other things to do first, and I just sent the breakdown over to them yesterday afternoon. We could set up a tentative meeting for early next week, if you want."

Arena was willing. But even while agreeing to return to the Old Grist Mill on Tuesday, Reardon knew that the earliest he'd be ready to give Tommy his "take it or leave it" position was on Friday of that week. If the drivers turned it down, the two-week strike notice Tommy had to give him would carry them through the election.

And that's how it worked out. Reardon cancelled the Tuesday meeting early that same day and lunched with Arena on Friday. He improved the wage package in each of the three years of the contract, but still held back a little of what he was authorized to spend in case there were any more surprises.

Tommy didn't disappoint him. "It's not all I wanted," he said, frowning, "but it gives me a fucking chance to sell it to the drivers if you'll throw in a two hundred dollar signing bonus."

Reardon hesitated, purposely, staring at Arena. "I'll tell you what I'll do," he finally answered. "Instead of my having to get back to you-know-who and discuss this all over again, I'm willing to do this: your guys get the package I already put on the table today, plus a bonus of a hundred bucks up front—and that's gross, before deductions—if they ratify this deal the first time around. If they reject it, the bonus is out the window, no matter what happens afterward. Write that down, so there's no misunderstanding." Terry waited for Arena to open his notebook and make the entry. "But you've got to give me an answer no later than next Thursday. If they turn it down, you can bring me the strike notice at the same time. Thursday will be the day, either way, agreed?"

"I could sell it easier with the fucking two hundred, but I'll do my best," Arena said.

So Tuesday got off to a great start when Tommy Arena came by unexpectedly with news of the ratification. Terry informed his boss, and got himself invited to lunch at the Biltmore.

80

He was still flying high an hour after lunch. That's when Jenna called and asked if he had time that night to stop by her apartment.

"The last time we did it I got a great idea on the Niro case," she told him. "I just have this feeling I'm close to finding the answer. I'm hoping lightning will strike again."

"I'll take that as a brazen excuse to have sex," he said. "But seeing that we work for the same newspaper, I'll show my loyalty and be most happy to oblige. I'll try and say 'Shazam' at just the right moment."

"You'll say what?"

"Forget it. You probably never heard of 'Captain Marvel' anyway. I'll get you some lightning without it."

* * *

Afterwards, when the fireworks had come and gone for Jenna and they were still lying in bed, she told Terry she couldn't come up with a single reason for anyone to walk into Chi-Chi's and gun down Al Niro.

"I'm convinced that the Tarantinos didn't care about his two-bit football operation. He was like a gnat on an elephant's back. The other guys taking bets around town are all small-time, just like Niro. Sal Tarantino calls them 'barroom bookies.' None of them was looking to push him out of Chi-Chi's and take that spot. In fact, no one else has set up shop there since the killing. Besides that, the man was never involved in drugs, either using the stuff or selling it.

"Niro's wife is positive he didn't have an enemy in the world. She says he told her *everything*. If he ever suspected that someone was out to get him, he would have let her know, she's certain about that. The two of them ate breakfast and dinner together every day, even on the nights he went to work at Chi-Chi's. I just can't find a motive, Terry, and neither can the police."

"Maybe the guy wasn't sent in there to kill Niro," he said, turning on his side toward her.

"What do you mean?" she asked.

"I'm not sure, but maybe it was an initiation of some kind. Could be the guy with the gun had to prove to someone he had the nerve to kill, that he could walk into a bar and do what he did. So he just waited until he got almost to the back door because he knew the getaway car was in the alley, and shot Niro sitting in the last booth. He probably could have just killed Richie instead since the two of them were right across from each other. Then Niro might still be taking bets in Chi-Chi's and you'd be here with me trying to figure out who it was that wanted Cardella out of the way."

Jenna didn't say anything. She just lay there, looking up at the ceiling. Several minutes passed. Terry reached out his hand and let his fingers walk around her stomach. She shook slightly with pleasure and gently lifted his hand away. Her expression didn't change.

"Do I smell rubber burning?" he asked.

She remained silent for another minute or so. And then suddenly she screamed out his name several times and was all over him. She kissed him on his lips and everywhere else on his face, talking to him all the while. "You did it, you did it. Oh, I love you, you're wonderful. I knew I was close. But you did it, you made me see it. You are absolutely Mr. Lightning. I love you, I love you."

"Quick, tell me what I did," he said, when she finally settled back.

"No, no, there's no time for that," she answered. "You've got to go home and I have to work on a story."

Terry feigned disappointment. "I see. I come over here as soon as you say you need me, and I do this wonderful thing, and my reward is that you don't want me to know what I did, but I've got to get out of bed before I see if I have another bolt of lightning to fill up your . . . eh, sky. Is that it?"

Jenna was already on her way to the bathroom. She didn't answer his question directly, but stopped long enough to smile at him and say, "If we could just do this often enough, I think I *would* get a Pulitzer Prize."

81

The lights in the bedroom were off. Bruce Singer could see Carol's form under the blanket as he walked quietly past the foot of the waterbed and sat down on his side of it to take off his shoes and socks. The bright red lights of the digital clock on the nightstand read 11:47. It was Tuesday night, exactly two weeks before the election.

"How did everything go?" he heard his wife ask.

"You still up?" But he didn't wait for her to answer. "It was a good day. The crowds have definitely picked up since that story about the Tarantino-Fiore connection. Hopefully, by some time tomorrow the *Herald* will have its latest poll out and we'll be able to see if we gained any ground in the last few days."

"Good," was all Carol said.

"If you're not half asleep, I've got some juicy information you might like to hear . . . about Fiore."

Carol opened her eyes, facing away from her husband, but didn't move. "What is it?" she mumbled.

"It seems he's having an affair."

She held her breath, afraid to ask, "With whom?" After a pause, she said, "Oh?"

Bruce got undressed and was putting on his pajamas. "Yup, with the wife of a company president who runs a wire plant. One of Doug's clients owns the place. Her name is Pat Hanley."

"I assume that's just a rumor." Carol made it a statement, not a question.

"It's not a rumor, it's a fact. But the only ones who know about it are you and me and the guy who gave me the tapes."

She turned toward her husband. "What are you talking about, Bruce? Tell me before you go into the bathroom."

He sat back down on the side of the bed. "A certain person knew that Doug was meeting this Hanley woman at a hotel and that they weren't just friends. It was in the same room all the time, one her husband's company kept rented for business guests who came to Providence. This person was given a key to the room, in case he had to use it. For his own reasons, he asked a detective friend of his to set up a tape recorder under the bed. The microphones were hidden in the lamps on the bedside tables. As soon as one of the mikes picked up a voice, the tape started to run. It's very good quality. He gave me eleven tapes, from May to September, so Doug was seeing quite a bit of the lady."

"Have you listened to them?" she asked.

"Parts of a few," he said. "Pretty pornographic sound bites, except when the maid comes in to clean and turns on the TV. They both seemed to enjoy themselves."

"What are you going to do with them?"

"I don't know. Maybe nothing. This guy wanted me to have them in case Fiore tried to pull something dirty before the election. He thinks Doug wouldn't hesitate to start telling lies about my personal life if the race tightened up and he thought that's what it took to win. But even if he did, I can't see giving these to anyone else. Why hurt the woman just to get back at him?"

"Not many people running for office would look at it that way." Carol hesitated before continuing. "I respect you for having that attitude. But who's this person that's so concerned about you?"

"Will you promise me it never leaves this room?"

"I promise," she answered.

"It was George Ryder," he said, and then told her why Ryder arranged for the tapes in the first place.

"Fiore doesn't know how lucky he is that Ryder found another job," Carol said, when he finished. "He'll never even know the tapes exist unless you get desperate and change your mind."

"Not much chance of that, but that doesn't mean I may not tune in to more of the action at the Biltmore once in a while." He started walking toward the bathroom. "Maybe I'll learn something new and exciting from the folks in Room 606."

For a while, as soon as the room number left Bruce's lips, Carol thought the heavy pounding in her heart would cause it to burst. She was certain that was the room in which Fiore made love to her. That meant she was on one of the tapes and that Bruce might find out about it at any time. *Oh, God, what had she done?*

When the alarm went off the next morning, she felt as if she hadn't slept a minute that night.

82

The only disagreement Richardson and McMurphy had on Wednesday was whether she should call police headquarters and let Gerry Quinn know about her story before it appeared in the *Herald* the next morning.

"It's your scoop, Jenna," he said. "You worked it out on your own and you've got no obligation to tell Quinn about it ahead of time. We don't know if he might just decide to take some action before the papers hit the newsstands tomorrow. He may want it to look like his detectives were thinking along the same lines."

But she insisted. She felt she had the chance to interview the Tarantinos only because Quinn interceded for her. That's what got her the start she needed on the story. Quinn asked her to keep him informed. Jenna wanted to keep her side of the bargain, and when she finally reached him, was glad she did.

"I hope ya on to something," Quinn said, after listening to her new theory of the case. "It's certainly another way of looking at it. But even if ya wrong, it may shake something else outta the trees. Good luck, kid, and thanks for letting me know aheada time."

* * *

Richardson's story was featured on the left side of the *Herald*'s front page and ran under the headline, "WAS CARDELLA GUNMAN'S TARGET?"

"Six weeks ago, an unknown assassin entered Chi-Chi's Bar & Grille in downtown Providence, hurried to the rear of the establishment and brutally murdered both Al Niro, a part-time bookmaker, and Richie Cardella, a Republican candidate for governor of Rhode Island (who succumbed to his massive wounds nine days later). Since then, the attention of the police and everyone else interested in the case has been focused on what reason anyone had for wanting Niro dead.

This line of inquiry was based on the fact that the killer was heard to say the words, 'We warned you' to Niro before shooting him. The assumption followed that Cardella became a victim because he was standing almost directly across from Niro's booth, answering a telephone call, and probably saw the gunman's face.

Investigation by both the Providence and State Police departments turned up evidence that Niro ran his gambling operation out of Chi-Chi's for approximately four years, taking wagers during the football season. Similar bookmaking operations, all on a small scale like Niro's, were found to exist in a number of downtown and area bars and restaurants. None of the other individuals involved in accepting bets in this manner have received threats aimed at persuading them to cease their activities. There is no evidence that Niro was actually threatened in such a way.

For this reason, the police now appear to be convinced that the Family which presides over big time gambling in Rhode Island from its headquarters on Federal Hill, led by Salvatore Tarantino, was not involved in the slayings that occurred.

Yet it has become clear that Al Niro had no other enemies who wanted him out of the way. Contrary to rumors that surfaced early, Niro was never involved in drugs in any way, shape or form. He owed no gambling debts himself and was not invested in any other kind of criminal activity taking place in the City.

Weeks of intensive investigation revealed only that Niro worked at his lawn maintenance/snow removal business on a regular basis during the day and supplemented his income marginally by taking small bets on football games at night from July through January.

That being the case, how do we explain the horrible events of that Monday evening at Chi-Chi's?

This reporter thinks we must begin to look at what happened with the premise that Richie Cardella was the prime target for the killer, and that it was Al Niro who suffered the loss of his life simply for being where he was.

While police can find no provocation for the murder of Niro, there is at least one possible motive for eliminating Cardella and taking him out of the race for governor: namely, that he was a strong proponent of State-sponsored casino gaming parlors, to be located throughout Rhode Island.

Cardella declared on numerous occasions during the primary campaign that if elected, he would support such legislation and fight for its enactment.

His position on the issue was diametrically opposed to that of Doug Fiore, against whom he was running to secure the Republican nomination for governor in the general election.

At the point that Cardella was gunned down, one week before the primary balloting, he was running five points ahead of Fiore in the polls and looked to be a winner in the election.

Who would profit by Cardella's death? This reporter is unable to point a finger at anyone or any group at this time because there is no evidence available yet to rely upon. But clearly, the interests of those who do not want to see the State become involved with casino gambling were dramatically served by Cardella's tragic removal from the gubernatorial campaign.

Was the Tarantino family involved? Did the order for Cardella's death come from Federal Hill?

It must be pointed out that the Family has not been charged with a single homicide in our State since Salvatore Tarantino took control of the operation on the death of Anthony Buscatelli in 1969.

The people of Rhode Island should also be aware that the Tarantinos have taken the Family completely out of many criminal activities in which its members were involved during the Buscatelli regime.

But as this reporter detailed four days ago, there was a strong friendship between Sandy Tarantino and Doug Fiore during their years together at Princeton University and Columbia Law School. Fiore and a spokesman for the Tarantino family have denied any close relationship since that time, but a different look at Cardella's death may prompt further investigation.

The scenario as I see it is this: someone decided to kill Cardella once it became clear that he would defeat Fiore. A professional hit man was kept on call to get to Cardella in an unguarded moment and in a situation offering a planned getaway.

Chi-Chi's was considered a prime spot at which to perform the act because Cardella frequented it regularly and there was an escape route through the back door and down an alleyway.

The person responsible for the crime knew the layout at Chi-Chi's and was also aware that Al Niro always occupied the booth closest to the back door. When Cardella was seen entering Chi-Chi's on Monday evening, the operation was put into effect. A car was sent to the alley behind the bar and the hit man was brought to the scene. He was familiar with both Cardella's and Niro's appearance, either from having known one or both of them or from having been shown pictures of them earlier.

The killer was told that Cardella would be at the phone in the rear of the restaurant, but was instructed to shoot Niro first, saying the words, 'We warned you' just before doing so.

Someone (from outside the bar, apparently) dialed the number of the pay phone at Chi-Chi's and asked for Cardella. At the right moment the assassin entered the bar and did the rest. The words he spoke were deliberately intended to manipulate the police and defeat the investigation.

This reporter is confident that the police will continue to explore all possible avenues in attempting to solve these murders, including, it is hoped, the one set forth in this space."

83

At 241 Atwells Avenue, Sandy Tarantino sat in his father's office along with another man who prided himself on being one of Sal's closest friends for years.

The man was awakened early that morning by a telephone call and alerted to Richardson's story in the *Herald*. As soon as he read it, he got dressed and called in sick at work. He disguised himself with an expensive toupee, horn-rimmed glasses and a paste-on beard, all purchased much earlier and kept ready for occasions such as this. In his closet, he found an old raincoat and a white Cape Codder hat that he could pull down over his forehead, just above his eyes. Before leaving home and driving seventeen miles to a mall in East Providence, he removed the telephone receiver from its cradle as he would do if an illness kept him at home in bed. At the mall, a taxi picked him up outside a "Benny's" department store and dropped him off in a small parking lot belonging to a building facing Atwells Avenue. He quickly made his way to the rear entrance of the building, punched the right combination of numbers into the coded lock next to the door, and entered. The stairway to the Tarantino offices was just as steep in back as it was in front.

As soon as Joe Gaudette sat down in the chair in front of Sal Tarantino's desk, he removed all parts of the disguise he put on earlier at home. He saw the light covering of white powder on the rash areas of the Mafia don's face and watched in silence as he took out his handkerchief and softly patted his cheeks and chin. When he finished, Sal spoke sharply to his son and the police captain whose help and advice he so often relied upon. "I told you, Salvy, and you too, Joe, I was against letting that Richardson come in here. The broad's poison, and she could cause us a lot of trouble, a lot of trouble."

"You've already said that a few times, Pop. Now that Joe's here, let's just figure out what we're going to do." Sandy was irritated with his father, but still spoke softly, with respect.

Gaudette moved his chair so that he could easily turn his head from Sal to Sandy. "Alright," he said, "maybe I can summarize where I think we're at. We know someone did a job on Niro and Cardella. We didn't know why and we didn't care who it was. It was a big break for Fiore and the Family and that's all we were concerned about. But now things have changed. Half of Rhode Island probably thinks that Cardella's death sentence came out of this room because that's what Richardson was saying between the lines. She made it sound like the Family is the only one that could have a motive. So we've got to move fast and try to get our hands on this guy real quick, before the election. I'll do what I can to expand the investigation when I go back to work tomorrow, but your contacts on this are a lot better than ours."

"Richardson's one smart reporter," Sandy said.

"I wish you'd figured that out before we let her in here," Sal answered, shaking his head.

A half hour later, a different taxicab pulled out of the parking lot behind Atwells Avenue with Joe Gaudette in the back seat. He was fairly certain that his close friend, Sal Tarantino, had nothing to do with Cardella's death. Still, he wasn't sure he would bet his life on it if it came to that.

When Gaudette left, Sandy drafted a letter on his word processor and showed it to his father. Sal read it and handed it back. "All on account of that goddamn broad," he said. "Without her, we wouldn't have this headache and Fiore would win going away."

Sandy unlocked a drawer in his desk and took out a listing of names and telephone numbers. He went over to the fax machine and sent the letter out 14 times.

My Honorable Brother • 377

84

THE FIRST OF THE two scheduled televised debates between Singer and Fiore took place that night. It was sponsored by The League of Women Voters and held in Sayles Hall on the Brown University campus. Each side received 200 complimentary tickets to hand out to its supporters. A limited number of Brown students with ID cards were allowed to attend.

All the questions were put to the candidates by three panelists. One of the two men was a senior editor at the *Newport Record*, the other a political reporter for the *Pawtucket Evening Times*. The third participant was the very popular female member of the WPRI-TV twin anchor team in Providence.

None of the panelists referred specifically to Jenna Richardson's front page story that day. A decision was reached earlier to refrain from questions that might cause the debate to deteriorate into charges and countercharges. As a result, no one interrogated Fiore directly about his relationship with the Tarantino family.

However, the *Evening Times* reporter attempted to get at the issue in a different way. "Would you tell us, Mr. Fiore, why you're opposed to casino style gaming under State auspices when that's the same stand that the gambling interests in Rhode Island obviously favor."

Fiore's reply was identical to what he was telling audiences around the State and to what he said in radio and newspaper interviews throughout the campaign. "That kind of gambling encourages decadence and would stifle Rhode Island's economic growth in many ways," he answered, enumerating the list of negatives, one by one. "It's only happenstance," he continued, "that what's best for the hard-working citizens of this State turns out to be good business for those who cater to people with a need to gamble."

Fiore delivered the answer in the most emotional tone he could raise. He then added, gratuitously, that as far as he was concerned, the campaign stories that appeared in the *Providence Herald* that week were one reporter's "flights of fantasy." Despite the announcement before the debate began that applause for any candidate was prohibited, Fiore's supporters registered strong approval of his remarks. The moderator again admonished the audience to refrain from such conduct.

At the conclusion of the 90-minute program, Fiore walked across the stage to shake hands with Singer. Cyril Berman had informed him in their debate preparation that the viewers always gave a point or two to the candidate who appeared the more sociable. While Doug was still smiling and talking to Singer, Grace and their daughter joined him. He kissed and embraced both of them. That was part of Berman's scenario also, as soon as he learned from Fiore that in all probability Carol Singer would not be present.

The Fiore family broke away from Singer and moved to the other end of the stage to greet supporters. Soon after, Rachel and Bonnie Singer, both of whom came home from college for the event, reached their father's side and offered their congratulations with kisses. But the single pool camera covering the post-debate proceedings stayed with the more photogenic Fiores for the better part of another minute before switching back to local programming at each of the three major channels. News anchors began soliciting various opinions from around the State as to which of the candidates came out on top. Thirty minutes later, consensus called it a draw and Cyril Berman was a happy man.

85

GERRY QUINN KNEW WHAT he was talking about when he told Richardson that her story about Richie Cardella being the prime victim at Chi-Chi's might shake some things out of the trees. In his thirty-five years as a cop, he saw it happen time and time again. An investigation went nowhere for months—in some cases, years—and then one new clue, prominently publicized, or brought to the attention of various suspects, succeeded in prodding a key witness to let the cat out of the bag in an effort to save himself.

On Friday afternoon, Jenna got a call in her office from Lester Karp. He started to remind her that he was treasurer of the Fiore campaign. She interrupted, saying that she remembered him well from having spent an entire day earlier in the month following his candidate around.

"I want to know whether I can speak to you off the record, Miss Richardson. I wouldn't want my name used if I gave you certain information. No, let me put it differently. I'll consider talking to you only if you agree to attribute anything I say to "a source claiming to have ties to the Fiore organization."

Jenna's gut told her that something good was on the way. "I can certainly do that," she assured him, "but I'd have to be convinced I was talking to the right Lester Karp."

"Of course," he replied. "I understand." He gave her his home telephone number and suggested she call the following morning, before 10:00 a.m. "I still want to think it over," he said, terminating the conversation.

* * *

Lester Karp's stomach hadn't stopped bothering him since he read Richardson's story on Thursday morning. At first he tried taking some Tums, but when that didn't give him relief, he switched to the stronger Gelusil tablets. Still, the nervous tension wouldn't go away.

Karp reached the same conclusion as Jenna as to what really happened at Chi-Chi's, but he arrived at that point at least two weeks before she did. The idea suddenly entered his mind while he was lunching alone in a downtown Providence cafeteria, and rapidly escalated to a conviction he couldn't dismiss. Now that the probable reason for the crime was out there for the public to read about, ponder, and in all likelihood accept, Karp was worried. The *Herald*'s finger was being pointed at the Tarantino family, at least by insinuation. If it did order the bloodbath that took place, there could be follow-up allegations that everyone holding a high position in the Fiore campaign was aware of the plan and assented to it.

Karp knew how badly the Tarantinos wanted to see Fiore win the election. He never spoke to either Sal or Sandy directly, in person or otherwise, since he was enlisted to work in the campaign by Russell Walsh; but he was in Berman's room at the Biltmore quite often while Cyril spoke to one or both of the Tarantinos on the telephone. There were ways Karp could tell the incoming call was from Sal or Sandy. For one thing, Berman never mentioned the other person's name during the conversation. And he habitually held his other hand close to his ear, as if convinced that it was the best way to keep the sound of the voice on the other end from being heard by anyone else in the room.

It wasn't difficult for Karp to imagine the concern behind the message being communicated to Berman on those occasions. It was enough to hear Cyril say, "It's risky, but I'll look into it," or, "I *know* how important this is for you." And Berman's reply was just above a whisper several times when he said, "I think you're right on that one. Let's win the election and afterwards we can worry about whether we should have done it."

Karp remembered the time Berman finished one of those conversations, turned to him and Russell Walsh and said, "If I ever tell you we're going to do something that sounds unethical, illegal, or immoral, call me on it. We promised Fiore he could have his clean campaign and I'm not looking for ways to beat Singer if they're dirty. Make me justify anything that smells to you like it has crossed the line. I may not change my mind if I disagree with both of you, and I may not even have the final say. That may come down to Fiore and the Tarantinos. But let's all be aware that the people who want Fiore in the governor's office talk as if they're willing to do anything to get him there."

If Richie Cardella was murdered because he stood in Doug Fiore's way, Karp wanted to be certain that everyone knew he wasn't a part of that decision. He was a successful businessman all his life, and was tapped for fund-raising by the Republican Party in earlier political campaigns because he had a multitude of friends who contributed when he asked. His contacts resulted in large sums given to the Women & Infants Hospital, the Museum of Art, and the Rhode Island Philharmonic Orchestra, each of which he served as a trustee.

Lester Karp was a respected name in the Providence community, and he didn't want even a hint of scandal attaching to it, especially now, near the end of a distinguished career. But even more importantly, if this tragedy *did* come off on orders from Federal Hill, he realized how dangerous it could be for the people of Rhode Island to have Fiore in office. The State's Governor would be beholden to killers.

The only thing Karp knew was that he wasn't involved in any conspiracy to end Cardella's life, but he wasn't certain about the others. He doubted that Walsh was brought in on something like that ahead of time. Walsh was more of a fringe player, like him. If he had to wager, he'd say that Berman wasn't part of the plan either, but he couldn't be sure. He recalled how shocked Berman seemed to be when news of what happened at Chi-Chi's came over their car radio that night, but he supposed it could have been play acting, all part of the game. Karp asked himself a number of times whether he thought Doug Fiore would go along with such a scheme. It disturbed him that he couldn't come up with an answer that allayed his fears.

* * *

Richardson called him at just after 9:30 in the morning. There was only one Lester Karp listed in the Providence directory, at the number he gave her. Still, she asked him a few questions that she knew no one but the real Lester Karp could answer. He understood the reason for what she was doing, and willingly responded. He told her the nickname he was given by Russell Walsh, the location of the window on his Lincoln that lost its power control and the name of the credit card she heard him say was the only card a person ever needed.

"You've got some memory there," he said, in a complimentary tone.

When Jenna asked what he wanted to tell her, Karp first had her confirm that she wouldn't use his name in any connection with the information he related. He explained that there were some things about the campaign only he and a handful of other people knew. Those things couldn't be revealed directly without the others speculating that he was very possibly the source. But he could suggest that she do some more investigating in a particular area that ought to lead her to the same facts.

"The only thing you're absolutely right about, Miss Richardson, is the relationship between Sandy Tarantino and Fiore. Make no mistake about it, the Tarantinos want him to be governor so he can veto any legislation that would let the State open up the kinds of casinos operated by the Family. They know from everything that's been said at the Statehouse that the vote on casino gambling would be very close either way. If it's passed, there wouldn't be enough votes to override a veto by the governor.

"I suspect that Sandy Tarantino talked Fiore into running for office and coming out strong against casino gambling, but I can't be sure of that. Fiore's got a huge ego and maybe he figured he could do the job as well as the three others who were already in the race before he announced. It's possible he called Tarantino first, just to feel him out about financial support, and ended up hitting the jackpot. The bottom line is that the Family put up a lot of money to get the campaign off the ground and keep it moving."

Jenna interrupted. "I checked out their contributions to him, Mr. Karp, and they weren't very large at all."

"Not the ones they knew the public would see," he replied. "You were hitting the nail on the head. The problem is that you couldn't bang it in far enough. I'll tell you what to do. Go back to those lists of campaign contributors. We file a new one every month. I'm sure you're aware that a person can give up to a thousand dollars to any candidate. Take a name, like Morgan for example—I'm making that one up—and go through all the lists. September's is already on file, by the way, even though the *Herald* hasn't published it yet. Count up the Morgans and see where they live. Maybe you'll find five of them at the same address, each giving the maximum amount. That could be the husband, the wife and three children. A little unusual, wouldn't you say? It would be interesting to see how recently the checking accounts for the children were opened.

"Or perhaps you'll see that the Morgan children are all married and that each of them and their spouses also sent in a thousand apiece. Another unusual giving pattern, you'd have to admit. It would be very revealing to know how many of those checking accounts started with cash that was hand delivered to the Morgans or others from a source on Federal Hill. Maybe you can't check some of those things, Miss Richardson. You don't have much time left anyhow. But people you speak to may give you some good information without realizing it. What do you think?"

"You're right, Mr. Karp, it's going to be a time-consuming thing to try and pin down. I'm not even sure how much the average voter would care about that sort of thing anyway. But I'll take a look at it. Maybe it will be a good post-election story, regardless of who wins. That still leaves me wondering why you called. It wasn't just to tell me *this*, was it?"

"No, that's not the main reason." There was a pause, and Jenna heard him exhaling into the phone.

"This part has to be strictly confidential, just something I want to get off my chest, but between you and me and no one else."

"Agreed, Mr. Karp."

"I don't know whether you're right or not about who was responsible for what happened to Cardella, but I agree with you that he was the target. The other guy, the bookie, was the one in the wrong place at the wrong time. That's what I've thought for a while already. It's important for me to say that if the Tarantino family had anything to do with it, I never heard a word about it ahead of time. Believe me, I would have called the police if I did." Karp paused again. "That's what I wanted you to know. What I told you about the finances was just to give you something else to go on in case Tarantino or Fiore was involved at Chi-Chi's."

"I understand. I'm glad you told me that, Mr. Karp. It helps a lot to know you feel I'm on the right track. Please don't hesitate to call me again if you'd like."

86

The rest of the week went by slowly, and each day Carol Singer waited for the other shoe to drop.

There was no doubt that she and Fiore made love in Room 606. The day after Bruce told her about the tapes, she walked over to the Biltmore to check the location of the room. She recalled that it was not directly on the corridor, but required her to step into an alcove before reaching the door. Carol took an elevator to the seventh floor and walked down the hallway to 706. It was just as she remembered, and Room 506 was in the exact same location, two floors below.

That meant, she realized, that as Bruce continued to listen to the tapes, he would suddenly recognize her voice along with Fiore's. He would hear her sighs and her moaning with pleasure as the two lovers engaged in whatever it took to satisfy each other. Carol anticipated her husband's shock and then outrage at the words and sounds burning his ears. It was impossible to avoid vividly picturing the confrontation that would take place between them.

Carol had already mentally rehearsed the response she would give him any number of times. The scene with Bruce permeated her consciousness at all hours of the day or night but it never came out the same way twice. At times she saw herself breaking down and begging for forgiveness. At others she defended herself and blamed him. He was at fault for pushing her into an affair by constantly neglecting her in favor of politics and his law practice. Depending on her mood, there was a different scenario for the inevitable encounter that would occur.

But there was no doubt in her mind that Bruce's awareness of her infidelity meant the end of their marriage. It troubled her deeply when she considered the total amount of pain she'd inflict on him were he to lose the election to the man who was sleeping with his wife.

Carol was also distressed about the situation with Fiore. She felt betrayed by his carrying on another affair at the same time, one she had no inkling of whatsoever. It forced her to wonder about the kind of man who needed more than one mistress. When they discussed their sexual fantasies one night, he told her that he always wanted to see what it was like to make love to two women at the same time. Carol wondered now whether his becoming a lover to both of them was a prelude to his thinking about bringing both Pat Hanley and herself into bed with him.

She had no idea when Doug's relationship with Hanley began. She thought that perhaps it was after she stopped seeing him, when he became a candidate for governor. If that's when it happened, Carol had only herself to blame for giving him that opening. He had every right to believe that their affair was over and that he could look for someone else.

But if he started an affair with another woman, why didn't he just leave Carol out of his life? Why couldn't he walk past her in the lobby of the Biltmore that night without saying a word? Why did he stop to speak to her and invite her up to Room 606?

Did she want to have anything more to do with Doug Fiore? Would she meet him again if he called? Carol wasn't sure of the answer.

87

Richardson's next column appeared on Tuesday, a week before the election. It summarized the additional information she gathered since articulating the view five days earlier that Cardella was stalked and murdered.

She noted that a spokesman for the Tarantino family—a lawyer from the firm of Fisher & Lovett, specializing in criminal law—issued a statement adamantly denying that his client had anything whatsoever to do with a plot to murder Richie Cardella, if in fact one existed. The police, Jenna pointed out, had neither arrested anyone from the Family nor charged it with any wrongdoing since the shooting occurred. She also indicated that her efforts to reach Salvatore Tarantino or his son were unsuccessful, and that no one from Fisher & Lovett was willing to answer any of her questions.

"I have learned from 'a source claiming to have ties to the Fiore organization,'" she wrote, "that the Tarantino family has allegedly funneled large sums of their own money to the candidate through other individuals whose names appeared on the lists of contributors. If that's true, it would be a violation of the Act governing campaign contributions and subject to criminal penalties. The Tarantinos are apparently working very hard on behalf of Fiore's election, and if he does succeed John Sacco in the governor's office, they are no doubt counting on his being ready and willing to veto any legislation authorizing State government to get into the casino gaming business."

In the limited amount of time Jenna had to review the different lists of contributors to Fiore's campaign and to make follow-up phone calls, she was unable to make a definitive case for the information given her by Lester Karp. In fact, she hadn't yet scrutinized the latest list she was able to obtain from the Secretary of State's office. But she pointed out for her readers that a number of individuals from different families around the State, entire households in some cases, were each documented as having made the maximum contribution to Fiore. She went on to infer that such a pattern of giving was unusual at best, and that further investigation was necessary on this aspect of the campaign.

Jenna brought her column to a close by calling on the police to do everything in their power to try and solve the Cardella killing before the election, just seven days away.

* * *

A separate article in that morning's *Herald* contained the results of a poll taken by WPRI-TV, in conjunction with the Alpha Research Associates polling firm during the 72-hour period ending at noon on Sunday. It indicated that Fiore's lead over Singer slipped to a mere percentage point. Considering the margin of error of two percent, plus or minus, in the poll itself, the race was a virtual dead heat.

Cyril Berman knew that the latest tracking numbers were all Jenna Richardson's fault. Based on his past experience, he assumed the race would tighten up in its final two weeks, but never considered that some external event would suddenly put Singer in a position to win. He didn't know what Richardson had in mind for the coming week, but figured it wouldn't hurt to threaten her employer with a libel action for her unfounded insinuations. Maybe that would at least slow her down.

88

On Tuesday afternoon, the third day after the end of Daylight Saving Time, it was already dark outside by 4:30. Sandy Tarantino stood by the window of his office, sipping a cup of espresso he ordered from the café downstairs. He was watching the traffic pick up on Atwells Avenue, most of it heading toward the Interstate just blocks away where it would divide north and south. Behind him, he heard the ringing on his fax line. Moments later, he was aware of the humming sound made by the printing element as the machine began to accept a message.

Tarantino was thinking about the Family's chances of keeping a casino gambling bill from getting through the State legislature in the event Doug Fiore lost the election. There was no doubt in his mind that the momentum was now with Singer, thanks to Jenna Richardson's reporting, and he figured that Singer's latest TV ad would keep things moving in his direction. It was powerful, reminding the voters that he fought in Vietnam while Fiore avoided the conflict through the influence of Rhode Island's notorious Buscatelli family.

Tarantino spoke to Cyril Berman by phone earlier that afternoon while Fiore was making a speech in Glendale. He hoped to hear that Berman had uncovered one or two bombshells he could use against Singer in the final days of the campaign. The news in that regard was disappointing.

"What we're down to now, Sandy, is that Doug has to do a fantastic job in the debate Thursday night. A lot of people are going to be tuned in to that one. And we've got to hope like hell the *Herald* gives him its endorsement for governor on Sunday."

"What are our chances of that?" Sandy asked.

"I'd say it's at least fifty-fifty," Berman offered optimistically. "I'm going on the fact that Fiore's position on gambling is consistent with what's appeared in the *Herald*'s editorials on that subject, and they feel pretty strong about it."

In Berman's view, there was no reason to conclude that Singer would get the paper's backing. He didn't think that was an automatic just because Richardson raised the possibility of the Tarantinos being responsible for Cardella's death. Her view was pure speculation, with nothing to back it up. He had a strong feeling that under those circumstances the senior editors at the *Herald* would choose not to give it any weight in their endorsement decision. "Hell, this is still America, Sandy," he said, "the presumption of innocence and all that."

Berman told Tarantino that he had an appointment to meet with Dan McMurphy on Thursday afternoon. "He's the editor Richardson reports to. I want to talk to him about the crap she's been writing and make a case for them giving their editorial support to Fiore. Maybe I can convince McMurphy that they owe it to us after all the slime ball stuff she's been putting in the paper."

* * *

Sal Tarantino came into his son's office through the adjoining door. "I'm getting out of here, Salvy," he said. "Maybe if I go home and lie down, I'll feel better." As he finished speaking, a single beep from the fax machine indicated that it completed its receipt of the incoming transmission. "You've got something on your machine there," he added, pointing toward the fax.

"I know, Pop, I was just waiting for it to end." Sandy went over and removed the two sheets of paper from the tray. He crumpled the cover page in his left hand and flipped it into the wastebasket as he looked at the letter addressed to his father.

"It's from Dave DePaolo in Cleveland. It's for you," Sandy said, extending the paper toward him.

"What does he want?" Sal asked.

Sandy read the letter. "It looks like he wants you to start feeling better right away. He says the man we've been looking for will be in Providence tomorrow morning."

Sal sat down, took out a cigarette without removing the package from his shirt pocket, and lit it. "That's good news. How do we get hold of him?"

Sandy looked at the fax. "He'll be on US Air flight 170, scheduled in at 9:52 in the morning. His escort wants to hand him over and go right back to Cleveland. DePaolo says we should have someone standing there holding a sign that says MR. CARTER-EXPRESS, so the escort will be sure he's giving him to the right person. Here, Pop, I think you ought to read everything he says."

Sal Tarantino scanned the letter. "Tell Rocco and Al to meet me in front of the Dunkin' Donuts near the airport at nine in the morning, with that sign you just mentioned. After we see this guy, I'll call you here." He dropped the fax back on his son's desk. "It's going to be hard waiting until tomorrow," he said.

89

Fiore's last appearance on Tuesday night was in Pascoag, in the northwest corner of the State. It was the last time they would do any personal campaigning in that area, and Cyril Berman scheduled a day full of meetings and speeches. They started in Chepachet at 8:30 that morning, at a businessman's breakfast, and made stops in Mapleville, Glendale, Slatersville and Bridgeton before winding up the evening in Pascoag at a Chamber of Commerce dinner. Berman told Doug to stand around and shake hands with everyone in the VFW hall who wanted to meet him. He knew they needed every vote they could get.

It was almost 10:30 when Fiore, Berman and Walsh emerged from the building and climbed into Karp's Lincoln. Karp moved the car out of the parking lot ten minutes earlier and was waiting in front, the heat turned up against the chilly, early November night.

"What a day," Walsh said from the front seat, not looking at anyone.

"It's almost over . . . it's almost over." Berman seemed to let the words out with a sigh. "Six more days and that's it. You feeling okay Doug?"

Fiore sat in a far corner of the back seat, his body slack, his legs stretched out in front of him. He was in a bad mood all day, saying very little while they were on the road, and moving off by himself whenever they stopped to take a break. It was as if he found it necessary to save all his energy for the next speech, the next receiving line. And he performed well in front of every audience, so Berman told the others not to bother him, to speak only if they were spoken to.

"We're going to lose this fucking thing, aren't we, Cyril?" Fiore's eyes stayed closed when he asked the question.

Berman was surprised by Fiore's use of the expletive. He couldn't recall hearing him swear once in the time they spent together. "It's too close to call, Doug. They give you a one point lead in the polls. That's better than being down a point. Singer would be happy to trade places with you. He's had the momentum lately but that can change fast. You've got to come on strong in the debate Thursday, and I think we're a shoo-in if you get the *Herald*'s endorsement this weekend."

"It would help more if someone pushed Jenna Richardson off the Newport Bridge, that bitch." Doug said.

Both Walsh and Karp laughed out loud in the front seat.

"Where the hell did she get that stuff about the Tarantinos putting up a lot of money? Who's the 'source' she's talking about? I thought we were the only ones who knew what was happening." Fiore's frustration was evident.

Karp felt some tightening in his chest. He thought Richardson did a good job disguising the basis for her story, but he didn't trust himself to get into a conversation about it. He was relieved to hear Berman say that anyone studying the lists of contributors carefully could speculate that some individuals were probably being helped to give to the campaign by others.

"The information could have come from any number of people," Berman added. "That includes personal friends of the Tarantinos who were hit up for money and knew exactly how it was being spent." He didn't suspect for a moment that Richardson was enlightened by either Karp or Walsh. "There are always people around who talk too much to a reporter without realizing what they're saying," Berman told them. "Not everyone out there with a Fiore sign on their lawn has smarts, Doug. And the only way you can try to get a reporter to name a source is to sue them if you can show damages. Forget about it."

They rode along in silence for a while. Fiore loosened his tie and then took a granola bar out of his briefcase. When he finished eating, he turned to Berman. "I think we've got to find something negative to say about Singer. The *Herald*'s not going to throw its support to me after those columns by Richardson. It doesn't figure. They'd be cutting her heart out if they did. We've got to come up with *something* that hurts

Singer really bad, even if we have to fudge the facts. Otherwise, we're going to lose this thing. You know I'm right, Cyril."

"I don't think we can do that," Berman replied quickly. "It's been a clean campaign on both sides. All the papers have said that you and Singer deserve a lot of credit for that. If you suddenly go negative, especially with stuff that turns out to be only half true, there could be a backlash in your direction. The media will pick up on it right away, and they'll be all over us in the press and on TV. I told you I've checked Singer out totally. He's a good family man, and he doesn't drink or chase other women. When he was lieutenant governor, he never asked for a kickback on anything or took one if it was offered. You ask anyone at the Statehouse and they'll tell you he didn't put five cents in his pocket that didn't belong to him. Believe me, Doug, he's squeaky clean. You're going to have to beat him on the issues, and you can do it."

Fiore closed his eyes again. "You may be right, but it was easy to go with a clean campaign while we were ahead. There was no pressure then to go after Singer with anything we could dig up, but there is now. I haven't gone through a half year of this shit to lose. I'll do whatever it takes to beat him, and if we can come up with something sensational, that's what everyone will be talking about. No one will be shedding tears about the end of a clean campaign. Just go to work and get something on that bastard fast while there's still time to do some damage. If we get the facts wrong, we can always apologize after the election."

Walsh and Karp looked at each other in the front seat. Both were aware of the sudden metamorphosis in Fiore's character as evidenced by his foul language and his declared willingness to do anything to win the election, even if it involved lying about his opponent. Their faces showed their concern with what was happening. Berman turned away from Fiore and was looking out the car window as it sped toward Providence. He knew there was nothing negative he could come up with about Singer, and even if he could, it would have to be the truth. He didn't believe in doing anything it took to win.

90

The Wednesday collections were over for Tommy Arena before noon. He counted all the money he was given by the freight deliverers, divided it in half, and put equal amounts in separate manila envelopes. The envelopes went back inside his briefcase, and he hollered "Ciao" to the restaurant owner as he left the store.

Walking toward his car parked at the end of the block, Arena saw a State Police cruiser pulled up behind it, with someone sitting at the wheel. He ignored it and went to unlock the door of his Oldsmobile. Suddenly, the horn from the cruiser sounded, startling him. Its uniformed occupant was waving his hand, signaling Arena to come over. He walked to the driver's window.

"Get in the car for a minute, Tommy. I want to talk to you."

"Do I know you?" he asked.

"It doesn't matter. Get in."

Joe Gaudette had waited almost an hour for Arena to finish his business. He received a relayed message at home the night before from Sandy Tarantino and learned of the fax sent by Dave DePaolo, the Mafia boss in Cleveland. Tarantino said that he expected his father to be meeting with their "guest" near the airport by ten minutes after ten the next morning if the plane arrived on time. He wanted Gaudette to know that depending on what Sal Tarantino found out, they might need his help right after that. Sandy instructed his friend to wait next to the series of pay phones in the parking area of the Howard Johnson

Motel on Jefferson Boulevard in Warwick at that time in the morning. He left word that he had the numbers for all six phones and would call him there as soon as he could.

Sandy reached Gaudette shortly after 10:30 that morning and brought him up to date on what Sal knew. They worked out certain details and a timetable for specific action to be taken on each end. "We don't want to fire the guy, Joe. We'd much rather see him resign. You understand?"

"I understand," he answered. "I'll be as persuasive as I can." Gaudette made a stop at a CVS Pharmacy, drove to the street where Arena's Wednesday morning collection "office" was located and waited there for him to come out.

Arena sat down in the front seat and saw the bars on Gaudette's lapel. "You're a captain, right?" Before getting an answer, he added, "So what the fuck crime did I commit?" He figured it had something to do with the collections he just made, and expected to be asked about the contents of his briefcase. His mind was racing to come up with a reason for having two envelopes full of money in his possession.

"Relax, Tommy, I'm just helping out a mutual friend of ours. Sal Tarantino's having a late lunch at the Marriott today with a few associates, and he wants you to join him. I don't know whether he wants to speak to you alone or with the other guys. He's thinking of retiring soon, you know, and he's starting to put everything in order. You can probably figure out why he wants you there."

Arena smiled. "You're a good friend of his, huh? Sonofabitch. That fucking Sal knows all the angles."

Gaudette nodded his head and smiled back at Arena. "So here's what's happening," he said. "Get back in your car and drive on over to the Marriott right now. We're going to wait for Sal in the Coach Room, one of the three conference rooms in the basement. He'll let us know where to go, where the meeting is." Gaudette turned on the car's ignition. "Get started now. I'll be right behind you all the way."

Arena said he had to call his office to let them know he wouldn't be in. He also had to tell his wife that he might not be able to drive her to the dentist at 3:30 that afternoon. Gaudette told him he could make the calls from the Marriott as soon as Tarantino let him know how long he'd be there.

Twenty minutes later they were in the Coach Room together and sat there another half hour, just killing time. Gaudette picked up copies of the *Providence Herald* and *USA Today* in the lobby news shop. Arena turned to the local sports page and soon began talking about the Providence Bruins hockey team.

"They never were any fucking good and they'll never get any fucking better. It don't matter who coaches them. That team has a curse on it. Every fucking game they try to invent a new way to lose. I wouldn't go see them play if the tickets were free. Waste of fucking time."

At one o'clock Gaudette said he'd call Tarantino and find out what was going on. "You stay right here," he told Arena. He returned five minutes later. "Sal wants you to check into a room under some phony name and pay in advance with cash. He said to use his money, that you should have some dough with you that belongs to him. Sal says it won't be long and that I should wait with you."

The two men returned to the lobby. Gaudette stood close enough to the registration desk to hear the clerk tell "Mr. Russo" he'd be in Room 429 as he gave him the key and a receipt. They went to the room and began waiting there, talking about the election. Fifteen minutes later Arena wondered out loud when Tarantino planned to have lunch. "I ain't had a fucking thing to eat since 6:30 this morning," he complained, "and I ain't called my wife or my secretary. I'm gonna do that right now." Arena got up from his chair.

"If you get on the phone, Tommy, Sal can't reach us. Then he may keep us waiting just for the hell of it. Give him a few more minutes. You can keep working up an appetite and it'll taste better when you dig in. Just relax."

At 1:45 Gaudette picked up his chair from next to the window and carried it to the other side of the king-size bed, closer to the door. He leaned back in the chair and balanced it on its rear legs. "Tommy," he said, "do you know a guy named Johnny Baldacci?"

"Who?" Arena asked, narrowing his eyes and bringing his left thumb and forefinger up to his chin.

"Johnny Baldacci. They call him Johnny Balls."

"No, I don't know him. I mighta heard the name once or twice but that's it."

"That's funny, Tommy, because he says he knows you real well. Says you gave him ten grand a couple of months ago for a few minutes work at Chi-Chi's."

"You're pulling my fucking chain. I don't know what you're talking about and I'm getting sick of waiting around here." Arena got up from his chair again.

Gaudette let his right hand drop down and rest on the butt of his revolver. He told him to sit down. Arena hesitated, and then returned to his chair.

"Let me tell you what I'm talking about because it's important you understand everything. You listening, Tommy?"

Arena didn't want to answer, but had no choice. "Yeah, I'm listening. Probably be a lotta shit."

"Your friend Johnny Balls came back to Providence today. He made a special trip so he could confess to killing Al Niro and Richie Cardella. I hear it's going to go down as first-degree murder, life imprisonment with no parole. That's his reward for turning himself in. No needle in the arm. Not that he had too much of a choice, you understand. His loose talk got him in trouble. That and throwing around more money than he earned. The Family in Cleveland picked up on it and had a heart-to-heart chat with him. I guess they convinced him it was better to spend the rest of his life in the pen than go through what they'd have to do to him for the trouble he caused the Tarantinos. Johnny didn't agree with that at first, but it wasn't hard to get him to see the light. Those hits at Chi-Chi's gave Sal and his Family a real bad name around here. You read the papers, Tommy, so you know what I'm talking about. Poor Johnny didn't have any idea how tough things were going to work out for him when he pulled the trigger. But as they say, that's the way the cookie crumbles.

"Now here's the part you'd be most interested in. Johnny told Sal Tarantino this morning how you called in the big favor he owed you from five years ago. That's when you swore to the cops you never saw the guy who robbed the freight warehouse in Cranston and shot the security guard on his way out. Danny Finnegan was the guard's name, remember, Tommy? He ended up in a wheelchair for the rest of his life. Imagine how surprised Johnny Balls was to run right past you, his

Teamster business agent, on the way to his car, holding a gun in his hand. And how grateful he was you covered up for him."

Arena had a pained expression on his face as Gaudette spoke, and shook his head back and forth as each new fact came out. Gaudette didn't give him a chance to interrupt.

"No wonder Johnny stopped driving a truck and took the job he had in Cleveland. He loves the work. Anything that lets him pack a rod and use it now and then. But unfortunately for you, Tommy, you tried to make it look like the Tarantinos were behind that scene in Chi-Chi's to get Al Niro out of their hair. That line about 'We warned you,' that was cute, but it didn't work. On account of you, the Family's had some rotten PR in the past two months, and Sal Tarantino's awfully unhappy about it."

"Like I told you before, that's a lotta shit and it's all fucking lies. I ain't seen Johnny Balls in years and I didn't ask him to fucking kill no one."

Gaudette ignored the answer and looked at his watch. He pointed toward the television and told Arena to turn it on. "Let's see what's on the news," he said. "Put on Channel 10."

At 1:58 an announcer from the WJAR news desk came on for a two-minute update. He repeated the story, "as first reported here earlier today," that a John Baldacci had voluntarily surrendered to the Providence Police and confessed to the murders of the two men, including gubernatorial candidate Richie Cardella, in Chi-Chi's Bar & Grille on the night of September fifth. He informed his viewers that the killer implicated another man, who allegedly paid him to commit the crime. The police were attempting to locate the suspect, he said.

As soon as the announcer went on to the next item, Gaudette said, "That's it," and pointed to the TV again. Arena shut it off.

"They're out there looking for you, Tommy. But Sal doesn't think you want them to take you in. Sal says he's got a lot of friends wherever the cops lock you up, and that his friends won't be nice to you. Not nice at all. He says you're all finished, Tommy, you've got nowhere to go. Your life's over. But Sal wants you to know he'll take good care of your wife if you make things easy for everyone. He'll see that Maria gets all the money you're carrying in your briefcase right now and that she'll always

My Honorable Brother • 399

have enough to live on." Gaudette stood up. "You understand what I'm telling you, Tommy?"

Arena looked like he was feeling sick. He slumped in the chair, and only his head moved as he spoke. "Baldacci's a fucking liar. Sal probably told him what to say to the cops." He closed his eyes and let his head fall forward slightly. There was a long pause as Tommy began breathing heavily. "This is too fast," he whispered. "I didn't wake up today to fucking die."

Gaudette waited a few seconds before answering. "Cardella probably felt the same way if he could still think after your man put a hole in his chest." He paused again. "What did you have against him, anyway?"

Arena kept breathing in as much air as he could and then letting it out noisily. His eyes opened and closed several times as he spoke. "He was gonna ruin my fucking life. He knew how close I was to Sal and how me and the Family did things for each other over the years. Richie and I got drunk together one night while we were negotiating a deal, and I let him know some fucking things I shoulda kept to myself. We were telling war stories, you know? When the feds were checking me out this summer, I found out they spent a lotta time with him. I figured he could give them stuff they couldn't get from no one else. When they put me down for a fucking hearing, I knew he was gonna be their star witness and cost me my job and everything else. I had no fucking choice."

"That's too bad," Gaudette said. "I hate to see friends turn against each other. But you don't have a choice today either, Tommy." He reached in his pocket, slipped on a thin plastic glove and threw a package of razor blades onto the edge of the bed, in front of Arena. "Sal's letting you go out in class. A nice room. Take a warm bath and make a couple of cuts. If you wait to do it the other way, the cuts will hurt a hell of a lot more and leave you in the same place. Sal guarantees it."

Arena stood up. His face was flushed. "Sal don't know why I did it. Let me go see him or at least get him on the fucking phone for me so I can explain. He'll understand. Him and me go way back. He ain't gonna want me to die when he hears what I got to say."

"Sit down, Tommy." Gaudette waited until Arena complied. "Sal's already made the final decision. He doesn't care why you did it. He only cares about the trouble you caused him."

Arena's briefcase was on the bureau. Gaudette used his gloved hand to move it to the bed and opened it. He took out the two manila envelopes. "You've got Sal's word on these and what I told you before. Let's go Tommy. It's getting late."

Arena folded his arms in front of him and then began hitting his right arm with his open left hand. He closed his eyes again and let his chin drop to his chest. When he spoke, it was as if he was saying the words to himself, not to Gaudette. "If I was locked up, at least I'd have the chance to make a confession."

"I told you before, you wouldn't last that long," Gaudette said. "But just to save the department some trouble, why don't you write a note and let them know what you did. Tell them you're sorry, if you want. That's the only confession you're going to be able to make." Gaudette took the notepaper from the night table on his side of the bed and threw it next to the razor blades.

Arena didn't move. "Do it right now," Gaudette told him, "or you don't do it at all."

Tommy laid the pad down on the small round table next to his chair and took the pen from his shirt pocket. He stared down at the paper for half a minute.

"Write what I tell you," Gaudette said, unwilling to wait any longer. He dictated the words slowly. "'I'm sorry for what I did to Richie Cardella. I'm sorry Al Niro had to get hurt. I hope their families forgive me. I pray to God for mercy.'"

Arena wrote what he was told and put down the pen. Gaudette was about to tell him to sign it, but realized it wasn't necessary. "Alright, Tommy," he said, pointing toward the other end of the room, "you've got to take a bath and then I've got to tidy up."

91

EVEN AS ADDITIONAL DETAILS were released by the police and she continued putting together her story, Richardson remained skeptical about the events that were unfolding so suddenly.

No one had yet offered any explanation as to why Tommy Arena would have wanted to kill Richie Cardella. Jenna couldn't believe that any labor dispute in which they represented opposing sides would provoke Arena to seek revenge of that sort on his adversary, even one in which a long and difficult strike occurred to the detriment of the Teamsters. She knew she'd be researching the *Herald* files on Thursday to find out whether Arena and Cardella ever locked horns in that serious a battle.

She wondered whether Johnny Baldacci was ordered to say he was hired by Arena to do the killing. Baldacci didn't hide the fact that he was a member of the DePaolo family in Cleveland. He told the police that Dave DePaolo advised him to turn himself in when he learned that a member of his Family had committed the murders for which the Tarantinos were being blamed. The questions that Baldacci answered made it clear that DePaolo's advice wasn't something he was in a position to disregard if he wanted to continue breathing. *On that basis,* Jenna thought, *Baldacci may have incriminated Arena because he was told to do so, even if he was really paid by the Tarantinos to execute Cardella.*

That wasn't the end of Jenna's misgivings. There was the concern that maybe Arena was forced to slit his wrists in the bathtub at the Marriott just to avoid a death more horrible than that. She recalled a similar situation in the *Godfather* movie, something the Tarantinos might get a kick out of imitating. The confession they found was in Arena's handwriting, but maybe he did it with a gun to his head. It was possible that he was set up and then forced to kill himself before the authorities could find him and ask questions about Baldacci's allegations.

Still, Jenna had to admit that all the pieces seemed to fit into place. The story about Baldacci broke first on Channel 10 at 12:28 p.m. and was all over the radio dial a few minutes later. The police assumed that Arena heard it while he was in his car and realized they were probably out looking for him. In that case, the only way he could have any privacy to think things through was to take a hotel room under an assumed name. At first, Jenna couldn't figure out why a man who was going to kill himself would lay out ninety-five dollars to use a bathtub at the Marriott instead of his own, but then realized that Arena didn't have the option of going home.

She learned that he checked into the hotel under the name of Carl Russo shortly after one o'clock. That made the timing right, as it probably took him ten minutes or so to stop for razor blades along the way. (Richardson already knew that neither the shop in the hotel lobby nor the dispensing machine on the fourth floor carried the brand of single-edged blades that Arena used to slit his wrists.) His car was in the back of the parking lot, its doors locked, and the keys were in his jacket in the room. The fingerprint people were still checking to see whether there were any other prints on the steering wheel or the door handle. Jenna gathered from what she heard that no one expected to find anything there. In fact, as Gerry Quinn told them during a short question and answer session at 7:30 that night, "Everything points to an out-and-out suicide, girls and boys."

There were three details about the hotel scene that disturbed her. First, Jenna couldn't understand why Arena bothered to take his briefcase up to the room if it was empty. Quinn couldn't answer that one either, except to speculate that it was a matter of habit for him to carry it wherever he went, to look like a businessman.

Second, it was difficult for her to believe that he wouldn't call his wife with some message before taking his life, even to say something like "I love you," or just "Good-bye." But, as she had to admit to herself, the shame he felt over being found out may have stopped him from doing it once he realized that his wife, a strong Catholic from what Jenna picked up, knew he caused two people to die.

Finally, Jenna was certain that if she intended to end her life that way, she wouldn't have failed to fasten the sliding chain lock on the door, to guarantee that there would be no interruption of the act. As it was, the maid entered the room at six o'clock to change the towels and discovered the body.

Richardson's phone rang. It was Reardon.

"Hi. Just wanted you to know I was getting ready to leave. It's almost nine in case you hadn't noticed. I'll buy the drinks if you've got your story done."

"This won't be finished until tomorrow, Terry. I've got to think about what it means, or what I might have to say now, considering everything I wrote about the Tarantinos last week. But I'd love a drink. Meet you in the lobby in five minutes."

* * *

For some reason he couldn't explain, Reardon chose to bypass the closer establishments and walk the three blocks over to Chi-Chi's. They sat side by side in a booth, near the front of the bar. He listened patiently as Jenna took the devil's advocate position that Arena was falsely accused of what happened and then forced to commit suicide before he could publicly deny the charge.

"Maybe the Tarantinos arranged this whole thing," she said. "They could do it easily. Baldacci was ready to say anything he was told, just to stay alive. All Sal Tarantino had to do was speak to Dave DePaolo in Cleveland. It's just been wrapped up too fast and too neat, Terry, don't you think?"

He didn't agree with her. He said that she had essentially broken the case open by realizing that Cardella was the target that night. "Don't you see what happened? Your story put tremendous heat on the Tarantinos, especially the way you connected the Family to Doug Fiore's campaign. The Tarantinos recognized the killings as the work of a professional— you told me that yourself after you met with them. They probably asked the other Families to check and see whether one of their men was AWOL on the Monday that Cardella and Niro were shot."

"And you think DePaolo found out about Baldacci?"

"Absolutely. It's my guess that Baldacci blabbed to someone about the job—maybe a girlfriend, who knows? Whoever it was didn't want to sit on that information, and told one of the DePaolos about it. The Cleveland family was able to do a big-time favor for Sal Tarantino when they learned the details. I'll bet they gave Mr. Balls a pretty good idea of how dim a future he had if he didn't come back here and tell the cops the truth. He knew the jig was up. He did what he did because he had no choice if he wanted to stay alive. If the Tarantinos weren't involved in Cardella's death, there's no reason to believe that Arena was set up by anyone. Case closed."

Terry finished the beer in his glass with a long gulp. "I guess now I know why Arena postponed our meeting that night."

Jenna looked at him quizzically. "What are you talking about?"

"Richie and I had a date to meet Tommy here at seven o'clock that night to talk about the drivers' contract at the *Herald*. Didn't I tell you that before?"

"No, you didn't. That means Arena knew that Cardella would be here. What happened?"

"I got a call in my office about 6:30 or so saying that Tommy would be fifteen to twenty minutes late."

"From him?"

"No. It was a woman. I assumed it was his secretary."

Jenna frowned. "I doubt she'd still be working at 6:30. Go on."

"I called Richie's office to tell him, but he wasn't there. I didn't bother to call over here and leave a message. I guess I figured he'd wait until we got here. It was after seven o'clock when I left the *Herald*. I heard all the sirens on my way over. A few minutes later Arena saw me as I was moving around the back of the crowd."

"Where was he?" Jenna asked.

Terry leaned over to his left so that he had a clear view out the front window of Chi-Chi's. "Almost directly across the street, in front of the deli."

Jenna got up and walked toward the door. She returned a minute later and picked up her briefcase. "The deli's still open. Give me ten minutes, okay?"

* * *

The manager of Saul's Delicatessen, whom Jenna asked to see, was Saul, the owner. She soon learned that Saul, his counterman Morris, and the waitress Marge were the same people who were working there the night of the shooting across the street. Jenna took a picture of Arena out of her briefcase and showed it to them. Marge recognized him immediately.

"He came in with another man," she recalled, "and they ordered coffee at the counter. A few minutes later he called me over and offered me a five-dollar bill to make a phone call for him. All I had to do was read a message he'd written down on a piece of paper, something about his being late for a meeting."

"Was it to a man named Reardon?"

"I don't know. He dialed the number, listened for a few seconds and then handed me the phone."

Marge's face showed the effort of struggling to recall everything. "He didn't look like the kind of guy who threw money around, but I knew there were plenty of reasons some people wanted to avoid talking with someone else. I didn't notice when his friend left because I was busy with a few tables. I think he was gone before this same guy in the picture used the pay phone again." She started wiping an area of the counter that already looked clean to Jenna. "Then it was just a few minutes afterwards that the police and ambulances were here on the street."

Richardson went over to the telephone. It hung on the wall in a corner of the store, just a foot from the front window, at the other end of the deli from the entrance. Looking across the street, she could see Chi-Chi standing behind the bar, talking to two men sitting on stools opposite him.

* * *

Jenna slipped back into the booth. "You're right," she told Terry, "case closed," and passed on to him what she just learned.

"Now that we can be sure Arena was involved," she continued, "the only question is why?" Jenna leaned on her elbow, her hand at her mouth. "Maybe it's got something to do with that federal hearing he was supposed to have next month. I'll check it out. Meanwhile, I have to throw a couple of big fish back into the water."

"What does that mean?" Terry asked, smiling at her.

"It means I've got to take the Tarantinos off the hook."

92

Cyril Berman wasn't waiting to see what Richardson put in her next column. As soon as word of the Baldacci confession came over the news, he put a call in to Dan McMurphy from Karp's Lincoln. Their appointment was moved up from three o'clock the next afternoon to ten in the morning. Berman wanted a full apology to the Fiore campaign for being linked indirectly to Richie Cardella's death. And he wanted it to come from the *Herald* itself, not just its blundering political reporter.

* * *

The entrance to the *Herald*'s third floor newsroom was located directly across the corridor from the building's two elevators. A receptionist sat at a white metal desk just outside the door, several feet away from a long wooden bench that provided seating for up to eight people. A venetian blind hung inside the door, its louvers pulled taut. The large glass windows of the room, on either side of the door, were coated with a green-colored substance that prevented anyone in the corridor from looking at what was going on inside. In the five minutes that Berman sat alone on the bench, waiting to be called, the movement of people in and out of the room was constant.

Shortly after ten o'clock the telephone on the blonde receptionist's desk buzzed twice. She put down the magazine she was reading, opened the door and pointed Berman toward Dan McMurphy's office. It was situated in the back of the newsroom, at almost the farthest point from where Berman stood. He could see from a distance that McMurphy's work area was framed by three glass walls, two of which extended into the newsroom from the side of the building and were joined in front by a third, in which the door was located.

The reporters, whose cluttered desks were arranged by twos, back to back, all looked busy either entering information into their personal computers or engaged in telephone conversations. They ignored Berman as he moved from aisle to aisle in his diagonal path across the room. No shades or blinds screened McMurphy from anyone working there.

McMurphy opened the door just as his visitor arrived at it. He introduced himself with a strong handshake, showed Berman where to sit, and moved to the large executive chair behind his desk. Berman intended to start slowly. He wanted to review the substance of Richardson's recent columns and then, after a brief reference to the remarkable events of the preceding day, move toward the extraction of an apology from the newspaper. Unfortunately, McMurphy never gave him the chance.

"If you're thinking of asking the *Herald* for some sort of an apology," the editor began, "forget it. I approved everything Richardson wrote, Mr. Berman, and it was right on the money as far as who the real target was that night. Her story broke the case wide open, which was to your candidate's best interest. Half of Rhode Island suspected that the Tarantinos were involved in what happened, and that wasn't going to help you in the election." McMurphy's eyes emphasized the point he was about to make as he stared hard at Berman. "Especially since Richardson uncovered how close your guy used to be to Tarantino junior. I'm sure she'll make it clear to our readers right away that Cardella's murder had nothing at all to do with politics. That's all we can do for you."

They talked for no more than ten minutes. Berman argued that the paper had already damaged Fiore's reputation with the unfounded insinuations that were printed. "The election's just five days away," he said. "I want to be sure before I leave here that the coverage won't continue to be unbalanced, weighted in Singer's favor the way it has been. Look, I'm not asking to see Richardson start repenting in print because the ridiculous things she imagined got shot down yesterday. Fiore can take care of himself on that score. But there are some damn important issues in this campaign. Fiore and Singer are on opposite sides of the fence on a number of things, especially the right way to fix the State's economy and the casino gambling issue. That's what they'll be debating more about tonight, and it's what you folks ought to get back to writing about in your stories."

Berman never intended to threaten the newspaper with a lawsuit, and McMurphy's opening salvo forced him to give up any hope of Fiore receiving an apology in a *Herald* editorial. What he set his sights on was reminding the news editor that his paper lauded Fiore's economic plan at an earlier date and spoke out against State-operated gaming parlors on a number of prior occasions. He was working his hardest to lobby McMurphy's support for a Fiore endorsement in the Sunday edition. When the conversation ended, McMurphy wished him good luck in the election but didn't accompany him back through the newsroom.

In the corridor, Berman was putting on his raincoat when a young man stepped out of one of the elevators. Its flashing green light indicated that it was going up. "Hold the door," the man said to another passenger, and hurried over to the receptionist's desk. "This is for McMurphy," he told her, handing her a large interoffice mail envelope from among a number he was carrying. "He's been calling the pressroom for it all morning, so let him know it's here. Tell him it's the Singer endorsement."

93

Room service brought lunch for four to Cyril Berman's suite at one o'clock that same Thursday. At first Berman thought it smarter to let Fiore go into the debate against Singer that night without the weight of the *Herald*'s endorsement decision on his shoulders. Later that morning, he changed his mind and revealed the bad news to Fiore, Walsh and Karp at the same time. He solicited their input, wondering out loud whether there was any route of attack Doug could take that they hadn't tried yet.

Karp was overjoyed at the events of the previous day. He was certain before then that his status and reputation were in free fall, hurtling toward the bottom of a pit. Suddenly, everything was made right again by the confessions from Baldacci and Arena. Karp could forget about the denials he composed and rehearsed many times in his head. Now he was only regretful that he possibly damaged the Fiore campaign by revealing information about its finances to Jenna Richardson.

"I think we've got to attack the *Herald*," Karp told the group. "A preemptive strike. As long as we know they're going to endorse Singer, Doug should make it sound like they were out to get him all along. He can find some way in the debate to give Richardson hell for raising all kinds of phony innuendos without any facts to support them. Then he could say that the *Herald* brass was obviously pressuring her to write those stories."

"Lester's absolutely right," Walsh said. "Doug shouldn't just let this thing die. He ought to take advantage of the fact that the whole State of

Rhode Island may be watching on TV tonight. I say he should demand an apology from the paper to the Tarantino family, and a separate apology to the Fiore campaign for even hinting that we were aware of a plot to kill Cardella."

"Good idea," Karp said.

"There's some danger in speaking up for the Tarantinos," Walsh continued, "but the fact remains that Richardson dragged them into the gutter before Baldacci showed up. I think the people would respect Doug for taking their side in this thing. The point I'm trying to make is that we want to convince the voters the *Herald*'s the one wearing the black hat for the way it handled this. If we can do that, there could be one hell of a backlash in our favor when they come out Sunday endorsing Singer."

"Doug?" Berman's voice indicated that he was open to any idea Fiore had. But silence followed, and he tried again. "It sounds to me like Lester and Russ are making a good argument," he said. "What do you think?"

Fiore filled his coffee cup with French fries and ate them as he paced around the room. "I'll say all that stuff if you guys want, but in my opinion it won't make much of a difference. We need something we can hit Singer with that will stick to him and make him smell, like dogshit on the bottom of his shoes. We're *losing* this fucking thing, and blaming it on Richardson and the *Herald* won't help us. The only thing everyone will remember next Tuesday is that Singer got their endorsement. Unless we can come up with something on him that will shock the shit out of the voters, that endorsement will kill us."

Fiore's use of crude language no longer surprised the men on his team. He spoke that way more often as the election got closer. Berman realized that his candidate's panic over the probability of losing the election was responsible for the way he spoke, but considered it wiser to simply ignore it than to make an issue of it. The bigger problem was that he knew there was nothing out there that would have the knockout effect Fiore was looking for. As he told Doug earlier, Singer came out "as pure as the driven snow" in everything they checked on him personally.

But he was concerned about what Fiore said and the anger in his voice when he talked to them. He had no doubt Doug had reached the point where he would use anything he could come up with, even if it was immoral or unethical (with the possibility of its also being illegal) to try and damage Singer in the eyes of the voters. Berman recalled Fiore's earlier show of panic just before the primary. He was eager then, even after learning that Richie Cardella was shot by an assassin, to go ahead with a negative campaign against Cardella in an effort to reduce his opponent's lead in the polls. He knew for certain now that where once Fiore set out and prided himself on running a campaign he could always be proud of, that objective was no longer in play. All he wanted at this stage was to win, at whatever cost to the truth or to his adversary. Cyril intended to tell Walsh and Karp what he thought and to warn them that Fiore could go off the deep end.

"Don't forget that Warwick, Portsmouth, and Pascoag have already come out for you in their editorials," Walsh was saying. "And we'll probably pick up some others this week. So the *Herald* backing Singer might just even things out." He knew how weak it sounded as soon as he said it.

Fiore stopped moving and looked at Walsh. "Tell me, Russell, would you trade Warwick, Portsmouth, Pascoag and a few maybes for the *Herald*'s endorsement?" The question reeked with sarcasm. When Walsh didn't answer, Fiore continued. "You'd give your left testicle to get it and so would I." There was silence from the others. Doug saw the opportunity to try and relieve whatever resentment his tone of voice had caused. "In fact, if I was as old as you, Russell, I'd give both testicles if it would help."

It worked, and everyone laughed.

"What about Singer's wife?" Karp asked innocently. "She's in your firm, Doug. Is there anything we can use against her that could rub off on him?"

Fiore paced halfway around the room before answering. "I don't think so. The ironic part is that she'd probably volunteer it if she had something. I happen to know Carol Singer would give anything to see her husband lose this race." Even as he spoke the words, the germ of an idea began taking hold, one that he soon believed could put him behind the governor's desk at the Statehouse.

94

The debate was scheduled to begin at eight o'clock and take place in '64 Hall on the campus of Providence College in the Elmhurst section of the city. Berman didn't schedule any speaking engagements for Fiore that afternoon. He wanted him to rest up and rehearse the answers he'd give to the questions they anticipated being asked. Instead of using a panel made up of writers and broadcasters, the debate sponsors decided to let all the questions come from preselected members of the audience attending the event.

When Fiore's three man "brain trust" left the suite to take a break at the bar on the Biltmore's mezzanine level, Cyril gave Doug two hours to relax before they'd return to go over the issues with him. Fiore telephoned Pat Hanley immediately and told her it was important for them to meet right away. She was delighted to hear his voice and agreed to be in Room 606 in a half hour. He used the time to put details on the idea he had minutes earlier.

They weren't able to be together for several weeks, but Hanley didn't need any apologies. She understood that the final leg of the campaign demanded all Doug's time. He embraced her and kissed her after she locked the door, and held her hand as they walked toward the sofa. They sat down next to each other and exchanged pleasantries for several minutes.

Fiore was eager to get to the point and made quick use of the first lull in their conversation. "Let me tell you what's happened, Pat," he began. "This has really come as a shock to me because I remember what you said the last time we were here when we were talking about Ocean State. You told me that business was a lot better than last year, and that according to Brad, everything was going fine. Now I find out it's not that way at all." He hesitated, watching a look of concern come over her face. She uncrossed her legs and allowed herself to settle deeper into the sofa.

"I got a call this morning from Irwin Platt," Fiore lied. "He gave me the bottom-line numbers for the first three quarters, and they stink." He had absolutely no idea what those numbers were, and was ready to avoid a direct answer if Pat tried to get more detailed information from him. He emphasized the word "stink," and knew it was best to let her draw her own conclusions.

"As if that wasn't bad enough by itself," he continued, "Platt found out that Brad's been spending a couple of nights a week gambling for a long period of time. Apparently, he goes to one of those gaming parlors the Tarantinos run. Right now, he owes about $10,000 they extended him on credit, and the Tarantinos are starting to get anxious about whether he can pay it off."

Fiore suddenly wished he had checked out the exact figure with Sandy before meeting with Pat, and then decided to give himself some wiggle room. "It may be a little higher or lower than that right now," he added. "I don't know whether Platt was up to date on the account or giving me the last total he got from the Tarantinos. What's more important is that Platt didn't say he suspects Brad of ever using any of Ocean State's money. That's the good news. The bad news is that he figures anyone involved in that kind of regular gambling has a major problem and can't be concentrating on the job he's getting paid to do. Platt sees a company in the red and a president who's got interests elsewhere. As of today he's leaning heavily toward shutting the place down, and he wants to know what I think."

Hanley let her head fall back against the top of the sofa. "Oh, my God," she said, almost moaning the words.

Fiore gave her plenty of time to think about what he told her.

"Get me a drink, Doug," she finally said. "Please."

He went to the liquor cabinet and made her a gin and tonic. There was no ice in the bucket. He started to pour one for himself also, but thought better of it. Pat took several sips before putting the glass down on the coffee table.

"When are you supposed to tell him?" she asked.

Doug sat down in the green wing chair across from her. "I've got to get back to him on Monday, this coming Monday, as if I don't have enough to do that day."

He paused, looking down at his feet, and then directly at her. "Look, Pat, part of what I'm about to say is going to upset you, probably upset you pretty bad, and I guess you'll hate me for having the nerve to do it. Believe me, the easiest thing all around would be for me to just tell Platt to put a lock on the door and throw away the key. That's the only honest answer to his question. But you told me once, a long time ago, that you'd do anything to help Brad keep this job. If you really mean that—and don't say you do until you hear me out—I'll go to bat for him. That means I'll do everything I can to convince Platt that somehow or other things will start turning around at Ocean State Wire if I'm the new governor."

"Doug, I can't imagine anything I could do that . . ."

He interrupted. "The easy part of what you've got to do is to speak to Brad tonight and get him to promise he won't do any more gambling at that club. Don't let on that you know how much he owes, or even that he's in debt at all. That might give him the idea that he's got to talk to Platt about whose money he's gambling with, and I can't think of anything worse right now. Anyway, the fact is that if I lose to Singer and casino gambling becomes legal in Rhode Island, he'll be able to go anywhere he wants to play the tables. But he has to understand that the Platts know what he's been doing and they want it stopped immediately."

"Brad will ask me how I found out. What do I say?"

"That's no problem. Tell him I called and told you because those were the orders they gave me. He may be unhappy about not being spoken to directly, and wonder why not, but he'll live with it. Now listen, Pat. What I *don't* want you to do, under *any* circumstances, is talk to him about how Ocean State has been doing. There are too many things involved, and most of what's been putting the bottom line in red ink isn't his fault. The Platts know that, and if they decide to keep it going, we'll all meet with Brad about what has to be done next year. Do you understand that?"

My Honorable Brother • 415

She nodded her head without speaking. Fiore got out of his chair and stood behind it, his hands resting on the finely curved piece of dark cherry wood that ran along the top and sides.

"You know, they say all's fair in love and war, and here I am at war with Bruce Singer. You've probably seen the latest polls. The finish line is right there, just a few yards away, and we're running a dead heat. That's supposed to mean that my chances of winning are as good as his, except for the fact that the almighty *Providence Herald* is set to endorse him on Sunday. That would put the nails in my coffin. I think those sonofabitch senior editors over there are more in tune with what I've been saying about the issues than what they've heard from Singer. The problem is that in their minds they've still got me mixed up in a plot with the Tarantinos to kill Richie Cardella."

"But those other men confessed," Pat said, almost arguing the point.

"Sure they did, and by now everyone in Rhode Island knows what really happened. But the *Herald* was in so deep with all that shit Jenna Richardson wrote in the last couple of weeks that they're too embarrassed or ashamed to come out and support me. You didn't see them apologize to me or the Tarantinos for any of that stuff in her columns. That says a lot."

"Then what did you mean about your war with Singer?"

Fiore returned to the sofa and sat down next to her. Looking at him, Pat could see the intensity in his face as he started to answer her.

"The issues in this campaign don't count any more. The only way I can beat Singer now is by getting something on him personally, before Tuesday. It has to be a situation he absolutely wouldn't want the public to know about . . . the kind of thing that would force him to fold his tent and withdraw from the race as fast as he could." He took a deep breath before continuing. "Now just listen to me. Let me tell you what I have in mind, because this isn't easy for me to say, and I wish to hell the goddam *Herald* wasn't pushing me to this point.

"I'm not sure you know it, but Singer's wife—her name is Carol—works for my law firm. She's a banking lawyer, not a secretary or anything. I'm sure she'll help me do what I'm going to ask you because she's very bitter about everything right now. Politics ruined their marriage. She didn't want him to run for governor. She actually begged him to stay out of it, but he wouldn't listen. I guess he made it clear that becoming governor meant more to him than staying married to her. So it's over for them, after twenty plus years, with two daughters in college. Carol would just love to see him lose what he wants the most."

Fiore hesitated a few seconds before delivering the punch line. "What I need, Pat, is for a photographer to catch Singer in bed with another woman, and I mean you."

She wasn't anticipating that kind of a bombshell. Pat gasped audibly and stared at him. After a long awkward pause, she reached for her drink on the coffee table.

Fiore knew he had to keep talking. The worst of it was out, and despite her obvious shock, she was still sitting there. The rest was a selling job, and he spoke quickly.

"I don't mean you should have sex with him. That's not part of it. He won't even know you're there until the flashbulbs go off and he sees what's happening. He may never even find out who you are. But as soon as we send him a copy of the picture, Singer will understand that the media will get to see it, and then maybe all of Rhode Island if he remains a candidate. He's going to want to bow out of the race right away. He'd probably call a press conference and say he's quitting for health reasons. He can claim it's something he just found out about but wants to keep to himself for the time being. My guess is that Singer's personal physician would be there with him when he makes the announcement. The doctor won't know what to say because there won't be any examination or tests run until later, when Singer's in the hospital. But someone in their camp will give the doctor an innocuous statement to read to the media; that in his opinion, depending on test results, it could be difficult for his patient to be an active governor if he's elected. Then he can cut off all the questions by raising the right to privacy under the doctor-patient relationship."

Fiore pictured the whole scene in his mind and wanted to smile, but held back. "Once the election's over, no one will really care what his problem is. He'll be yesterday's news. Singer will take some time off to make it look good, and then go back to his law practice."

Pat wasn't thinking yet in terms of a "Yes" or "No" answer to his proposition. She was still into her role in the scenario he just described. "How could I possibly be in bed with him without his knowing it?" she asked.

Fiore was calm now, ready for the questions he figured she would raise if she stayed around to hear his plan. He began moving around the room as he answered her.

"It's easy," he said. "Carol would get him to sleep here in the hotel with her for one night. I'm talking about tomorrow night, Friday. Or Saturday at the latest. She'll come up with some pretext she can use to get him here. Singer will do it because he'll figure it may help to keep them together after the election. You'll be in the adjoining room. Tell Brad tonight that you're so angry with him about his gambling you've decided to stay at the Biltmore for a couple of days and think things out. He'll be too ashamed to try and stop you. At some point after Singer falls asleep, you and Carol will switch places. Ten minutes later the room lights will suddenly go on, you and Singer will sit up in bed in time for the flashbulbs, and the contest for governor will be over."

Fiore was pleased with himself. His plan was put together in just minutes, after lunch, and he was certain that all the pieces fit perfectly. If Pat and Carol cooperate, he told himself, he didn't have to worry about the *Providence Herald*.

Pat raised another problem. "What if something goes wrong? Singer might wake up when we switch or before the photographer gets there."

"That's a chance we have to take. Besides, I'm not worried about it. Carol told me he sleeps like a rock. But if anything goes wrong, I'll take the hit. And here's my part of this. If you'll do what I've asked, Brad's off the hook no matter what happens. I'll see to it that the Tarantinos wipe out the debt he owes them, whatever it is, and I'll tell the Platts I'm convinced it would be a mistake to shut down the plant. You do your part, and I'll do mine." Fiore felt he already had her on his side.

Pat let her head fall and covered her face with her hands. "You shouldn't be asking me to do this, Doug. I'm not a whore." As soon as the word escaped her lips, she began to sob.

Fiore went back to the sofa and sat down, leaving some space between them. He tried to talk softly, persuasively. "I already told you there'd be no sex involved. I wouldn't ask you to screw the guy just for me . . . and I don't think getting in the same bed with him for ten minutes makes you a whore."

"It doesn't matter whether anything happens or not," she said, rubbing her eyes. "It's just the idea of the whole thing." She stared at him. "How am I supposed to feel about the fact that I'm the one destroying his career by being in the picture with him? And what if the picture ever became public? What would that do to *my* marriage?"

"Like I said before, all's fair in love and war. He'd do the same thing to me if he had the chance."

It was as if he hadn't heard the questions she asked. Pat realized that his only concern was with winning the election at all costs, even though the costs were Singer's and hers, not his. Her feelings and the potential consequences she might suffer meant nothing to him. "So you want to take advantage of what we have and use me to fight your war," she said.

Fiore heard the bitterness in her voice and felt he might be losing her. "I'm not trying to take advantage of you, Pat. I'm just offering you a deal. Brad needs my help to keep his job, and I need something from you to get the job I want. He's dead in the water if I don't say the right thing to the Platts, and you'll still have to figure out how to pay off the Tarantinos."

He stood up, took one step away from her, and then sat back down. "The worst thing that happens to me is that Singer wins and I keep making four times as much money in my firm as I would as governor. It just so happens that your relationship to Brad and to me puts you in the position you're in and lets me come to you with this. If you help me, you help him, and you help yourself. Even Carol Singer gets something out of it."

"What makes you so sure she'd do it?" Pat was losing some control over her voice. "You're asking her to put her husband in the most humiliating and shameful position of his life, to set him up for this thing. She may be angry about what he's done to her and that they may be getting a divorce, but is she going to stoop this low just to get even? Could she live with that for the rest of her life?"

Fiore looked at Pat and nodded his head up and down. He couldn't let her know about his relationship with Carol and how certain he was that she would do whatever he asked. "The answer is 'Yes,'" he said. "You haven't seen Carol Singer with her husband once during this whole campaign. And you won't see her there tonight, at the debate. She's absolutely through with him. She hates him for destroying what they had and for what it will do to their kids so he could be in politics. If I ask her for this favor, she'll do it."

My Honorable Brother • 419

Pat got up, walked a few steps away from the sofa and turned back toward him. "I can't believe this whole conversation," she began, and the tears came again. "I'm sick to my stomach that you'd even talk to me about doing something like this. I don't know what to say. Maybe it all means that it's time for Brad and me to get out of Providence, and to hell with Ocean State Wire. No job is worth this."

She went to the closet and got her coat. Doug started toward her but Pat told him to stay where he was. "You can call me tomorrow morning and I'll give you my answer." She turned and left the room.

* * *

Fiore suddenly felt warm. He took off his jacket, poured a glass of tonic water and drank it down. He went into the bedroom, sat down on the side of the bed and then let himself fall backwards, his heels still resting on the floor.

With his eyes closed, he pictured the scene in the hotel room that would overwhelm Bruce Singer in a matter of seconds and force him to quit the race. There he was, being jolted out of his sleep by the sudden light in the room, the rapid-fire clicking of the camera's lens and the flashing bulbs that accompanied it. Singer was wearing red and white vertically striped flannel pajamas. He reached over to the night table for his glasses and then realized that the woman in the nightgown next to him wasn't Carol. She was a stranger, someone he'd never seen before. As he started to get out of bed, the photographer ran from the room, slamming the door behind him. Instinctively, Singer hurried over to the door and fastened its chain lock. He seemed to remember doing the same thing earlier in the evening, before he and Carol went to sleep. When he turned back toward the bed, the stranger had the sheet pulled up to her neck. "Who are you?" he yelled. "Where's my wife? What's going on here?"

Fiore chuckled at the scenario he envisioned, and sat back up. He went to the telephone and dialed the number for Carol Singer's line at Walters, Cassidy & Breen. When she answered, Doug invited her to the Biltmore to have a cup of coffee with him. Carol said she had a closing taking place and was due back in the conference room in ten minutes.

"What's up?" she asked.

Fiore told her about the endorsement Bruce would be getting from the *Herald* on Sunday. He said it would add to the momentum building for her husband since the stories in the paper linking Doug to the Tarantinos and Cardella's murder. "He'll beat me on Tuesday, Carol, no getting away from it. The only way I can win is if Bruce decides to withdraw."

She laughed and was about to ask what made him think Bruce would ever do that. But she held back, suddenly wondering why Doug even brought up the thought.

"I've got to get him out of the race before election day, and there's only one way to do it. Listen to what I have in mind. It will take just a few minutes."

Carol listened, without interrupting, as he laid out the plan he already discussed with Pat Hanley. She considered the whole idea incredible. *This is absolutely bizarre,* she thought to herself, hearing that Fiore wanted to catch Bruce in bed with Hanley while he was unaware that Bruce had tapes of him and Hanley screwing in Room 606 for months. She had a mind-boggling thought that maybe both of them would have to withdraw at the last minute. Then suddenly she grasped the fact that Fiore would be asking her to acquiesce in his wild scheme.

When he finished describing what had to be done, Doug took Carol's consent and participation for granted without waiting for any reply. He simply asked her if she could get Bruce to stay at the Biltmore on Friday night.

Carol was devastated by Fiore's plan and his obvious certainty that she would be a willing participant, but she felt paralyzed at that moment to offer any response. Her mind wouldn't let her find the right words to communicate to him. She needed some time to reflect on what he said, but for right now his question hung in the air.

"I think so," she answered, "but I can't be certain. I believe his schedule has him going to Portsmouth, Middletown and Newport tomorrow, so it might depend on how late they get back."

"You don't think he'd give you some excuse to avoid it?"

Again, Carol thought it best to just go with the flow of the conversation and keep her emotions to herself. "I doubt it. He'll probably still want me to help him with something in the campaign before Tuesday or at least be there with him if he gets to make his victory speech. So he'll want to be accommodating."

"Terrific."

But she couldn't resist asking Doug about Pat Hanley. "Why is she willing to do it?"

"Because her husband's in deep shit at Ocean State Wire & Cable, and she knows I'm the only one who can bail him out. It's a trade-off. She hasn't said 'Yes' yet—the proposition hit her like a ton of bricks—but I'm pretty sure she will. I've got to call her tomorrow morning. But why don't you call the Biltmore today and reserve two adjoining rooms for tomorrow night. Hold them for Saturday, too, in case there's a last minute problem. I'll speak to you in the morning after I reach Hanley, okay?"

"Okay."

"By the way, do you want to meet her before the action starts?"

"I don't know. Let me think about it."

He hung up the phone and went to get his jacket in the other room. "Fuck you, *Providence Herald*," he said out loud.

95

THE DEBATE THAT THURSDAY evening was another draw, according to the media analysts. Both Fiore and Singer had their agendas, the issues they knew they had to articulate for the audience. Each was skillful at turning certain questions around and using them to send the appropriate message. Of the two, Fiore seemed more relaxed, walking around the stage as he answered questions from both guests and students in different parts of the auditorium. But it appeared that Singer, more or less anchored to one of the stools provided for the candidates, received as many rousing ovations as his opponent.

Clearly, however, the loudest applause of the evening came when Fiore addressed part of an answer to "any journalism students who may be sitting out there tonight."

"I want you to recognize how innuendo, based only on a vivid imagination, as in the stories that ran the past two weeks in the *Providence Herald*, can almost destroy a reputation or libel an innocent party. It makes no difference whether that innocent party is a young lawyer running for governor of this State or an unpopular Family on Federal Hill that is well known for its interest in gambling. If you don't have the facts, stay out of the newspaper."

Fiore waited for the applause to die down and for the audience to rivet its attention on him again before he concluded his answer. "I want to tell those in attendance here and the tens of thousands watching on television that I remain outraged at what the *Herald* has done. At this point, ladies and gentlemen, I don't care whether the newspaper endorses me or not." As expected, that got him a standing ovation from his supporters.

When the forum ended, the two candidates walked toward each other for the obligatory handshake. This time Singer's daughters reached the stage to embrace their father as quickly as Fiore's family was there to greet him. The Singer team, minus an important member, understood that with the race in a dead heat it couldn't give Fiore any further advantage than what the presence of his wife by his side already provided him.

* * *

There was a fresh pot of coffee, along with a small chocolate cheesecake from Alden Merrell, waiting when Singer and his daughters arrived home from the debate. Carol greeted them as they came in, and told her husband that he performed wonderfully. "You looked much more sincere than Fiore in the close-ups," she said.

"How come you watched?" he asked. The question was friendly, not malicious in tone.

"Oh, you know, with election day getting so close, I've got to start making up my mind who to vote for." She smiled at her family and led the way into the dining room.

"Did they give any new polling numbers tonight?"

"I didn't hear any, Bruce. What's the latest?"

"Through Tuesday night Daddy was down by a point," Rachel said, "but with that plus or minus two points stuff."

"What do you think?" Carol asked, passing a cup of coffee to her husband.

"I think we're in good shape right now, but I'm not sure what will happen in the last two days. If I had to bet, I'd say the *Herald* will endorse Fiore. That was great strategy he used against them tonight."

Bonnie Singer, the older and less attractive of the two girls, was already cutting herself a piece of cheesecake. "And if Fiore gets in, he'll probably make his friend Sandy Tarantino the chief of staff."

They all laughed.

A little later, as their daughters were clearing the table, Carol told Bruce that she wanted to talk to him upstairs about Friday night before he went to sleep.

96

Jenna Richardson actually gave the Fiore campaign more than it expected in her Friday column, and more than her strong intuition was willing to privately concede.

No one was able to satisfy the questions she raised about the presence of Arena's empty briefcase in the hotel room, the unlatched chain on the door and the failure to call his wife on the telephone before slashing his wrists. Nevertheless, she summarized the Baldacci confession and said that both the Providence and State Police were convinced that Tommy Arena took his own life. It happened without any form of coercion, they agreed, as soon as he learned that Baldacci fingered him as the man behind the killing of Richie Cardella.

Richardson told her readers that she reviewed all the public documents in the federal case that was pending against Arena. She said there wasn't any clear evidence that a decision for or against Arena in that matter depended solely on the testimony expected to come from Cardella, who was listed as one of several government witnesses. She pointed out, however, that the Justice Department conceded that it was considering a withdrawal of some of the charges ever since Cardella's death. Arena's suicide made everything moot.

"It can now be concluded," she wrote, "that the Tarantino family had nothing to do with the loss of life at Chi-Chi's that night in September. As reported earlier, the Family has not been charged with murder or any felony having to do with violent crime in over two decades. That record deserves much applause, but Rhode Islanders must remind themselves that the Tarantinos still rule illegal gambling in the State. That being the case, the Tarantinos are obviously desirous of seeing Doug Fiore elected governor inasmuch as his views against State-sponsored gaming casinos would perpetuate the need for the kinds of services and facilities offered by them.

"Yet in all fairness," the column continued, "Fiore's position on that issue has strong support around the State from many thousands of individuals who are less concerned with what the Tarantinos would gain than they are with what open and legal casino gambling could do to the fiber of their communities. The issue may well be the one that decides the election."

Jenna editorialized a bit at the end. She urged the voters to put the Cardella tragedy behind them and judge the candidates for governor on their past records and accomplishments, their positions on the issues that affected Rhode Island most deeply, and on the gut feeling each citizen brought into the voting booth about the character of the two nominees. Dan McMurphy decided to let her get away with it.

* * *

The Fiore campaign was concentrating its efforts in Warwick, West Warwick and Cranston that day.

When Cyril Berman read Richardson's column over breakfast in the morning, he gave a mild "Yahoo" to Russ Walsh, who was there with him. "The only thing she left out was that everyone should just ignore the *Herald*'s endorsement and vote for the man they like the best. Right, Russell?"

"Better yet, Cyril, vote for the candidate whose wife cares enough to show up at the debates." With that, Walsh gave Berman a thumbs-up.

97

Doug Fiore had a number of calls to make that Friday morning and couldn't use the phone in Lester Karp's Lincoln for any of them.

At ten o'clock, when he finished the last of several private conversations with supporters who gathered at the Holiday Inn at the Crossings in Warwick for a 50-dollar a plate breakfast, Fiore called Pat Hanley from a lobby telephone. He was nervous when she answered, realizing that everything depended on her willingness to go along with his plan. Pat was somewhat abrupt, but her voice was not unfriendly and she agreed to do what he asked.

"Thanks, Pat, you won't regret it. What you've got to do is check into the Biltmore by six o'clock tonight and ask the clerk for the room reserved in your name. Carol Singer will be in the adjoining room, and unless there's a change for some reason, the switch will take place right at midnight." Pat had a few questions about procedure, and Doug spelled out the details.

He hung up and called Frankie Scardino in the office. Scardino's secretary said that he wasn't expected in until eleven o'clock. Fiore told her to give her boss the message that he would be calling back at 11:45 sharp, and for Scardino to be sitting next to his telephone at that time. He got back to the switchboard and asked to be connected with Janice Rossman. Instead, after half a dozen rings, her assistant picked up and said that Janice would be available later in the morning, at about eleven. He hung up without telling her who was calling.

When he reached Scardino later on, Fiore asked him where he was the night before.

"I slept out," Frankie answered.

"Well, I'd appreciate it if you and Janice would still try and get to work by nine o'clock, okay? You're supposed to be running a law firm."

"She forgot to set the alarm, Doug."

"And you had to have one more this morning, right?"

"I won't let it happen again."

"Let it happen all you want, but just make sure you're in the office between nine and five on weekdays."

Scardino didn't say anything.

"I called to find out if you know any private investigators."

Frankie recalled that the bank where he used to work retained one on an irregular basis to check on certain employees, but said that he couldn't recommend him.

"Well, speak to Richard Rubin. I'm sure he must use one or two investigators in his divorce practice. I want whoever it is to be ready to enter a particular room at the Biltmore tonight, at exactly ten minutes after midnight, and take pictures of the man and woman in bed. Tell him he's got to get the film developed overnight and to make half a dozen copies of each picture, 8 by 10s. If he wants extra for that, pay it. Arrange to pick up everything from him by eight o'clock tomorrow morning. Then wait for me to call you at home—no, never mind, take the stuff to the office and I'll reach you there."

"I'm curious, Doug. Is this personal or political?"

"Some of both. As soon as I know the exact room number, I'll call you back."

* * *

Lunch was over, and the members of the Post Road Development Association left the Johnson & Wales Airport Inn to return to work. Fiore found a telephone near the restrooms in the basement and called Carol. He never doubted that she would be able to convince Bruce to stay in Providence that night. She didn't disappoint him.

"He'll get here about ten," she confirmed. "We'll be in Room 1021. The adjoining room is 1023."

"Do this for me, Carol, because I've got to get going to my next appearance. Call the Biltmore and have 1023 reserved in Pat Hanley's name. She'll be checking in before six o'clock. You ought to introduce yourself to her as soon as you can and maybe even rehearse how the switch will take place." He knew the word sounded all wrong as soon as he said it. "I don't mean a rehearsal, but . . . you know, just so you're both on the same wavelength."

"So we don't bump into each other and wake up Bruce," Carol retorted.

Her attitude didn't amuse him. Fiore thought he could detect a trace of self-contempt in the way she said it. He should have just let it go, but didn't.

"Look, you told me a dozen times how you feel about him for getting back into politics, and you said the marriage was gonzo on account of it. I figured you'd rather see him lose than win, and I sure as hell prefer to win than lose, so why hate yourself over it? He doesn't mean anything to you anymore."

Carol let him finish, not disputing what he said. *What difference did it make?* she thought. She knew it would all come crashing down anyhow as soon as Bruce heard all the pillow talk that took place in Room 606.

"What time will the photographer come in?" she asked.

"At ten after midnight," he told her. "Does that work out alright?"

"It'll be fine. What time do you get done tonight?"

"The dinner's at seven, so I'd guess by nine-thirty."

"I want you to call me, Doug. I'm going to need some support."

"Don't worry. Everything will be okay. I'll call, I promise."

* * *

Cyril Berman didn't know what got into Fiore that afternoon and evening. But in his speeches, handshaking, and general presence Doug was suddenly more spirited, and exhibited greater energy than he showed in several days. The people who came to listen to him thought he would make a great governor, and Fiore responded as if he knew the job would be his. Even though Cyril realized that the conduct he was witnessing was probably the result of Doug's good performance at the last debate and Richardson's column that morning, he had an uneasy feeling about it—something he couldn't put his finger on—that wouldn't go away. Still, while it might only be wishful thinking, he began to believe they could actually overcome the *Herald*'s endorsement of Singer.

98

It was a very stressful but interesting Friday afternoon for Richardson, and she was telling Terry Reardon all about it as they sat in a booth at Player's Corner Pub. The place was rapidly filling with the "Thank God It's Friday" crowd.

"I mean, what it comes down to, is that I was being grilled by the seven most powerful men at the *Herald*—and they *are* all men, as you know—about the ten major candidates in the election. First, Sacco and Whitley for the Senate, then Williston and Droney and their opponents for the House seats. I thought Singer and Fiore would come next, but they reversed it and discussed lieutenant governor ahead of them. It was really exhausting, Terry, almost four hours without a break."

"What kinds of things did they want to know?" he asked.

"What *didn't* they want to know," she replied. "It was absolutely everything, from whether the candidate seemed to have a vision for the future, to what I thought about his or her view on a particular issue; how I sized up the important people on their staffs; whether I trusted one candidate over another; how they came across when they spoke to an audience; whether they looked me in the eye when I interviewed them, etcetera, etcetera. They were interested in intelligence, character, articulateness, sincerity . . . you name it, they asked about it. And when you're sitting there looking at the publisher, the executive editor, the managing editor, two assistant managing editors, the editorial page editor, and Dan McMurphy, you better have all the answers ready."

"Were they asking each other questions too?"

"There was just a little bit of that while I was there. Most of what they said was in picking up on some of my comments. But I could see that when they finished with me, they were about to start going at it among themselves over who they'd endorse on Sunday."

"Would I be right in guessing that you had more questions thrown at you about governor than the others?"

"Easily, that's probably why they saved it for last."

"Any comments from them on that one?"

"Some nice words from the big boss on my staying with the Cardella story, but also a couple of warnings about how we were operating a little fast and loose on the potential libel issue. Overall, I'd say they gave me from an A-minus to a B-plus."

"And who do they figure you'd like to see them endorse for governor, or do I risk getting my lights punched out by asking?" Terry put his hands up in front of his face, as if protecting himself.

"They definitely know I'm in Singer's corner," she said, "although they don't seem to understand why Fiore's too slick as far as I'm concerned. I guess you have to be there. But I'll tell you what I got the biggest kick out of. It's the way they go through it to reach their decisions, how much effort goes into it. They have the assistant managing editors draft the language for the *Herald*'s potential endorsement of *every* candidate in the race. Each draft is edited, photographed, and put on a press plate, ready to run if they decide to use it. Everyone at the meeting had a paper copy of all the endorsements. When I got through answering their questions about the Senate race, for example, they asked me to read the endorsements for Sacco and Whitley. All they wanted to know was whether there was anything in either one that I would change if I could choose one candidate over the other."

"Hmm, ve-dy-in-tu-res-ting," Terry said, mimicking the character of the German soldier he remembered from the old *Laugh In* TV shows, "but shtupid, yah?"

"No, it's actually a great idea," Jenna answered. "It forces you to look for every good point you can find in a candidate. Then, when you read the whole thing, it gives you a feeling about whether that person really adds up to much. They had me do the same thing for each of the five races. And do you know what, Terry? The only place you find two people who are equal to each other in just about every way is in the governor's race. I wish you had seen the endorsements for both Singer and Fiore, but I had to leave them there, of course. Oh well, you'll get to read one of them on Sunday."

"And that reminds me," he said, resting his arms on the table and slowly moving his head forward, like a turtle cautiously emerging from its shell, "were you giving some thought to getting laid tonight?"

Jenna looked at him blankly, let out a deep breath as if his question had totally annoyed her, and shook her head warily from side to side. But Terry knew from the smile that began to appear on her face that she wasn't saying "No."

* * *

It was the first time in years that Sal Tarantino was still in his office after three o'clock on a Friday afternoon. But as much as he wanted to get an hour or two on the golf course before going home, there was an election coming up in four days and final plans needed to be put in place.

Sandy was on the telephone all morning with many of their contacts around the State. They discussed weather forecasts for Tuesday, the most recent local polling results and plans for transporting Fiore supporters to the voting booths. With each of them, Sandy stressed the need for as many campaign workers as possible to be on the streets with Fiore signs. They were to start on Saturday morning and not stop until all the polling places closed at eight o'clock on election night.

The two Tarantinos walked over to the Blue Grotto for a quick lunch. Each ordered mussels marinara, a small salad and coffee. While they ate, Sandy gave his father all the latest information, along with some details on what the final days of the campaign would cost.

"I thought those drivers and sign carriers were all volunteers," Sal told his son.

"I did too, Pop, until the bills came in after the primary. They get as many college kids as they can, at no cost, but then they have to use a small army of moonlighters at five bucks an hour."

Still, a lot of the news was good, and Sal was excited. Richardson's story about the Tarantino family started his day off on the right foot. "We're still in the fight, Salvy, so we've got to give it everything. I'll get on the phone when we get back and tell those guys to spend whatever it takes. It sure would feel good to have the governor in our pocket if we need him."

99

Carol Singer picked up the telephone in Room 1021 before it rang a second time. It was 9:40 p.m. She was watching a movie on television but couldn't concentrate on it. "Doug. Thank heavens you called. I just heard from Bruce a little while ago, and he's not coming here tonight. He got one of his terrible migraines in Newport and he's out of it. They're all staying there overnight."

"Shit!" The word sounded harsher to Carol than it ever had. "Did he say anything about tomorrow?"

"Yes. He promised he'd do it tomorrow night if I still felt like it."

"Did you tell Pat Hanley yet?"

"No, I didn't say anything. I wanted to let you know first."

"Have you spoken to her at all?" he asked.

"Yes, we talked a little. She's very nice."

"Well, why don't you let Pat know about the change. I'll call off the photographer."

"Doug, I've got a wonderful idea."

"What is it?"

"I was thinking, after Bruce called, that this may be the last chance we have to see each other. We've never been able to make love and then be together for the night. This room is all paid for, and I don't have to go home because Bruce won't be there. Why don't you come and stay here tonight?"

Fiore thought about it. He was horny enough, that's for sure, and he felt it might be good to get rid of some of the tension that had built up in the last week. But Grace was expecting him. He called her at six o'clock and she told him she baked a chocolate rum cake, his favorite dessert.

"I'd love to Carol, but it could cost me my marriage." He meant it as a quip.

"Then we'll be even, Doug. What I'm doing for you will take care of mine."

He didn't want her to start thinking about changing her mind. But if she got angry with him, she might, and then everything could go down the tubes. He would put the blame on Berman, and tell Grace that Cyril insisted on meeting back at the Biltmore to review all their strategy for the final four days. He would say that if they were still at it by midnight, he'd sack out on Berman's couch and get home for an hour or two first thing in the morning.

"Okay," he said, "I owe it to you, Carol. I'll be there by 10:30."

* * *

Carol purchased a bottle of Bombay Gin—Doug's favorite—and some tonic water at a liquor store before checking into the hotel. She filled the plastic bucket with ice cubes from the machine in the corridor on the tenth floor, and poured two drinks as soon as Doug arrived. She was wearing a cream colored Italian silk negligee under a white terry cloth robe that was loosely belted. Fiore hung his jacket in the closet, noticing the man's suit hanging inside a plastic wrapper. A white shirt and tie lay on the shelf.

He still needed to unwind from the long day. Besides, for the first time with Carol, there was no rush. This wasn't just another hit-and-run job. The whole night lay ahead of them. Doug sat up in bed, a pillow behind his head, while Carol chose a chair off to the side. They talked about a number of things. The words spilled out fast, followed every so often by short silences that threatened on occasion to become embarrassing.

"So you like Pat Hanley," he said.

"Yes, I do. But I think you have to be careful."

Doug smiled. "Why is that?"

"Because that woman has a crush on you. I'm sure she'd like to get you into bed."

He feigned skepticism. "Come on, you're not serious. She likes me because I've helped out her husband, but I don't think she sees me as a sex object."

"I think you'd be surprised," Carol said. "And speaking of sex objects, are you almost ready?"

"Yeah, I guess so. Why don't you get in bed and I'll take a quick shower."

"Okay, but hurry up. I've been ready for the last hour."

* * *

"Why are you still dressed?" Carol asked. There was a mock pout in her voice as her fingers found the bulge in the undershorts Doug had on when he came out of the bathroom. They kissed for several minutes, pleasurably but not passionately. He lifted himself slightly and Carol helped him pull the shorts down over his knees. He let them rest above his ankles instead of kicking them off.

She touched his penis easily but he pulled her hand away.

"What's the matter?" she teased. "I'm entitled."

He sucked a little breath through his teeth. "Too tender," he said. "You do that with your fingers and I'll show you my 'Old Faithful' imitation."

She giggled and leaned over, kissing both sides of his chest.

"Why don't you sit up," he said.

She got up on her knees, next to him.

Doug reached his hands up to the straps of her negligee. "Is this coming down or going up?" he asked.

Carol began raising the nightgown slowly. "Close your eyes," she said. "No peeking."

He ran his fingers in the triangle of hair that was already exposed, and watched as the negligee moved up over her breasts. When it was off, Carol let the soft silk fall on his face. He put it on her side of the bed, pulled her toward him and began kissing her nipples alternately, back and forth.

"This is my windshield wiper move. What do you think?"

Carol kept her head raised, until he stopped. Then she looked down at him. "Could you do that if you had two windshields instead of one?"

"What do you mean?" he asked.

She straightened up, still on her knees. "I just had the sexiest thought. It even sent a shiver right through me. You know that fantasy of yours, about making love to two women at once? The more I thought about it and pictured it in my mind, the more I began feeling I wanted to try it sometime, but only with you. And it just hit me that it would be perfect right now if we got Pat Hanley in here with us. We've got all night to try whatever we want. I bet she'd say 'Yes.'"

Her words left him speechless. His two mistresses were sleeping in two adjoining rooms, without their husbands. It was fertile soil for his fantasy, but the thought of even hinting at a ménage à trois never occurred to him. He quickly reminded himself that neither of the two women knew he was intimate with the other. But here was Carol suggesting that the three of them have sex together. He wasn't sure how to react.

"It's after 11:30," he said. "Pat's probably sound asleep. And if she isn't, suggesting that she join us might upset her to the point of changing her mind about tomorrow night. She'll worry about getting into bed with Bruce and finding me there too." Doug laughed at that. "I think we'd better forget about it."

"Pat Hanley isn't a prude, Doug. Far from it. Women can tell these things about each other after just a few minutes. She might say 'No,' but she'd probably be thrilled that we asked her. I'll tell you what. Let me knock quietly on the door and see if she's awake. If she doesn't answer, that's that. If she's there, I'll tell her I've got you prisoner in here and ask if she wants to come in. There's no harm in it if she's not interested." Carol reached over for her nightgown and slipped it back on.

Fiore didn't know what to say. He wondered how Pat would react to finding him in bed with Carol. Not only the idea that he was sleeping with another woman, but that he was actually screwing his opponent's wife. What was Pat going to think of Carol, seeing her willing to set a trap for her husband that would cost him the election, and having this relationship with Doug at the very same time?

And yet the idea of having both these women in bed with him was overwhelming. He knew there might never be another chance like this to have his greatest fantasy come true. It was as if fate had started him in an affair with Carol and then introduced Pat so that at one precise moment, this very night, he could lie between two beautiful women and do whatever he wanted with either of them.

Fiore saw that Carol was turned on by the idea as much as he was. It was hard for him to understand why one woman wanted to be there, watching another twist and tremble with pleasure as the man focused his attention on her and shared all of his body with her in a ritual that immersed the two of them entirely. He thought it might be a lesbian sort of thing involving two women who weren't comfortable getting into bed together and making love. With a man present, they could find ways of giving pleasure to each other while ministering to his desires also.

He watched as Carol walked toward the front of the room, opened their half of the double door on the opposite wall, and knocked. When Pat answered, Doug saw the light from her room before Carol disappeared behind the closed door. Several minutes passed before she returned, holding onto one of Pat's hands. As they approached the foot of the bed, Fiore pulled the sheet up to his waist.

"Pat said she'd rather be with us than watching Jay Leno," Carol said. "And guess what I also found out?"

Before he could say anything, Pat spoke up. "I just told Carol that we've been together before, Doug. I wanted to be honest."

"So we should all be more comfortable than as if we were strangers," Carol added. "Come on, let's get into bed." She returned to her side, to his right, on the window side of the room. Fiore was grateful that neither woman was upset at learning of his relationship with the other.

Pat took off her robe, dropped it on the floor and joined the other two in the king-size bed. "The three musketeers," she quipped.

"But with only one sword," Carol replied, giggling.

They all laughed. Their humor was beginning to loosen him up. Doug put an arm around each of their shoulders. "I suppose you're all wondering why I called this meeting," he said.

"Probably just to see the latest in women's lingerie," Pat said, turning toward him.

"When you could have just asked Victoria's Secret for a catalogue." Carol was laughing as she spoke the words. She sat up in bed. "It is now midnight, the witching hour. So which witch is it going to be first? I think I have seniority." She lifted her nightgown up over her head.

My Honorable Brother • 437

Pat raised herself to her knees. "Unless he wants to do something with one of us witches on each side. I think they call that a sandwitch, w-i-t-c-h."

"And I think Jay Leno should be watching *us*," Carol said. "We've got some great material here. But let's see, before we took a break Doug was showing me his windshield wiper number. If you want to join in, you'll have to you-know-what." As she spoke, Carol pulled the sheet back down to Doug's ankles. Pat took off her negligee.

Fiore looked up at the two women, waiting for him to start the action going. He raised his hands and fondled Carol's breasts with one, Pat's with the other. Carol's breasts were larger, but Pat's nipples stood out firmer, making the fingers of his left hand more aware of them as he passed each hand back and forth from one breast to the other.

He sat up and Carol got on her knees also, just across from Pat. He moved his head in a semicircle, from right to left, first kissing Carol's breasts, then doing the same with Pat, then going back again from left to right. He repeated the movement several times. "Love those wipers," Carol said. She called Pat over to her side of the bed so that they were both on Doug's right.

His eyes were closed and his mouth was pressed hard on one of Pat's breasts when the light near the door first went on. Pat's scream, and the way she pulled away were what alerted Fiore to the activity in the room. He looked toward the door in time to see flashbulbs go off before he raised his right arm to cover his face. There was a man standing partway between the light and the bed. "Good," he heard the figure say, and then saw him run toward the door. The light went off and the door opened at almost the same instant. A moment later, it slammed shut.

"What the hell was that?" Doug cried out. He moved to his left and got his feet over the side of the bed, but had to bend over and pull up his shorts before he could run. He opened the door and looked out, but the corridor was empty.

Fiore fastened the chain lock before walking back toward the bed. Someone had turned on the lamp near the window. Carol had her nightgown on and was sitting on the edge of the bed, holding Pat in her arms. Pat had her face buried against Carol's chest and was sobbing.

"Get me her robe, Doug," Carol said.

He picked the robe up from the floor, put it around Pat's shoulders and stood there watching them.

"It's ten after twelve," he said. "That's when the photographer was supposed to show up. I told Scardino to tell him not to come tonight—that it was off until tomorrow—but something must have gone wrong. Frankie probably left a message with someone else, and the guy never got it. Shit! . . . *shit!* . . . *shit!*"

Pat pulled her head away from Carol and began wiping the tears from her face with the robe. "Damn it, I didn't need a dress rehearsal," she said, "especially when I wasn't expecting it."

"That was just terrible." Carol tried to comfort her, pushing some hair away from Pat's eyes.

Fiore sat down on the bed. He looked at Carol. "I guess neither of us remembered to put the chain lock on the door."

"I was sure you had done it," she answered.

Pat stood up. "I'm okay now. I'm going to my room. I hate to disappoint you guys, but I couldn't get back in the mood again. Not after that."

Carol reached across the bed and got Pat's negligee. "I'll go with you and make sure you're all right," she said.

"Goodnight, Doug," Pat whispered.

"Goodnight, Pat. I'm sorry about what happened. Someone will pay for this. I'll call you tomorrow."

The two women walked through the adjoining doors into the other room. A few minutes later, Carol returned. "She's crying again, Doug. It was very traumatic for her. I'm going to sleep in there tonight just in case she needs me. I feel responsible for the whole thing. Do you have an itinerary for where you'll be tomorrow?"

"Yeah, I've got it in my jacket. I'll leave it here on the bureau. Call me as early as you can. I want to be sure that everything's arranged for tomorrow night. Do you think she'll have a problem doing it?"

"I doubt it. It's different when you know what's going to happen. Besides, she must still feel pretty desperate about what you're going to do for her in return."

"Yeah, that's right, I forgot that."

"Goodnight."

"Goodnight," he answered. "And don't worry about those pictures. I'll get them tomorrow and destroy everything."

"I wasn't worried," Carol said, and closed both doors as she returned to Room 1023.

My Honorable Brother • 439

100

On that same Friday night Jenna stopped at the Twin Oaks on her way home, determined to give that "interesting stranger" from her horoscope of a month earlier another chance to show up. She sat at the bar, trying to follow a *Seinfeld* rerun that was in competition with the general din around her. A man took the seat next to her, looked over and said, "Hi."

She smiled and returned his greeting. She could see that he was about her age, fairly good-looking even with glasses, and more shy than forward.

"I believe I know you," he said. "Don't you write for the *Herald*?"

It always flattered her to be recognized, but she didn't want to identify herself too quickly. "Yes, I do," she answered.

"We actually spoke to each other for a few minutes about a year or so ago. It was at the Hopedale Nursing Home in Kingston. You were visiting a relative there at the same time I was and you asked me some questions about the care my mother was getting. I remember reading the articles you wrote about some of the bad stuff going on in the industry. By the way, my name is David Prince."

"And I'm Jenna Richardson. It wasn't really a relative of mine, just a nice old man who lost most of his marbles and couldn't speak up when they didn't treat him right. I had to pretend to be family in order to sit in his room all that time and watch what went on. How's your mother doing?"

She died about four months ago, but that was right on schedule with what the doctors had given her. She had kidney problems."

"I'm sorry."

"Thanks." He noticed that there were no rings on her left hand. "I've also read your columns on the election. Some of it was like reading a novel, the way things kept changing and how I felt about certain people. Who do you think will win the race, I mean for governor?"

Jenna didn't want to say she hoped it was Singer. That would let him think there was a bias in her writing, and there was still one more column to turn out. "It's so tight now, I think whoever gets the *Herald*'s endorsement will be the favorite, despite what Fiore said in the debate last night. Did you watch it?"

"Yes, the whole thing. He came on real strong against your paper, but I had the feeling it was because he didn't expect to be endorsed anyway. Otherwise, there was no sense in going out of his way to make an enemy. I think he's a pretty slick character, too slick for me. I don't want to see casino gambling become legal but I'll vote for Singer and take my chances. Anyway, I'll go put my name on the waiting list if you can have dinner with me tonight."

Jenna could see that the restaurant was packed. Everyone was there to forget the week that just passed and to let their hair down. She knew from experience that they'd have to wait almost two hours before getting a table.

"Thanks, David, but I've got too much to do tonight and I'm following the candidates around tomorrow. That means early to rise." She was about to tell him she'd take a rain check.

"Then let's do it next week," he said. "I'll be in New York on Wednesday and Thursday, but my plane gets in at six Thursday night. How about meeting me here at seven?"

She already had plans to see Terry that night, but she liked this guy. "What do you do, by the way?" she asked.

"Computers," he said. "My partner and I have a small company and we install software exclusively for Oracle. We program the software to do whatever Oracle's customers want it to do."

Jenna expected him to pull out a card and give it to her, but he didn't. For some reason, that impressed her. It was as if he was willing to risk their friendship on her believing what he said.

My Honorable Brother • 441

"Okay, Thursday night at seven." Jenna knew she wouldn't kid Terry about the reason for breaking their date. She was sure he'd understand and even tell her he hoped it worked out well. "But if something comes up, call me at the *Herald* before six and let me know." She wasn't about to give him her card either. They shook hands and she left.

On the drive home she couldn't help singing the words to "Someday my prince will come." And she loved the fact that the stars had made it so obvious.

101

The law offices of Barrows and LeBlanc were located in a four-story renovated building on the canal side of South Main, two short blocks away from the landmark golden dome of the Old Stone Bank. A furniture wholesaler, with a first-floor showroom and three floors of warehouse space was the sole occupant of the premises for more than two decades, but the skyrocketing cost of rentals in the rejuvenated area forced him to find a new location in a less developed section of the city. Barrows and LeBlanc was the largest of three law firms that moved in as soon as the restoration was completed.

At a few minutes after nine o'clock on Saturday morning, Carol Singer and Pat Hanley stepped off the elevator into the firm's third floor reception area. Moments later, George Ryder was there to greet them. The two former partners hadn't seen each other since Ryder's last day at Walters, Cassidy & Breen in September. He kissed Carol on the cheek, shook hands with Hanley when they were introduced, and led them to a conference room overlooking the water and the Providence skyline.

"How's Brad doing?" Ryder asked, as Hanley sat down.

Pat only knew what Doug Fiore told her about George Ryder: that this man was incapable of controlling her husband's impassioned agenda during the negotiations with the Union. She came to the meeting with a lack of confidence in his abilities.

"Still struggling," she answered.

"I'm glad they settled the last contract without a strike. Give him my regards."

"I will."

Ryder had a large white envelope with him. "I picked this up from my friend an hour ago," he said, looking at Carol. "I haven't opened it."

She asked to see it and he pushed it across the table. On the front, in large lettering, was the name "Ellison Woodrow," with the words "Private Investigator" below it. The flap of the envelope was taped down on both sides.

"There's a letter opener in the drawer," Ryder said, pointing toward the credenza at one end of the room, and he started to get up. But Carol had already inserted a fingernail under the tape in one corner and was slowly tearing it open. Before reaching inside, she slid the envelope a little to her left, where Hanley was sitting.

The pictures were excellent. In each one, Doug and Pat's faces were unmistakable. Carol's head, which she turned toward the window as soon as the light went on in the room, was seen either directly from in back or in just a partial profile. She couldn't be recognized as the other woman in the bed.

In each of the four shots, Fiore had a bewildered look on his face, lying in bed, nude. Pat, on her knees and facing the camera, was showing the front of her body. It was clear that the other woman with them was also undressed, her breasts still partially visible from the side as she hid her face from the camera.

Carol and Pat smiled at each other after looking at the photographs.

"Shall I?" Carol asked, her eyes on Pat as she moved her head once in Ryder's direction. Pat nodded affirmatively, and Carol passed the pictures back to him. He gazed down at each of them quickly, and then back at the two women.

"Your friend did a good job," Carol said. "And he came exactly on time. I had my eye on those numbers on the clock every second."

"What do you intend to do with these?" Ryder asked.

"If you're still representing me, George, it's what *you're* doing with them."

"I've only thought of this as a favor so far, but if there's something more you have in mind, perhaps it would be better to establish a lawyer-client relationship just in case anyone wants to ask me any questions."

"Let's think of it as that kind of relationship from the time I called you on Thursday," Carol told him. "You represent both Pat and me."

"Fine. Okay, what's next?"

"Here's Fiore's itinerary for today," Carol replied, handing him a small memo-sized piece of paper that had the Biltmore's name inscribed on it. "He'll be back and forth between Cranston and Warwick. Cyril Berman is his campaign manager, and he's always there with him. Find Berman and tell him you represent Pat. Show him the pictures and let him know where and when they were taken. When he asks you who the other woman is, don't tell him it's me. Just say that Fiore knows. Advise him that Pat is ready to make copies of these pictures available to the media unless Fiore withdraws from the race. Make sure Berman understands that Fiore had a plan with Pat to set Bruce up for the same kind of pictures, and that she's ready to spill her guts to everyone about the whole thing."

Carol turned partway toward Pat as she continued talking. She lowered her voice and spoke slowly. "One more thing, George. If Berman speaks to Fiore and then tells you that Doug says he never saw Pat before last night, tell him to let Fiore know that Pat has tapes of all the bedroom conversations they ever had in Room 606 at the Biltmore."

"Bruce told you?" Ryder asked.

"Yes," Carol said.

She could see the bewilderment in Pat's eyes. She reached over and squeezed her hand, sending a message that there was no need for Pat to say anything. When she turned back to face Ryder, she caught the smile at the corner of his lips.

"Is there a deadline on this?" he asked.

"Yes." Her reply was resolute. "I've been thinking about that. I want to give him enough time to establish a reason for getting out. It seems to me that about the only thing he can come up with this late that people will believe is a medical explanation of some sort. He has to have the chance to see his doctor today and put it all in motion. Tell Berman there are two deadlines. There has to be an announcement by eight o'clock tonight that Fiore has called a press conference for Sunday. And they've got to meet with the media tomorrow morning, no later than eleven, for him to withdraw. If they're late on either one, Pat goes public with the pictures. How does that sound?"

"Sounds great to me," Ryder grinned. "Shall I tell Woodrow to have the copies ready or do you want to wait and see what happens?"

"Spend the money, George. We want to be ready to roll if Fiore thinks we're bluffing."

"Where can I reach you?" he asked.

"Room 606 at the Biltmore," Carol replied. "And if either of us sounds a little sloshed when we answer the phone, it's because we will be."

102

BERMAN AND RYDER SAT together in the back seat of Lester Karp's Lincoln. Karp and Russell Walsh were asked to make themselves scarce for a while. Fiore was inside The Gables, a restaurant in Warwick, getting ready to address that city's Post 1813 of the Veterans of Foreign Wars. He would praise their bravery and tell them they hadn't risked their lives on the battlefield for a Rhode Island that would take money from the poor in State-run casinos instead of biting the bullet and doing whatever had to be done to stimulate a real economic recovery. His elderly audience, welcoming the attention, would ignore the fact that he avoided the Vietnam War through a questionable deferment, and give him a strong ovation.

The pictures caused Berman to whistle through his teeth. He listened patiently to everything Ryder said, trying to think of a way out of the mess created by his client. Berman didn't want to face the fact that his hundreds of hours of work could end with a whimper instead of a bang because of this ugly development. But his gut was roiling and told him that the ballgame could be over. He remembered with dismay that when the press forced Gary Hart to withdraw as a presidential candidate, all it had for leverage was a picture of Donna Rice sitting on his lap and a shaky allegation that he spent a night with her. Getting caught in bed with two women, for all the world to see, after plotting to entrap his opponent in a similar fashion, put Fiore in a much higher league of his own.

"Are we off the record, Mr. Ryder?" he asked.

"Certainly, if you want to be."

"I had a feeling right from the beginning that there wasn't a zipper strong enough to hold Fiore's prick in his pants."

Ryder smiled.

"But tell me the part about Hanley and Bruce Singer again."

Ryder repeated the scheme Fiore worked out to get Singer caught in bed with Pat Hanley. He explained why she felt she had to go along with it. "All she knew was that at midnight she was supposed to open the doors separating the two rooms, go into the other room and get in bed with the man who was there. Fiore said it would be Singer." Ryder's version of the facts made no mention of Carol's involvement.

"How did Fiore know that Singer planned to be staying at the Biltmore last night?"

Ryder downplayed the question. "My guess is that when he hatched the plan, he got Singer's schedule from someone in the media."

Berman turned to look out the window and tried to dissect everything Ryder told him. He felt that the story was still fuzzy around the edges. "So you're saying that Singer cancelled out, Fiore found out about it somehow and told the Hanley woman he'd be staying there himself. She agreed to share his bed for the night and then arranged for a photographer to show up and take pictures. Is that it?"

"I guess that's it."

Berman rubbed his chin with his hand. "It's hard to figure. She stood to gain nothing for herself or her husband by doing this. In fact, she had to know that Fiore would want revenge and do whatever it took to make sure her husband lost his job. That's what I'm having trouble understanding."

Ryder was ready to offer the answer. "You know that old expression, 'Hell hath no fury like a woman scorned.' She told me she was so upset at the position Fiore put her in—actually blackmailing her and being willing to humiliate her for what he'd get out of it for himself—that she just wanted to strike back at him any way she could. When Singer couldn't make it to Providence and Hanley knew she'd be alone with Fiore, she got the chance and moved on it. I guarantee you this lady's not worried at all about what happens next."

"Then why did she bring another woman into it with her?"

"Who said *she* brought the woman?"
"Didn't she?"
"You can ask Fiore that question."
"And who is she anyway?"

That was more than what Ryder could divulge. "I'd have to say it's pretty inconsequential," he replied.

Berman was through. "All right. I'll speak to him as soon as the lunch is over. Can I keep these pictures?"

"No. You can show them to Fiore and then I've got to have them back. I'll wait in the Ford wagon over there."

* * *

Doug Fiore wasn't sure what was happening. He arrived home from the Biltmore at seven o'clock that morning, showered, changed into a heavier suit and read part of the newspaper with his breakfast. Later on, before driving to the Airport Hilton where he arranged to meet Berman and the others, he called Scardino at home. Frankie's wife said he wasn't there, that he and several of the senior partners were spending the weekend in Boston on a retreat to discuss the firm's operation. He asked for the name of the hotel where they were staying, but she had no idea what it was.

Fiore was certain that Scardino didn't mention any Boston retreat to him, and doubted that Ed Jackson would initiate one without clearing it with him first. He went to a file in his study where he kept the names of everyone employed by Walters, Cassidy & Breen. He returned to the kitchen with Janice Rossman's home telephone number and was dialing it when Grace came into the room. Doug hung up the receiver casually, remarking that he was unable to reach Berman all morning.

At the Hilton, Fiore told Walsh he wanted to use the men's room before they got on the road. He called Rossman again and asked her where Frankie was.

"I don't know, Mr. Fiore," she said, sounding as innocent as she could. "He told me he was going to a meeting in Boston."

"Listen to me carefully, Janice. If I find out you're not telling me the truth, I'll fire you on the spot."

Rossman hesitated. "Can you hold on just a minute?"

"I'm holding. Go get him."

Scardino came to the phone. "Sorry Doug. She was afraid to say I was here."

"Did you call that goddam photographer?" he asked.

"It's all taken care of. I left a message on his machine, switching it to tonight at the same time. Don't worry, he'll be there."

Fiore bent down inside the phone booth and pulled the receiver to his ear. He had it as low as it would go, about six inches below the metal counter. "Well, if he's coming tonight, why the fuck did he show up last night?" he shouted.

Scardino didn't know what to say. "I can't figure it, Doug. Let me find out and call you back."

"I can't wait here. I've got to get rolling with Berman. When you reach him, tell him to put the goddam negatives in an envelope and deliver them to you. I want them in my hands tonight. You can bring them to East Greenwich when I get home. Are you going to be at Rossman's all day?"

"I planned on it."

"What is that cunt trying to do, make partner?"

* * *

In the back of the Lincoln, outside The Gables, Berman handed the envelope to Fiore. "I'm afraid I've got to show you this."

Fiore looked at the pictures. "Who brought these? Frankie Scardino?"

"No, a lawyer named George Ryder. He's sitting in the Ford over there." Berman pointed across the street. "He says he represents a woman named Pat Hanley, and that she's ready to go public with these pictures right away unless you withdraw." Berman recited all the details he was given almost an hour earlier.

Fiore's head was spinning. He thought he was beginning to understand what happened. Ryder was obviously out for revenge ever since Doug forced his resignation from the firm. He probably became very friendly with Pat Hanley through Brad during the union negotiations, and somehow learned about Doug's relationship with her. Then Pat blabbed to him about the Singer business at the Biltmore after Fiore told her the plan he had in mind. Now Ryder was capitalizing on it, and no doubt the bastard helped her set things up for pictures of them in bed together. He figured Ryder knew that Carol would be with them last night.

"Did he say anything about sending these to Grace?"

"No, he didn't, but they probably figure she'll find out like everyone else if you don't play ball."

"What do we do, Cyril?"

"I guess we go somewhere private and try to reach Sandy and his father. Ryder didn't say who the other woman is in the picture. He was playing cat and mouse. Do you want to tell me?"

Fiore was certain that Berman would explode with anger if he knew it was Bruce Singer's wife. It scared him to think of how Sandy and Sal Tarantino would react if they became aware of her identity. Doug couldn't handle that right now. "No one you know," he said, "just a friend of Hanley's that happened to be around."

Berman opened the door of the Lincoln and started across the street. Ryder got out of his car.

"He asked whether you sent these to his wife."

"We haven't yet and hope we don't have to. If he gets out by the deadline, she'll never know about them."

"We've got to make a few phone calls. Where can I reach you if I have to?"

Ryder took one of his cards out of a billfold. "I'll be at the office until four and I'll be home after five." He wrote his home number on the back of the card and gave it to Berman.

"If he pulls out, we get the negatives, right?"

"Absolutely, and all the pictures are destroyed. You have my word on that."

"If I ever need a good photographer, I'll know who to call." Berman turned and headed back toward the Lincoln. He saw Walsh and Karp watching him from the corner of the street. He waved his arm, signaling them to return to the car.

Ryder watched Berman open the back door and get in. He wasn't sure whether Fiore was looking his way, but gave him a mock military salute anyway. Then he climbed back into the station wagon, sat there and felt terrific.

My Honorable Brother • 451

103

THEY WERE DUE FOR an appearance at the Rhode Island Mall in Warwick at two o'clock. Knowing it would be mobbed on a Saturday afternoon, Berman planned to have Fiore walk around in his shirtsleeves, shaking hands with as many shoppers as possible. Karp headed toward I-95 as soon as they were all in the car.

"Drive back to the Biltmore, Lester, there's been a change. Russell, get on the phone and leave a message with one of our coordinators at the mall that Fiore will be detained indefinitely." Berman saw Walsh begin turning around toward him in his seat. "Don't ask any questions now," he said. "I'll fill you in on what's going on as soon as I can."

In his suite, Berman followed the instructions he was given when first hired to manage the campaign. He dialed a number, identified himself to the man who answered and told him to tell Joe Gaudette where he was and that he wanted to speak to their good friend as soon as possible. "It's an emergency," he added.

Berman didn't want Fiore in the room when he spoke with Sandy Tarantino. It was a time for the utmost candor. He didn't want to have to pull any punches in order not to upset his protégé, and planned to ask Fiore to leave when Tarantino returned the call. But it wasn't necessary. After ten minutes of painful silence between them, Doug got up and said he would join Walsh and Karp in the lounge. The call from Tarantino came about fifteen minutes later, and Berman told him everything that happened that day.

"Christ, I could kill the sonofabitch," Sandy said. "How many times did we warn him?" He paused for a moment. "So what do you think, Cyril? Is there any alternative to him announcing his withdrawal?"

"Yeah, maybe we can convince him to do the same thing Tommy Arena did." He waited for a chuckle or any sign that Sandy got the humor in his last remark, but there was only silence on the other end of the line. Berman had no reason to suspect the very tender nerve he struck.

"I'll have to speak to my father about this. If he agrees there's nothing else to do, will you be with Fiore at the press conference tomorrow morning?"

"I don't think we should wait until then," Berman said. "The *Herald*'s endorsement of Singer will already be out. Doug's withdrawal afterwards will look like sour grapes to a lot of people, no matter what reason he gives. They'll figure he knew he didn't have a chance of winning anyhow."

"What are you recommending?"

"I'm in favor of getting him to a doctor this afternoon, Sandy. It fits in with the fact that he skipped his appearance at the Rhode Island Mall. Let him complain about feeling strong stomach and chest pains. He'll have to be admitted to the hospital for tests. We'll leak word that he's in there, in a lot of distress. I'll call a press conference tonight and meet with the media late, like at ten or eleven o'clock. That way they won't have time to write a big story for Sunday's paper.

"I'll tell them there were consultations with Fiore's doctors about the pain he's been experiencing for the past several weeks. It'll sound like three forms of cancer by the time I'm through. I'll say that when Fiore learned a definitive diagnosis could take as much as ten more days and that his doctor warned the situation could be very serious, he decided it wouldn't be fair to the voters for him to remain a candidate. He recognized that a major illness could prevent him from doing his job as governor. Then I'll ask the *Herald* not to run its endorsement of Singer, under the circumstances. If it's not too late to change the editorial page, there's a chance they'll go along with it."

Tarantino listened to everything Berman suggested without interrupting him. "Stay where you are, Cyril. I'll get back to you." He called his father at home from the same pay phone and repeated the story. "I think we ought to figure out a place and meet with him right away, Pop."

"What good will it do? He's already dead in the water."

"I want to hear exactly what happened and find out who the other woman was. I'd like to be close enough to push my hand in his face, depending on what he tells us. And maybe there's still something we can do."

Sal Tarantino was disgusted. "If I ever get my hands on your friend, Salvy, I'll have one of the boys put his balls in a vise and turn the handle. But it don't make no difference who else he had in bed with him. Even if it was Singer's wife, who Berman told us he was dicking last year, it wouldn't help. As soon as word got out, everyone in Rhode Island would feel bad for Singer and line up to vote for him. Forget it. I couldn't have anything to do with that pervert now even if I thought we could figure a way out of this. We'll just have to take our chances. What the hell is wrong with people these days? Tell Berman to get it over with tonight and unload that piece of shit. That means you and I will have to go in and make some calls from the office tomorrow."

After Tarantino called back, Berman dialed the lounge and told the bartender he wanted to speak to Lester Karp. When Karp picked up the phone, Berman asked him to send Fiore upstairs right away.

"Here's the scenario, Doug," Cyril said, and laid it out for him. "Hopefully, your doctor's not playing golf this afternoon. Tell him your chest and your stomach both hurt like hell, that it's been happening a lot over the past month, but nothing as bad as this. You can say you've been having some dizzy spells too. If he asks questions, make up anything you want, just so it sounds like you're in a lot of pain. Let him know where you are and say that I think we should call an ambulance."

Berman hesitated a few seconds before sliding the telephone to the other side of the coffee table. Doug looked at him with glazed eyes, as if hoping for a miracle to happen before he dialed information to get his doctor's number. Berman had no sympathy for him—actually despised him completely at that moment—but restrained himself when he spoke. "The campaign for governor is over, Doug. It's down the drain. All we're trying to do now is protect your family and keep you from going down as the biggest asshole in the State's history. If that means anything to you, you'd better do a good acting job. The tests they do and the pictures they take at the hospital won't show anything wrong with you, but they can't tell you you're not hurting if you say you are. My suggestion is that you keep hurting badly, at least through Tuesday."

454 • Bob Weintraub

104

When the Rhode Island subscribers to the *Herald* opened their front doors that rainy and windy Sunday morning to pick up their papers, which were encased in a double plastic wrapper to keep them dry, they found two significant election items.

The first was a headline above the *Herald* masthead, in the space normally reserved for late Saturday night sports results. It declared in bold two-inch letters, "FIORE HOSPITALIZED, PULLS OUT OF RACE." It referred the reader to a story on page nine of Section A. There, Jenna Richardson wrote about the late night press conference that took place in an auditorium of the Rhode Island Hospital. She described the scene in which Fiore's campaign manager, Cyril Berman, was surrounded by the candidate's wife and other campaign leaders. In a voice cracking with emotion, he told the assembled members of the media that Fiore instructed him from his bed in the intensive care unit to withdraw his name from the contest for governor.

Berman informed the group that Fiore complained of various ailments, including chest and stomach pains, headaches and nausea on a number of occasions within the past month. He brushed them off initially as merely signs of the stressful campaigning he was doing. The pain became intense in the past several days, however, and the candidate was concerned that the diagnosis of any serious illness would impede his ability to take on the strenuous tasks of the governorship. In those circumstances, Fiore thought he owed it to the citizens of the State to bow out of the race at this point instead of waiting another day or two and chancing some chaos in the election on the part of those who didn't know his status.

"Berman assured everyone," she wrote, "that Fiore's personal physician, Dr. J. Carlo Chiarenza, was heading up the team of doctors who were examining him. They were studying the results of various tests, along with X-rays and magnetic resonant imaging photographs taken that day, and discussing other tests they thought would be helpful in reaching a diagnosis." Berman was uncertain, he said, as to when Chiarenza would be able to make himself available to reporters.

Several media representatives posed the question, in different ways, as to whether Fiore's decision was too hasty in light of the fact that his doctor wasn't able to pinpoint the cause of his painful symptoms. In response to each, Berman patiently stated that Fiore wanted desperately to lead Rhode Island out of its long economic slump, but couldn't abide the possibility that he would be elected and then be unable to properly serve.

"'Let me sum it up this way,' Berman said. 'Fiore understands that the people are being asked to choose between Singer and *him*, not the Republican candidate for lieutenant governor who would move up to the State's highest office if Fiore wins the election and is then forced to resign because of his health.'"

Richardson concluded her story by focusing on the double set of bizarre events. "The first one took Richie Cardella out of the race during the primary campaign when he had a fairly significant lead. The second has now given the election to Bruce Singer by default, even though the most recent polls showed the two candidates for governor to be running neck and neck. This has certainly been an election to remember."

The other major piece of election coverage was on the editorial page. A short note, signed by the publisher, informed the *Herald*'s readers that although Doug Fiore was no longer a candidate for election, the paper's senior editors still saw fit to run the endorsement of him that was approved just two days earlier. He noted that the decision was reached after an extensive examination of the positions advanced by Singer and Fiore throughout the campaign.

The publisher wrote that in the *Herald*'s view, "the issue of state-sponsored and administered gaming casinos, fiercely opposed by Fiore, is of overriding importance to the State of Rhode Island. We encourage those who are against such legislation to send a message to the State's lawmakers by pulling the Fiore lever when you vote."

The endorsement itself ran just below the publisher's communication.

105

Bruce Singer celebrated at home that Sunday morning by making poached eggs. It was his favorite breakfast, and one of the few things he ever learned to cook well. Carol joined him in time to measure out the right amount of fresh beans for the coffeemaker.

Word of Fiore's withdrawal reached Singer and everyone else just after he finished a speech to the High Technology Association of Rhode Island in the packed Capital Room of the Pawtucket Holiday Inn the night before. After that, party leaders converged on the motel and an impromptu victory gathering stretched into the early hours of Sunday. Carol simply whispered "Congratulations" to him when he got into bed just before 3:00 a.m. and said she was too tired to talk about what happened.

Sitting at the kitchen table, they discussed whether he should continue campaigning for the next two days. She listened to Bruce express his sense of obligation about keeping the commitments he already made, despite the unforeseen events of the previous day. There was no reason to discourage him from doing so.

"You should also find some time to call Grace Fiore and inquire about Doug," she said. "Or drop by Rhode Island Hospital and visit with whatever family members are there. I'll send a 'get well' card to Doug from both of us."

* * *

Frankie Scardino's wife took a message for him late that morning from Mark Reed of the Reed & Reed Detective Agency. He was corroborating the fact that no pictures were taken at the Biltmore Hotel on Friday night. He also said that his photographer carried out the assignment on Saturday night at the appointed time, only to find that there was no one occupying Room 1021 when he arrived. The agency would send out a bill that week, and he hoped they could be of service in the future.

Scardino didn't know anything about Fiore's hospitalization and withdrawal until he was in his car driving home on Sunday afternoon. He and Janice spent Saturday evening watching several porno movies before going to bed, and she didn't subscribe to any newspaper for home delivery. Scardino explained to his wife that the Reed & Reed Agency photographer was supposed to take a picture of a Fiore family surprise party, but that it had been called off when Doug went to the hospital.

* * *

The phones at 241 Atwells Avenue were busy most of Sunday. Sal Tarantino was heartened by the *Herald* publisher's encouragement to the voters on the casino gambling issue. That went a long way toward persuading him to spend the money to get as many ballots cast for Fiore as possible. He and Sandy authorized their contacts and operatives throughout the State to hire drivers to get people to the polls and to keep workers on the streets with Fiore signs. They gave instructions to change the signs by writing in the words FOR NO STATE CASINOS under VOTE FIORE.

Sal was locking up on their way out of the office that afternoon. Sandy was already halfway down the stairs. "Salvy, tell me how much business you think is going to Fiore's law firm from the different companies we're invested in."

Sandy stopped and turned around to wait for his father. "My guess, Pop, is that it averages at least half a million a year."

"Then I'll tell you something. I'll be very disappointed if the number doesn't go down to zero as soon as possible."

* * *

By Sunday evening, Dr. Chiarenza realized that there was nothing seriously wrong with his patient, despite Fiore's continued complaints of random pain in different parts of his body. However, in discussing his findings with Grace Fiore and Cyril Berman, both of whom arrived in the waiting room about 8:00 a.m. that day, he began to understand the enormous personal consequences for Doug in the event he was declared fit and ready to leave the hospital too soon.

In those circumstances, Chiarenza wanted no part of a freewheeling exchange with the media. Instead, he agreed to issue a statement to the effect that he was unable to locate any damage to Fiore's heart thus far, although pain in that area still persisted. The statement included an assurance that his patient was also being diagnosed for other types of infections or disease that could be giving rise to his overall discomfort. Fiore might be able to leave the ICU on Tuesday, the release stated, but made it clear that he would remain in the hospital for an indefinite period until all the necessary tests had been administered and analyzed.

Privately, Chiarenza told Berman that he thought it all boiled down to stress. "I'm sure Fiore would have felt fine as soon as the election was over. It's a shame he gave up his chance to be governor. This guy has the balls to do the things that ought to be done in Rhode Island."

"You're right, Doctor," Berman told him. "The problem is he also has the balls to do what a lot of guys just fantasize about."

"I don't understand, Mr. Berman."

"It's too hard to explain. Let's just say that what happened to Doug Fiore in the last few days is a fucking tragedy and leave it at that."

106

On monday afternoon bruce Singer phoned Carol at her office. He told her he'd be finished with his final campaign appearance about seven o'clock and wanted to take her to dinner at The Mills Falls in Barrington. "I called over there and the owner said it's pretty quiet on Monday nights. How about meeting me at home at 7:30 and we'll go in one car?"

The evening passed quickly and pleasantly. They spoke a lot about their daughters and how mature they had both suddenly become. Bruce was aware of the fact that his being governor would introduce some difficulties for Bonnie and Rachel, especially in their social activities. "Fortunately," he said, "between college and grad school, they'll be able to spend most of their time outside Rhode Island. That should help." Carol was pleased with his sincere concern for the girls' happiness.

He told Carol he heard that Fiore was going to be released from intensive care the next day but would stay in the hospital for an additional battery of tests. "Before Saturday," he said, "I never would have believed that Doug Fiore would put someone else's interests ahead of his own, especially when there was so much at stake for him personally. It just goes to prove that people can always fool you, no matter how well you think you know them."

Carol didn't want to say anything that might keep Bruce on that subject. She just nodded her head, as if in agreement.

Bruce knew she would crave at least one bite of some chocolaty dessert with her coffee, and insisted she pick one from the menu. "Don't worry about it. I'll finish whatever you leave," he told her. She gave in to the chocolate suicide cake and they smiled at each other over her decision.

As Carol put down her coffee cup, Bruce reached over and took her hand. He put it on the table and covered it with his own. "I want to ask you something I've been thinking about recently," he said. "We both know how you felt about my running for governor and how distant it left us over the past six months. But doing this is my life, Carol, and that's why I couldn't listen to you when you begged me not to get into the race. I had to hope that eventually you'd begin to see things from my point of view.

"Since I became a candidate, I've tried to figure out what it is that bothers you about the whole political scene. Campaigning *is* a long and horribly difficult ordeal, but it's the only way the voters out there can ever get to know enough about the candidates to make them want to pull the lever for someone. Anyway, the one thing I did learn is that I can go through the whole thing without having to disrupt your life as well by having you with me. So I want you to know that if I run for reelection, or anything else, I'll never ask you to give up your time to support me.

"I'm going to be governor for at least the next four years. There are so many things I want to do, and I'll need an awful lot of help. I want to ask you to consider something, not because you're my wife, but because you're such a terrific lawyer. I'd like you to think about leaving your firm and heading up the Office of Industrial Opportunity. Attracting private industry into the State is going to be one of the most important jobs of my administration. That's how we can put Rhode Island back on its feet, and you're the most talented person I can think of to handle it."

Carol didn't anticipate any kind of offer to join State government. She knew that her days at Walters, Cassidy & Breen were numbered. Fiore would figure out at some point, if he hadn't already, that she was the one who arranged for the photographer that night and then coaxed him into bed with Pat and herself. Once he realized what she did to him, he'd stop at nothing to get her out of the firm.

She could start building some support among the partners for a showdown with Fiore later on, but she knew it wouldn't be worth it. He would resume his position as managing partner as soon as he returned to practice. That would give him any number of ways to make her life there miserable. Besides, Carol really didn't want to ever have to look at Doug Fiore again.

But she couldn't do what Bruce was asking. Sooner or later, while playing the tapes for a lark, he was going to hear her making love to Fiore in Room 606. That would end their marriage and any other kind of relationship along with it. The irony was that she began to have a rekindled feeling for Bruce in the final stages of the campaign. She felt his sincerity deeply as she watched him answer questions during the two TV debates. Her respect for him grew immensely when he made it clear that he wouldn't use those tapes for his own advantage and risk the problems they could create for Pat Hanley. And he honored her objections by campaigning on his own, never once suggesting that it would help him immeasurably if she accompanied him to an important event.

Bruce sensed that Carol wasn't ready to answer him yet. "There's another lawyer we know that I'm going to ask to join my administration," he continued. "George Ryder. He's one of the most experienced labor lawyers in the city. He probably knows every important union official out there. We've got to have a few years of labor peace—especially in the private sector—if we're going to pull ourselves out of this recession. Ryder's the man I'd want to send in when it looks like the two sides need someone to help them reach a fair settlement. He's been through the nitty-gritty of that stuff for years, and many of my AFL-CIO supporters told me that George is someone they all trust."

"I think you're right," Carol said, "and I bet he'd love it."

"I just don't want him to feel it's something I'm offering him because he brought me those tapes."

"I'm certain he wouldn't, Bruce. George never thought in political terms like that. He did it because he didn't trust Fiore and wanted you to have some ammunition in case Doug tried to pull something dirty on you at the last minute."

Bruce nodded his head in agreement. "It doesn't really matter because I destroyed all the tapes the week after he gave them to me. I didn't want them sitting there, tempting me to use them under any circumstances. If they ever became public, it could have ruined too many lives."

Carol's heart leapt at Bruce's words. She was almost overcome with the relief they brought. Suddenly, so unexpectedly, she could let go of the fear she was living with since he first told her about the hidden microphones in Room 606. Now, he would never turn on the recorder and find out that she was intimate with Fiore. He wouldn't discover that hers was another one of the lives that could have been ruined. She realized that it was a chance to start all over again.

But was it a good idea to work for Bruce? Could she handle a job that would necessarily bring her into daily contact with politicians battling to be in on any deal that would bring a new office building or manufacturing plant into his or her district? Could she work in that atmosphere, or would her general loathing of the political process affect her ability to carry out the task and impair Bruce's goals for the State? At that moment, Carol knew only that she wanted to do whatever would help their marriage.

She took her hand out from under her husband's and then placed it on top of his. "I'm flattered that you think I could do that job for you, Bruce, I really am. And the truth is that I had already made up my mind to resign from WC&B. It's become a much different place from the law firm I went to work at fifteen years ago. There were too many times in the past year when I stepped off the elevator in the morning and dreaded going to my office. Maybe it's what the recession did to make so many lawyers the way they are today—cutthroat about everything and having so little fun—or maybe it's just me. But I'm going to be out of there before the end of the year.

"The answer to your proposition is that I'll think about it. This has all happened so fast. Before I do what may be good for Rhode Island, I want to be sure I'm doing what's best for us. But I'll only give it some thought on one condition."

"What's that?"

"That I can be with you and the girls when you make your victory speech tomorrow night."

"It's a done deal," he said, resting his other hand on top of the hand that held his.

107

It was a bolt out of the blue. Pat Hanley could barely contain her joy when Brad told her about it early Tuesday evening.

"I just didn't want you getting your hopes up and then possibly being disappointed," he said. "I knew I had to get away from Rhode Island before I ruined everything for us. The stuff that happened down at the plant depressed me to the point of where I didn't want to come home and spoil your nights. That's why I got started gambling, just to have someplace to go where I wouldn't be bothering anyone.

"Then I could see it getting out of control, so I began checking the industry want ads and applied for a few different jobs. The last two times I was away overnight wasn't to see customers. I wanted to be at my best for interviews at Conrad Wire. The Japanese own it now, and they think my ideas for turning it around and making money are terrific. They called today and offered me ten thousand more than I'm making now, plus a super bonus if we hit certain targets. So what do you say we sell the house, pay off our debts and go back to Pittsburgh?"

Three hours later, Brad was sound asleep on the couch while Pat watched the election coverage. Everyone she voted for that day was on their way to winning.

The station switched to Bruce Singer delivering his victory statement from the Grand Ballroom at the Marriott. As the camera moved away from Singer and picked up the others on the podium, Pat saw Carol standing behind her husband, along with her daughters, smiling out at the excited throng. Pat smiled also, and blew her friend a kiss.

She thought back to Thursday afternoon when Carol called her at home and introduced herself as the other woman in Doug Fiore's plan to have a private detective take pictures of Hanley in bed with Singer. They shared with each other the shame and humiliation they felt at being asked by Fiore to put themselves in that position. Pat explained how her husband's job at Ocean State Wire & Cable was in Fiore's hands. In turn, Carol said that although Doug assumed she would do anything to hurt Bruce out of spite for his running for governor, it wasn't true.

As they spoke, the contempt they shared for Fiore and his willingness to use them in that way reached a boiling point. It was then that Carol devised a plan that would trap him, instead of Bruce, if Pat was willing to join her in pulling it off. They took a hard look at all the risks, including the release of the pictures for publication if Fiore called their bluff and refused to withdraw from the race. Before Hanley committed herself, Carol confessed that she and Fiore were lovers.

"I think you ought to know that," she said, "because I'm aware of your own relationship with him."

Pat didn't ask Carol how she knew of it, but she respected her for being honest, and agreed to join in the plan at the Biltmore on Friday night. Now she could return to Pennsylvania, knowing that she and her new friend probably affected the history of Rhode Island. "And all for the better," she said out loud.

When Singer was through speaking, Pat turned off the TV. "Come on Brad. Wake up. It's time to go to bed."

108

IT WAS AFTER MIDNIGHT by the time Jenna Richardson finished her column for Wednesday's *Herald*. Her day started at eight o'clock that morning with the first of a handful of visits she made to polling places in and around Providence to interview workers for each of the underdog candidates in the election. Jenna wanted to know who they were and how they felt about holding signs or passing out campaign flyers for office seekers who were already written off on the basis of polls taken by the various media.

After dinner she attended Bruce Singer's victory celebration at the Marriott and was able to ask him a few questions while in the receiving line that formed to congratulate him. When Carol Singer was introduced to her, Richardson wondered why such a charming woman didn't make any earlier appearances in the campaign. Then she recalled Mrs. Singer's reply, "I hope not," when Jenna inquired six months earlier whether her husband would be a candidate for governor. *Maybe she hates politics as much as I do,* she thought.

Jenna took a taxi from the Marriott to the recently opened Westin Hotel. She arrived just in time to hear John Sacco thank his exuberant campaign workers for helping him defeat David Whitley in the Senate race. Afterwards, Sacco shook hands with her as he mingled with the crowd and invited her to call for an interview toward the end of the month.

"I'll need a little time off first," he said.

"So won't I, Senator," she answered.

He gave her a big smile and turned away.

Richardson returned to the newsroom and wrote several drafts of her column before she was satisfied with it. She left room for some facts and figures to be added when the final election results were known, but complemented the necessary coverage with several human-interest features. She took the copy out of the printer and brought it to Dan McMurphy's office. The shades were drawn on all three of his picture windows, surprising her. The office was dark when she entered but she could see her way to his desk.

"So what do you think?" Dan's voice came from one of the sofas to the right of his desk. "It's okay, you can put on the light," he said. "I just needed a short nap."

Jenna was flustered for an instant but recovered quickly. "What are you still doing here?" she asked. "I thought Barry Parker was sitting in for you tonight."

"He is, but I figured I ought to be around when your temporary assignment on the political desk came to an end. Otherwise you wouldn't know what to do tomorrow when you got out of bed."

She chuckled. "It wouldn't have been a problem. I was planning to sack out all day."

"In that case I'd have to dock you for the time. Of course, you could withdraw that statement and give me the chance to tell you to take the day off."

"Easiest decision I've had all week. Tomorrow's on you."

McMurphy sat up on the couch. "Drag a chair over here, Jenna, and sit down." He waited for her to get comfortable. "Well, it was some election year, wasn't it?"

"Do I hear an 'I-told-you-so' coming, Dan?"

"Yeah, I guess so, but I think I deserve it. Ten months ago the call on this one was a real long shot."

"You don't have to remind me. I didn't exactly agree with you at the time."

He smiled. "No, you didn't, that's for sure. But you went out and worked your tail off anyway. Your instincts for the things that were happening out there were incredible. You weren't always right on the money, but you gave the people of Rhode Island facts they probably otherwise wouldn't have known and you made them think hard about who they were going to put in office. In short, you did a hell of a job and I'm proud of you."

She thought about being flip and asking if that translated into more money, but held off. "Thanks, Dan," she said.

"Which brings us to your next assignment. Did I mention to you that Butch Concannon was leaving us after Thanksgiving? *The Daily World* hired him to work in Boston. That's a real plum for him."

Jenna knew that Concannon worked in the sports department under Al Silvano. She was quite certain he covered all the games of the State's two major professional teams, the Pawtucket Red Sox and the Providence Bruins. "You tried getting me into the men's locker room once before," she said. "It's still not funny."

"I'm dead serious," he answered, and looked the part. "Al Silvano's predicting that the Bruins will go to the Calder Cup finals and the Red Sox will play in the International League World Series. There's going to be tremendous fan interest in hockey this winter and baseball next summer. Silvano wants someone with imagination who can come up with unusual stories, keep the hype going all the time and sell papers. That's you he's describing."

Jenna suddenly realized what was at stake. McMurphy was talking about a year in the sports department. That meant days and nights covering mostly boring games. It required travel to any number of dull cities and being stuck there for days at a time. Worst of all, it called for constant interaction with rich, spoiled athletes who would mumble the same inanities about how fortunate they were to have done well and led their team to victory. She could still enjoy watching a game at Fenway Park now and then, but that was it. Hockey and baseball reporting weren't going to become part of her resume. She *wouldn't* do it even if it meant having to leave the *Herald*.

"There's no way I'll agree to that, Dan. Politics was one thing, and I'm up to here with it, but I'll never do sports." She paused a second before adding, as deliberately as she could, "Under no circumstances." She looked him in the eye, knowing the axe could fall at any moment if he felt she was being disloyal. What began with his raving about her work was in danger of ending with her having no work at all.

"I knew you'd had enough of the political arena," he said. "Then the managing editor sent word he wanted an in-depth follow-up on what you wrote about whole families making campaign contributions to the same candidate. He's excited about it. Thinks it may have gone beyond the Tarantinos and that it could be a blockbuster story. But I didn't dare assign it to you. Something like that could take months to investigate and break. More politicians and campaign managers to interview and check up on. All those John Q. Publics who'd be afraid to talk to you or tell you the truth, worried about what could happen to them. You'd be back in that whole scene all over again. I wasn't about to punish you for the good job you did. The next day Silvano came in and talked to me about the help he needs in sports. We're shorthanded here already, Jenna. For now, my hands are tied."

Her reputation for being quick at separating truth from bullshit didn't come undeserved. She saw through McMurphy's ploy at once. "You old bastard," she said, pronouncing each word slowly and distinctly.

His repute was earned also and took in a lot of territory. He knew she understood everything he said. "Then it's a deal," he shot back. Her eyes gave him the answer, and he kept talking. "I made notes about a few campaign treasurers you might want to talk to, starting with Lester Karp who handled contributions for Fiore, and some things to look for. They're under the paperweight on my desk. This story could really be a candidate for a Pulitzer. In fact, I'm ready to bet you'll get one."

What Jenna didn't tell McMurphy was that she intended to speak to him about investigating the very same story. Now she could use her willingness to take the assignment as a bargaining chip for some other story down the road.

"How much money are we talking on that bet?" she asked.

"I'll put up ten dollars," he said.

"It's a longer shot than the one you hit on. Tell you what, Dan. I'll owe you fifty if it happens."

"That's a deal, too." He paused. "But you know what, sucker? I'd have taken even money." He gave her an exaggerated wink.

As Jenna left his office, they were both hoping he'd win.

109

On wednesday afternoon Cyril Berman checked out of his suite at the Biltmore. The regular doorman whistled down a cab for him and helped him with his suitcases. Berman put a twenty-dollar bill in the man's hand as he shook it for the last time. He told the driver to take him to Rhode Island Hospital. On the way over, he opened his *Herald* and reread some of the election coverage.

Singer had received 55 percent of the Statewide vote from those citizens who voted for governor despite Fiore's withdrawal. But amazingly, in the Greater Providence Metropolitan Area, where most people read the *Herald* on a daily basis, Fiore had come in ahead of Singer, 58 to 42 percent. Berman realized that those voters were sending out word to their representatives that they didn't want to see the State get into the casino gaming business.

Berman knew the Tarantinos were very happy with the results. Sandy called him in the morning to say good-bye and to thank him for heading up the campaign. Berman apologized for being wrong about the *Herald*'s choice for governor. He told Sandy that Dan McMurphy explained to him that morning how they drafted a complete endorsement for each candidate before reaching a final decision on whom to support. It was just Berman's bad luck to be leaving McMurphy's office when the "Singer endorsement" was brought in.

"Don't let it bother you," Sandy said. "My father may have wanted Fiore to withdraw even if we knew the paper planned to recommend his election. He's not big on guys who go for a ménage à trois. Besides, it looks like the legislature will get the message that the people don't want casino gambling. We think we'll be in good shape."

At the hospital, Berman told the driver to wait for him. He asked for Fiore's room at the information desk and took the elevator to the fourth floor. When he entered, Doug was watching an old rerun of *The Addams Family* on television.

They talked for almost twenty minutes before Berman said that he had to get going in order not to miss his flight. He tried to leave Fiore with the message that he came out of the campaign a hero to the general public for the reason he withdrew. "You can think about running again four years from now. For a guy in politics for the first time, you had one hell of a strong campaign. And it looks like you got the Tarantinos what was most important for them all along."

The two men shook hands and Berman started to leave. He stopped at the foot of Fiore's bed and asked whether there was any chance Doug would tell him the identity of the other woman in the pictures. "I'm just curious," he said.

Fiore looked at his campaign manager and smiled. He didn't have to worry anymore about Cyril lecturing him. "What if I told you it was Bruce Singer's wife?"

Berman put his hands in his pockets, took a long look out the window at the interstate in the distance, and then looked over at Fiore again. "First, I'd say you were a liar. I can't imagine that either of you would be dumb enough to be in bed together and have someone else there who could talk about it.

"Second, I'd say that if you were telling the truth, we could have gone to Singer with the pictures. If I let him know the other woman was his wife and made sure he understood you'd give her name to the media if the story broke, I'd bet anything he would have persuaded her and the Hanley woman to back off, for the sake of their children, if nothing else.

"And finally, I'd say that if the *Herald* or any other news outlet in Rhode Island got hold of those pictures and went with the story, we would have accused Singer of using his wife to set up the whole thing for his own benefit. Why else would any woman in her position and in her right mind get involved in something like that? Then the people of this great State would have had to decide whether to vote for the guy who they figured laid the trap or for the poor bastard who was trapped into getting laid." Berman paused. "And on a question like that, Doug, the poor bastard wins every time. So instead of lying here recovering from nothing, you'd be in bed at home getting over the biggest and best hangover of your life from the victory party you would have had last night."

Berman watched the smile disappear from Fiore's face. He could only pity him. "But I get your message," he said, "and you're right. There's no reason now for me to know who it was."

ACKNOWLEDGMENTS

A GOOD FRIEND IS one who will read the draft of your book, whatever its length, not knowing whether it will ever be published, but certain that he/she will be asked, "Did the first chapter grab you?" "Did the story hold together at the end?" and of course the crucial "Did you want to keep turning the page?" I offer my thanks to Dale Marcy, Myron Uhlberg, Victor Freedman, and Barney Hass who turned all the pages, gave me their candid opinions and urged me to keep working until I got it right. When there was still some ground to cover here and there, my amazing literary agent, Peter Riva of International Transactions, Inc., always put me on the right path. Thanks Peter.